CHECKMATE

CHEC

A Tom Doherty Associates Book   New York

CHECKMATE

KARNA SMALL BODMAN

CHECKMATE

Copyright © 2007 by Karna Small Bodman

This book is printed on acid-free paper.

A Forge Book
Published by Tom Doherty Associates, LLC
175 Fifth Avenue
New York, NY 10010

www.tor.com

Forge® is a registered trademark of Tom Doherty Associates, LLC.

Library of Congress Cataloging-in-Publication Data

Bodman, Karna Small.
    Checkmate / Karna Small Bodman
        p. cm.
"A Tom Doherty Associates Book."
    ISBN-13: 978-0-765-31542-7
    ISBN-10: 0-765-31542-4
    1. Scientists—Fiction. 2. Cruise missile defenses—Fiction. 3. Terrorism—Fiction.
4. Washington (D.C.)—Fiction. 5. India—Fiction. I. Title.

PS3602.O3257 C47 2007
813'.6—dc22

                                                                    2006031203

First Edition: January 2007

Printed in the United States of America

0 9 8 7 6 5 4 3 2 1

For my husband, Dick Bodman—
the hero in all my stories

ACKNOWLEDGMENTS

The story of *Checkmate* was inspired by President Ronald Reagan's Strategic Defense Initiative (SDI), which he announced while I was serving on his staff in the White House. I will always be grateful for the opportunity to travel to arms control talks and summit meetings with the Soviets and experience, first-hand, the power of an idea—his idea of missile defense. More recently, I am indebted to the people at the U.S. Missile Defense Agency, especially the cooperation of Rick Lehner.

When it comes to technology, my best advisor was—and is—my husband, Dick Bodman, whose engineering background and fascination with computers led me to the key elements of my heroine's invention. Thanks as well to the developers of CryptoLex authentication technologies.

Conducting research gave me a special appreciation for the writings of Bernard Lewis and Gerald F. Seib, the many position papers developed by the Heritage Foundation, the Center for Strategic and International Studies, the American Enterprise Institute, and the pages of *The Wall Street Journal*.

One of the President's military aides, Tom Carter, provided personal observations and insights. William Luti of the National Security Council staff added historical context. And Roger Singh gave me a special understanding of the cultures of India and Pakistan.

For clever phrases and observations, I'm indebted to Karen Breidert, Tony DeRosa, Anne Wexler, John Carlson, and especially my father, who used to lecture us at the dinner table about the merits of individual responsibility and how free enterprise is simply the enterprise of free men.

To special friends who gave their constant encouragement and support—Pat Foss, Fran Luessenhop, Judith Mulholland, Kay Heller, Shannon Fairbanks, Sue Bailey, Connie Broomfield, and Lorri Purin; and finally to my agent, Susan Crawford, and my editors, Natalia Aponte and Paul Stevens, whose patience and perseverance resulted in this debut novel—thank you all from the bottom of my heart.

CHECKMATE

CHARACTERS

THE PRINCIPALS

Lt. Col. Hunt Daniels, Special Assistant to the President for Arms Control
and Strategic Defense
Dr. Cameron Talbot, Project Director, Bandaq Technologies

BANDAQ TECHNOLOGIES STAFF

Stan Bollinger, Chief Financial Officer
Melanie Duvall, Vice President of Corporate Communications
Gen. Jack Landsdale, Chairman and Chief Executive Officer
Dr. Raj P. Singh, scientist
Ben Steiner, research assistant

ISLAMIC MILITANTS

Abbas Khan, Lashkar-i-Taiba leader
Jambaz Muhammad Sharif, cell member
Rachid, cell member

WHITE HOUSE STAFF

Austin Gage, National Security Advisor
Jasmine Ito, Director of Intelligence Programs

Ted Jameson, Special Assistant to the President for Near East and South Asian Affairs
Lucy Shapiro, secretary to the NSC Advisor
Stockton Sloan, Deputy National Security Advisor

MEMBERS OF CONGRESS

Betty Barton, California congresswoman
Davis Metcher, Maryland congressman

OTHERS

Amir Ahmed Bhattia, Ambassador of Pakistan
Dr. Nettar Kooner, Sterling Dynamics Chairman and Chief Executive Officer
Arun, Sterling Dynamics computer programmer
Roxanne O'Malley, receptionist for Congressman Davis Metcher
Janis Prescott, Deputy Director of the FBI
Senator Farrell, Special Envoy

1

The White House—Monday Early Morning

"A cruise missile attack? Good God!"

"Exactly right, Mr. President. At least it was armed with a conventional warhead." The National Intelligence Director pulled a satellite photo from his leather folder and handed it across the Situation Room conference table to his Chief Executive. "You can see the damage. An entire army base destroyed. Hundreds may have been killed. We're still getting casualty figures from the Indian government."

"Where is this base?" the President asked as he studied the high-resolution photo.

"On the Indian side of the Line of Control in Jammu and Kashmir. Not too far from the epicenter of that big earthquake. As if those people didn't have enough problems," the Director added.

"Did the Paks do it? I can't believe they'd be that stupid. They know India will retaliate. And with both sides having nuclear weapons . . . this could make earthquake havoc look like second-grade recess."

The usually unflappable National Security Advisor, Austin Gage, weighed in. "The Pakistanis are going ballistic over this. I've already had a plea from their Ambassador asking us to set up a call between you and their President.

They're denying everything. They say that after fighting three wars with India, they're in no position to start anything. Besides, you know they've been trying to tamp things down for months. They've restored bus service across Kashmir—"

"Then again, those damn militants keep blowing up the buses," the Intelligence Chief interrupted.

"Then where in the hell did that missile come from?" the President asked.

Austin shook his head. "That's what we're trying to find out."

"Well, get about it then. It's one thing to have a bunch of Islamic militants staging attacks on villagers. Hell, they've been doing that for years. But a cruise missile attack? That takes brains, experience. They're computer guided. You don't just have some deranged terrorist picking one up and figuring out how to program and launch the damn thing."

"We know, Mr. President. We've got our best people on it," the Intelligence Director said.

"About the press, sir," the Chief of Staff said. "They're already clamoring for details."

The President glanced down at the photo again. "The press? Amazing that they even know where Kashmir is. Most of them probably think it's where they make sweaters."

Austin shrugged. "You've got a point there. We should have more by the noon briefing. I suggest we try to hold down the hysterics if we can." The President nodded. "Now about that phone call for the President of Pakistan?"

"Set it up," the President ordered. "But first get me some talking points on possible suspects and how they could have gotten their hands on a sophisticated missile system."

"We're on it, sir."

The President stood up, effectively ending the meeting.

The three men gathered their notes and headed for the door of the basement conference room. As they filed out, each one uttered the same phrase, "Thank you, Mr. President."

"I want you to find the bastards who launched that missile," the President called after the trio. "And figure out if they've got any more of them."

2

Rockville, Maryland—Monday Morning

"We've gotta shut her down!" Stan Bollinger announced as he marched into the office of the retired general and current CEO of Bandaq Technologies. The short, wiry CFO tossed a sheaf of papers on the desk and pointed to the page on top. "Just look at those numbers, Jack. That crazy project of hers is sinking our bottom line. How much longer can we be that woman's personal ATM?"

Gen. Jack Landsdale stared at his Chief Financial Officer. "You must be joking! Shut down our missile defense line just when she's had a breakthrough?"

"So her computer game worked once. In simulation," Stan scoffed. "That could have been a fluke." He strode over to the tall windows and looked out at the park across from their corporate plaza and added with a wave of his hand, "Besides, once in a row won't cut it with our shareholders."

"Wait just a damn minute," the general bellowed. "I've known Cameron Talbot since she was a teenager. I've watched her graduate at the top of her class at Stanford and breeze through M.I.T. She's a computer genius with an IQ higher than your stock price will ever be."

"Yeah, and I hear 'IQ' stands for *Ice Queen* where she's concerned," the CFO challenged.

"God damn it! How exactly does her personality impact on your precious P&L statement?"

"It doesn't. It just makes it easier to fire her," Stan said, pacing across the room.

"Look, I can read the numbers as well as you can. But you have to admit that if she can make her program work to actually take control of a cruise missile and redirect it, our entire military is going to be screaming for her technology, to say nothing of other countries who will want it for their own protection."

Stan stopped and turned in mid-stride. "I'm not so sure. The boys at the Pentagon have blown over a hundred billion bucks on all kinds of missile defense projects over the last twenty-five years. And they still only work once in a while. Remember *Brilliant Pebbles*?" The general had started to interrupt when the CFO continued, "More like stupid pebbles if you ask me. Congress is getting fed up with all of their red ink, and when I give my quarterly report to the board in two weeks, you can count on their being up to here with the whole idea, too."

General Landsdale pushed the papers aside and cleared his throat. "First of all, that hundred billion was spent trying to stop big ballistic missiles. Cammy's working on smaller, guided missiles that can carry chemical, biological, even nuclear warheads. It's a whole different concept. You know that. And second . . ." The general paused for emphasis. "I'm still the boss around here."

"Not for long," the CFO muttered.

"So my retirement's coming up. But as long as I sit in this chair, I will make the decisions on which lines get funded and which ones are closed down . . . if any."

"Then I assume I can count on you to answer all the budget questions at the board meeting?" Stan asked derisively, shooting his French cuffs as he stood in front of the desk.

"We may have answers by then." The general checked his watch and thought for a moment. "She's preparing a new simulation right now. If she can lock on to a dummy missile again, there's going to be a lot of crow on the cafeteria menu."

"Tell you what. Why don't we both check in on this *new simulation* and see whether she can finally reduce our burn rate here."

"Right this way," the general ordered as he got up, buttoned his jacket, and headed toward the door.

"Come in," Cameron Talbot said absently, her eyes trained on her computer screen. The door to her lab opened, and when she turned around she was surprised to see her boss, Gen. Jack Landsdale, with Stan Bollinger, his CFO, in tow. She took one last sip from her coffee mug, realized the coffee was cold, and set the mug down next to a stack of tablets filled with calculations. She quickly saved her screen and brushed a few strands of blond hair back under her headband. "What's up? I was just getting ready for another test run of Q-3."

"We know," the General said, motioning for Stan to pull up a chair. "We've been talking about your project, and we'd like to see the next simulation. Any new progress here?"

Cammy eyed the CFO and saw him staring at the bank of computer screens and piles of notes and books spread around the room. He had never ventured into her lab, and she wondered what brought about this sudden interest in her work. She'd never liked the man. The way he barked out his orders around the company made her think he had some sort of Napoleonic complex. And he was obsessive about numbers. She wished he could be as passionate about concepts like throw-weights as he was about EBITDA. *Earnings Before Interest, Taxes, Depreciation, and Amortization,* she reflected. What a total drag. His whole demeanor was so austere, she had told a friend that their CFO had one thing in common with Clint Eastwood. He was stone-faced with hair combed or stone-faced with hair mussed up.

Cammy pointed to her computer screen and answered, "I've been working on a new set of algorithms. If I can just get them to analyze the frequency a command center is using to communicate with a missile, I can use the same frequency to lock on to it and take control."

"And you think you can do that now?" the general asked expectantly.

"Almost," she said. "I'm working . . . my whole team is working on it every day now. I really think we're close."

"Close only counts in horseshoes and hand grenades," Stan declared. "I think George Wallace said that once."

The general waved dismissively and focused on the screen. "So are you going to fire this thing up and try another simulation?"

"We were planning another one for later today, yes," Cammy said. "Why?"

"We want to watch," the CFO said.

"Oh," Cammy said tensely. "Now isn't really the best time." She glanced down at the figures on the tablets, mentally calculating how long it would take to experiment with her latest formulas. She reached up and twisted a strand of her hair. *I'm not ready for this*, she thought. *Maybe later. Maybe tomorrow. Not now.* Ever since her first triumph when she'd been able to lock on to a simulated weapon, she'd been working for weeks to re-create the conditions. And she'd failed. She had the ideas. She just couldn't seem to translate them to her hard drive. The concepts were just in her head. And right now, her head was pounding.

"So, how about a little show-and-tell?" Stan prompted.

Cammy heaved a sigh, swiveled her chair on the tile floor, and picked up her intercom. "Ben, could you come in here, please." Her palms were damp as she smoothed her beige slacks and pushed up the sleeves of her white sweater. A young man dressed in beige chinos and a navy polo shirt pushed through the door. He stopped abruptly when he saw the CEO and CFO seated in the corner. He glanced at Cammy with raised eyebrows.

Cammy exchanged a look with her key assistant. She had hired Ben Steiner the previous year. He was a computer whiz, and he had come up with a whole slew of calculations and ideas for Q-3. He was proving invaluable to her. He was awfully smart, but rather one-dimensional. Everything except his computer skills was kind of medium. Medium height. Medium brown hair. Medium build. There was nothing sharp or defining about him. She often thought that his face was what you'd get if someone faxed you a picture and you were low on toner. Then again, she thanked her lucky stars that there was nothing low about the guy's energy level.

"Ben, we've got work to do. Mr. Bollinger and General Landsdale are anxious to see our progress on Q-3—"

"But we're not quite—"

"Never mind where you are, or where you think you are," the CFO intoned. "It's time we got some action out of this division. Now does this Q-3 thing work or doesn't it?"

There was silence in the room. Finally, Ben dropped into a gray desk chair and rolled over to the second computer. "Guess we'll give it another try."

Cammy pushed a button. A white object jumped onto the upper corner of her screen and began moving across at an angle. Her fingers flew over the keys; the staccato patterns on the two keyboards were the only sounds permeating the tension in the room. She entered a sequence of numbers as Ben made a series of calculations. Cammy typed faster and looked up to see the object reaching the center of her screen.

"Damn," she said under her breath. "What's its C^3?" she muttered, racking her brain for another sequence. She tried again, but the little object kept moving. "Ben, anything?"

"Not yet, boss. Last algorithm . . . thought I had that sucker . . . try another . . . nope."

She tried to ignore the flashes of pain across her forehead as she stared at the screen and entered another list of numbers. The small white object was on a downward trajectory when she shook her head. "New input. I need new input," she called out to Ben.

"I know. I know," he said. "I'm trying. It's too fast. Need more time."

"We haven't got any more time. The missile is about to hit its target and we can't . . . damn." She watched as the white object hit the bottom of her screen and disappeared altogether.

"Zilch . . . zip . . . zero," Ben said as he pushed his chair back and folded his arms.

"And that's what your budget is going to be if I have anything to say about it," Stan said, as he got up from his chair and headed for the door.

"What do you mean?" Cammy said, pushing away from her console and hurrying toward the CFO.

He turned abruptly to face her. "What I mean is that I've got to shut down this division because it's not producing. That's what I mean."

The shock on her face brought the general to his feet. "Cammy, listen."

"Listen to what? Listen to how he's going to close me down after all these years of trying to develop a fabulous new technology? Close me down when we're right on the edge of a terrific discovery? Close me down when we might have a missile system that actually *saves lives* rather than one that just kills a bunch of people?" She put her hand on the general's arm. "Don't let him do that, Jack."

Stan Bollinger grabbed the doorknob and twisted it. "Show's over, folks. For the record, nobody *lets* me do anything. I think the board will have to decide this one. But if it were up to me . . . ," he turned and gave Cammy a stern look, ". . . yes, I'd shut you down in a heartbeat." He opened the door and called over his shoulder, "And now, I've got real work to do."

Cammy slumped down in her chair and saw the dejected look on Ben's face. She paused and turned to the general. "So does this mean we're through? You're really going to give up on Q-3?"

The general ran a hand through his graying hair and thought for a moment. "Stan doesn't have the power to shut you down . . . not yet anyway. I'm still running the show here, but you know I'm scheduled to retire, and Stan is the heir apparent. He's right about one thing though. If we can't show more progress on this missile defense idea of yours, the board may agree that we've got to cut our losses."

"So we've got a couple of weeks till the meeting?" Cammy asked.

"Two weeks max. But there are a few things we can do right now."

"Such as?"

"First of all, the satellite and radar division is ahead of schedule. I'm going to pull Raj Singh off that line and reassign him to your staff on a temporary basis. He may have some new ideas on how to get your computer program to react faster once a missile is launched. And with a little more time, you may be able to figure out the frequencies."

She hesitated. Work with Raj? She didn't like the idea. She knew he was smart, but she wasn't sure she could trust him. She figured Ben might have misgivings, too.

"Ben, what do you think about working with Raj?" she asked.

"I don't know. Guy's smart. No question. But . . ."

"But what?" the general demanded.

"What Ben means," Cammy answered, "is that Raj has his own priorities. He heads up another division, and he's been trying to get his own budget increased for months now. Why should he help us when he'd get the lion's share of R & D money if we get slammed?"

"Don't be ridiculous. We're all working for the same company. We all want this place to succeed. We all want to get this whole missile defense system working so it ties into his satellite and radar and then get the Pentagon to buy the whole shebang. You know that."

Cammy looked up. "His satellite and radar systems can be used independently. He could partner with Sterling Dynamics on their missile systems. Or he could sell them separately." *And he could compromise Q-3 once he learns my routines here*, she thought to herself.

"We're not doing any deal with our major competitor. Where did you get that idea?"

"You know Sterling has been trying to replicate some of our systems. I told you about the guy they hired who tried . . ."

The general softened his tone. "Yes. I know. The man tries to sweet-talk you into telling him about Q-3, and when that doesn't work, he goes to work for Sterling."

It still hurt when Cammy thought about Ken. The bastard. She had met him at a defense symposium. He had seemed so attentive. And she had to admit he had been rather attractive. After a few dinners and a weekend at his place in Middleburg, she had fallen for him. Hard. Then the questions came. They were subtle at first. He said he was so interested in her work, how she had come up with the idea of Q-3, how it stood for its three components of satellites, radar, and computers working together to take control of a cruise missile once it was launched. But her project was classified. She never talked about it outside the office. Then when he finally figured out that he wasn't going to learn anything about it, he dumped her and went to work for her nemesis, Sterling Dynamics. She had been devastated. For a while anyway. Ever since then, except for her own small staff, she had preferred to work alone.

"So you trust Raj to come over here and save my project?" Cammy asked.

"That's step one," the general said.

"There's a step two?"

"Yes. This is a long shot, but there's a hearing before the House Armed Services Subcommittee on Wednesday morning. They're in the process of putting together one part of the Defense Authorization Bill. I'm going to see if we can get on their docket for that hearing. If we could get an earmark for this technology, we'd have enough R & D funds to keep going. At least for a while."

"That sounds like a good plan," Cammy said.

"I'm going to call the Chairman. But I want *you* to handle the testimony."

"Me?" Cammy exclaimed. "I've never testified before a Congressional Committee. I've never even given a speech, Jack. Why in the world would you put me in front of that bunch?"

"Because you're the one who created Q-3. It was your idea, your research, your simulation that worked."

"Once."

"When it worked that time," Ben said, "guess we should've TiVo'ed it, huh?"

"Wish we had," Cammy murmured.

"Yes, once," the general said. "And so you're the best one to explain why it's important for the United States to have a system that can neutralize a guided missile if it's launched against us or our allies."

"But I can't . . . I mean, I don't have time . . . I'd have to write the . . ."

"Stop it, Cam. Stop the excuses. If you can impress the Committee, and I think you can, there's a chance we can keep going here. Bollinger will have to take a pass and the board will, too. At least for now."

3

Kashmir, Foothills of the Himalayas—Monday Afternoon

"We will control the Islamic bomb!" Abbas Khan announced as he sat cross-legged on a worn rug and stroked his neatly clipped beard. "That missile strike today was only the beginning of our grand plan."

"And it worked, Khan Sahib," a young man called out from the back of the dusty room. A roar of approval rose from the dozen other members of the cell, their shouts echoing off the cement walls of the small bunker.

Their leader held up his hand commanding silence. "The missile worked just as it was programmed. Our new brother, Rashid," he turned and nodded to the man on his right, "has joined us and he deserves our praise."

"The praise is to Allah," Rashid said with a slight nod. "And we must not forget that our other recruits from ISI helped steal those missiles along with their launch vehicles from that Pakistani depot."

"Yes, it was brilliant. A brilliant plan," the leader agreed. "But as I said, this strike was only the start. We have much work to do. Plans to devise. Assignments to give out."

The air in their concrete headquarters suddenly was heavy and tinged with apprehension for the men crowded into the small space. They waited and followed their leader's gaze out a small window where a fine mist enveloped snowcapped mountains. Their view was marred by piles of rubble and a twelve-foot-high fence off in the distance.

"This place, this homeland, this should all be ours. But no. Look at that fence with its wire and metal and electricity. Here we are, still recovering from the Ramadan quake of 2005, still trying to rebuild our villages, and the Indians are spending their time building fences. They think their stupid fence will keep us out. They think it will prevent us from staging any more attacks on the other side."

A few of the cell members laughed at his description and one remarked, "They now know they were wrong."

"Just as wrong as the Israelis were when they built their fence to keep the Palestinians out of their rightful land," Khan continued. "At least the Jews were condemned for their fence. But who is condemning Delhi? Who, I ask you?"

He looked around the room and scrutinized the faces of the young men leaning against the dark walls, offering him rapt attention.

Abbas Khan took a sip of his sweetened tea and continued ominously. "We are smarter than our Palestinian brothers. We will not try to fight the big countries alone. That would be foolish, and we are not foolish men. No. We will continue to stage our attacks in India, but we will see to it that Pakistan gets the blame. Then India will have to retaliate."

The men nodded and mumbled their agreement. They had heard this before. Many times. They had fought together for years, trying to drive the Indians out of Kashmir. India and Pakistan had fought wars over this land. Nothing was ever settled. They knew they'd only take control if they had a new strategy, a daring new plan. And Abbas Khan was about to lay it all out.

"We will see to it that India and Pakistan go to war . . . again . . . but this time, with both sides having nuclear weapons, the feckless bureaucrats at the UN will scream for a cease-fire. They will demand elections. Fine. Our people are *Muslim*. All of Kashmir is *Muslim*. We will have their election . . . once . . . because we will win."

Again, the men nodded.

"And when we win in Kashmir, we'll pick up the pieces in Islamabad and take control of the government and," he paused for effect, "we'll also control—"

"The bomb!" the young men cried in unison.

"Yes, *Inshallah*! And you, Jambaz . . ." He turned to the young man on his left. "While we work here, you will work in America on a most important assignment . . . one that will allow us to defend ourselves when missiles start flying." He leaned forward and pointed to a stack of papers on the low table in front of him. "This is your passport. These are your new identity papers. Everything you need has been arranged."

Jambaz reached for the documents. Of all the members pledged to free their homeland from the clutches of India, of all the militants from the old ISI network, old al Qaeda cells, and Taliban sympathizers who were going to work together to take control of Pakistan's nuclear arsenal, he was the one chosen to go to America. He didn't know what his mission would be. But he knew it must be important. He wouldn't ask questions now.

He had traveled there before. He had studied their ways. He had learned their language. So, of course, he should be the chosen one. For it was the saying of Muhammad, Peace Be unto Him, "It is your own conduct which will lead you to reward or punishment as if you had been destined therefore."

4

Capitol Hill—Wednesday Morning

"The meeting will please come to order."

Chairman Davis Metcher of Maryland sat behind his raised podium with an American flag behind him and his nameplate in front. He struck the gavel and began the hearing before the House Armed Services Subcommittee on Military Research and Development in the Rayburn House Office Building. In the brightly lit hearing room, the Chairman's brown suit was almost the same shade as the tall mahogany doors. This was their regular Wednesday morning session.

"Let me remind the Members that the microphones in front of you are live, so when you are conferring with staff, please be cognizant of that fact."

He pulled his own microphone a bit closer and looked down at the witness table where an attractive young woman in a navy suit, her blond hair held back with a navy barrette, sat confidently reviewing a set of notes. An older gentleman with a full head of salt-and-pepper hair sat next to her, leaning over to whisper some last-minute comment.

This could be interesting, the Chairman mused. *We usually get generals and CEOs at these hearings, not striking women who would look right at home in a Victoria's Secret catalogue.* He wondered what she was doing here. He checked his roster again. *Maybe she's the old man's assistant. Must be.*

He cleared his throat. "Today, the Committee is pleased to welcome the Project Director of Bandaq Technologies, Dr. Cameron Talbot." He nodded to the gentleman. "Sir, you may begin."

The woman looked up and smiled. "Excuse me, Mr. Chairman. *I* am Dr. Cameron Talbot, Director of Project Q-3."

There was a murmur around the room as several of the Members chuckled and Congresswoman Betty Barton of California gave the Chairman a sidelong smirk.

"Mr. Chairman," Dr. Talbot began, "Members of the Committee. It is an honor to be here, and I am grateful for the opportunity to testify on the development of our new technology which, with your help in funding for research and development, can become an integral component of the President's National Missile Defense system."

Chairman Metcher sat back in his black leather chair and began to enjoy the performance. *Nice legs,* he thought. *Good thing we decided not to put skirts on the witness table or else we wouldn't be able to see the skirts under the table.* He refocused his attention on what the lady was saying.

"A copy of my full testimony and funding request have been placed in the record, but I will give you an executive summary of our progress. I am accompanied by retired Air Force general Jack Landsdale, Chairman and CEO of Bandaq Technologies. We both will be happy to answer your questions, keeping in mind that the details of our project are classified. However, we would be available to arrange a private briefing on the operational structure for Members who may wish to schedule a closed hearing."

I'd like to have a closed hearing with that one, Davis thought. *And Bandaq hasn't kicked anything into my reelection campaign yet, even though they're in my district. Maybe I can kill a couple of birds here.*

Air Force lieutenant colonel Hunt Daniels, detailed from the Department of Defense to the White House National Security Council, sat in the last row of black leather chairs arranged behind the witnesses and quietly listened to the proceedings. As Special Assistant to the President for Arms Control and Strategic Defense, he, with the assistance of his staff, had the job of keeping up with nuclear proliferation as well as the latest technology in defensive systems.

He had known about Bandaq's project. It was his business to know. He had even heard about Dr. Cameron Talbot. But he had pictured some cyber-geek with wire-rimmed glasses and a pocket protector who had a curved spine from hunching over a computer screen all day long. Boy, had he been wrong. He watched intently as Dr. Talbot read the summary.

" 'As you know, back in 1999, an act was signed into law which states, "It is the policy of the United States to deploy as soon as is technologically possible an effective National Missile Defense system capable of defending the territory of the U.S. against limited ballistic missile attack (whether accidental, unauthorized, or deliberate)."

" 'In 2004, our country began to deploy the first layer of that system—ground-based missile interceptors at Vandenberg Air Force Base in California and Fort Greely, Alaska, that work in conjunction with advanced tracking radar located on Shemya Island in the Aleutians. Later those systems will be supplemented with ship-based interceptors and floating radar.

" 'These initial systems are meant to protect us from large, long-range ballistic missiles aimed at the United States by such countries as North Korea and China. Pakistan has similar missiles and, of course, Russian missile technology has spread at an alarming rate.' "

Hunt couldn't help staring at Dr. Talbot. From his angle, he had a view of her profile. High cheekbones, narrow nose. A very tidy package. The only unruly thing about her was her hair. It was pulled into some sort of clasp, but little tendrils had crept out and were framing her face. Yes, she was kind of pretty, in an angular sort of way. He snapped back to attention as she continued to read her testimony in measured tones.

" 'But, Mr. Chairman, we have new technology that is not focused on ballistic missiles. It is an entirely new concept to identify and redirect guided or cruise missiles—the type of shorter-range weapons that can be fitted with conventional, biological, chemical, or even nuclear warheads. New computer- and GPS-guided missiles are being produced, along with other radar- and radio-controlled weapons. Several rogue countries already own some of them, terrorists could acquire them, and defensive programs we now have in place are not exactly reliable.' "

She was right on that score, Hunt thought. Nobody had figured out a way to target an incoming cruise missile with any kind of decent kill ratio. He wondered how she thought she could pull it off. *Wait. Did she say "identify and redirect"? How is that possible?* He listened.

" 'Our system is named Q-3 for its three components: satellites, radar, and computers, and we are excited about its potential to protect Americans here and abroad in these difficult times.' " Dr. Talbot then paused and nodded to the Chairman.

Davis Metcher stopped gazing at the speaker and turned to his left. "The Chair recognizes the Gentlelady from California, who has the first question."

"Thank you, Mr. Chairman," said the Congresswoman. "Now, Dr. Talbot, thank you for coming before the Committee today. Your new project certainly sounds interesting. And if it really works, I can see how it might be useful in places like the Middle East or perhaps in regions like India and Pakistan where things are heating up with that missile strike on Monday. However, first I would like to know if you have had any successful test trials of this new technology?"

"We have had some success in simulation, but not in the field as yet, Madam Representative. But you see—"

"And in light of this lack of . . . successful trials . . . I am not sure I can, in good conscience, vote for R & D funds, especially when we have so many more pressing priorities such as troop strength, shipbuilding, and especially the worldwide fight against terrorism, to say nothing of our concerns over an expanding deficit. And so, considering these other necessities, for us to simply hope for some pie-in-the-sky . . . literally . . . technology to suddenly work, well, I'm afraid I'll have to see better results than this."

"May I respond, please?" Dr. Talbot looked directly at the Congresswoman. "We are only in the initial stage of development of our technology. But we are so confident that this new approach is the right approach, we ask for your patience. We do understand your priorities.

"On the subject of troop strength, I would suggest that a first priority would be to protect our forces in the field, which this program could do.

"As for shipbuilding, yes, of course our Navy needs newer and better ships. And yes, the Navy already has a sea-based missile defense program, the Aegis system, or SM-3. But, as you know, it has experienced many failures and has cost millions of dollars to launch defensive missiles. In fact, just one such kill vehicle has hit its target in the last several years."

The Congresswoman leaned away from her microphone, brushed a strand of brown hair off her forehead, and stared impassively as Dr. Talbot continued.

"And in the fight against terrorism, Project Q-3 could be a key to neutralizing these new missile systems that many countries in the Middle East and elsewhere are trying to acquire.

"Now as for the deficit, may I remind the Committee that current programs which fund defensive measures such as the Patriot PAC-3, along with the Aegis, call for one of our missiles to be launched against an enemy missile. A bullet hitting a bullet, if you will. Those missiles are expensive, very expensive, whereas our technology does not require the launch of a missile. Ours is a computer program designed to intercept an enemy missile by locking onto its guidance system."

Good God! thought Hunt. *This really is new. In fact, it's pretty wild.* He couldn't take his eyes off the confident woman who was now winding up her rebuttal.

"And finally, may I point out that Q-3 is precisely the type of program that could—"

The Chairman interrupted as his Legislative Aide passed him a note. He leaned forward to speak into his microphone.

"Excuse me, Dr. Talbot. Unfortunately, there is a vote on the floor, so it will be necessary for us to recess. Each member has a copy of your testimony. If we have further questions, we will contact you or General Landsdale."

With a knock of his gavel, the meeting was adjourned.

"Good job, kiddo," the general whispered as he gathered his papers and shoved them into his briefcase. "I hope to hell we can pull this off."

As the Members and staff stood up and began to clear the room, Hunt Daniels slipped out the back door and made a mental note to send Dr. Cameron Talbot an e-mail asking for his own personal briefing on Project Q-3. He had studied a lot of missile systems, but he'd never seen one like this. The more he thought about it, though, the more he doubted it could ever work.

5

Washington, D.C.—Wednesday Morning

Jambaz Muhammad Sharif leaned over the wooden desk where former students had scratched their initials into the rough surface. He had moved into this chilly apartment four blocks from the American University campus and was spending most of his time staring at his computer screen, its eerie glow the only light in the room. He hadn't bothered to turn on the metal floor lamp in the one-room efficiency that served as his temporary quarters. He was anxious to check for messages. He had entered the chat room of the assigned company Web site and then proceeded to a private room. It was a clever way to communicate and very hard to trace, as long as he didn't repeat it too often. He knew the agents looked for patterns, and he wasn't about to oblige them.

It was there in the private chat room that he met his leader, Abbas Khan. It was there that he received updates on his cell back home and on other members of his beloved militant group, Lashkar-i-Taiba. It was there that he would receive his instructions, his assignment that would aid their plot in Pakistan as well as their cause in Kashmir, seeking to drive out the Kafir from what should have been a Muslim-ruled country.

A few rays of morning light filtered through the window in the kitchen area. A microwave and toaster took up most of the space on the linoleum counter, while plates and mugs of unfinished tea cluttered the chipped enamel sink. He wore black pants that were baggy on his thin frame. His favorite dark green T-shirt hung loosely over his waist. Green was the color of Islam, the most holy, the one true religion. Didn't God's messenger, Muhammad, Peace Be unto Him, say, "Islam is the head, prayer is the backbone, and Jihad is the perfection"?

Yet, in order to continue the Jihad, they must have clever plans and good weapons. Jambaz wondered if his mission involved weapons. He knew the Americans had sophisticated systems that his people wanted. But the Americans also had a lot of other things his people didn't want. After all, this was a culture that debased its women, imported drugs for its young men, and plundered the resources of other countries under the guise of its corrupt capitalism.

He hated the Americans with their smug superiority. And yet, he was here because he knew how to blend in, gain their confidence, and be trusted. For didn't his very name, Jambaz, mean "honest and truthful"?

He had observed all of their laws so as not to be noticed. After 9/11, the American agents tried to crack down on his fellow Muslims, rounding up and interrogating thousands, deporting hundreds, and shaming them all. He would not be caught in such traps.

His cell had waited patiently for the predictable outcry from the so-called human rights groups. And when the complaints and lawsuits were filed, the agents had to back down for a while. They were not allowed to use profiling at airports. Even suspected terrorists who had been arrested were given lawyers. It was then that Abbas Khan had applied for a renewed student visa for Jambaz.

He was here now, dutifully enrolled at American University, signed up for classes in computer science and even American history. That was a joke, but Abbas Khan must have felt it would look good on his application. He had his books. He was quiet. He broke no laws, for the Muslim proverb instructs, "A stranger should be well mannered." He was a stranger, and so he was well mannered and careful. Always careful.

He wondered how long would he have to wait to carry out his mission? How long would he have to live in this place before he could return to his home in Dardapora, the village in the Kashmir Valley that had been given to the filthy Indians back in 1947? Dardapora, where so many had died in their fight for freedom from their oppressors. Dardapora, where half the people were widows, including his mother and his sisters. Dardapora, a name that means "Village of Pain."

He felt pain when he thought about his family, how his father had been part of the attack on the Indian Parliament in 2001 but later died at the hands of the Indian police. India and Pakistan had almost gone to war over that attack. That had been the purpose of his father's group when they staged it. They had wanted another war.

There had been three wars since the British pulled out, two of them over Kashmir. That area with its shimmering lakes, valleys, and foothills of the Himalayas should have been part of Pakistan. The people were Muslim. India was Hindu and yet the hated Maharaja Hari Singh, who ruled a section of it at the time, along with the traitor Sheikh Abdullah, his Muslim Prime Minister, decided this region should be a part of India. They must have been paid off and offered protection in exchange for their allegiance to India. And so, from that day forward, the Muslim people in the eastern half of Kashmir were ruled by the Kafir in Delhi.

Kashmir was beautiful. Kashmir's mountains were more majestic than anything in Europe. They were more impressive than the Alps. Kashmir was where all people used to go to enjoy its treasures. Not now. Not anymore. Now it was filled with land mines and roving soldiers and seventy thousand graves. It was like Beirut or Baghdad. Travelers used to go there, too. But not anymore. And yet, he couldn't wait to go back and fight to free his people and establish a proper caliphate run by a proper religious leader.

Pakistan used to help them. Pakistan had set up the training camps and the schools, the Madrassas where he had gone at the age of seven to learn the word of Muhammad, Peace Be unto Him. But now, the Americans had pressured the government in Islamabad to close some of the camps and schools and outlaw his group, his loyal Lashkar-i-Taiba.

So now they would work outside the system. They had even changed their name to Jammat-ul-Dawa, which meant "Preaching Core." He still liked the old name, which stood for "Army of the Pure." It didn't matter what they called themselves; they had contacts and support from many members of Pakistan's Inter-Service Intelligence agency, the remnants of al Qaeda, and several other militant groups. They would all work for change.

He looked at the words on the screen once more. There was a new message. Now there were instructions about how he would play an important role in the unfolding scenario. They told him to wait a little while longer because "an infidel is working on a project, and she has not completed it as yet." As soon as it was finished, he would be instructed how to take control of it.

6

The White House—Wednesday Late Morning

Who the hell shot off that missile? Hunt wondered as he shifted in his leather desk chair and rubbed his eyes. The door to his outer office was closed to shut out the noise of the constantly ringing telephones and fax machines. He had been reading the briefing papers from the Defense Intelligence Agency, the National Security Agency, and the CIA, complete with a cover memo from the Director of National Intelligence, for the past hour, and he didn't like what he saw. Every staff member whose shop had anything to do with Southeast Asia, weapons proliferation, or terrorism issues had been scouring their sources for the last two days trying to figure out who had the brains, or lack of them, to lob a cruise missile that just might ignite a nuclear war.

He glanced at his speed dial and punched the fourth button on the phone.

"Ted Jameson here."

"Hey, Ted, it's Hunt. You got a minute?"

"Sure. In fact, I was just about to call you."

"Oh yeah? Why?"

"Come on down. I want to show you a report I just got from a back channel at ISI."

"Is it big?"

"Sure looks like it."

"I'll be right down."

Hunt gathered up his reports, tossed them into the safe, and spun the dial. He grabbed his leather folder, a must-have for everyone in the building. He never knew when he'd be yanked into a meeting and might need to take notes. He nodded to his secretary and headed out toward the office of Theodore Jameson, Special Assistant to the President for Near East and South Asian Affairs.

Hunt liked Ted, even if he was a bit stuffy at times. Then again, the man had spent his life in academia, either teaching or doing research over at the Center for Strategic and International Studies between assignments for various administrations. He had served in the State Department and on the National Security Councils of two presidents. And when their party was out of office you could also find him on MSNBC or Fox News earning a thousand bucks a pop as an analyst.

As Hunt hurried down the long hallway of the Old Executive Office Building, he glanced at the doorknobs. He had always been a history buff, and when he got word of his transfer to The White House, he had made it a point to read up on its architecture and culture. Finding particular rooms where certain treaties had been signed or important conferences had played out had turned into a bit of a hobby. He reflected on the fact that the Empire building had been built in the late 1800s for the State, War, and Navy Departments. The offices of each department had their own distinctive insignia on the knobs of every door. A pair of anchors on the doorknobs meant that office had been assigned to Navy personnel. His office had doorknobs from the War Department. That figured.

He headed along the black- and white-tile corridor with its sixteen-foot ceilings, cast-iron pilasters, and columns and turned down the ornate curved staircase with the brass railing on the top of the banister. He remembered the story about the curved brass and how it had been added when Secretary of War Taft had slipped on the steps and asked for an extra rail.

As he jogged down the stairs, Hunt figured he could get all the workout he needed just going to meetings rather than hitting the health club in the basement. After all, the OEOB had two miles of corridors.

The building was home to the official office of the Vice President, although he had a small office in the West Wing along with the other big boys such as the Chief of Staff, the Press Secretary, and the National Security Advisor, Austin Gage. But most of the staffs of the Office of Management and Budget, the speechwriters, the political office, the advance team, and the NSC were here, along with the medical folks, and even the frame shop.

The OEOB was just across the West Executive driveway from the West Wing, so the two buildings combined were known as "the White House." Hunt was proud to be working here. An assignment at the Pentagon was fine, but being detailed to the White House staff was an honor, even if it meant being on call 24/7.

He opened the door to Ted's office. The secretary looked up and smiled. "Good morning, Colonel Daniels. Go right in. He's expecting you."

Ted glanced up from his briefing papers. "Pull up a chair, Hunt, and take a look at this."

Hunt slid his lean six-foot-two frame into a dark green leather chair, shifted forward, and grabbed a report. He read it quickly and muttered, "Oh shit! Three cruise missiles? Stolen? How in the hell . . . ?"

Ted leaned back and gripped the arms of his chair. "My contact says it had to be a clever inside job. No militant group just waltzes into a Pakistani depot and makes off with those missiles *and* their launch vehicles. Problem is, we don't know who took them, where they are, or what they want to use for target practice. But considering the problems over there, my best bet is one of those militant groups that's been killing and harassing those poor people on the Indian side of Kashmir for decades. They're getting more and more sophisticated in their approach. Sometimes they get as far as Delhi and Bombay. Well, it was Bombay then. Now it's Mumbai. Anyway, remember that attack a few years back on the Indian Parliament?"

"Yeah, I remember that. We were afraid they'd go to war over it."

"We dodged the devil on that one. But now that both sides have been trying to cool things down with talk about more trade and opening the highways again, the militants don't like it. Those guys don't want peace. They want their land back."

"You know, I've been focusing on North Korea, Iran, and Syria. Now we're all crashing around trying to figure out India, Pakistan, and Kashmir." Hunt uttered a sigh and glanced at the mound of papers on Ted's desk. "Those militant groups . . . you'd think that one day they'd wake up and figure out that that their own people aren't all that hot for this whole Jihad routine. I mean, after all the elections in Afghanistan, Iraq, Palestine, Kuwait, Egypt . . . and all the talk about democracy . . ."

"It's not that easy. Democracy presupposes an ordered society," Ted suggested.

"Okay, so it takes a while."

Ted took a sip of coffee and leaned back.

Hunt continued, "It's bad enough to worry about a bunch of terrorists getting ahold of a couple of cruise missiles, but look at the other weapons they've got over there. I mean, India's got the Prithvi nukes. Pakistan's been testing that Shaheen 2 that can send a nuclear warhead to Delhi, and they won't sign on to a no-first-use deal. I'm afraid they could decide to stage a pre-emptive strike because India has so many conventional forces, and they may want to get a head start."

"And there's another problem. A big one," Ted said. "I'm afraid the Indians feel that if we can hit a country like Iraq that's far away because we *suspected* they had nukes and terrorists, why can't they hit a neighbor they *know* has nukes and terrorists?"

Hunt raked his fingers through his hair. "The thing is, I think there are a hell of a lot of military types in Pakistan who are sympathetic to the guys in Kashmir. Think about what could happen if that bunch took over . . . and controlled the nukes."

"Controlled the nukes? No way." Ted pointed to another paper on his desk. "ISI says they have pulled back from supporting the extremists."

"Obviously, that's not working," Hunt said. "They used to back them all the time. Then when things got rough, they did it secretly. Now they may say they're backing off, but it doesn't look that way to me."

"The President publicly banned most of those cells," Ted countered. "The other thing is that Pakistan has been spending a third of its budget on defense, and their economy is just now starting to improve, so there's a lot of pressure to kick in money for economic development instead. That's why we've seen the olive branches to India."

"But that just makes the militants even madder, to say nothing about that crackdown sometime back on A. Q. Khan and his boys who were selling their nuclear technology all over the place." Hunt paused for a moment and added, "So you think it's a rogue group. I think it goes deeper than that. But what's the bottom line here? Do you think we can get India to hold their fire until we figure out who launched that missile?"

"Who the hell knows? I will say this, though. If the reports are true, and they took three weapons, we've got to find those other missiles and fast."

"Look, I want to head over and talk to Stock about this and give him a heads-up on the other two missiles."

"I hear he's pretty tied up with the Japanese state visit. I don't think you'll get in today."

"I'm going to try. I also need to brief him on that House Armed Services Subcommittee hearing this morning."

Ted got up from his desk and walked with Hunt to the door. "And how was it? Anything new going on?"

"Actually, yes. It's amazing. And you would have been blown away by the woman giving the testimony."

"Woman?"

"Yep. Seems she's the Project Director over at Bandaq Technologies, and she's got a new technology for missile defense."

"We've blown an awful lot of money on that stuff lately, and nothing works very well. Why would hers be any different?" Ted asked.

"I'm not sure. But if I can carve out some time, I'm going to head over there and try to find out. I'll tell you one thing, though. If this thing does work, it could change a hell of a lot around here."

"What do you mean?"

"Well, if her stuff is for real, it means the President's layered network of defense systems turns into a real shield for all kinds of missiles."

"I'll believe it when I see it," Ted said skeptically.

"Okay. Fine. But the way I see it, if there's ever a war going on and one side gets ahold of this thing, it completely alters the balance of power."

7

Rockville, Maryland—Wednesday Early Afternoon

Cameron Talbot held her cup of coffee in one hand and reached for the door to her lab with the other. She saw General Landsdale in the hallway. "Afternoon, Jack."

"Hello, Cammy. Good job on the Hill this morning."

"Except for that spontaneous round of indifference I got from the Congresswoman," Cammy said.

"Forget about her. I've already had calls from two other Committee Members asking for more information on Q-3."

"Let me guess," she said. "Was one of those calls from Davis Metcher?"

"One and the same."

She shrugged and walked inside with the general in tow.

"You know, he did seem pretty interested during the hearing," Jack said. "And don't forget, he *is* the Chairman." He studied her expression. "Do you have a problem with him?"

She hesitated. "No, I guess not. But you do know about his reputation."

The general gave a half smile. "Oh, you mean how everyone says that 'Metcher' rhymes with 'lecher'?"

"That's him."

"Well, I'm sure you'll manage. Just remember, we *need* his vote," he said firmly.

The general knew a lot about how government worked. He had spent thirty years in the Air Force. He was still fit, though his face had the weathered look of the gray manzanita branches Cammy used to collect on Stinson Beach when she was a kid. Her family had lived at Travis Air Force Base outside of San Francisco, where her dad was an air force pilot. The general had been the Base Commander.

When her father was killed by an advanced version of the AIM-9L Sidewinder missile that malfunctioned on board his F-16, the general had handled the paperwork and tried to comfort the family. But Cammy had been devastated. She still had dreams once in a while about fiery plane crashes, and she still hated to fly.

She had tried to get over it. She had even studied aeronautical engineering and got her Ph.D. at M.I.T. That was when the general retired from the Air Force, took the job as CEO of Bandaq, and offered her a job. She had accepted right away. But now, four years later, she was having such problems with her current project, she wondered if it would ever be developed and deployed.

Cammy set down her coffee. "Did Metcher say what he wanted exactly?" she asked. "I mean, I don't think he's the type to delve into too many operational details."

"He said he wanted to come out for a briefing. Said it might be on short notice, depending on what's happening on the Hill. Oh, and he mentioned that he was 'impressed with your demeanor' at the hearing," Jack said, "and he asked when we were going to stage a test in the field."

Cammy pulled her chair out, sat down, and switched on her computer. She clicked on Outlook and began to scan her e-mail.

"Cammy, I said Metcher wants to know about a field test."

She kept looking at her screen and said, "A test in the field? I'm not prepared—"

"Prepared? You've been *preparing* for this for months now."

She turned around to answer, "I like to follow the rule of the six p's."

"And they are?"

"Proper Preparation Precludes Piss-Poor Performance," she stated.

The general crossed his arms and stared at her. "I hear you. But now you've got to hear me. We need another good simulation. We need to schedule a field test. We need to brief Committee Members, and we need to get support from the board. Got that?"

"I've got it," Cammy said with a shake of her head.

"I know it's all coming to a head now. But if you can impress the Committee, we just might be able to get a decent chunk of money out of the defense budget. And it'll probably come right out of Sterling Dynamics' appropriation. They had a pretty good lock on the missile contracts until you came up with Q-3, and I have to admit I like the idea of giving those guys a run for their money."

Suddenly Cammy pursed her lips. "You know how I feel about that company. I mean, it was one of their missiles that killed Dad. You can't forget that."

Jack reached over and touched her shoulder. "Wait a minute, Cam. You know the investigation didn't prove anything."

"Maybe not to you. But the fact is, it misfired, and you know that Dad was too good a pilot to have made a mistake."

"You may be right. But that was ten years ago. Times have changed. Sterling has a whole new line of defensive missiles now."

"And I'm going to do everything I can to put them out of business," she said firmly.

"I doubt that we'd put them out of business, but we could give them a bit of grief," the general conceded.

"Speaking of grief," Cammy said, "when do you think Stan Bollinger will be taking over? I mean, is it a done deal?"

"I'm thinking of leaving at the end of next month. And yes, he'll be the new boss. The board has always been impressed that he had worked on the acquisition side of the Pentagon, you know."

"Okay. So he's got the five-sided building on his résumé. But I hate the idea of being his direct report."

"I'm sure you can work with him. This has always been a pretty collegial place."

"Maybe. For most of us. With Stan Bollinger, we're still on a last-name basis." She cocked her head and added, "Why do I think his middle initial must be 'O'?"

"Let's get back to the basics. We're all feeling the pressure. You more than most." He turned and headed for the door. "I really think you can pull it off, though. I never would have hired you and put you on Q-3 if I didn't think you could do it. We've invested a ton of money in this system. I don't want to lose it." He added, "And I don't want to lose you, either."

8

The White House—Wednesday Early Afternoon

Time to brief the brass. *If the brass is available,* Hunt thought. The last time he tried for an unscheduled appointment he couldn't get past the secretary. She was a regular Praetorian guard.

Hunt shoved his notes into his leather folder and headed out of the OEOB across West Exec to the awning over the door to the basement of the West Wing. The Secret Service agent sitting at the desk just inside the door took note of Hunt's security badge and nodded. The agents knew the staff by sight but always checked the badges through habit and training. After all, there were often reassignments and turnover to consider.

Hunt walked into the lower reception area, past the staff entrance to the Situation Room, and turned left. He checked out the dozens of photos along the walls, pictures of the President, his family, and visiting dignitaries. The photos were changed every few weeks, replaced with newer ones showing more recent events around the building or the Presidential entourage on the road.

Hunt walked up the blue-carpeted stairs to the first floor, turned down a short hall, and stopped at the desk of Lucy Shapiro. The dark-haired assistant was the picture of efficiency. Her black suit jacket covered all but the top button of her red silk blouse. A small arrangement of fresh tulips sat on the corner of her desk, replaced daily by the White House florist. Lucy had worked for National Security Advisors and their Deputies in four successive administrations, Democrat and Republican. She knew everyone and everything. Or at least it seemed that way.

Her Rolodex was as up-to-date as the files of the famous White House telephone operators who could find any member of the Administration at any time on any given day. And if they couldn't find you, you were in big trouble.

Legend had it that President Eisenhower needed to get ahold of one of his emissaries in the Middle East. When told that he was off in the desert somewhere, the White House operators had someone tape a note on a tree in an oasis. The guy found it and called in.

"Good afternoon, Lucy. Is Stock in?"

"Yes, he's in, Colonel Daniels. I assume you have something important, as you're not on his calendar," she said briskly.

"You're right, as usual. Can I get him for a minute?"

Lucy glanced at her computer screen and then at the wall clock. "He's got a meeting with Austin in fifteen minutes, and he's on the phone right now. But wait a minute, and I'll see what I can do."

"Thanks, Lucy. Things look pretty busy out there," Hunt said, motioning over his shoulder toward the West Wing reception area.

Lucy sighed. "Yes. As if it's not enough that we've got a Japanese state visit going on, there's an environmental group in the Roosevelt Room that's worried about some sort of eel extinction, and a Congressional delegation that's pushing for wind power. Sounds like an appropriate group on that score, though."

"Same old, same old," Hunt said as he smiled at the brusque lady with the impeccable manners and compartmentalized mind. "I heard that the Japanese wanted to have a bunch of their sumo wrestlers meet the President outside the Oval Office."

Lucy sniffed. "Can you imagine! Four-hundred-pound near-naked men rolling around in our Rose Garden? Not for this White House, I can assure you."

Hunt chuckled. "I know. I know. That one came up at our morning staff meeting, and we decided to boot it over to the Secretary of State."

"Yes, I heard. Let those seventh-floor diplomatic types handle that one." She glanced down at her phone and picked up the handset. "Colonel Daniels is here with something important, sir." She paused, then turned to Hunt. "You can go in to see the Deputy now, but mind the time."

He winked at her. "Thanks, Lucy, catch you later." He walked over to the open door of Stockton Sloan, Deputy National Security Advisor.

A graduate of West Point, Stock had a stellar military career. When he retired, he was quickly recruited by the current National Security Advisor, Austin Gage, to be his number two man, and serve as his eyes and ears around the agencies.

"Good morning, Daniels," Stock said as he placed a red folder on top of two others on his desk. "Feels like a three-ring circus around here today. So, have you got something new on that missile strike?"

Hunt pulled up a chair and opened his leather folder. He had jotted down several points he wanted to raise with Stock. He'd keep it brief.

"The big news is from one of Ted's ISI contacts. Seems one of their depots is missing three cruise missiles along with their launch vehicles."

"Now it's three?" Stock exclaimed. "Are they sure the other two are gone and it's not just some paperwork foul-up?"

"Gone. He says they're gone."

"Do they have any idea who . . . ?"

"Not yet. But it sure looks like whoever stole them has a lot of support inside the government. Ted's not so sure about—"

"Jesus Christ!" Stock interrupted. "Does ISI have any leads on who fired the first one? Anything they're telling us, that is?"

Hunt checked his notes and shifted forward. "Ted's working his contacts. And I've checked with CIA, NSA, and State. No firm leads yet. No claims of responsibility, either."

"Well, stay on it." Stock checked his watch and frowned. "I've got a meeting in a few minutes."

"I know." Hunt got up from his chair and said, "Just one more quick point. It's about that new missile defense technology Bandaq is putting together. Ironically, it's supposed to work against cruise missiles."

"Cruise? Not ballistic?"

"Nope. Cruise and all the guided missiles. It's a computer program that evidently takes over the guidance system of the missile."

"How the hell would they do that?" Stock asked, his face suddenly becoming animated.

"I don't know . . . yet. But I'm going to head over there as soon as I can get away to check it out."

"I did see a short article in *Air Force Times* saying their Project Director was going to testify at the hearing, but there weren't many details."

"She was there with her CEO because they're trying to get R & D funds in the new defense budget."

"They'd better hurry up."

"I know. After I see if this thing is for real, I'll let you know, and maybe we can give it a push with the Committee."

"For this one line item? No way," Stock said, raising his eyebrows.

"Why not? Nancy Kennedy's legislative shop could alert a few Members when they're on the Hill. They'll be up there a lot this week anyway. Look, I know we're trying for a major increase in defense spending and some Congressmen are balking—"

"Balking? I'd term it major roadblocking."

Hunt glanced down at his talking points again. "Besides, there's an important thing here when it comes to the budget."

"Which is rapidly getting out of hand," Stock said.

"Okay, I know. But Q-3 . . . that's the name of the project . . . Q-3 is cheaper because it doesn't have to send up a missile to knock down one of theirs. It's all done with computer programs. And think about it. If this thing really works, can you imagine a better deterrent than having an enemy even *think* that we could neutralize their missiles?"

Stock leaned back and steepled his fingers. "*If* is a big concept for a small word. On the other hand, if the damn thing does work, there'd be a helluva market for a system like that. Taiwan wants missile defense against China. India's trying to buy Israel's Arrow system. And, of course, you've got Japan worried about North Korea, so they're contracting with Sterling Dynamics for their missile system."

Stock turned and pulled a red folder out from the middle of the pile on his desk and continued. "And on that subject, I'm sure the Japanese Prime Minister will want to talk about it in the meeting with the President this afternoon." Stock paused and glanced over at Hunt again. "Now on this Q-3 thing, go out there and get me an assessment."

"Will do."

"And one more thing. As soon as we get anything on those stolen missiles, I want you to stay on top of that one . . . and I mean yesterday! The President is leaning hard on India not to retaliate, but if another one is launched, all bets are off."

"Right. I know."

"In his briefing this morning, the President said he's thinking about appointing a Special Envoy to go over there and try to get peace talks back on track. He also mentioned that the big 350th anniversary celebration of the Taj Mahal is coming up and he's got visions of some sort of a treaty being signed right there with the world watching."

"That would be a pretty fancy photo op," Hunt said.

"And come to think of it, an advance team could pull double duty on this . . . set up the negotiations, but also talk to the defense people in both India and Pakistan about those damn missiles."

"Good idea. Want me to get on it?"

Stock nodded. "Let's get ahead of the curve here. Do some preliminary planning. Get me a list of names for the team . . . someone from the Pentagon . . . CIA . . . guess we'll have to include State," Stock said with a frown. Everyone knew Stockton Sloan had great disdain for the diplomatic approach when direct action could be used instead.

Hunt made a few notes in his folder and headed for the door. "I'll have a Decision Directive ready by COB."

If he was going to check with all the agencies again, summarize his findings, and pull together an advance team by Close Of Business, he'd better get hustling. He turned and left the office, feeling a bit like a juggler in that circus that Stock was talking about.

9

The young man burst into the office of the CEO waving a copy of the *Air Force Times.*

"Have you seen this, boss?"

Dr. Nettar Kooner, Chairman and CEO of Sterling Dynamics, swiveled around in his maroon leather chair and faced the young man. "Damn right I saw it. This could mean big trouble."

"That's what I thought when I read about the hearing. The question is, will Bandaq's program really work? But even if it does, we might be able to delay it or kill it."

"I wish we could, because if it does work, it could mean big problems for our bottom line. Our new production of defensive missiles could be obsolete, and that means millions down the drain."

"I know. But on the other hand, we've still got the foreign contracts, especially the Japanese. Those could save that division."

Dr. Kooner got up from behind his sleek cherrywood desk and glanced over at a series of photographs lining the wall of his spacious office. There were pictures of a rocket launch, one of another rocket being loaded onto a C-17, and yet another helicopter shot of a series of missiles lined up outside their main production facility.

Two other frames held certificates awarded to Dr. Nettar Kooner showing a master's degree and Ph.D. in engineering from the University of Allahabad, the famous school founded in 1887, alma mater of Nobel Prize winners, home to Jawaharlal Nehru, first prime minister of independent India.

Dr. Kooner was proud of those degrees. Proud that his family, part of the wealthy clans of Calcutta, had sent him to that university to continue developing the family dynasty of business and political leaders. And here he was, almost at the pinnacle of his career. Or was he?

He turned to his Executive Assistant, a young man he had brought over from New Delhi to be his right-hand man. The fellow was smart and loyal. He also had another trait that Dr. Kooner admired. He knew how to conduct an investigation into his competitor's pipelines. He knew how to cut corners without jeopardizing a contract. The man could be ruthless. And right now, that could prove invaluable.

"The Japanese still want our missiles to protect them from the North Koreans, and, of course, we still have the Taiwanese in our back pockets in their standoff with the mainland. But our big problem now is going to be the Pentagon," the CEO said.

"I don't think they'd renege on your handshake deal."

"With the deficits they're running, I wouldn't make any wagers."

"Then again, Bandaq's technology may not work."

"Doubtful. Why would they spend years developing a system that fails? The general isn't that dumb. In fact, he's one of the craftiest guys in the business."

"Well, what if we developed the same . . . or better . . . technology?" the young man asked, a gleam in his eye.

"Fat chance. That woman they've got over there is some sort of computer genius with systems our guys have never conjured up. We tried to get a line on them once, but that backfired." He paused and added, "However, I think you may be on to something." He glanced down at his calendar and issued an order. "Set up a meeting with the I-team. I want to start a crash project."

"You got it, sir."

"The problem is, right now we've put all our chips on the new high-speed rocket that can destroy an enemy missile within five minutes of launch."

"I know. In the boost phase."

"Precisely. But it's expensive. And it'll be even more expensive if we have to scrap that line and start over."

"On the other hand," the young man suggested, "you were talking about the foreign contracts. If this Q-3 thing really does work, maybe we should think about whether we could get ahold of it . . . make a deal with Stan Bollinger. You know, cut a joint venture with Bandaq . . . and maybe get it to Delhi."

"What? And hand a fat contract over to the general so his stock soars while ours ends up in the toilet?"

"I just meant . . . well, you know . . . with all the problems they're having in Kashmir, Delhi might need our help."

"I can't think about that right now. I've got to figure out how to get the Committee to fund our line and squeeze out Bandaq's. I don't think there's room for both of us in this year's MDA budget."

"Do you want me to work up a plan?"

"What do you think we pay the boys in the K Street office for?" Kooner said, furrowing his brow.

"I know, sir. It's just that it seems to me this is going to take higher-level input than a Vice President of Government Relations."

He scrutinized the young man. "On second thought, you may be right. This one's going to require a good deal of personal attention. And I think I know exactly where to start."

10

Cammy stared at the first computer screen showing the projected trajectory of a missile launched from some distance away. The second screen was a graphic demonstration of her software activity, with a chart of adjustments acting like a virus invading another computer. The third screen was where she was typing in her instructions.

Sometimes she felt like the commander who sent the Trojan horse filled with hidden combatants into enemy territory. By embedding her own combatants, she could surprise the bad guys and take over the city or, in her case, the onboard computer inside the missile. At least that was the plan.

She had been reworking the algorithms, trying to ignore a pain in her wrist that had been bothering her lately, when she heard the knock. General Landsdale opened the door. "Excuse me. Sorry to interrupt, but I just had a call from a Lieutenant Colonel Daniels from the White House. He says he exchanged e-mails with you about the hearing."

Cammy looked up from her keyboard and sighed as she pushed away from the desk. "Yes, he was there. And he sent a nice note."

"Well, he's on his way over. You need to break away to give him a briefing on Q-3."

"It's classified."

The general snorted. "Don't be ridiculous."

"I know. I know. He's got clearance."

"Damn right. Those NSC boys have code word clearance higher than any number you can count."

"I knew that," she said.

"And this guy's probably got TS/SBI for SCI, for God's sake."

"Would you care to translate?" she asked, straightening her headband.

"It means Top Secret/Special Background Investigation for Sensitive Compartmented Information," the general explained patiently. He paused for a moment and added, "I doubt if he has a Yankee White clearance, but that doesn't matter to us."

"That's the highest level?"

"Yep. Just for the President's closest advisors. The ones who can have access to him anytime. Those guys have a Zero Defects clearance."

"I guess that means they don't even have outstanding parking tickets." Cammy observed. "Okay, okay. He gets a briefing. How much disclosure this time? I mean, do you want me to tell him about how it worked once, but then the last three simulations have failed?"

"This briefing could be important to the company. This guy's in the catbird seat at the NSC, and a little push from the White House legislative affairs staff could really help us with the Committee."

"I know. Guess I'm just pressed for time."

The general walked over and looked down at her computer. "Cammy, it worked once. Focus on the positive here."

Cammy stared at the first screen again. "Jack, I'm so focused, I should do ads for Kodak."

The general headed for the door. "At least you can keep a sense of humor here."

"Barely."

"Daniels will be here pretty soon. Let me know how it goes. I'll be in my office the rest of the day."

Cammy tried to concentrate on her program again, but something about the e-mail exchange with Colonel Daniels had bothered her. It reminded her of the disastrous affair she'd had with Ken. Why couldn't she forget the man? He had seemed so interested in her. Too interested, as it turned out. She pushed the memories aside when the interoffice phone rang. She swiveled her chair and picked it up. "Dr. Talbot here."

"There's a Lieutenant Colonel Daniels in the lobby for you."

"Okay, thanks. I'll be right out."

She saved the screen, straightened a few papers on her desk, and headed to the front of the building. When she pushed through the double doors, she saw a tall man with broad shoulders looking out the window. He wasn't wearing a uniform. Instead, he wore a navy suit with a blue and white striped shirt. *Straight out of the windows at Brooks Brothers*, she thought. When she got closer and called out, "Colonel Daniels?" he turned.

With a square jaw, high forehead, and brilliant blue eyes, his face was striking. She wondered why she hadn't noticed him in the hearing room.

He took three long strides and extended his hand. "Yes, and I know you are Dr. Talbot."

"Cammy," she said as she shook hands. "Everyone calls me Cammy."

"And my name's Hunt."

"This way then. I'll show you around." She peered into the retina-recognition lens and waited for the door to click open.

"Pretty tight security around this place," he said, examining the black box installed next to the double doors.

And we're going to keep it that way, she thought. "Yes, it's a pretty good biometric system. I think it's better than the fingerprint or voice-recognition programs. But then I doubt it's any tighter than the White House," she said as she led the way down the hall.

"Guess that's right. I don't pay much attention to it with all the Secret Service types around to worry about who's coming in and out."

"I've never been to the White House, so I haven't seen it."

"Well, maybe we can rectify that one of these days." He followed her into her office and stared at the long row of computer screens and keyboards. "This place looks like USSTRATCOM."

"You mean the Command Center at Offutt Air Force Base?" she said as she motioned to a chair.

"So, have you been there?" he asked, pulling the chair closer to her console.

"No, haven't been there, either. What's it like?"

"It's a big show-and-tell place with eight screens."

"Well, I don't have quite that many. Scoot over here, and I'll give you a quick outline of our project."

He sat down next to her and watched while she began to key in some initial data and the first screen sprang to life. Something inside him was starting to spring to life, too. He had a vague sense of the scent of vanilla. *Must be her shampoo or soap or something.*

What the hell. What was the matter with him? He was here on official business. She was a scientist, and he was here to get up-to-speed on a new technology, not get distracted. She did look kind of intriguing, though. A combination of an all-business demeanor with an almost but not quite friendly façade. He wondered if she was one of those "Mensa" types who didn't suffer fools gladly. *It doesn't matter,* he told himself. She may be attractive, but right now he had a job to do. And he'd better get about it.

He snapped out of his reverie and turned to watch the computer screen. "So do you want to explain what's happening here?" he asked as he saw her fingers fly over the keys.

"Sure. Just a second." She made some more adjustments and then pointed to the first screen. "Okay. First, the U.S. radar and satellite tracking devices sense that a missile has been launched."

"Yes, we have lots of those sensors. Ground based and space based."

"Right. But we have special radar and satellite teams that can tie into those sensors and notify my Q-3 project here. Obviously, time is critical, and we're working on ways to cut down on the time delay between a satellite sensor and our tracking system. There's at least a sixth of a second delay from a satellite. I can't afford anything more than that. Not when the missile is going so fast. Anyway, we've got teams that handle that part. We've got a guy from India, Dr. Raj P. Singh, in charge of that division," she said. "And he'll be moving in on our division, too," she muttered.

"Raj P. Singh? Don't think I know him. But there are a lot of Indian guys in this business."

"I know. Must be something in the gene pool."

"The new CEO over at Sterling Dynamics is from India."

Cammy winced when she heard the company name.

"I've met him," Hunt continued. "Pretty impressive fellow. He's got a bunch of guys from his university on the staff over there."

"So I've heard. Anyway, our satellite team sees the missile and relays its course here."

"Sounds good so far," Hunt said. "Then what?"

"Okay, so as soon as we get the signal that there's an incoming missile, Q-3 kicks in."

"What a minute," he said. "How do you figure out what kind of missile it is?"

"That's the tricky part. I've had to research just about every type of missile and anti-missile device that I can find, develop a huge database of their operational signatures as well as their critical parts, and then build ways to counter these weapons. Here, with one of the newer computer-guided missiles, I try to evaluate its C^3," she said as she gestured toward her bookshelves crammed with papers and manuals.

"Its Command, Control, and Communication."

"That's right."

"So you see that there's an incoming missile. Then what?" he asked.

"Then we try to lock on and communicate with its onboard computer. We use fast-calculating algorithms to figure out what frequency it's listening to. If it's listening to a single frequency . . . no problem. If it's a variant of spread spectrum, that's where the magic of algorithms works."

"Spread spectrum. Wasn't that invented back in World War II?"

"Yes, by an actress, Hedy Lamarr."

"Hedy Lamarr? I've seen her in some old movies. She was a big star, but I had no idea she had anything to do with spectrums."

"She was one of my idols when I was a kid. I heard the story about how this movie star had invented a radio guidance system for torpedoes, and I thought it was really neat."

"So you wanted to grow up and be like Hedy Lamarr?" he asked, thinking that with a face like that, this scientist could have made movies, too.

"Only to act on ideas, not on the screen," Cammy replied.

"I wonder how she got the idea?" he asked.

Cammy turned away from her computer screens to face him. "Let's see. As I remember the story, she was born in Austria and married some rich guy who made munitions and planes. He was into control systems, too. So she probably learned a few things from him. But he was a big Nazi sympathizer. He never wanted her to be an actress. He wanted her to stay home and just entertain his friends. Like Hitler and Mussolini."

"I'll bet they liked her act," he said.

"I suppose. But she didn't like those guys. And it turns out she didn't like her husband very much, either. So she left him. That was before the war. And she finally got to America and got a movie contract.

"Then she met this smart guy who was a concert pianist. I think they were neighbors in Hollywood. Anyway, they got to talking about serious stuff, and she told him about an idea she had about radio control and frequency hopping."

"Frequency hopping?" he asked. "How did they make it work?"

"They figured out that if you could coordinate rapid changes in radio frequencies, it would be like a whole new secret communication system. And because the guy played the piano, he came up with the idea of piano rolls. You know, those things with little slots in them?"

"Sure. I've seen those."

"So they used these rolls with slots in them to synchronize the frequency changes in the transmitter and the receiver."

"So each end had a piano roll to use to figure it out."

"Pretty clever, huh?"

He nodded. "Right!" He was enjoying this.

"Well, later they got into electronics rather than piano rolls. But they got a patent. Our military used their idea. And we call it spread spectrum."

Cammy turned back to the computer screen. "Okay, back to business. So we get inside and analyze the missile's control program. The term is 'reverse engineering.' You start at the shell and work back to see what makes it go. At that point, one thing you can do is figure out if it has enough fuel to get back home and not drop down on a friendly site."

"And if there is enough fuel . . . if it hasn't gone more than halfway to its target, you can what? Send it back where it came from?" he asked, staring at the screen.

"That's the general idea. Kind of like a boomerang."

"Jesus! This is wild. But go back. Go back to where you figure out the frequency and how to communicate with the computer. How do you take control of it?"

She hit a series of keys and pointed to the second screen. "Okay, now watch. I send a computer software routine that acts like a virus invading the computer on board the missile. That virus interferes with what is controlling the missile and substitutes the commands I give it. So I become, effectively, the pilot of this missile."

He'd seen a lot of guidance systems, but nothing like this. He couldn't believe it. But as he stared at the screens and started to analyze the process, he began to understand the concept.

"But what if it's not pre-programmed but guided real-time by a command and control center?" he asked.

"We're working on that, too. Watch." She hit more keys and a series of wiggly lines moved across the second screen. "See, it's like a worm that goes into the missile, crawls around, and figures out if it's communicating with its originator. If it is, the worm, like the other embedded computing routine, can then first invade the originator and put the transmitting program out of commission and just send the missile home. Or it can send signals back to us as to the location of that control center. And then our guys can take it out. You know, bomb it or send some troops over to get rid of it."

"What if the remote command center figures out it's been invaded before we get around to destroying it?"

"They won't have time to write new software," she explained. "They've just lost their payloads."

"But later," he asked, "when they figure out their system's got a virus, so to speak, wouldn't they be able to disable it?"

"Maybe, maybe not," she said. "Our software has to be so hardened and have such a strong shell that the bad guys can't hack their way in. Think of it like an illness. The body can't fight back at a new virus because it doesn't know how it works. It takes time. And in a battle situation, they simply don't have the time."

"Yeah, like SARS or something," he ventured.

"You got it, Colonel." She turned her chair around and crossed her arms. "So what do you think?"

"What do I think? I think it's incredible."

"Now we just need the Armed Services Committee to agree with you," she said.

He nodded. "But, does it work? I mean, you said at the meeting that you haven't had a chance to test it in the field."

She hesitated. She had explained the system but not how she wrote the software or how she really took control of the missile. How much more should she tell this guy? How trustworthy would he be? Did he have some hidden agenda she had no clue about? He already said he knew the head of Sterling Dynamics. She got that image of Ken again with his ever-present smile. She tried to push the picture away, but it kept intruding in her mind's eye at the most inopportune times. Like now. Ken had been attentive. Just like Hunt. Ken had seemed so interested in her work. Just like Hunt. And Ken had never been intimidated by her Ph.D. title like so many other guys she had met. What now? What were Hunt's motives?

She knew that missile defense was high on the President's list of priorities. He had pushed for an increase in the budget for the Missile Defense Agency at DOD and had highlighted the program in his last State of the Union address. But hers was kind of a special project. It was new. It was different. And it could be threatening to some of the status quo types, especially to the guys over at Sterling who manufactured the missiles used to shoot down an enemy attack. If her project succeeded and got funded, the Pentagon wouldn't need Sterling's big "bullets that hit bullets" anymore. Or would they? Again she thought about how Hunt had said he knew the people at Sterling. Of course he'd know them. Was he in their back pocket, too, and just here to check out the competition?

She suddenly realized that Hunt was looking at her, waiting for her answer.

"Test trial? As I said, we haven't gotten quite that far yet. It's worked here in the lab."

"What's holding up a test against a live missile?" he asked.

"Well, we're dealing with a lot of variables here, like what kind of missile will they send up? How soon can we figure out its signature? How fast can we learn to communicate with it? Are the algorithms spending too much time analyzing one series of possibilities when they should be switching to the next, and all of that? I mean, it's something we're working on all the time here. And now we're getting a lot of pressure from the Committee to schedule a trial." *To say nothing of the pressure I'm getting from my boss and the* CFO *to put up or shut up*, she thought to herself.

"And?"

"And what?"

"And when do you think that will be? I'd like to be there."

So he wanted to be there. He wanted to be at a test that just might blow up in her face and send the stock of Bandaq down the tubes.

"Well, we've been talking about that. I'm trying to get the kinks out so we can go for the test in less than two weeks now."

"Two weeks? That sounds good. That means you'll be just in time for the markup of the defense bill. Anything later than that, and I'm afraid you'll have a problem. For this year anyway."

"Yes. I know."

"And I assume you'll be using the Atlantic Testing Facility?"

"The Atlantic? Yes. That one."

The demonstration was over, but the colonel made no move to leave. She had given him what he wanted. Most of it anyway. But he had something she wanted. She glanced at the wall clock and made another calculation.

"It's almost one, and I was just thinking. I'm about to head down to our cafeteria for a quick bite. I can't take much time. I'm pretty slammed here. But if you want a sandwich or something, the food's pretty decent."

He checked his watch, looked up, and gave her a slow grin. "I've got a bunch of stuff today, too, but why not? A quick sandwich would be good."

She switched off her computer and grabbed her purse. "Follow me."

They picked up their trays and silverware. Hunt reached for a roast beef sandwich and bag of chips while Cammy picked up her usual fruit salad and yogurt.

"Here, let me get this," he said as they walked to the register.

"Oh, thanks."

They took a small table by the wall. "There are a couple more things I wanted to tell you about Q-3," she said as she put her food on the table and set the tray aside.

"Such as?"

"Well, first, from a budget standpoint, I wanted to go over the idea that with our system, you don't have to send up a missile to hit another one. I mean, we're talking about saving millions of dollars with every launch."

Hunt stirred some sugar into a glass of iced tea and agreed. "Yeah. I remember that from the hearing. But you still have the cost of the radar and satellite system tie-ins."

"Well, sure. All of the missile defense systems have detectors. But ours still saves a ton."

"That is a point. Of course right now the Hill is screaming about deficits. Well, some of the members are anyway."

"I know. But Q-3 is really different." She went on to explain how he could think of it as a Trojan horse invading enemy territory. He wolfed down his sandwich as he listened to her explanations.

"And so with the cost savings and the unique capabilities of Q-3, do you think the White House will back us on this one?" she asked.

"You mean with the Hill?"

"Yes. We hear that Davis Metcher hasn't made up his mind yet on whether to earmark the project. We know there are a lot of demands right now, but we need those R & D funds to keep going." *And I need to get the funds to keep my division alive*, she thought.

He hesitated when he saw her hopeful stare. "I don't know yet. A lot will depend on that test. Oh, by the way, when you were going through all of this, I thought of one more question. An important one."

"Shoot."

He took the last bite of his sandwich. "Let's say this scheme of yours works. Could it take control of our own cruise missiles? And if it could, what if our adversaries got ahold of it?"

"I've thought about that. First of all, remember I told you I've been studying all kinds of missile systems. At least what I could find out."

"Yes."

"Well, what we're designing is really aimed at what foreign countries are producing now."

"And ours are more sophisticated, so you wouldn't be targeting our stockpile. Is that it?"

"That's it. At least for now."

"Okay. Look, I'm going to go back and talk to some people about this."

She raised her eyebrows, "But . . ."

"Don't worry. It won't go further than the NSC." He checked his watch again and said, "It's getting late. I have to get back to D.C." He reached in his wallet and took out a card. Then he grabbed a pen from his inside pocket. "Here's my card. And let me give you my private cell." He wrote down the number. "If you need anything or have any questions or problems, really, anything at all, give me a holler, will you?"

She took the white card and studied the embossed gold emblem on the top. It looked like an eagle with part of a flag below. She read his name and title. There was no address. His office number was on the lower right side. At the lower left, it simply read, "The White House."

"Nice card," she said as she slipped it into the side pocket of her purse and got up from the table.

"Standard-issue," he replied.

As they walked out, she never noticed that someone else was watching them. Intently.

11

Washington, D.C.—Thursday Afternoon

"Today, we will analyze how the desire for freedom of religion played a key role in the settling of the original colonies."

The history class at American University was under way. Jambaz was taking notes, trying to look interested when everything he was hearing annoyed him.

Freedom of religion. What is that? There is but one God, Allah. And Muhammad, Peace Be unto Him, is His messenger.

Across the room a young girl with big dark eyes and long straight black hair was looking at Jambaz. When he caught her eye, she gave him a wry smile. He quickly looked down at his notes. Why should he even notice a brazen woman like that? She didn't cover her hair. She had no respect.

The professor noticed her. He called on her when she raised her hand. "What about the Muslim religion?" she asked. "You've only talked about the Judeo-Christian ethic. But we have a lot of Muslims in this country, so how do they fit in?"

Jambaz jerked his head up to study the professor, a man of about fifty with a bald head and eyes that darted back and forth as he vied for the attention of his students.

"Yes," the teacher replied. "There are many who believe that Islam is the one true religion. Many are coming to this country, getting jobs, and fitting in quite well. But they did not settle this country. They had nothing to do with the formation of our laws. In their religion, their God is Allah, and everything a true believer does is dictated by their religious leaders. Here in America, we believe in the separation of church and state."

What a stupid man he is with his Judeo-Christian basis for laws. The Jews and the Christians. As far as Jambaz was concerned, they would all burn in hell. Perhaps he could hasten that process and get a few of them to burn first here on earth.

He knew that he would go to heaven, where the rewards in Paradise were great. For didn't the Prophet Muhammad, Peace Be unto Him, say, "The smallest reward for the people of Paradise is an abode where there are eighty thousand servants and seventy-two wives"? And aren't "wives" described in the Qur'an as "having resurrected them as virgins, full of love, well matched to those who have attained to righteousness"?

Yes, he would go to heaven. But not yet. He had more to do before he would receive his rewards.

Back in his apartment, Jambaz logged on to his computer and again entered the private chat room. He had taken many precautions. He was now using the "Pretty Good Protection" program, which gives the sender and receiver a 128-digit password. Even if NSA tried to track their communications, he was certain it would take weeks to break the combination. He was careful not to repeat his patterns too often. He was clever. He was smart. He could always elude them.

He had thought about using a wireless connection at the Starbucks café on the corner. But when he went there and scanned the area, he saw the cameras and knew they could coordinate a video with the time someone logged on to a computer. No, it was safer to stay here and work alone.

A long message was there waiting for him. He stared at the words and carefully copied the lengthy instructions from his leader. He felt the adrenaline level rising, his breath getting shorter, as he scrutinized the letters so carefully arranged.

An hour later, he studied the translation he had devised. The first launch of their stolen missiles had received wide publicity and praise back home. And yet no one had yet figured out that his cell had fired it.

"We are hoping that India concludes that Pakistan fired the missile since

it came from Pakistan's arsenal," Khan wrote. "India has many cruise missiles they can launch, and the repercussions will be enormous if they decide to fight back."

The message went on to explain that there was a chance India might retaliate against one of Lashkar's locations, if they figured out who really
staged the attack. But there was an answer for that. Jambaz would provide
the answer.

Jambaz stared at his notes. *He* would provide the answer? Here in
America? How could he do such a thing? He read on.

His leader referred to an earlier message and wrote, "The new technology developed by the infidel scientist may now be ready. She has received
publicity because she testified at a Congressional hearing. From all reports,
it would be simple to transport her new software program back to our cell.
You must find a way to procure this invention for the protection of all of
our people and for the glory of Allah."

There they were. The words giving Jambaz his orders. Interesting that
they involved a woman. If a woman had been selected to tell their story to
the American Congressmen, it must be because she was pretty. These Americans only thought about exploiting their women and parading them around
for their own ends. She must have many men backing her up, doing the real
work. But no matter. He would follow the instructions.

He read the last line of his orders. "If the message cannot be obtained
quickly, the messenger must be destroyed to preclude our enemies from
obtaining it. This must not happen. You must succeed."

Jambaz glanced over at his small bookshelf now crammed with textbooks, religious writings, his beloved Qur'an, newspaper clippings, a dictionary, and a few supplies. There were no pictures on the walls. Pictures
were forbidden in strict Islam. There was no music here. That, too, was forbidden. But that was fine. He needed quiet to think, to plan, and to plot.

He sat at his desk and reviewed his notes. He turned back to his computer, clicked on Explorer, and typed in www.Switchboard.com. He typed
in two names and got phone numbers, addresses, as well as maps showing
their exact location. *How foolish these Americans are, putting their telephone books online.* He then carefully removed the black American Heritage dictionary from the shelf and frowned. *American Heritage. Not my
heritage!*

He put the heavy book aside and reached behind it to remove the small
Browning 9mm handgun he bought at a gun show. It had been so easy

showing his fake ID. He had walked right out with the gun and kept it hidden ever since, waiting for exactly the right moment when he might need it.

Now that moment had come. He checked the clip, slipped the Browning into the pocket of his black pants, grabbed his keys, moved out into the hall, and quietly locked the door.

12

Rockville, Maryland—Thursday Mid-Afternoon

Cammy looked up at the wall clock and figured she could use a cup of coffee. She had spent the last few hours poring over calculations, and she needed a break. She saved her notes, grabbed her purse, and headed out the door.

Down in the dining room she saw her friend Melanie Duvall, the company's Vice President of Corporate Communications. The woman was dressed in a slim black skirt and lavender sweater. A gold chain with a medallion hung around her neck.

"Hi, Mel. Pretty sweater. So what's going on in your shop today?"

"Just getting some press releases together about our satellite project. How about you? Anything I can publicize?"

"Not yet. Still trying to make Q-3 score again."

Melanie flashed her hazel eyes and pushed a wisp of ebony hair off her face. "A little encouraging press release about its potential might hold the interest of the Hill right now. Gotta keep our name in the forefront. You know the line, 'If a tree falls in the forest . . . '"

" 'And no one hears it . . .' Yeah, I know," Cammy replied. "Just give me a few more days, and I'll try to have another story for you." She reached for a coffee mug and said, "Isn't this the day you're getting your car serviced?"

"Glad you asked," Melanie said. "I just checked, and they're kind of backed up, so they wanted to know if I could leave it for a day or two. Can I grab a lift home with you?"

"Sure, if you don't mind leaving late. I've got a ton of work to do, and I'm under the gun now to finalize this thing. Dealing with a string of failures can be downright depressing."

"Hey, c'mon. We're making progress here, and Q-3 is just about to jump off the drawing boards. I can feel it," Mel said encouragingly.

"No wonder you're good at your job, always putting the best face on things when everything's going to hell in a handbasket."

Cammy paid the cashier and was looking around the dining room when she spotted a slender, dark man sitting alone at a corner table. "Well, I might as well get it over with," she said, staring across the room.

"Get what over with?" Mel's eyes lit up as she followed Cammy's gaze. "What's going on?"

"I have to talk to Raj. Now that he's nailed his satellite project, the general is reassigning him to my team. Says we could use an extra pair of hands right now."

Melanie leaned over in a conspiratorial fashion and whispered, "I wasn't going to tell anyone, but tonight I'll tell *you* about that man's hands. They're amazing."

Cammy eyed her friend, glanced at Raj and then back at Melanie. "What are you trying to tell me, Mel? That you and Raj . . . ?"

"Mmm-hmm," Mel said. "The man's divine. We've been seeing each other, but I didn't want to say anything because, well, you know how gossip gets around this place."

"Intriguing," Cammy said. "You and Raj. I never would have thought . . . then again, the man is rather polished. And he doesn't appear to have any pierced body parts," she added.

"Get real, Cam," Mel chided.

"In all the time he's worked here, I never heard anything about his private life. He always seems so quiet and still."

"Still waters indeed," Mel said with a knowing nod. "And speaking of men, who was that hunk you were having lunch with earlier?"

"Oh, you mean Hunt."

"Hunt? So who's Hunt?"

"He's the guy from the White House who sent me an e-mail about my testimony. Remember? I told you there was some guy who was in the audience and wanted to come over for a briefing."

"That's not just 'some guy,' my dear."

"I guess."

"Good God! He looks like that lawyer on the old *JAG* reruns."

"Yes, I suppose he does. Sort of. But look, Mel, I gave him a briefing on Q-3 because I could use his help in getting our funding. I mean, if we could get a little support from the White House legislative staff, well then I might really have a story for you."

"Wow. The White House! That would be terrific. When are you going to see him again?"

"I haven't got any idea. But he did give me his cell phone number . . . said to call if I needed anything."

"Okay. You keep in touch with that one. I'll keep in touch with Raj and . . . well, who knows?"

Cammy held her mug and headed across the room. If she could talk to Raj privately for a while, she might get a better sense of his priorities and whether he'd be a help. Or a hindrance.

Dr. Raj Prakash Singh was sitting alone, finishing his tea, reading the latest issue of *Technology Review*.

"Hi, Raj, glad I caught you. May I sit down?"

The young Indian scientist looked up and smiled, his large brown eyes beaming a welcome. "Please do, Cammy. I haven't seen you for a while. You have been tied up with Q-3," he commented in his precise British accent.

" 'Hog-tied' might be a better description. We had that Congressional hearing yesterday, you know."

"Yes, I heard about that. The word around the labs is that you took on the lady from California and came out the winner."

"I wouldn't go that far, but we did have a pretty good exchange. Anyway, we're really pressed now to get a major field test scheduled. The general says your satellite team is ready."

"Yes, this is true."

"Jack also said he was going to reassign you to my team for a while. Has he talked to you about that?"

"Yes. He called and asked if I could make the switch. If that is all right with you, of course."

She had to admit the guy was smooth, asking her opinion, as if she had a choice.

"I know you've been with the company for what . . . two years now?"

"Yes."

"And before that?"

"I was doing research on defense programs for ITI."

"On their satellites?"

"Yes. But I always wanted to come to this country. And when your government expanded the E1 visa category . . ."

"The one where we let in the smart scientists and business types, right?"

"Yes, but it also includes athletes, artists, others," he said deferentially.

"So obviously, you qualifed."

"Thankfully, yes."

"Did you work for any other American company?"

"No. General Landsdale hired me. This is where my loyalty lies now."

"I see."

"You must understand. I have been working on defensive projects for years, and now with Q-3, it is exciting to be a part, perhaps a small part, in seeing it succeed."

As Cammy finished her coffee, she thought he seemed sincere enough. The trouble was, it would take time to figure out if the man would be a partner . . . or a parasite. And time was running out. In the last analysis, she sure could use another pair of eyes examining her algorithms. Pair of eyes for her. Pair of hands for Melanie. This could get really interesting.

"About working with my team," she said. "Would tomorrow morning be too soon?"

"Not at all. Not at all. I will come to your lab at eight o'clock."

13

The White House—Thursday Late Afternoon

"The President needs this room in thirty minutes," Austin Gage warned, "so let's get a move on here."

The National Security Advisor, Stockton Sloan, Ted Jameson, and Hunt Daniels sat around the gleaming hardwood table in the Situation Room of the White House. Jasmine Ito, the Director of Intelligence Programs, opened the door and slid into a chair next to Ted.

Hunt felt quite at home in this complex of small offices, a technical center, and this conference room in the basement of the West Wing. He was in it at least once a day. The conference room, commonly called the Sit Room, measured just twenty-four by seven feet and was pretty compact and simple compared to Hollywood depictions.

Besides the table and leather chairs that could seat two dozen people in a pinch, it was equipped with TV sets and two-way videoconferencing capability. Its only decoration was the large, round Presidential seal on the wall.

Hunt often conferred with the thirty or so handpicked technicians and watch officers who worked in teams around the clock, just outside the Sit Room. They were the ones who received cables and Internet updates, reviewed intelligence from State, Defense, the CIA, NSA, and other agencies, read news wires, and monitored TV headlines.

They had to work fast to synthesize and summarize it all into two daily intelligence reports prepared for the President and top White House officials and route over a thousand messages a day to various staff members. They also set up, monitored, and arranged translations for Presidential phone calls and teleconferences with other heads of state.

The faces changed pretty often, though. It was a tough job. So tough that the officers only served a two-year tour of duty there. But during those two years, they turned out to be the levelheaded ones. During the horrific events of 9/11 when all the other White House people were ordered to leave the building for fear of another attack, the technicians refused to go home. They stayed and worked throughout the crisis, just as they had every other day of every other crisis.

Folks like that hadn't always been stationed in this basement. He'd heard that the Situation Room complex was created by President Kennedy after the disastrous Bay of Pigs affair in 1961. JFK wanted a more up-to-date on-site intelligence center. He wanted it right there at the White House so he wouldn't have to rely on reports that might be delayed from the State Department or the CIA.

Later, Lyndon Johnson had the habit of going down to the Sit Room at all hours to monitor events in Vietnam. And during the Gulf War, the first President Bush would check in between four and five every morning to read the latest intelligence.

The technicians were first with the news, first with the analysis, first with the reports. Usually, but not always.

Hunt remembered one story that went around about the female NSC staffer who was dating a Minister at the Swedish Embassy. Early one morning, he placed a call to her office to thank her for making him dinner the previous evening. In the course of the conversation, he said that he had been having a strange morning with phone calls back and forth to Stockholm about one of their power plants receiving weird readings. They had to evacuate the plant when some of the workers showed excess radiation.

She had gone back to the Situation Room and asked the watch officer to please check out any developments east of Stockholm. Two hours later, the officer raced into her office and exclaimed that they had just figured out that a disaster had occurred at a place called Chernobyl. Some of the staff joked that if she had been dating a Russian, the United States might have found out about it even sooner. Then again, staffers weren't allowed to date Russians. At least not in those days.

Now the NSC Advisor used the Situation Room for his early-morning staff meetings and small conferences like this one, and he had been managing various crises from this secure location for years. He unbuttoned the coat of his blue pin-striped suit and reviewed the paper in front of him.

"India is saying that the cruise missile fired at their military compound in Jammu and Kashmir killed one hundred eighty-four and injured sixty more. Place is destroyed, and they've been meeting to discuss retaliation against Pakistan. As you know, the President has talked to the leaders of both India and Pakistan, asking for restraint. But there's precious little trust on either side. This is your basic disaster in the making. If another missile is fired and Delhi strikes back, we could see nuclear weapons being launched for the first time since Nagasaki!" He turned to Jasmine. "Any success in pinpointing the launch site?"

The Japanese-American scholar answered briskly, "Not yet. We're trying to determine if it came from Pakistan or Kashmir. We don't have any assets in the Kashmir area, no actionable intelligence at this time. What we do know is that the main group fighting for the past several years in the Kashmir region is known as Lashkar-i-Taiba. They keep changing their name, but we're using the original for now. We're compiling more data. I'll have it for you shortly."

"Ted? Anything from your ISI contacts?"

"ISI agents are all over this because the Paks are petrified that India really will strike back."

Austin nodded. "Ambassador Bhattia came rushing over here an hour ago. The man was apoplectic. He's swearing that Pakistan did not fire the missile. He says it's got to be one of the militant groups, but he doesn't have any idea how they got it."

Hunt broke in. "No idea? Give me a break. We all know that there were three missiles stolen, not one. The whole point is that this first one was a Pakistani missile, fired from Pakistani soil, or at least the Pakistani-controlled area of Kashmir. And that means that if it was one of those al Qaeda type groups, then Islamabad has an army depot with lousy security *and* army troops that collaborated with the bad guys. In other words, Bhattia's ass is in a sling. Uh, sorry."

"Never mind," Austin said, "my view as well. Stock, what's your take on this thing?"

The Deputy had a grim look on his face. "I don't give a damn about Bhattia's excuses. We've got to focus on New Delhi and make sure the Indians don't fire back." He passed around copies of a memorandum. "Hunt, put this Decision Directive together about sending an advance team over there to set things up for a Special Envoy. The President's going to name someone pretty soon, right?"

Austin answered, "Yes. He's going through the motions and clearances right now. I think he's leaning toward Senator Farrell. At least Farrell did a pretty good job when he was head of the Foreign Relations Committee. He's only been out of office two years, so he's still pretty up-to-speed on things."

Stock nodded his approval. "Good choice." He glanced down at the memo. "So as you can see, Hunt's got a list here of people for the team. Ted, you're an obvious choice to go with him on this one. You know the area."

Ted said, "Yes. Hunt and I talked about the list. We need to keep it small. I think he's right to get one agent from the CIA, one from State, and one from the DIA."

"Even with the reorganization, Defense controls the lion's share of the intelligence budget, so they can jolly well send their best analyst and pony up for the plane," Stock said.

"I agree with that," Austin replied. "The list looks good. Hunt, you firm up the plans and get ready to leave in a couple days . . . if we have a couple of days. I'm going to get the President to call the Indian Prime Minister again and talk to him about the envoy and our push for peace talks. We need time to get you all in there and get both sides up for some sort of agreement. And while you're there, you can work with the Indian Defense Ministry and ISI to try and locate the rest of those damn missiles." He turned to his left. "Ted, get me talking points for that phone call."

Ted made a note and nodded.

Austin continued, "Stock, see if you can get an emergency SIG together to examine all the intelligence from the area. Jasmine can chair it. Get a report together for Hunt's team before they go over there. And, Jasmine, keep pushing for intel on those terrorist groups and their relationship, if there is one, to ISI."

Hunt was taking notes. In spite of the gravity of the situation, he had to smile at the suggestion of yet another Senior Interagency Group. They set them up all the time with players from the different departments. The only trouble was that there were so many of them, they were kind of like

Congressional commissions. They tended to proliferate like kudzu. One of the NSC staffers had even circulated a list of suggested names, like Priority Interagency Group (PIG) or even Presidential Review Interagency Group (PRIG). Hunt snapped back to attention.

"Let's wind up here, unless there's anything else . . . ?"

"If you have just one more minute," Hunt said, "I wanted you to be aware of another matter. At least this one is more in the good-news category."

"I could use a little good news right now," Austin said. "What is it?"

"There's a brand-new technology being developed over at Bandaq that's pretty revolutionary. I mean it could be."

"Could be?"

"Yes. They'll be testing it soon. It's for missile defense."

"Our systems are already being deployed."

"No, this isn't for ballistic missiles. It's for cruise missiles. Like the one the crazies just launched."

"We've got the Patriot," Austin said.

"The Patriot doesn't always work," Hunt countered. "Anyway, I just wanted you to know that we're watching this one because it might be better."

Stock interjected, "I saw a news story on this one. Actually, it does look pretty promising. Hunt wants our legislative shop to give it a push on the Hill."

Austin paused as he was gathering up his papers. "We can't do that right now. Congress is complaining about the deficit as it is. The Armed Services Committee is swamped with requests for R & D money for everything from bazookas to blimps."

"A request for blimps?" Hunt asked. "I haven't heard about that one. But I gotta say that I'd sure rather see money for Bandaq than for blimps."

Austin cut him off and pushed back from the table. "You've got enough on your plate for the moment. Your first priority right now is averting a nuclear war."

14

Congressman Davis Metcher was visiting his district. It was important to spend time in the district, talking to the people at the Chamber of Commerce, the labor unions, the Masons, the Rotary Clubs, the universities, and even the folks at the local diners. He especially liked to go to the diners during the campaign when the TV reporters showed up to interview *real* people.

He never completely figured that out, though. What's *not real* about a member of the Jaycees or a secretary at a biotech company? He could never seem to get the cameras to follow him to those places, but he went there anyway. He had to cover all the bases. He needed all of their votes because he was in a very tight race this time around.

He had served four terms in Congress, almost eight years now, and he was even thinking about running for the Senate down the road. First, he had to pull off a win again in November. But now a local district attorney who had put away a bunch of white-collar types had ended up on the news almost nonstop for weeks. And then when his name had become a household word, the bastard comes out and announces he's running for Metcher's seat in Congress on a law-and-order campaign.

Well, good for him. But who does he think he is? The only politician around here who cares about law and order? Sure, that's important, but it's not the only issue around these parts. It's not enough just to crack down on a few lowlifes, even if they do run companies. He needed to look at the other companies who were playing by the rules and give them a few breaks so they could buy more equipment, depreciate it faster, and create more jobs.

And if the companies were doing well, that meant more campaign contributions for his coffers. He tried to hit all the big ones, but he especially liked to talk to the pharmaceutical companies. They were always pretty generous because they had so much to lose. Now with the government gearing up to get cheaper drugs for seniors and vaccines for kids and everyone else trying to import them from God knows where, their profits were heading south.

As he drove up Canal Road toward the Beltway, he punched a number into his cell phone. His Legislative Aide answered on the first ring. "Joe? Davis here."

"Yes, sir. What can I do for you?"

"Just wanted to check how you're coming on that new drug bill."

"To extend the patent rights?"

"Yeah, that one. Have you finalized the language yet?"

"I've been using some lines from the old bill that Lieberman introduced a while back."

"That didn't go anywhere."

"I know. But now we may have a shot. Long shot, but a shot. I got some new industry figures I can play with."

"Like what?" Metcher asked, turning onto the crowded Beltway and maneuvering past a truck in the far right lane.

"I figure it can cost up to two billion dollars to do all the research, trials on animals, and everything to develop a new drug. And then for every dozen or so, only one makes it through the FDA rigmarole."

"So obviously, they need to jack up the price when they get one to market to recoup their costs."

"Well, sure."

Davis checked his side mirror and jumped over into the left lane to veer onto I-270. He silently cursed a silver Mercedes that almost cut him off. "So it costs beaucoup bucks to develop. Everybody knows that. Trouble is, it probably only costs a few cents to churn it out, and by then everyone from Medicare types to Third World huggers demands lower prices."

"Yeah. But at least your bill will give them a little respite before the generics take over."

"I like it. See what you can do to finish the draft, and I'll start shopping it around. I gotta go now. I'm almost at Bandaq."

"That defense outfit with the fancy new technology?"

"We'll see just how fancy it really is."

Pulling up to the sprawling three-story complex, he parked in one of the visitor slots, shifted his bulky frame out of the car, and shivered in the early-spring air. Rows of poplar trees bordered the walkway and swayed in the breeze as he hurried into the reception area. He usually took an aide with him on these district visits, but he was hoping for some time alone with the pretty blonde, so he hardly needed a staffer or even a driver hanging around.

"May I help you, sir?" the receptionist asked cheerfully.

"Congressman Davis Metcher to see General Landsdale," Davis replied, focusing on the attractive young woman.

She turned away from his stare. "Certainly, sir. Let me ring him for you. If you'll just wait over there," she said, pointing to a bank of leather chairs by the window, "I'm sure he'll be right out."

"Thanks, my dear. But I like the view from here just fine," he said, smiling broadly.

She turned away again and punched a number into her phone. "General, Representative Metcher is in the front lobby . . . yes . . . thank you . . . I'll tell him." She swiveled back to Metcher. "He'll be out in just a moment. As I mentioned, there are comfortable chairs over there, and information on the company is on the coffee table."

"Thanks, I'll have a look." He could take a hint. The girl wasn't quite up to his standards anyway, he told himself. He was used to the young women on the Hill who fawned over the men in positions of power. They were always trying to get one step ahead of the game. Playing up to a Congressman, especially a single one, seemed to be their number one goal. And who was he to deprive them of their hunting pleasures?

He sauntered over to the table, picked up a copy of Bandaq's Annual Report, and began to leaf through it, looking for a photo of the blonde. There it was, toward the back, along with photos of the other top scientists in the place. God, she was pretty. Seemed a bit aloof, but he was sure he could bring her down off her high horse if he could just get a few minutes alone with her.

As for the general, Metcher had plans for him, too. There just might be a way to get a little of the general's help in the fund-raising department. This could turn out to be a stellar visit, killing two birds, just as he had planned.

"Congressman Metcher. Good to see you again." General Landsdale came striding into the reception area, hand outstretched.

"Thanks, General. Nice building you have here."

"Yes, we like it. Come on back, and let me give you a quick tour." The general looked into the security device and ushered his guest through the large double doors. They proceeded to several of the labs, the general giving a cursory explanation of the new technology as they went. He introduced the Congressman to several scientists and explained the significance of the radar- and satellite-based sensors and then continued back down the hall.

"That was interesting. But where is this Dr. Cameron who testified before my Committee?" Metcher asked with a glint in his eye.

The General paused. "She's working on Q-3. You know we're working hard to get that field test scheduled."

"The test? Oh yes, that one. We talked about that in the Committee. We do need to know if this thing is reliable."

"It does work, I assure you," the general ventured. "I mean, it has worked here in the lab, but I know your Committee wants to see concrete results in the field."

"You say 'it has worked here in the lab.' How many times has it worked . . . or failed?"

"This is a highly classified project, sir. I wouldn't want to say too much about the results just yet."

"Come, come, General. You know you can trust me. After all, this company is in my district. You employ a lot of my people here. I want to see your boys . . . and girls . . . nail this thing."

"Yes, I'm sure you are right. You see, Dr. Cameron did have one success when she locked on to an incoming missile and was able to redirect it."

"Sounds good so far. But you said she only did it once?"

"Well, since then, she's been trying to re-create those conditions . . ."

"And she's failed?" Metcher said, raising his eyebrows.

The general led the way into his own office, delaying an answer to the question.

"Did you say she's failed?" the Congressman asked again as he followed the general into the spacious suite of the CEO.

"I'm not sure if we should call them failures. It's all part of the continuing research process."

"But the bottom line is that every time she tried it again, it failed. Right?" Metcher asked as he settled into a large wingback chair in the corner.

The general sat down opposite him and looked him squarely in the eye. "Look, we're at a very critical stage right now. Yes, we've had some reversals, but it's important to us that this be seen as just part of the process. We want to emphasize the unique features of the technology that Cammy . . . uh, Dr. Talbot . . . has created here. It's a real breakthrough. That's why we need your earmark on that Defense Authorization Bill. Do you think you can help us out here?"

The Congressman saw tiny beads of sweat on Landsdale's upper lip. "As I'm sure you know, there are lots of competing ideas out there, lots of other companies who are trying to get a line item in the budget. Why, just this morning I had a visit from Dr. Kooner. I'm sure you know him . . . the new CEO over at Sterling Dynamics?"

"Yes, we're well aware of the competition. But our technology—"

Metcher held up his hand. "Yes, yes, I know. Your technology is different. Now I'm not saying we won't fund it. What I am saying is that it might be tough in this atmosphere. You know the problems with the deficit."

The general shifted uneasily in his chair as Metcher continued. "But I'll see what I can do. And on the subject of deficits, I seem to be running a bit of a deficit myself. In my campaign organization, that is."

"Yes, I'm sure times are tough for all the candidates these days. It's not easy to raise money."

"You see, I've got a tough competitor this go-around. But with my seniority . . . I'm sure the district wouldn't want to start all over with that DA."

"Oh, I'm sure you're right. In fact, in the general election, I wouldn't think you'd have any trouble at all," the general said reassuringly.

"I don't want to take any chances, of course."

"Of course."

Metcher leaned forward, getting ready to make the ask. "So here's what I'd like to do. I'd like to offer you folks here at Bandaq an opportunity to host an event. Something special for you and your people. Your officers could donate the maximum of twenty-one hundred dollars each, with another twenty-one hundred from their wives, and then it could be bundled as an aggregate donation to the primary. Then the law allows you all to donate another twenty-one hundred . . . each . . . to the final campaign. And as for the company's PAC . . . I assume you have a PAC . . . ?"

The general gave a slight nod.

". . . and so your PAC could kick in five thousand to the Party for a good get-out-the-vote effort."

"Well, I'm not sure we could do all of that. Our company policy doesn't allow us to pressure any of our employees to donate to any specific political campaign. We feel it's important for them to be able to manage their own budgets and choose their own candidates."

"Of course, of course, my boy," Metcher said genially. "On the other hand, I'm sure they all realize the importance of having a friend in Congress, to say nothing of a very good friend as a key member of House Armed Services."

There. He had made it plain as day. He sat back in the chair, quite satisfied with the direction this conversation was taking. He wasn't nearly as satisfied with the direction his first priority had taken, however. He still wanted to see the very smart, very pretty, but evidently very busy Dr. Talbot. "Tell you what. Don't make a decision today. Give it some thought."

The general looked somewhat relieved and started to get up.

Metcher hauled himself out of his chair as well and said, "Before I go, I really would like to have a quick word with Dr. Talbot, if that wouldn't be too much trouble."

The general paused to check his watch and said, "Of course. We'll stop by her lab. I'm sure she can take a short break."

"Good enough," Metcher said as they filed out of the office.

"Come in," Cammy called absentmindedly as she focused on the second computer screen and hit some keys. She didn't want to be interrupted, but she figured the knock was probably Ben with a quick question.

"Sorry to bother you, Cammy," the general said, opening the door, "but Congressman Metcher insisted on seeing you before he left the building."

Cammy swiveled her chair around and saw the man with the paunch below and the lascivious eyes above. *Great*, she thought. *Just what I need today.* She plastered a half smile on her face as she got up from her chair to shake his hand. "I must say it's good to see you again, sir." "Mustn't I," she muttered under her breath.

"Please," he said as he appeared to be appraising her slim figure clad in beige slacks and a white sweater, "call me Davis. After all, I am *your* Congressman."

"Uh . . . yes . . . I guess you are . . . sir."

Metcher turned to General Landsdale and said, "Now that we see the little lady has a moment, there are a few questions I wanted to ask her about her project. You don't really have to stay. I'm sure I can find my way out."

As the Congressman was turned toward the general, Cammy gave a quick shake of her head in Landsdale's direction. "No problem," the general said. "I would never leave such an important visitor wandering around the premises all alone."

Cammy picked up the ball. "Here, Congressman, uh, Davis. Why don't you sit down for a moment and let me show you the trajectory of the missile I'm targeting in this exercise."

Metcher didn't give a damn about trajectories or missiles or exercises right now. What he wanted was to get this little filly alone and see if he could talk her into a bit of private time down the road. "The trajectory," he mumbled as he pulled a chair close to hers and glanced toward her keyboard.

The general leaned against the doorjamb and kept quiet as Cammy began an extremely businesslike description of her keystrokes.

"And so you see, sir, what we're trying to do here is embed . . ."

I'd like to embed something myself, Metcher thought as he watched her nimble fingers move over the keys.

"You might think of this as a Trojan horse," she continued.

Trojan, he mused. *I'd like to think about a Trojan, but not the horsey kind.*

"And so we take over the onboard computer and redirect it—"

Metcher cleared his throat. "Yes, yes. Very interesting. Tell you what, Dr. Talbot, or may I call you Cameron?" he asked in a low voice.

Cammy didn't turn around. She kept plying the keyboard as if her next move were the most important of the day. "Most people call me Cammy . . . sir."

"Yes, Cammy. Well, the general and I have been talking about putting together a little event for my campaign, and I thought you and I could talk about that. You seem like the organized type. You just might be the perfect person to help set up this little shindig."

She turned in her chair. Enough. That was enough. She could barely stand to be in the same room with this man, to say nothing of sitting so close to him that she could smell the martini he'd obviously had for lunch. She got up and walked toward the door and adopted a firm tone.

"I'm sure the event will be lovely, but I don't think I would be the right one for that job, sir. As you can see, I'm totally occupied with this project. And we all want to get ready for the field test, so your committee can see some good results."

What a brush-off, Metcher thought. *This little wench has the nerve to brush me off like I was a speck of dust on her pristine white sweater. Well, we'll just see about this.* He got up from his chair and marched toward the door.

"Sorry about that, my dear. And here I thought we might be able to work together . . . on something."

General Landsdale opened the door and led the way out as he shot Cammy a disapproving stare. "Congressman Metcher, I'm sorry if Cammy is a bit preoccupied these days. But you can understand how focused she has to be on the technology right now."

"I'm sure," Metcher grumbled.

"However, we have several other very capable members of the staff who just might fill the bill when it comes to organizing an event. I'll check around and see what we can do."

"You do that," Metcher said as he pushed through the double doors to the reception area.

"Thank you for coming all the way out here today," the general said, holding out his hand to say good-bye.

The Congressman gave him a quick handshake and said, "No problem. Now I've got to get back to town. I have a couple of drop-bys tonight. You know how it goes."

"I certainly do." The general walked him to the front door, opened it, and the man strode outside, walking as quickly as his large frame would allow.

The CEO stood there for a while, convinced that his protégé had just screwed up their only shot at funding for Q-3.

15

Rockville, Maryland—Thursday Early Evening

The traffic on I-270 was moving along at a decent clip as Cammy and Melanie headed home. At seven o'clock it wasn't too hard to negotiate the route to the Beltway. At five, this road would be a parking lot. Then again, Cammy never left the office at five.

She was thinking about the uncomfortable encounter with Davis Metcher, wondering if she'd made a strategic error when she didn't jump at the chance to plan his little fund-raiser. Sure, she needed his vote. But right now, she needed time in her lab even more.

Melanie interrupted her thoughts. "Cam, before we get to the heavy gossip, want to hear my nomination for dumb recipe of the week?"

Cammy sighed. After a day like this, she'd never match Mel's lighthearted attitude, but she could try to be civil. "Sure. When you said you were going to start collecting recipes for a restaurant you want to run someday . . . I never thought you'd find such idiotic ones."

"Everyone knows I'm a frustrated chef at heart. Besides, a little comic relief never hurts, especially when we work in such a serious place."

"So, what have you got this time?" Cammy asked as she signaled and changed lanes.

"Yak stew with green olives and lemon." Melanie giggled and added, "I found that one in the *Sunday New York Times Magazine*. And for dessert . . . how about oatmeal ice cream?"

Cammy made the turn onto the Beltway and shook her head. "I wonder where you find a yak?"

"I have no clue. And here's another one I saw in *The Wall Street Journal* that some San Francisco restaurant is pushing. It's called baby leek and chanterelle *dhosa*."

"What the heck is that?"

"They grind up fermented rice and make it into a crepe and fill it with leeks and mushrooms. Then for dessert, there's sweet potato cheesecake."

"That sounds like Thanksgiving leftovers."

"Probably," Melanie said with a grin.

"Well, I trust that if you ever do open your own place, you'll have the good sense never to offer any of that."

"Don't worry. I just like to keep on top of the competition. Okay, enough nonsense," Mel said. "Tell me about Q-3."

"My failures are classified," Cammy deadpanned.

"You're forgetting I've got a security clearance."

"I know. Just testing."

"In fact, I'm probably the only chef . . . well, I call myself a chef even though I guess it's just a hobby at this point . . . so I'm the only chef, except for Julia Child, with a security clearance."

Cammy turned her head. "Julia Child?"

"Sure. I really miss that lady. Anyway, she started out in World War II as a member of the OSS? You know, the crowd that started all the spy stuff that then turned into the CIA?"

"I know about the OSS. I just didn't know Julia Child was in it," Cammy said.

"She sure was. In fact, I think she served in India and China and then later went to the Cordon Bleu in Paris after the war."

"India and China? Those are countries I've been studying. China has been testing a new DF-31 missile along with a submarine-launched JL-2. And India has been trying to buy the Arrow Anti-Missile System from Israel."

Melanie rolled her eyes. "I always wonder how you can keep all those systems in your head."

"Systems are my business. I have to study what everybody else is doing or else I can't keep up."

"I guess so," Melanie replied. Then she shot her friend a smile and added, "You know, years ago when I said I couldn't keep up, they put me in a slower group."

"Sometimes I wish I had that luxury," Cammy said, half in jest. "I'm so slammed right now. With Bollinger screaming about budgets and the general demanding a field test, I keep telling everybody it's going to work when I really feel like the Queen of Denial."

Melanie started to laugh. "C'mon. You mean that country song about floating on a river of lies? It can't be that bad."

"It is, but I'm trying to keep a lid on it. If the Congressional Committee finds out about all the failures, we won't get the R & D funding. And if we do schedule a field test and it fails, the board will shut me down."

"But they can't do that," Melanie practically shouted. "You've been working on this for . . . what . . . years?"

"That's the whole point. Stan says he can't keep carrying this project on the books if it's not going to pan out. Talk about pressure."

"And what about the Congressional Committee?"

"Well, for starters, I've had to deal with Davis Metcher."

"Metcher the Lecher?" Mel asked.

"Guess everybody knows about that guy."

"How could they not know? Seems that every time I have dinner downtown, I see him with a new twenty-something on his arm. And that guy is way beyond his 'sell by' date."

Cammy had to laugh in spite of her mood. "He came by today, and I kind of blew him off. I know we need his support, but if we pass the test, he'll have to vote for us. After all, we're in his district. A point he made loud and clear." She checked her rearview mirror and changed lanes again. "At least I've got Raj on my team now. Do you want to tell me about him?"

Melanie leaned back against the car seat and closed her eyes. "He's just dreamy."

Cammy glanced over and said, "Are we going to have a Hallmark moment here?"

Mel opened her eyes and looked chagrined. "It's just that chocolate brown hair and those deep dark eyes. He's taller than most men I've dated. And his manners are so . . . refined."

"Well, I do know what you mean about his mannerisms. He must be from one of those upper castes, considering the schools he went to."

"For sure. His family is really connected. And you should see his house. It's over on Foxhall Road."

"Foxhall? I thought there were only mansions and embassies over there," Cammy said.

"He's got one of the mansions. In fact, when I first saw it, I asked him if he had his own zip code."

Cammy chuckled and headed toward their condo building in the heart of Bethesda. "I must say I'm glad to have Raj on board." As she said it she had an image of herself bobbing around in a sea of calculations, and Raj Singh was a life vest. In the end she might not need him, but she felt a little bit better just knowing he was there. Then again, she said a silent prayer that he wouldn't deflate her plans.

"I could talk about Raj all night," Melanie said, "but tell me about this White House guy."

"What about him?"

"Are you going to see him again?" Mel asked.

"I have no idea. I mean, I hope he'll give us some help with the funding, but we didn't arrange another meeting."

"Well, if you do see him again, I do have a suggestion."

"And that would be?"

"About your wardrobe."

"What's the matter with my wardrobe?" Cammy asked.

"Are you kidding? It ranges from beige to ecru to bone to white."

"So?"

"So, if you're going to attract a man, you have to attract his eyes as well as his brains, you know."

Cammy shrugged. "First of all, I just met this guy. Second, it's a business contact. Third, I don't have time to think about men right now. And fourth, who says men don't like beige or white?"

"Okay, so you're not trolling. But just for argument's sake, it would be an interesting experiment to try you in teal, kelly green, or even red once in a while."

"C'mon, Mel. I'm a scientist, not a peacock."

"I know. But it wouldn't hurt to have you look like something besides an egret."

Cammy had to laugh as she pondered her friend's description. Did she want to see Hunt again? Actually, yes. Being with him in her lab and talking over lunch had been the first time in ages . . . the first time since Ken . . . that she had felt . . . how had she felt? Alive and slightly off balance. It was kind of like someone had switched her usual TV show to a different channel and she couldn't find the remote.

"Tell you what," Cammy said. "If this guy calls again, I'll consult with you so I don't encounter some sort of wardrobe malfunction."

This time Melanie laughed. "Fair enough."

She pulled into their condo garage and gathered her things from the backseat. As they got on the elevator, Mel said, "Hey, thanks for the lift. I'm not sure how long those guys are going to keep my car."

"No problem. Let's head in at seven thirty tomorrow."

"Good plan. And hey, I didn't really mean to be critical of your clothes. I was just . . ."

Cammy waved her hand and punched the numbers for their floors. "Don't worry about it. You're probably right."

The elevator door opened and Cammy got out. She called over her shoulder, "Have a good one, Mel. See you tomorrow." She walked down the carpeted hallway to her apartment, took the key out of her purse, opened the door, and stopped cold.

16

The White House—Thursday Early Evening

Working late at the White House was nothing new. Most of the staff worked well beyond the evening newscasts, and Hunt was no exception. In fact, he had a late appointment with Ambassador Amir Ahmed Bhattia of Pakistan, who had called an hour ago requesting an urgent meeting. *The guy knows he's on a short leash*, Hunt thought to himself. *He's probably trying to worm his way back into our good graces.*

Hunt checked his watch and saw that the Ambassador wasn't due for another ten minutes. He stared at the stack of classified documents on his desk and pulled the top one off the pile.

As he began to read the *National Intelligence Estimate*, he realized it mirrored his concerns about the whole India-Pakistan region. It looked like the bureaucrats at State, the CIA, NSA, and other corners of the intelligence-gathering machine were all scouring their sources for information on the recent missile attack and other incursions in the Kashmir region. It was obvious that these militants were making every effort to scuttle the fragile peace process that had been developing between India and Pakistan.

Meanwhile, according to the intelligence summary, the Paks were fighting one another, with the political opposition parties vowing not to allow their country to recognize Israel, cooperate with the United States on peacekeeping operations, or completely stop the infiltration of the Islamic militants into Kashmir. And there was continuing concern that the government hadn't been able to totally slam the door on the sale of nuclear secrets by the last of their rogue scientists in spite of arresting a whole slew of them.

As he scanned through the document, he saw that the NSA had new details about how Pakistan and India were both focusing on missile defense technology. It said, "Those governments as well as outside factions may be organizing teams to either buy or steal systems in Asia and possibly the United States."

"Jesus Christ!" Hunt exclaimed out loud to his empty office walls. "What the hell is this?" It was bad enough that certain groups in that area were snapping at one another again like unruly rottweilers. Now it looked like their feuds might involve American companies and American citizens.

He heard a door open. "Colonel Daniels?" An educated voice emanated from the outer office. Hunt got up and went to meet his visitor.

"Good evening, Your Excellency. You're working late tonight."

The tall, urbane gentleman with hair the color of mahogany was wearing a double-breasted dark blue pin-striped suit and looked like he could have just arrived from Oxford . . . or Wall Street. He extended his hand in greeting. "With all of these crises in my country, I get very little sleep these days."

"Come in and sit down, Mr. Ambassador, and tell me what brings you to my office at this late hour."

They settled in two wooden armchairs in Hunt's office, and the Ambassador began. "First, may I say that we were very pleased with the comments your President made to *The New York Times* about his hopes for peace throughout our region. His support is much appreciated."

"Thank you, Mr. Ambassador. I assure you, all of us would like nothing better than to see a reduction of tension in your part of the world. As you know, we are working with New Delhi to forestall any retaliatory action. In fact, I'll be traveling to India next week to try and set up some talks. The President wants to send a Special Envoy over there if we can get everyone to the bargaining table. You can help us with that."

The Ambassador nodded. "Yes, I will do what I can. However, I am afraid that there are those who are working for an opposite goal, and that is why I am here tonight."

"Please go on," Hunt said, opening his leather folder, preparing to take notes.

"There is a group that, in the past, has called itself Lashkar-i-Taiba."

"We know," Hunt said. "Our State Department declared it a terrorist organization back in December of 2001."

"You are quite right," Ambassador Bhattia said. "And we, too, have stopped supporting this group."

"Completely?" Hunt asked skeptically.

"My government has adopted a policy of nonsupport. In fact, we froze their assets. And yet, we know that they still receive funds from many places."

"What places?" Hunt asked.

"Donation boxes are put in stores, in mosques, not only in my country but in many other countries. The money is everywhere. And it makes its way to this group, among others."

"So they still get a lot of money, but no military help?" Hunt asked.

"That is correct. Not from us. They used to have rallies celebrating their martyrs. Now they have to work underground. And yes, it is true that years ago our ISI helped them, especially in their struggle for Kashmir. They would simply turn a blind eye to the incursions over the Line of Control."

"And are they now turning a blind eye to the theft of cruise missiles?" Hunt asked directly.

"I assure you, Colonel Daniels, we knew nothing of this plan. The Army Commander is pursuing a full investigation, and we now believe that it may have been this Lashkar group that staged that raid. We do not have proof yet, only rumors."

"If you can prove it was Lashkar and not some action ordered by anyone in your government, that might help to assuage the Indians." Hunt made some notes in his folder. "Tell me more about this group."

"Several years ago they killed a number of Hindu pilgrims. That was a tragic event and one that my government does not condone. However, it has been difficult because we all fought together against the Soviet occupation of Afghanistan. Your government, my government, the Islamic militant groups. We were all allies then. And Lashkar-i-Taiba had especially close ties to the Taliban and to al Qaeda as well."

Hunt interrupted, "And then after 9/11, when everything changed and we went after the Taliban and al Qaeda, your little group was stranded, right?"

"Not my group, I assure you. But yes, they were cut off . . . but only for a while. Now they are reorganizing and getting more support. And they are changing their tactics, too. They used to dress as Indian soldiers, get into the Indian villages, and kill many innocent people. Now they are branching out. We believe they had ties to the group that set off the bombs in the London subways some time back. So yes, they are expanding, gaining new recruits, and becoming much more sophisticated."

"You mean besides figuring out how to steal and launch cruise missiles?" Hunt asked.

"Yes, and this is why I wanted to meet with you tonight. You see, in addition to planning more attacks with those missiles, if they really have them, we believe that they may have inserted one or more of their members here. Here into the United States."

"Here? Where?" Hunt demanded.

"ISI has been tracking several members of this group, and there is one particular individual who has not been seen in Pakistan or in Kashmir recently. We believe he may be here. Others may be here as well. But this particular man has experience traveling on a student visa. He has done it before."

"A student visa?" Hunt asked. "But the INS has cracked down on most of those."

"Yes, we know. However, he is very clever. He has been a student in past years, and we believe he may have applied to return. We have intercepted some e-mails, but they keep changing their methods of communication. This man is extremely intelligent and has learned your language and your customs. He can blend in well."

"Do you have any idea where he is?" Hunt asked.

"If past is prologue, he would return to Washington, because he once attended your Georgetown University. He probably wouldn't go back to the same school, though. He used a different name then. He has many aliases. We don't know, but we are investigating and will keep you informed, of course."

"Why is he here? Do you think he could be scouting out targets for another attack on our country?"

"I wish I knew the answer to that question. We do know that the goal of Lashkar is worldwide Jihad and an end to Indian occupation of what they see as their land in Kashmir. The other big problem is that Lashkar is one of the groups that have tried to assassinate our President."

Hunt was writing furiously in his leather binder. He looked up and asked, "One single guy, if he's alone, must be on some sort of special mission. The question is, what is it?"

"Yes, that *is* the big question. If his cells are stealing our missiles, perhaps he is here to steal other things they think they need. I do have one more bit of information for you."

"What's that?"

"A name. We have a name. Jambaz Muhammad Sharif. As I said, he has also used other names. But that is the real name."

Hunt wrote it down, paused, and frowned. "Lashkar-i-Taiba. Isn't that the group that threatened to attack the Taj Mahal back in 2002?"

"I believe it was one of the groups. But they were never able to do that."

Hunt closed his notebook and got up from his chair. "Mr. Ambassador, let me thank you for bringing this information to our attention. I will take up your concerns and your offer of help with our National Security Advisor. And I will see what our other agencies can do about this Mr. Sharif."

"Thank you, Colonel Daniels." The Ambassador stood up and shook hands again. "If we learn any more on any of these subjects, we will relay it to you immediately."

Hunt walked the man to the door. "Yes, please do that. These are difficult times, Your Excellency."

"Difficult times indeed," the Ambassador lamented. "I bid you good night."

17

Bethesda, Maryland—Thursday Early Evening

Cammy stared at her living room in stunned silence. Taupe cushions from her chenille sofa were all over the floor. Cabinet doors were open. Books had been pulled from the shelves and scattered over her carpet like shells on a storm-tossed beach. A lamp was knocked over. Even the painting of the Golden Gate Bridge hanging over the fireplace was askew. A pair of tall ficus trees stood sentry in the corners, the only objects in an upright position. She held her breath as she took a first tentative step across the threshold.

She listened intently, her heart pounding. Nothing. She cautiously made her way into the kitchen where plates were lying on the counter. *Plates? Who looks at plates?* She opened a drawer and gave a small sigh of relief when she saw her grandmother's sterling silver still lined up inside.

She turned around and walked into her bedroom. Her closet door was open. Hangers had been pushed aside. Her bed was torn apart and her computer was . . . gone. *Damn! Why would somebody steal a computer that could only be hocked for a couple hundred dollars and not take the silver that's worth thousands? Kids maybe? Not druggies. They'd know better what they could fence.*

She suddenly turned toward the bathroom. *What if? No. Nobody's hiding behind the shower curtain. This isn't a B movie. This is my life. And right now, my life is a disaster.*

She looked around again, studying the scene, analyzing whether anything else was missing. She didn't think so. She reached for the phone. *No. Better not touch anything. Maybe the cops can find some fingerprints.*

She backed out of the bedroom, turned toward the front door, pulled her cell phone out of her shoulder bag, and punched in some numbers.

"Mel? I've got a problem here. Can I come up?"

"Problem? What's wrong?"

"Somebody broke into my apartment."

"Oh no," Mel cried out. "And you're down there alone?"

"Whoever did it is probably long gone."

"But how do you know? Maybe he's still here in the building. We should call the police."

"I know. I know. I want to think first. I don't want to touch anything down here right now. I'm coming up there, okay?"

"Yeah. Sure. But geez! I can't believe somebody got into our building."

"That part doesn't surprise me," Cammy said. "Our security isn't exactly high-tech. I'm on my way up."

Melanie was waiting in the doorway when Cammy got off the elevator. "This is awful! I never heard of any burglars in this building. What did they take?"

"My computer."

"That's all?" Melanie asked, leading the way inside and motioning for Cammy to sit down at her kitchen table.

"I think so, but whoever did it really trashed the place."

"How bad is it?"

Cammy signed. "At this point, it could be designated a Superfund site."

"Oh Lord! What about your jewelry or your silver?"

"Silver's still there," Cammy said, settling into the oak-wood chair. "I didn't take time to look for the jewelry. But if he didn't take the silver . . ." She paused. "You know, it's weird, isn't it? Why would somebody only take my computer . . . unless . . ."

"Unless what?"

"Unless he wanted what was in my mind and not what was in my drawers . . . so to speak," she added with a half laugh.

"How can you be so calm at a time like this?" Melanie asked. "Aren't you going to call the cops?"

"Probably. In a minute. It's just that . . . you know those lectures we get all the time at the office about our classified projects and industrial espionage?"

"Well, sure, but look, Cam, you're still upset about the Ken doll, aren't you? Just because some schmuck tries to use you to figure out what you're up to, that doesn't mean that some burglar is trying to steal Q-3."

"I don't know. And no, I don't mean Ken, although one thing he did do when he left was put me on my guard."

"Trouble is, when he left you, you left the field."

"What field?"

"The male field. You haven't let another man come near you since that guy played his little game."

"So? Once burned, twice shy, and all of that. But this isn't the time to discuss my love life, or lack of one. What I'm worried about is my professional life. The question is—could someone be trying to get a line on Q-3 or anything else we're working on? That's what worries me right now."

"You don't keep anything classified on your home computer, for Lord sakes," Mel said.

"Of course not. But not everybody would know that."

"Anybody with half a brain would know that."

"Don't be too sure. Remember that CIA guy who got caught with secret documents on his computer in Virginia, or wherever he lived?"

"Oh yeah. Guess you're right. So are you going to call the police or what?" Mel asked.

"I may have a better idea."

"You must be Melanie," Hunt said, stepping through the door.

"That would be me."

He walked in and extended his hand. "I'm Hunt Daniels."

"And I'm impressed," Mel said as she shook his hand.

Cammy came out of the kitchen. "Hunt, thanks for coming over. I wasn't sure if I should call you, but—"

"No problem. Fact is, you're working on a classified project that we think is pretty important and any trouble—"

"We?" she interrupted.

"I've briefed our guys on this, and they told me to keep an eye on it. So that's what I'm doing. Tell me about the break-in."

"Wait a minute," Mel said. "You guys want something to eat before you go play Sherlock?"

Cammy shook her head. "Thanks, but I'm not hungry now. Maybe later."

"Right now I think we'd better go assess the damage," Hunt said.

"Want some help?" Melanie asked.

"No, that's okay," Cammy answered quickly.

"Well, when you figure it out, come on back up and I'll fix you something."

"I don't know how long we'll be. But thanks. I'll call you," she said.

Cammy had always been comfortable in her apartment with its tall ceilings, antiques, English country chairs, and green plants. The whole effect was meant to be that of a quiet retreat. A total contrast to her edgy computerized office space that looked more like a Sharper Image store than a homey workplace. But as she opened the door for Hunt, it was obvious that this wouldn't be any kind of retreat for quite some time.

"Oh shit!" Hunt muttered, as he eyed the chaos. "Place looks like Medusa." Cammy absently straightened her headband and began to walk around the room. Hunt gingerly stepped over a pile of science textbooks. Looking down, he asked, "What's with these? Did you keep them from grammar school?"

"No," she replied. "I tutor kids in science sometimes."

"Oh. Good move." He walked back to her bedroom and saw that there were shoes tossed from the open closet. "Did you have any jewelry or anything valuable in here?"

"Just a few pieces from my grandmother's estate. I had them in a box up there," she said, gesturing toward the closet.

"Check it," he ordered.

She looked up at the shelves. Several boxes had been moved around. She reached for the one labeled "High School Yearbooks." She held her breath as she pulled it down and lifted the lid. Inside the box, right next to the book from her junior year, was the little jewelry case. The ruby earrings and bracelet were still inside. "They're right here," she said with a sigh. "At least he didn't get these."

Hunt took a look at the jewels. "Pretty snazzy. Better put them back. Wouldn't want to lose those."

"You're right," she said as she returned them to their hiding place.

"So, is there anything missing besides your computer? Anything at all?"

She surveyed the rooms once more. "I don't think so," she said evenly.

"Okay. They just took the computer. What did you have on it? Anything to do with your work?"

"Q-3? God no! That's classified."

"I know that. But did you have any notes? Anything that could tie you to the project?"

"No, nothing. I keep all of that at the office. And if I do any work at home, any calculations or anything, I just save those to a disk, take it to the office, and delete everything here. And I don't do that very often."

"So what was on it?"

"Well, I had all my personal stuff. My e-mail, pictures. And my Quicken. I do all of my bills online, and it has all my records, my tax files, my bank accounts."

"You've got good passwords for everything?"

What's the matter with this guy? she wondered. *Does he think I'm clueless? I work with computers and passwords all day long.*

"Of course," she said. "And I've got a good firewall program, too. I've got a restricted access program called CryptoLex."

"That's a new one on me. How does it work?"

So Mr. Know-it-all doesn't really.

"I have this gadget. It's called a Mobio. I keep it on my key chain."

"So what does it do?"

"I put my thumb on it. It recognizes my thumbprint and nobody else's. And if it's mine, then it unlocks my computer, so to speak, and lets me use it."

"What if you lose the Mobio thing?" he asked.

"Whoever had it wouldn't have my thumbprint, and the computer will only react to mine. It's a new system."

"I wish we had something like that at the White House," he said. "Then again, we're a bureaucracy. Seems like we're always a few steps behind you folks in the private sector." He raked his fingers through his hair and thought for a moment. "Wait. You said it unlocks your computer. What if this guy removes the hard disk and puts it into his own computer?"

"I've got that covered, too," she said, stepping over some of the shoes. "A while ago, I got a patent on another idea. If anybody tries to unscrew it or take out the hard disk, it fries itself."

"Sounds like the old self-destruct tape on *Mission Impossible.*"

"Yes. Kind of like that. Anyway, whoever stole my computer isn't going to get anywhere."

"You can bet he'll spend a lot of time trying, though."

They moved into the kitchen, where she stared at the plates again. They were spread out all over the counter. "Why would anybody want to look at my plates?" she asked.

He surveyed the scene and replied, "If you were going to hide disks, where would you put them?"

"Hmmm. Interesting thought." She turned to face him. "What do you really think this is all about?"

"I can't say exactly. But there's a lot going on, here and overseas, with all kinds of people trying to get a handle on missile defense projects."

"I know. I've been doing research for ages."

"And now you're working on a new project that could put a lot of the boys with the missiles out of business."

"And so you think this is an act of industrial espionage where someone's trying to steal my idea?"

"Steal it or stop *you* maybe. It could be someone from another company, or it could be agents from some other country trying to get their hands on your system for their own use."

Cammy slumped down in a chair, a sliver of fear creeping up her spine. He seemed to know a lot about this. What wasn't he telling her? "So you think that I'm the target of some scheme and this was not just a random burglary?"

"Could be. This was probably just their first stop. If they hit pay dirt here, they wouldn't have to try to hack into Bandaq."

"They'd never be able to do that," she said confidently. "You've seen our security systems. And if you think I've got a good firewall here, you should see what we've got over there." She thought for a moment, then added, "Of course, I'll have to notify our Internal Control Officer first thing tomorrow. I'm not going to call him tonight."

"Maybe you should."

"I said I'd wait," she snapped. "Besides, he can't do anything about it tonight anyway."

"Okay. But look, this is important. I don't want to tell the police that you're working on a classified project. We don't need this plastered all over the newspapers. One article was enough."

"I haven't called them yet. I was hoping you might know someone who could handle this. I mean, if it is espionage, what about the FBI or CIA?"

"I do know a few people who might be interested, but for starters, we'd better call the police and get them to dust for prints and see if there's anything else they can find."

She reached for her purse on a side table and fished out her cell phone again. "I'll do it."

At the loud knock on the door they both jumped up from the kitchen stools and rushed to open it. Cammy gave the officers her story and stood aside while the team scoured the place for prints and clues. She answered questions, filled out forms, and offered the men a cup of coffee.

After the officers examined every piece of furniture, drawer, and hanger, they politely withdrew, leaving information on whom to call if Cammy had any other type of trouble or discovered that anything else was missing. They also told her to install a dead bolt.

"Oh God! We never called Melanie," Cammy said as she reached for the kitchen phone. She dialed the number. "Mel, it's me. The police came and looked around. They're gone now."

"I was just thinking, why don't you sleep up here tonight? Just bring some clothes and your toothbrush or something."

"Thanks. I may have to do that."

She turned to Hunt. "She wants me to stay up there with her tonight."

"Woman was reading my mind. There's no way you should stay here tonight."

He walked over to her answering machine, where a light was blinking. He was about to push the PLAY button when she stopped him.

"What are you doing?" When she first saw that her apartment had been trashed, she had felt violated. Invaded. Now, for some reason, she felt that Hunt was invading her space as well.

"I just thought there might be a tie with the burglar," he explained. "You know, maybe he called first to be sure you weren't home."

"Even if he called, he wouldn't leave a message."

Hunt didn't reply.

Cammy glanced around the kitchen, then up at the wall clock. It was ten after ten. In the midst of the chaos, she had an odd thought. "Did you ever notice how every ad for every clock or expensive watch always shows the time as ten after ten?"

Hunt followed her gaze. "Ten after ten? What do you mean?"

"It makes a smiley face. They probably always want their products to look happy. Rather ironic."

"Ironic because we're not smiling?"

"Not much to smile about around this place," she said with a despairing glance. "I really should clean things up." She had started to stack a few plates when Hunt grabbed her arm.

"You can do that later."

Why is this guy always ordering me around? I have enough men doing that at the office, she thought. "Look, I appreciate your coming over here. I called because I thought maybe you could suggest some federal agents who could look into this, but I . . ."

Hunt took another look around and frowned. "I said I might, but it'll take a while. And until we figure out if this guy's coming back, you'd better get the hell out of here."

18

Washington, D.C.—Thursday Midnight

The Metro comes to a stop at Union Station a few blocks from Capitol Hill. One man gets off and takes the escalator to the main floor of the restored Washington train station. A cacophony of sounds usually bounce off the marble floors and ninety-six-foot barrel-vaulted ceilings all day long when commuters, shoppers, and diners pour through the doors and jam the gate areas. With 130 shops and restaurants and a nine-screen movie theater, it's a hub of noisy activity.

But not at midnight.

Now the janitors sweep up the detritus of a thousand travelers. A couple of teenagers with backpacks sit on gray plastic chairs waiting for an overnight train. And a night manager locks a restaurant off the main lobby and disappears through the revolving doors to the street.

The man walks past the newsstands with their metal grates pulled down, the empty shoe shine booths, and TV monitors listing the train arrivals and departures. He heads to a bank of pay phones next to Gate G, checks his Tag Heuer watch, leans close to the phone on the end, and waits.

No one notices when the phone rings. The call is generated from an

STD/ISD booth thousands of miles away. He grabs the receiver and says in a low voice, "Yes, I am here."

"When will Magellan arrive?"

"The explorer will be ready within a few days."

"And the boomerang will be next?" It wasn't so much a question but a command.

A slight hesitation. "It will take more time."

"We have very little time. We are in an emergency situation here. You must improve the timetable."

"I know. I have heard the reports. I know about the attack. Will there be retaliation?"

"It is being discussed right now."

"I shall do my best."

"We can count on you?"

"You have my word."

"For the Motherland."

"For the Motherland."

"Desh Bhakti, my friend."

"Desh Bhakti."

He hangs up the phone and walks out into the station, his footsteps echoing down the nearly deserted hallway. He takes the escalator down to another waiting Metro car, gets on board, and heads for home.

19

The White House—Friday Morning

"Colonel Daniels?" A twenty-two-year-old staffer wearing a blue button-down shirt with the sleeves rolled up raced into the office, his ID badge flapping across his chest. "Here's your News Summary. Sorry it's late, but we got sandbagged this morning with all these stories coming out of India and Pakistan," the young man said breathlessly.

Hunt was a bit irritated. He'd gotten home late the night before, after trying to help Dr. Talbot, and he was still miffed at her attitude. *Okay, so she was upset about the break-in. But she could have shown a little gratitude when I busted my ass to get over there.* He looked up from his briefing papers and grabbed the summary. "About time. I thought you guys distributed this thing at six. And right now it's, what, almost seven?" he admonished as he glanced at his watch.

"Like I said, Colonel, sorry about that. We come in at two A.M., you know."

Hunt started to scan the front page of national headlines and said, "I know. You guys have a lousy shift. But we've got a brewing crisis on our hands, so see if you can get us any new stories on that region or on the missile defense issues I called about. As soon as you see them, okay?"

"You got it, sir. I'm on it," the young staffer said, backing out of the room.

Hunt flipped open the summary and found a reference to an item in *The Washington Post*. He read the short paragraph. "The promising new technology for a missile defense system being developed at Bandaq Technologies has hit a snag. An individual with knowledge of the classified project would not discuss how it functions but indicated that problems had developed. After an initial success, every subsequent simulation has failed. In addition, there could be trouble on Capitol Hill when it comes to funding for the project since its long-term benefits are in doubt. Bandaq Technologies' spokeswoman, Melanie Duvall, refused comment."

Damn! Hunt slammed the pages down and reached for his second cup of coffee of the day. *What the hell's going on? Who would leak this stuff when it involves a potentially vital project? Could it have come from one of their competitors? One of the other defense contractors?* he wondered. *But how would they know about the simulations? No, that doesn't sound right. Who else has an ax to grind?* He reached for the phone.

"Good morning, Bandaq Technologies," the receptionist said brightly. This was one of the few companies that used a real-life human being to answer their phones. Hunt liked that. None of that "if-you-know-your-party's-extension-dial-it-now" shit.

"May I speak to Dr. Talbot please? It's Colonel Daniels calling."

"One moment, Colonel Daniels."

He took another sip of his coffee while he waited.

"Hunt, good morning. How are you?" Cammy said.

At least she sounds like she's in a better mood today, he thought. "Fine. I'm fine. I wanted to be sure you were okay staying at Mel's last night. No more burglaries in the building? No more visits to your place?"

"Not that I know of. Thanks for asking," she replied evenly.

"Good. Well, second, have you seen the *Post*?"

"You mean that piece on the Federal Page? Yes, I saw it. We've all seen it. What a mess! Mel's upset about it. When the reporter called yesterday asking about our simulations, she merely said she had 'no comment at this time.' But if we can get a couple of good test runs, she's got a whole press plan ready to go."

"Figures. But that article. Where did they get that stuff?"

She hesitated and then said, "I have my suspicions, but I'm not really sure."

"Suspicions?"

"Well, yes," she said warily. "Congressman Metcher was out here yesterday. I guess with all the trouble last night, I never mentioned it."

"Davis Metcher? From the House Armed Services Committee?"

"Yes. The general gave him a tour."

"You don't think he . . ."

"I don't know. I mean, I shouldn't really say. Nobody knows, but I can't think of anybody else who would do it. It's classified."

"Of course. But Metcher? I wonder why? I mean you guys are in his district. Why would he want to sink a project in his own district, for God's sake?"

"I don't know. At least I don't think I know," she said haltingly.

"Wait a minute. Did something happen while he was there?"

"What do you mean, something?"

"I mean, did he see anything fail? A simulation or anything?"

"No. The general handled the briefing . . . took him around, introduced him to some of the teams, and then he brought him by my office for a few minutes."

"And what did he say? Did he ask you about the project or the field test?"

"Not really. I tried to give him an abbreviated show-and-tell, but he seemed more interested in fund-raising for his campaign."

"Fund-raising?" Hunt blurted into the phone. "You've gotta be kidding."

"No. that's what he was talking about. And he wanted me to help with some event."

"And what did you say?" he asked carefully.

She sighed. "I have to admit that I kind of blew him off, but I tried to sound businesslike. I don't have time for that stuff. Besides, I can't stand even being near that guy."

She can't stand to be near him? What kind of dream world does this woman live in? he wondered. *Metcher holds all the cards when it comes to funding her project and she blows him off? Bad move.* On the other hand, he could just picture the scene. Cammy working at her desk, Metcher, the Hill's leading skirt chaser, licking his lips, trying to make a move on her. Hunt felt his stomach tense up. He didn't like it. He didn't like the image of another man, especially a guy like Metcher, coming on to Cammy. Wait. What was that all about?

He wasn't involved with her. He'd only seen her twice, and yet she had this weird effect on him. He liked her looks, but sometimes she really pissed him off. *Get a grip, man,* he told himself. Trouble was, he wanted to see her again and he was running out of time.

"Cammy, tell you what. Let's not worry about the article right now. It's a bit of a setback, but I think we can handle the fallout. I mean, it said Q-3 had worked in the lab. Remember it referred to an 'initial success,' so let it be. We don't want anyone talking about it and getting this thing into the next news cycle."

"I know that. I never deal with press stuff anyway. That's Mel's department."

"Okay, look, there's something else I wanted to talk to you about."

"What is it?"

"I've got a lot on my plate right now with this India-Pakistan thing about to blow up in our faces."

"Does anybody know who fired that missile over there?"

"Not yet. But they're sending me over to Delhi in a few days to check it out."

Cammy leaned back in her desk chair and tried to stifle a groan. The man had his domineering side. Then again, he was the only one she knew in the White House, and she could use his help on her funding problems. And if the burglar showed up again, she doubted the police would do anything more than they did last night. Basically nothing. "So when do you think you'll be back?" she asked.

"Not sure. You've probably seen the reports about how the President is appointing a Special Envoy to go over there and try to get peace talks going again."

"Yes. Senator Farrell, right?"

"Yeah. He's getting his act together right now. Our team has to get in there first and set things up. But put that aside for now. I was thinking about your problems. I've got some ideas on the break-in, and maybe there's a way we can short-circuit the earmark situation with the House Committee."

So he was focusing on her situation after all. "But how? I think I really killed it with Metcher."

"He'll get over it. In fact, his type usually likes the chase anyway. Besides, the guy might be a jerk when it comes to women, but at the end of the day, he usually votes right."

"It's just that without a test in the field . . . one that works . . . I don't think we'll get a dime out of that Committee."

"Maybe. Maybe not. Hey, I gotta run, but what say we kick this around tonight after work. You free?"

What now? The man sounded like he wanted to be helpful. Yes. But here he was inviting her out for dinner or some sort of late-night meeting. She had a nagging feeling. It just seemed a bit too personal . . . premature . . . pre-something. She hesitated and wound the phone cord around her fingers. "Uh, I'm afraid not. I told Mel that I'd take her out to dinner as a sort of thank-you for letting me bunk in for a few days."

"I see. Well, I've got to spend some time with Ted . . . he's one of the guys here at the NSC who's on the advance team with me. We've still got a lot of planning to do, so I'll grab a bite with him. Maybe we can talk again tomorrow."

She hung up the phone and stared at it. *It might have been nice.* She shoved the telephone aside as she tried to push the image of Hunt with his straight-line grin from her mind. If she could turn him into an ally, a businesslike ally, that could be useful. But anything more than that? Now? No way.

20

Washington, D.C.—Friday Noon

The muezzin's cry echoes from the top of the 160-foot-high minaret throughout the Kalorama neighborhood. He is calling the faithful to prayers at the Washington Islamic Center at the corner of Massachusetts Avenue and Belmont.

Scores of taxicabs line Belmont and nearby Tracy Place as their drivers head inside the elaborate limestone building with mosaic inscriptions of verses from the Qur'an written in blue Arabic script just above the five entry arches.

As Jambaz enters the mosque for Friday prayers, he feels anxious. Just that morning he had read a headline in *The Washington Post* that announced the bad news from his country. "In Kashmir, Abuses Bruise Hopes for Peace." The next line read, "Complaints against Indian Security Forces Rise." When he had read the article, he was infuriated that the Indian security forces had arrested a respected Muslim doctor and tortured him for three straight days, charging him with aiding militant groups in the region. He knew the doctor, and he also knew the man was not involved in their movement.

The article went on to say that complaints about abuses by the Indian forces had doubled in recent years. No wonder his cells were gaining new recruits every month.

The longer he thought about the situation in Kashmir, the more he began to see another angle to these developments. Since their cruise missile strike, the Indians were vowing revenge, refusing to free any political prisoners, and their remaining forces were redoubling their counterinsurgency campaign. This meant that the promised negotiations to end the hostilities were going nowhere. This was good. More attacks meant more retaliation. More retaliation meant more destabilization. More destabilization meant the government of Pakistan could fall. And when that happened, *Inshallah*, their cells could take over and put their ultimate plans, the ones involving control of the nuclear stockpile, into operation.

Jambaz took a deep breath and began to prepare himself for prayers. He began a series of bows, kneeling, and prostration and repeated the words, "Praise be to God, Lord of the Creation. You alone we worship, and to you alone we pray for help." He needed to be at peace with Allah. He needed to restore his equilibrium and his energy, for he had a big job to do tonight.

21

Bethesda, Maryland—Friday Early Evening

The first hint of spring in downtown Bethesda brought out the crowds. Couples walked hand in hand, searching for an outside table at the Austin Grill. Throngs of teenagers ambled toward the Bethesda Row Cinema. And a jazz trio played a New Orleans blues tune in front of Barnes & Noble.

Across the street, Cameron Talbot pulled her Honda up to the Valet sign where the attendant opened her door. "Welcome to Mon Ami Gabi," he said as he helped her out of the car.

"There must be a thousand people out here tonight," Melanie said, sliding out of the passenger seat.

And a thousand reasons I should be working in my lab and not out on the town, Cammy thought. The sidewalks had a mini Mardi Gras atmosphere, but it was hard for her to mask her somber mood. Her day had been a series of struggles. Raj had come in to help with her calculations, and she had suggested they pool their resources and develop an integrated budget strategy so she could get Bollinger off her back. Raj hadn't agreed. He just said he'd think about it and wanted to focus all his time on Q-3. And then when they tried a new simulation with Ben, it went completely off track, and all Ben said was that he wanted "another Mulligan." At least the kid had kept his upbeat attitude.

Even though she was out with a friend, she couldn't shake her sense of unease, as if an ill wind were blowing instead of this pleasant night air.

They pushed through the heavy glass door and headed to the Maitre d' of the popular French bistro. They were ushered to a small table in the back room near a wall of windows that looked out at a side walkway. The rest of the room was encased in dark wood panels flanking honey-colored walls. In that area, the din had lowered to a dull roar. "At least we'll be able to hear ourselves talk back here," Cammy said, reaching for her menu.

"And we have a lot to talk about!" Melanie replied while she scrutinized the wine list. "You want to share a bottle?"

"Huh?" Cammy said. "Oh, I don't think I'll drink more than a glass."

"You know, one of these days, I'm going to get you to loosen up a bit."

"Sorry. Guess I've been pretty preoccupied."

"Preoccupied? I know things are tough right now. It's just that I wish I could get you to relax once in a while. You're always so serious," Mel said.

"And you always say that. But think about it. It isn't as if we work at Toys "R" Us. Although sometimes I have to admit it feels like *our* toys are broken half the time."

Melanie chuckled. "Oh, c'mon. Lighten up. Just this once. We're out on the town and, come to think of it, I'm amazed you suggested it."

Cammy sighed. "I just wanted you to know how much I appreciate your taking in a roommate."

Mel adopted a serious expression. "It's only until they catch the burglar. Then we'll get back to normal."

"*If* they ever catch him, you mean," Cammy said with a frown. She looked over Melanie's shoulder and saw a skinny olive-skinned man staring at her through one of the windows. She glanced away. "Here comes the waiter. What do you think we should have? You're the chef. What wine goes with Jell-O?"

"You must be looking at the children's menu," Mel said with her trademark smile. Then she turned and pointed to a small serving cart by the next table. "See that? It's their wine-by-the-glass cart. You can sample different bottles till you decide what you want. But I'm going to order a glass of their Cote du Rhone."

"That sounds okay. What about the steaks?" Cammy asked.

"My favorite is the steak bordelaise. It comes with caramelized onions and mushrooms in a red wine sauce and a whole plate of *pommes frites* that are to die for," she gushed.

"Guess that kills the no-carb thing for tonight."

"Tonight I'm going to blow it all off and really enjoy myself."

"You don't need to lose weight, you know," Cammy said.

"I'd like to drop five or ten pounds. Then I could be like Cassius."

"Cassius?"

"Sure," she said. "The guy with the lean and hungry look."

"Speaking of a hungry look, some weirdo has been watching us." She inclined her head toward the windows.

"Where?" Mel asked, twisting in her chair.

"Don't look. You'll just encourage him. No, wait. I think he's leaving."

"What did he look like?"

"Strange. Middle Eastern type."

"Oh, they're all over the place. Ever notice how they ogle women and party when they're in this country? Stuff they wouldn't dare to do back in Saudi or Syria or wherever they should be. Talk about hypocrisy."

The waiter served the wine and took their orders. Melanie took a sip and continued. "There are an awful lot of those Muslim types back home in Paris. My parents say that thirty percent of all the babies born in Europe now are Muslim. They're gonna take over one of these days."

Cammy nodded glumly.

"But on a happier note, in France people have less heart trouble than we do here. And they say it's because everybody drinks red wine." Mel raised her glass. "So drink up."

Cammy pondered the idea. "I'm not so sure."

"Not so sure about what?"

"How about this?" Cammy said. "People who drink red wine get more headaches, and so they take more aspirin. And aspirin wards off heart attacks."

"Oh geez! There you go," Mel said.

"What do you mean, there I go?"

"You do that all the time."

"Do what?"

"Figure out some backdoor way to analyze something."

"I do?"

"Sure. Guess that's why you're the scientist and I'm the PR Department.

And on that subject, remember, as soon as you nail the simulations, I've got some press releases ready to go—"

"I know."

"And I'm working up a feature story with a great lead about 'young scientist has major breakthrough.' Then the Committee will take notice and—"

"We'll get our R & D money," Cammy finished the sentence. "I don't know, Mel. I've never been into personal publicity. I remember something my dad used to say about that."

"Yeah? What?"

"He said, 'I'd always rather have people ask me why my statue was *not* in the town square than why it was.' "

Mel eyed her friend. "Well, let's see how it goes. Maybe I can get *Scientific American* to publish a piece about how to love a kinetic warhead or maybe the story of lonely drones."

22

Bethesda—Friday Early Evening

They'll be there for at least an hour, Jambaz figured as he backed away from the window and slowly inched his way along the wall of the restaurant toward his car. He had parked in a big lot across the street where he felt lucky to find a spot. Allah was smiling on him this evening.

He was in no hurry tonight. He knew that eventually they would finish their dinner and have to drive home. They had given their car to the valet, and since those guys were notoriously slow to retrieve vehicles, Jambaz knew he would have plenty of time to get to his car, back out of his space, and get into position.

This little respite gave him extra time to think and to plan. He reached in the pocket of his black pants and fingered the cold piece of steel hidden in the folds. It gave him a surge of confidence.

He took his time. No need to go back to the lot for quite a while. He loitered at the corner and read the posters advertising the latest movies at the Bethesda Row Cinema. He stared at the photos of men draping their arms around scantily clad women. Another poster showed an explosion of some sort with a mountain in the background. Kashmir.

The picture reminded him of his Kashmir. If he had his way, there would be explosions everywhere, except in his beloved Kashmir. And what he was about to do tonight would put them one step closer to their goal.

23

Bethesda—Friday Early Evening

"Here we are, ladies. One *salade maison* and one *frissee* with crumbled blue cheese and balsamic vinaigrette," the waiter said, laying the white plates on the table. "And another glass of wine?"

"Sure," Mel answered. "We're through working for the day."

The waiter picked up a bottle from the wine cart and refilled their goblets. When he sashayed away, Cammy took a bite of her salad and said, "It's hard to think about anything *but* work right now. I've got so many bad things going on with Bollinger and budgets and burglaries—"

"Good alliteration, Cam. Wanna write releases for me?" Mel quipped.

"Hardly."

"Well, we could talk about that White House guy. He's not bad."

"Look, I don't mean to be a broken record here, but I'm in the market for a brand-new technology, not a brand-new man in my life."

"I know. I know. But I have this feeling that every time you meet a nice guy, you figure either he's a spy or he doesn't measure up to your father or something."

Cammy stopped with her salad fork in mid-air. She thought back to the days when her father used to help her with her science projects, especially the one where she built a model of a NASA spaceship. And when she came home with the results of some complicated math test, he would smile, give her a hug, and draw a big star on the top of her exam paper. The memories used to be happy. Now, they were painful.

She also remembered the day she got the phone call. The day they told her his plane had crashed. The day her whole world had crashed, too. She turned to her friend, her eyes glistening. "You're probably right, Mel. You never knew my dad, but he was the best."

"Hey, look. I didn't mean to get all maudlin here."

"I know you didn't. It's just that he was so important to me . . . to all of us. And then he left us."

Melanie reached over and put her hand on Cammy's arm. "Oh Lord, I didn't mean . . ."

Cammy straightened in her chair. "I know. Sorry about that."

"And one other thing. Remember, he didn't *leave* you. He was killed in an accident. There's a great big difference, you know."

Cammy let out a breath. "You're right. It wasn't his fault."

"It was nobody's fault," Mel said.

"Well, I wouldn't exactly put it that way."

"What do you mean?"

"I still think it was the fault of Sterling Dynamics."

"Sterling? You never told me that."

"It's kind of hard to talk about it, although Jack knows how I feel. He was there when it happened."

"I know. But what did Sterling have to do with it?" Mel asked.

"They made the missile that misfired and crashed his plane."

"My God! Then what happened?"

"They filed a lot of paperwork, and there was an investigation. But you know the bureaucracy. Anyway, the more I hear about the defense budget now and how they're competing with us, the more I remember their history, their first-generation missiles, and I can't seem to get it out of my mind," Cammy said, taking a sip of her wine.

"You've got to let it go, Cam. There's nothing you can do about it now. You've got to get on with life," she said gently.

"You mean get a life?" Cammy asked with a wan smile.

The waiter approached with two gigantic oval plates. "Oh, look. Here come the steaks," Mel said. "Wait a minute; there's my cell." She reached for her phone and chatted for a few minutes while Cammy tried to balance a bunch of *pommes frites* on her fork.

"That was Raj," Mel said as she shoved the phone back into her bag. "He suggested I come stay at his place for a couple of days. Then you can have my condo all to yourself. It really is pretty small. You know the old line, 'there's barely enough room to lay my hat and a few friends.' "

Cammy said, "Dorothy Parker, right?"

"One and the same."

"Okay, so you'll move to his place. When?"

"Tonight," Mel said, her face glowing. "Think you could drop me off after dinner?"

"Sure, but don't you need some clothes or something?"

"Actually, I have a few things there already," Mel said casually. "I mean . . . well . . . I've been there before."

After dinner, Cammy paid the check and they walked outside and waited while the valet delivered their car. As Cammy headed down Bethesda Avenue, she never noticed the black Volvo that followed right behind.

24

Georgetown—Friday Early Evening

Hunt's gray stucco house with black shutters and white trim was on P Street, just off Wisconsin Avenue. The street was lined with maple trees, punctuated with old-fashioned street lamps, anchored on sidewalks paved with weathered red bricks. Gray stone urns filled with red geraniums flanked the stairs leading up to the black front door with a large brass door knocker at the top and a brass mail slot at the bottom.

When he heard the knock, Hunt opened the door and nodded to Ted Jameson.

"Thanks for coming by. Hope your wife doesn't mind."

"No. She's not home," Ted said, hanging his coat on the banister.

With a wife who was a commissioner on the FCC, Hunt had always thought of the Jamesons as the quintessential Washington couple. They were the type who survived the changes in administrations and seamlessly gravitated to various positions of power. Members of the *Frozen Chosen*, as Hunt called them.

"Oh, has she got some event tonight?"

Ted shifted uncomfortably and cleared his throat. "I haven't talked about it, but she's gone."

"Gone? Gone where?"

"Just gone. We . . . well . . . we split up a couple of weeks ago and—"

"Jesus Christ, man. You never said anything."

"It's not exactly the sort of thing . . . I mean, it's not your problem. She just got fed up with the long hours and all. She wanted to quit. Have a kid. Well, you know how it is."

"Sort of. I mean, my wife left me. Guess it goes with the territory sometimes. But you two. You always seemed so, I don't know, so professional or something."

"That's what I thought. But with all the late hours, the travel. I've been calling, trying to get her to come back." He shook his head. "What do you suppose the divorce rate is for guys like us?"

"Never counted. But hey, you want a beer?"

"Yeah, thanks." He followed Hunt into the kitchen. "It's kind of strange. Just last year we were talking about maybe finding a bigger place. We were going to look around here. We both liked the history." He pulled up a bar stool and hunched his shoulders. "Course that's all history now."

Hunt opened the refrigerator and scanned its meager contents. He handed Ted a Bud Light and opened another one for himself. "Speaking of history, JFK lived on this street for a while. That was before he went to the White House."

"I heard he had five different houses around here."

"Yeah. John Edwards used to live just down a few blocks. John Kerry's still over on O Street. Some of the time anyway."

"So who lives next door? Anybody interesting?"

"Well, I've got a really conservative lady who lives on one side and a socialist on the other."

"Since when do you have time to discuss politics with your neighbors?" Ted inquired as he took a swig of his beer.

"I don't. But you can tell by the dogs."

"The dogs?"

"Sure. Lady has two terriers named Maggie and Winnie."

"Maggie and Winnie?"

"That's for Margaret Thatcher and Winston Churchill."

Ted shrugged. "So what about the socialist?"

"He's got a hound named Vlad."

"Vlad?"

"Vladimir Lenin."

Ted gave him an amused look. "You ever have a dog?"

"Had a bunch when I was a kid. Then when I was married, we had a German shepherd till I went overseas."

"What was his name?"

"Montana."

"Montana?"

"For Joe Montana. He was my favorite quarterback," Hunt explained.

"Oh yeah, the 49ers. So whatever happened to him?"

"Joe or the dog?"

"The dog, you idiot."

"While I was gone, my ex let him out and he got hit by a car."

"Bummer."

"You better believe it. Lots of things she did were bummers. But we don't need to rehash that tonight. Not with your news. We've got a lot of stuff to talk about."

"Right," Ted said. "The Indian Ambassador is making noises about special demands before his people will sit down with Bhattia's people."

"What special demands?"

"First, they want an official apology for the missile attack."

"But Pakistan didn't launch it," Hunt said.

"No, they only lost it."

"What else?"

"Delhi wants more action on locating the other two missiles."

"So do we," Hunt said. "And speaking of wants, I wanted to try Mexican tonight. I called in an order. Hope that's okay."

"Sure. From where?"

"You know that place over on Wisconsin?"

"You mean the one that's painted the color of Pepto-Bismol?"

"Yeah, that one. Lousy ambiance, but the food's pretty good, so I figured it would be better to have them deliver so we can eat here."

"Good plan."

They took their beer into the library, where Hunt sat at his desk and Ted pulled up a brown leather chair in front of it.

"Where'd you get the sign?" Ted asked, and then read the words on a small plaque next to a lamp. "The secrecy of my job prevents me from knowing what I am doing."

"Yeah, well . . . my ex gave me that one some time ago because I never told her anything I was working on. She used to bitch about that . . . said I should learn to communicate."

"If she had that sign made, at least it shows she had a sense of humor."

"Sort of," Hunt replied. "Come to think of it, that's about the only thing of hers I decided to keep around this place." He took a stack of papers from the desk and handed them to Ted. "Take a look at these. They're background on the guys we're hooking up with in Delhi this weekend."

Ted scanned the pages, started to make notes in the margin, and pulled his chair closer to the desk. "Okay, so our first appointment at the Indian Ministry, first priority, is to stop any retaliation against Pakistan for the cruise missile attack. Second is to find the two other missiles before they can attack again."

"I don't know how many of the Indian forces are out looking for those damn things, but it'd better be most of them. Same for Pakistan's boys. One piece of news. Bhattia came by last night to tell me that a member of a particular terrorist group, Lashkar-i-Taiba, might have slipped into the country."

"Wait a minute. Bhattia thinks one of those terrorist loonies is here? Where?"

"He could be right here in Washington. He was a student here some time back. I'm trying to get a better line on this guy. I've talked to a contact at Homeland Security and another one at the FBI. They're all trying to find him."

"What do you suppose he's doing here . . . if he really *is* here?"

"Don't know. Bhattia didn't know, either," Hunt replied.

"Does he think this Lashkar crowd stole the missiles?"

"They're high on the list right now. But they move around a lot. And if they did steal the missiles, remember, they've got two left."

They heard a loud knock. Hunt got up from his chair and reached for his wallet. "Must be the Mexican. . . . I'll get this." He took the bags, paid the delivery boy, and headed to the kitchen. "C'mon. Let's eat in there while it's hot."

Ted picked up the two beers and followed. "Speaking of missiles, what's the latest on your lady friend with the new invention?"

Hunt shot his friend a worried look. "She had a helluva problem last night."

"Last night? What happened?" Ted asked.

"Somebody trashed her apartment and stole her computer."

"You're kidding. Where does she live?"

"In a high-rise in Bethesda. Security's probably not that great, so who knows? But obviously, somebody wanted something awfully bad to tear up the place like that."

"What did the cops say?"

"Figured it was just some local burglary, but I doubt it. She's had some publicity on that project of hers and—"

"And you think somebody was trying to get a line on that?"

"I know it sounds weird, but her computer was the only thing missing. And she had a lot of other nice stuff around."

Ted unwrapped a tortilla and spooned some ground beef, refried beans, and guacamole into the center. "This robbery does sound strange. I mean, I'm sure the woman doesn't keep classified information on a home computer."

"Of course not. But if the perp is a foreigner, he might not know that."

"Jesus! You think?"

"Look at the facts. Three cruise missiles are stolen. One is launched. Lady invents a missile defense system for the same kind of missile. Bad guy comes to town. Somebody tries to steal her technology. Or at least it looks that way. It all sounds too coincidental. And I just don't believe in coincidences."

"On the other hand, it could be a case of industrial espionage," Ted said. "I mean, it's pretty far-fetched that some Pakistani . . . or Kashmiri . . . is right here in D.C. . . . has figured out where to look, and actually broke into that woman's apartment. How strange is that?"

"In this business, nothing surprises me anymore. Here, have some salsa."

Hunt twisted his bar stool around so he could get another container from the bag. "Trouble is, we can't afford any more surprises. We've got an American scientist under siege—"

"Uh-huh . . . and a bad guy running around town breaking and entering . . . a bunch of terrorists armed with cruise missiles, and Indians who want to start World War III."

Hunt looked up. "And that's just this week."

25

Cammy drove down Bethesda Avenue and turned left onto Arlington Road while Melanie kept up a steady stream of stories about Raj and his attributes. "Those big brown eyes and that fabulous accent," she said dreamily. "And he has the most impeccable manners. I mean, he treats me like a queen, and I'm not used to that. Not with American men anyway."

"I guess he's just the opposite of that guy you went out with last month . . . whatever his name was."

"Oh yeah. Total contrast. He was the kind of guy who clapped after the first movement of a symphony and had no clue how to eat escargot."

"I didn't realize you were so serious about Raj. I've been working with him, and no question, the guy is brilliant. Then again, he's always so . . . quiet. Contemplative. That's one way to describe him. I'm never sure what he's thinking."

"When he does say something, he's kind of spiritual," Mel said. "We got to talking about India and where he was born and about being a Hindu."

"What did he say? I don't know much about Hinduism."

"He told me about how it's the oldest religion. They have gods and goddesses and do a lot of meditating. So yes, he's quiet sometimes. That's his nature. Then there's the belief in reincarnation."

Cammy passed the Safeway and headed down toward Little Falls Parkway. "I've heard stories about previous lives. There have been a lot of books written about things like that weird feeling you get that you've been someplace before or know exactly what somebody is going to say because you've heard him say it before. Know what I mean?"

"Absolutely. But Raj says it goes way beyond that. He says that things that happen to you in a previous life can have an impact on this life."

"What kind of an impact?"

"Oh, things like fears or how you get along with people."

"What do you mean?" Cammy asked as she checked her rearview mirror. There was a lot of traffic. Par for the course on a nice night. There was a black Volvo on her tail. *Guy's following awfully close. What's his problem?* She refocused on what Melanie was saying.

"Let's say you have a fear of heights, for example. Maybe it's because something bad happened to you in a previous life, like falling from a cliff or something."

"Not a pretty thought," Cammy said. *And I have a fear of flying. Not because of an accident in a previous life, but because of a tragedy in this life.* She shook her head, trying to clear the all too familiar image of her father's jet engulfed in fire plummeting to earth.

Mel was still talking. "Now there are good things, too. You know how it is when you meet someone for the first time, and sometimes you really hit it off and feel like you've known that person all your life, but you never really did?"

"Sure. That's happened," Cammy said. "Kind of like when I first met you."

"There you are!"

"So what's that supposed to mean?"

"It means that maybe we knew each other in a previous life. That's my impression of our discussions anyway. Actually, I'm not sure whether Raj believes all of that or not. He just tries to explain it to me. Then he told me all about Karma."

"Isn't that your spirit?"

"No. It's kind of the sum total of all the things you do. The good and the bad. And if you do more good deeds, you come back at a higher level in the next life."

"Did Raj talk about all the tensions between the Muslims and Hindus over there?" Cammy asked, steering onto the Parkway.

"Oh sure. I mean with that big missile strike and the troubles in Kashmir."

"Is he following all of that?"

"Of course. He's got relatives who are pretty high up in the government. They all want to attack Pakistan, but they've been holding off, at least for now."

"You know that's what Hunt is working on," Cammy said.

"The guy at the White House? I thought he was interested in Q-3."

"Well, he is, but his whole area involves missile defense and nuclear proliferation and if India and Pakistan go to war again . . . well, can you imagine what could happen?"

Melanie shook her head and glanced out the window to the right rear view mirror. "I know. They both have nukes. Hey, Cam . . ."

"What?"

"Better get in the right lane. Looks like some jerk is coming up fast right behind us."

Cammy checked her rearview mirror again. "What's going on? He's really hightailing it." She shifted lanes just as a black Volvo careened up to her left rear bumper and smashed into it. "Oh my God!" Cammy gasped, and fought for control. Her car was skidding off to the right as the Volvo pulled up next to them. Its right window opened and the driver took aim with a small handgun.

The embankment was steep. The Honda slid off and headed down into a gulley lined with trees. The right side crashed into a thick tree trunk and finally came to a jarring halt as air bags exploded around the two women trapped inside.

26

Bethesda—Friday Evening

"Mel?" Cammy whispered cautiously. "Are you okay?"

Nothing.

Cammy tried to move her head. It hurt. Her shoulder hurt, too. She ached all over. She reached up with her left hand and felt her forehead. It was wet. Blood was seeping into her eyes. She tried to wipe it away as she called out again in a labored breath, "Mel? Mel? Talk to me, Mel." She tried to lift her right arm to touch her friend, but it was pinned by the air bags.

It was dark. Tree branches were fanned across the windshield, and as her eyes adjusted to the gloom, all she could see was Mel's body slumped against the door, her head lying against the window at what seemed like an odd angle.

Oh God! Maybe she's just knocked out. Maybe she just hit her head. Yes. Yes. That must be it. Please, God, let that be it. Cammy's head was throbbing. Her throat was dry. At least the air bags were deflating now, and she was able to reach down and undo her seat belt. She leaned over and touched Melanie's shoulder. "Mel? Can you hear me?"

Nothing.

I've got to get out of here. I've got to get help.

She felt weak as she tried her door. It was stuck. She shoved her left shoulder against it, winced, and tried again. This time it cracked open. She pushed harder and slithered out onto the rocks at the bottom of the gulley. She looked up and saw lights on the road and wanted to cry out. But she was so far down in the trees, she knew no one could hear her.

Help. I have to get help. Cell phone. If I can only find my cell phone. She tried to get up, but her knees buckled. She reached over to pull on the back door and finally wrenched it partially open. She leaned through the opening and rummaged around on the floor until she felt her purse. She and Mel had put their bags on the backseat, and everything had slid onto the floor during the impact. She pulled the purses out, slid back onto the ground, and felt a wave of dizziness as another drop of blood clouded her eyesight. She forced back the nausea and reached for her phone.

In the dim light of a quarter moon she tried to make out the numbers, but darkness had closed in. She touched a key. Then everything went black.

"Hello? This is Hunt Daniels." There was no reply. He tried again. "Hello? Anybody there?" He pushed his cell phone closer to his ear, but all he heard was the sound of traffic way off in the distance. "What the . . ." He pulled the phone down, looked at the little readout, and saw that the call came from Cammy's number. "Cam? You there? Cam? Answer me."

"What's going on?" Ted asked.

"I don't know. She called me from her cell. Now she's not there."

"Maybe something else came up and she tried to end the call. She'll probably call back. Give it a minute."

"No. She's not like that. Damn woman can be infuriating sometimes, but from what I've seen, she's very deliberative. I mean, she's not flighty or any of that." He listened again. Intently. He thought he heard breathing. "Something's wrong. Something's gotta be wrong."

"Where is she?"

"I'm about to find out." Hunt hit a series of keys on the cell and activated the new GPS feature. He studied the display on the small screen. "Holy shit!"

"What is it?"

"She's on Little Falls Parkway in Bethesda."

"Where on the Parkway?"

"Almost to River Road. There aren't any restaurants there. She said she was out to dinner. Must be in her car. Oh Jesus! I know that road. Off to the right side, it drops off. Way off. I'm calling 9-1-1."

Two police cars, a fire truck, and an EMS van pulled to a stop at the top of the ravine. With blue and white lights flashing, groups of men made their way down the embankment, hauling tools and two stretchers. First, they pried open the right front door of the car, and the EMS crew began to check Melanie. From the angle of her head they suspected a neck injury and immediately put her into a cervical collar. Next, they gingerly lifted her out, strapped her on a medivac gurney, and began to claw their way up the hill.

Another medic knelt down next to Cammy, took her pulse, and shone a light into her eyes. She moaned softly. "This one's just coming around," he shouted. The young man began to swab her face and muttered something about a gash on her forehead. Cammy couldn't see. The blood had caked on her eyelashes. When she tried to raise her head, the medic said, "Take it easy, miss. We need to get you both to the hospital." He cleaned her eyes and started to put a bandage on her forehead.

"Hospital?" Cammy murmured. "Where? Mel? Where's—"

"Easy now. We're going to get you out of here." He shouted to his partner, "I need the other gurney here."

A tow truck arrived just as a green Jaguar screeched to a halt in front of the fire truck. Hunt leaped out and raced to the van. He saw Melanie's inert body being pushed inside. "Is she . . . ? Where's the other one?" he demanded, craning his neck to look inside the van. It was empty. "There was another woman with her." He motioned to a policeman. "I said where is she?"

"Who are you?" the Police Captain said, walking up to Hunt, notebook in hand.

"Colonel Hunt Daniels. White House. I said, where's the other one?"

"Down there. Better shape. They're bringing her up now. Do you know this woman?" he asked, pointing to Mel as she was being loaded into the van.

"Yes, I know them both. Is she . . . ?"

"We don't know yet. Unconscious. Concussion maybe. Maybe worse. Taking her to Sibley. We'll take them both."

Hunt started down the ravine when the Captain grabbed his arm. "No need to go down there. They're bringing her up. Pretty big mess down there. Must have lost control or something. Need to talk to the other one."

Hunt eyed the Captain, taking his measure. The last thing he needed was a long interrogation here. He needed to get both women to the hospital and fast. He said to the policeman, "She wouldn't lose control."

"How do you know that?" the officer asked, taking notes. "And how come you're here?"

"Cammy called me. Well, she tried to. I got their location, and I'm the one who called you."

"Okay." He made a note of that. "And she's Cammy who?"

"Dr. Cameron Talbot," Hunt said impatiently.

"She's a doc?" the Captain asked.

"Different kind," Hunt replied. "I'm going down," he said as he turned, pushed his way through some bushes, and started to negotiate the steep incline.

He stumbled over a branch and then saw the medics strapping Cammy to some sort of board. "Cammy?" he called out.

She opened her eyes and mumbled, "Hunt? How . . . ?"

"Lady, don't move your head. We're taking you up now. Try to relax, okay?" the medic said.

"But where's Mel? She's hurt. I know she's hurt," Cammy pleaded.

The headlights at the top of the ridge illuminated parts of the ravine. Hunt could see a bit of blood oozing from under the bandage they had slapped on Cammy's forehead. Her blouse was torn; her hair was tangled. He couldn't tell if she was badly hurt. "They're taking Mel to Sibley. You, too." He trudged up the hill next to her stretcher and put his hand on her arm. "It's gonna be all right, Cam. We're getting help for both of you."

At the crest of the hill, Cammy whispered, "Mouth so dry." One of the medics reached inside the van and produced a bottle of water. Hunt took it, twisted the cap off, and gently held it to her lips.

"Gotta get this other woman to Sibley," the Captain said. Then he saw Cammy take a drink. "But I need to talk to you, uh," he consulted his notes, "Dr. Talbot."

"But I have to go with Melanie," Cammy murmured.

"You seem in better shape than that one. Can you answer a couple of questions? Then we'll take you over there."

"But I want—" Cammy insisted.

Hunt intervened. "Captain, can't this wait? The van is leaving. They both need attention. I'll follow. You come in your car. We can talk when we get there."

The Captain shook his head and grunted. "I need statements on this whole thing."

27

Kashmir—Friday Night

"Here, have some mutton, my friend," Abbas Khan beamed as he handed the plate to the young man seated across from him. "We have interesting news tonight. While we eat, we can read about our successes. They are all here. Right here in the bible of the capitalists. That's what we call it. Here, look." He handed over a copy of the Asian edition of *The Wall Street Journal* where a headline screamed across the page, "Al Qaeda Gaining New Support." The second line read, "Amid Crackdown in Pakistan, Cells Form Among Middle Class."

Rashid began to read aloud, " 'Across the country, police say more than two dozen small terrorist cells, most linked to al Qaeda, have been formed in recent months. Educated, middle-class Pakistanis run many of these new groups. An increasing number of the middle class are alienated by a pro-U.S. stance that they believe sacrifices Pakistan's own interests.' They are writing about our cells, are they not, Khan Sahib?"

"Yes. They now know of our power to recruit from among the educated classes, not just the graduates of the Madrassas. And it is true what they write about the stupid government in Islamabad doing the bidding of Washington. But not for long. I have a report on our latest attack on the

President. Eleven dead. More injured. Soon they will realize that they are on the wrong side. They will see that the people no longer support them and their invading allies. Soon we will be in a position to take over the entire government, and then we will be in a perfect position to dictate *to* the Americans, not take orders *from* them. And then we will put our educated members in the positions of highest power. You, Rashid, you can be one of those leaders. You are a university graduate, a trained scientist," the leader said, smiling broadly at the younger man. "You have carried out many assignments for us. You have performed well because you are smart."

Rashid adopted an obsequious pose. "I thank you for your confidence, but many others in our cells are well educated."

"Yes. We recruit only the best, although I am beginning to wonder about Jambaz."

"Jambaz Muhammad Sharif? There is a problem?"

"I have no report . . . yet. I am waiting to find out if he has fulfilled his mission."

"Surely he will report in very soon, Khan Sahib. He is far away, and perhaps he is in danger."

"He should know enough not to put himself in danger. He should follow my rules and get his job done."

"But he has traveled to America before. He knows their language. He has always been careful and thorough. I'm sure there is a logical explanation for his silence."

The cell leader munched on a piece of meat and met Rashid's eyes with a steady gaze. "I have given him a most important assignment, but now I wonder if he was the right man."

"What do you mean?"

"He has performed well in the past. That is true. But he has been seeking more and more power among us. And you know the wisdom of Imam Ali, Shiite though he was."

"Which wisdom?"

" 'He who seeks authority should not be given authority.' "

"Yes. I know. But perhaps there is some explanation. I am sure we will hear shortly. He told me he must be careful with his e-mail messages as the American agents are looking everywhere."

The older man nodded and stroked his beard. "You may be right. We shall wait." He then took the newspaper and turned to another page. "But while we wait for his report, we have work to do here. See this other article?

It is about the American advance team which is coming to New Delhi and will later travel to Islamabad to arrange peace talks. Peace talks. What do these insignificant dogs who send their soldiers to start wars . . . what do they know about peace talks?"

Rashid glanced at the paper, his eyes lighting up. "They are coming in a few days. Do we have time to stage an attack?"

"That is my plan. They think they can send infidels over here to tell us how to run our lives, our governments, our wars. We will show them who runs things here."

The young man nodded and said, "Do we have time to target them with our remaining missiles?"

"No. We will not waste a missile on a small team of low-level bureaucrats. We have plenty of conventional weapons to use on such scum."

"Of course you are right. But what about the missiles?"

"I have ideas for the missiles."

28

Washington, D.C.—Friday Night

The cry of a child behind the flimsy curtain jolted Cammy as a doctor applied disinfectant and stretched a fresh bandage across her forehead. The smell of alcohol, the groans of an old man being wheeled nearby, and the harsh overhead lights combined to create a surreal and dire atmosphere. *I've got to get out of here. I've got to find Melanie. Find out if she's badly hurt.* The child let out another wail. *I wonder if Mel is crying, too.* No one had told Cammy anything. They had just brought her into the ER where this doctor was fussing over her head wound and probing for other injuries.

"Any more dizziness now?"

"A headache. That's all," she replied. "But can't you tell me anything about Mel? Melanie Duvall?"

"Sorry. Somebody else is handling that case."

"I have to know if she's going to be all right," Cammy protested.

"Dr. Talbot?" The Police Captain pushed the curtain aside. Hunt was right behind him along with a nurse clutching a clipboard.

"Cam, how are you feeling?" Hunt asked anxiously. "They've got a bunch of forms they want us to fill out."

"Forms? Forget the forms. I have to see Mel," Cammy said, her voice rising.

"Just wait a minute, miss," the policeman interjected. "I want to know what happened out there."

"Sir, please," the nurse interrupted. "We need information on this patient and also on Miss Duvall. Her family—"

"Her family," Cammy practically shrieked. "What's wrong? Why do you need . . . ?"

"Cammy, calm down," Hunt said, putting his hand on her shoulder to steady her. "She's just doing her job."

"And I'm trying to do mine," the Captain said, irritation creeping into his voice. "I'm sure the docs are looking after your friend. Now, can you just tell me what happened? How your car ended up in that ravine?"

How can these people worry about filling our forms and filing reports when I don't know whether Melanie is even alive? Cammy shot a worried glance at Hunt, who nodded for her to answer the question.

She took a deep breath. "It was a black Volvo, I think. Yes, that's what it was. It was behind us for a while. Then it came up really fast."

"I don't suppose you noticed a license number or who was driving?"

"No. No license number. It all happened so fast."

"So he came up behind you. Then what?"

"Then he crashed into us."

"He crashed into your car?" the policeman asked, scribbling in his notebook.

"Yes. I got into the right lane, but he kept coming, and then he hit us. And I think his car backfired or something. I heard this noise, but my car went over the edge," she said in a halting voice.

"So he hit you from behind?"

"Not exactly. It was more like . . . like almost next to us. Like he was shoving us off the road. You know how you see some people do that in movies? They come up next to a car and bump it, and it goes over a cliff?" She shuddered.

"Yeah. So now it's Dirty Harry driving in Bethesda?" the Captain asked sarcastically.

"That's what the lady said," Hunt intervened. "I think you'd better start looking for a black Volvo with a dent on its right front side"

"We know our business, Colonel. We'll take care of it."

Hunt wondered why he felt like a kid in a sandbox playing king-of-the-hill with the town bully. All he wanted to do was get Cammy out of here and go check on Melanie. They didn't need to sit around and answer a bunch of questions. So the guy had a report to make. She told him what happened. Enough.

"Wait a minute. So your car goes over the edge. Then what?" The Captain gestured toward Hunt with his pen. "You call this guy?"

"No. I mean, maybe I hit redial or something. I don't know because I must have passed out."

The doctor peered at the bandage on her forehead again. "Nasty gash. At least nothing's broken. No more problems here?" he asked Cammy, effectively ignoring the Captain's questions.

"I got the call," Hunt explained. "And I tracked her down on my GPS. That's when I called 9-1-1."

"Okay. Okay. I got it. But I've got nothing on the other driver. Do you know how many black Volvos there are in this town?" He shook his head and muttered, "Never find the guy." He turned to Cammy once more. "So nothing on the guy? Was he alone? Do you remember that?"

"Yes. Alone. His windows were dark. Tinted, I guess. And I think there was just a driver. But I wonder . . ." She glanced up at Hunt, who nodded almost imperceptibly.

"You wonder what?" the Captain demanded.

"Last night someone broke into my apartment and stole my computer. Tonight somebody tried to run me off the road. Do you think . . . ?"

"A burglary last night? Did you report it?"

"Of course she did," Hunt said. "Sure looks to me like the lady is the target of somebody."

"What did the investigators say last night?" the Captain asked.

"Nothing much," Cammy said, staring down at the wrinkled sheets on the bed.

"And you two think this was the same guy?" The Captain shook his head. "A lot of crazy people in this town. But sounds more like a drunk driver to me." He slapped his notebook shut, pulled out a card, and handed it to Cammy. "If you remember anything else, call us."

29

Washington, D.C.—Friday Night

Jambaz pulled his Volvo into the small garage he had rented on New Mexico Avenue, a block from his apartment. He'd thought about trying to get another car, but he wanted to save his cash. Besides, his car was black. There were many cars just like this one lining the streets all around the university. He studied the dent in the fender. Not too bad. He wasn't worried about the car. He *was* worried about the woman. He wasn't sure whether he had been successful in disabling or destroying his prey.

As he hurried back to his apartment, he figured that by watching her building he would learn soon enough if she had survived the crash and was still working on her project. If she was, what was the expression? A cat with nine lives? Yes, that was it. And he had some thoughts on how to cut that number.

Once inside, he powered up his computer and checked for messages in the chat room. Abbas Khan had contacted him once more with news of his brothers. They had staged a few more attacks against government figures in Islamabad, were organizing a "surprise" in New Delhi for an American advance team, and had tried another assassination attempt against the Pakistani President.

If only they could eliminate the traitor and get control of his nuclear arsenal. The mere thought of such a triumph was exhilarating. Yet it was too soon to contemplate such victories. Others were in charge of the grand scheme. As for him, he had to finish his job. Khan was pressing him for a report. He could not make a report. Not yet. But soon.

He reached for the classified section of *The Washington Post* and leafed through the want ads. There in the middle of the page was exactly what he needed.

30

As Cammy handed her admission form over to the receptionist, a pair of doors swung open. A doctor came out and scanned the waiting room.

"Are you related to Ms. Duvall?"

Cammy jerked her head around and stood up. "No, but she's my friend. I was with her in the car. Is she badly hurt?"

The doctor replied in a serious tone, "We can't say just yet. She's still unconscious."

"Still unconscious? Oh no! How bad is it? Will she be okay?"

"We're doing a CT scan on her now."

"What are you looking for? What do you think? When can we see her?"

"Not for a while, I'm afraid. She'll be in an ICU. We'll have an intracranial pressure monitor in her head. We'll be watching her very closely."

"In her head?" Cammy exclaimed, and looked over at Hunt, who was standing protectively at her side.

"Does she have any family in the area?" the doctor asked.

"Everyone is asking about her family," Cammy said. "No. They live in Paris. I'll take responsibility. She was with me." She stopped and added, "And it's all my fault."

The doctor raised his eyebrows as Hunt chimed in, "Cammy, please. A guy crashed into your car. You were *not* responsible."

"He was aiming for me. I'm sure of it."

"Ma'am, this isn't the time to talk about who's responsible for what. We have our hands full here. I suggest you folks go home and get some rest."

"But when can I see her?" Cammy pleaded.

"She won't be back in the ICU for a little while. If you really want to wait, there's a coffee bar in the lobby and the cafeteria is always open. Now if you'll excuse me." He turned and pushed a lever on the wall. The doors swung open and he disappeared.

Hunt took Cammy's arm and led her out of the waiting room. He motioned to the receptionist. "We'll be outside for a while." He leaned down and said to Cammy, "You sure your head is okay? You could have spent the night here, you know."

"No. I'll be all right. Just a few bruises. It's Mel I'm upset about."

"I know. Maybe they'll have something in an hour or so. Do you want some coffee or something?"

"I guess so. But you don't need to stay."

"I'm staying," he said firmly. "Besides, this gives us a chance to talk, if you feel up to it."

She nodded glumly and followed him to the coffee bar. He ordered two mocha lattes, paid the clerk, and headed outside into the evening air.

"It's still pretty mild tonight. Let's go sit over there." Across the driveway was a small garden with a stone fountain at one end. In the middle there was a weathered wooden gazebo with benches inside. They sat down together and began to sip their coffee.

"Do you think she'll make it?" Cammy asked forlornly. "I saw her when they brought her in on that stretcher. She looked so pale."

"I know, but then again, those fluorescent lights in there make everybody look pale, if you ask me."

"Guess so. The real question is who—"

"You mean who is the guy who ran you off the road, and is it the same guy who broke into your apartment?"

"Well, of course," she said. "Sure sounds like he's using me for target practice. But why? I can see that somebody might try to find out how Q-3 works or try to steal it . . . even if it's not quite a proven system . . . yet . . . but why would they try to get rid of me?"

"I don't know. You'd think that if somebody really *is* trying to steal your project, they'd wait until you've got it up and running, then take it, not knock off the inventor. It just doesn't make much sense."

"Unless they're trying to make sure nobody else gets it," Cammy ventured.

Hunt stared at her, shifting a bit to sit closer to her. "I suppose that's possible, but I'm just not sure I can connect the dots here. Trouble is, I'm leaving town pretty soon."

"Yes, I know."

He'd leave and she'd be alone again, she reflected. There didn't seem to be much he could do to help her. Not with the burglary. Certainly not with the car crash. He had said he had some ideas, but he seemed strangely bereft of them now. Maybe he wasn't as high up in the government as she'd thought. When she lived on the air force base, a lieutenant colonel was fairly important. At least the officers knew how to get things done. But officers in the Pentagon and the White House were probably a dime a dozen. Even the Chairman of the Joint Chiefs rarely got much ink in this town. What could she possibly expect from Hunt? Then again, he was here, trying to be helpful.

"Uh, Cam," Hunt interrupted her thoughts. "You said Melanie's folks live in Paris. What about your family?"

She told him she had grown up on air force bases. She explained that her father had been a fighter pilot when they lived at the base in California. When Hunt asked how she got interested in missile defense, she described the night she was watching television with her dad. The President was on the air giving a speech about a brand-new initiative. That speech had made such an impression on her. It was March 1983 and the President had talked about missiles and how they posed a big threat because once they were launched, we didn't have any way of stopping them. All we could do was fire another one back at the enemy and probably kill lots of innocent people in the process.

She remembered how the President had said he had a new idea. An idea about saving lives rather than avenging them. It was an idea about destroying missiles before they got here, and he called on the scientific community to figure it out. It was that night she had announced that she wanted to become a scientist. She wanted to grow up and figure out how to stop the missiles.

Then she told Hunt how her little brother had made fun of her, saying, "Nobody can do that, unless he's Superman or something. And besides, you're just a girl."

Hunt chuckled at the story. "So that's how you became a scientist, huh?"

"Well, I was only nine. I had to go to college first. But yes, I guess that's how it all got started. It's funny how kids get ideas, you know?"

"Sure. When Kennedy made his speech about going to the moon, I think he spawned a whole generation of kids who wanted to be astronauts. Think about it. Kids don't know something can't be done, so they just decide to do it."

"I guess."

"So where's your dad now?"

"He was killed."

"Oh God, Cam, how?"

"A missile. He was a test pilot. It misfired."

"Damn! No wonder you're working on missile defense. You've got as good a reason as anybody."

She was silent for a while. Hunt knew it was getting late, but he didn't want to leave. Not just yet. To hell with the office. He wanted to stay right here and help this woman who had occupied his mind ever since he had met her. *Was it only two days ago?* He checked his watch and stood up. "Tell you what. Stay here for a minute. I'm going to go check. See if there's any news about Mel."

Cammy started to get up, but he gently pushed her back down on the bench.

"No, just relax. I'll be right back."

She drank the last dregs of her coffee, not even noticing that it was cold. *There he goes again*, she thought, *always telling me what to do. Sometimes he treats me like a child.* She was thinking about how she had felt the night before when he had ordered her around her apartment. But before she had a chance to analyze her reaction, he came loping across the little park and sat down again.

"Any word?"

"Nope. Sorry. Receptionist doesn't have anything new, and the doctors are tied up. Let's give it a little more time."

She fidgeted on the hard wood bench. The waiting, the not knowing, it was all so hard. At least she had someone to talk to. Here was a man who was trying to be helpful. A man who was staying with her through this god-awful night. But what did she really know about him except for a job title?

"Tell me about you," she said softly. "How long have you been in the Air Force?"

"Long time. I started out in pilot training."

"Like my dad."

"Well, yes. I love to fly. Still do . . . on the weekends whenever I can get away. But I was sent overseas a bunch of times."

"Did you have a family that went with you?"

His eyes were guarded. "Yeah, I did once. I mean, I was married for a while. But she never went with me. She didn't dig the military life. I was gone a lot, and she wasn't used to that."

"So what happened?" Cammy asked.

"After a while, she left," he said calmly, finishing his latte and squeezing the paper cup.

"So where'd she go?"

"To New York. Got herself remarried to an investment banker who's probably home most of the time. Now I suppose they spend their week-ends in the Hamptons at the Meadow Club and Shinnecock. Places like that."

"I've never been to the Hamptons," Cammy said.

"It's nice enough out there, if you like that sort of thing. Hey, enough of that. Let's get back to the here and now. I've been meaning to ask you about Bandaq. How did it get a weird name like that?"

"Oh, that. It's kind of an odd story. It was a long time ago. These two guys were bare-boating in the Caribbean, lounging around on the deck of a sailboat. They kicked around some ideas about a new technology com-pany. And when they decided how to put it together, they were drinking banana daiquiris. So . . . Bandaq."

"Sounds about right to me. Do you ever go sailing?"

"I love to sail." *I'm just afraid to fly,* she thought. "What about you?"

"I like it, just haven't had the time for that and flying, too. Oh, but once in a while a bunch of us from the NSC get away for a ball game."

"Baseball?"

"Yeah, the Washington Nationals. Our Legislative Director and her hus-band are big fans. I've got a friend who works for the team, so sometimes I snag some infield tickets for everybody." He paused for a moment. "Maybe, after all of this is over, you'd like to go with us," he ventured.

"Maybe," she said cautiously.

He grabbed their empty coffee cups and started to get up. "What say we check in with the doctors again? They may not know anything, but then again . . ."

Cammy sighed and stood up. "You're probably right. It could be a long night. But I have to find out."

He tossed the cups into a nearby bin as Cammy murmured, "She's got to come through this. She's just got to."

31

The doctor cleared his throat. Hunt and Cammy bolted upright.

"What's happening? Any news?" Hunt asked.

The doctor looked tense. "The nurse said you were still waiting."

"How is she? Can you tell us anything?"

"I'm sorry, but she's still unconscious. We'll have to keep monitoring her."

"When can we see her?" Hunt asked.

"She's in the ICU. You can see for yourself, but just for a few minutes."

They made their way to the special unit where Cammy saw Melanie surrounded by machines, wires, and beeping noises. Her skin looked pasty white except for several cuts and the beginning of discoloration around her eyes and forehead. A nurse hovered nearby.

Cammy leaned over. "Mel? Mel?"

No response.

She squeezed Mel's hand.

Nothing.

My God! She looks terrible, and it's all my fault. Cammy's eyes grew moist as she stared at her friend and said a silent prayer. She pointed to a gray metal chair in the corner. "Can I sit with her?"

"I'm afraid not. Not in an ICU. I'm sorry," the doctor said.

"How long do you think . . . ?"

"We have no way of knowing. There's nothing you can do now. And as I said before, why don't you go home and get some rest. But be sure to leave your numbers at the front desk."

Cammy took one last look at her friend, then at the machines, and finally raised her troubled eyes to Hunt. He gave her a sympathetic nod, put his arm around her, and slowly ushered her out of the room.

They headed over to the parking lot. He helped her into his car and she sank down in the tan leather seat. "Oh my God, Raj."

"The guy at the office?"

"Yes. Mel was supposed to go to his place tonight. He called her. I completely forgot." She dug into her purse, pulled out her cell phone, and dialed Raj's number. She explained what had happened, where Mel was, and that she was unconscious. He said he had been frantic all evening and had been trying to call Melanie's cell phone. She said that she had put Mel's purse in the trunk, so never heard it ring. He said he would be at the hospital first thing in the morning to check on her. He also mentioned that he had been working on some new algorithms and if she felt up to it, they could try another simulation tomorrow if she wanted to come into the office or first thing Monday. She said she'd check in with him later. She closed the phone and put it away.

How can he think about algorithms when the woman might die?

"Tell you what," Hunt said, turning left out of the lot and onto Loughboro Road. "What say we swing by your building, you pick up some clothes and come to my place?"

"Your place?" Cammy was stunned. What was this all about? "I'm staying up in Mel's apartment. I'll be fine there."

"Maybe. Maybe not. Look, we have no idea who tried to nail you tonight, and I don't like the idea of your staying there alone. If this guy has been trailing you around town, he knows where you live. And until we can get some protection . . ."

"I think I'd better go to a hotel. There's an Embassy Suites near our building. They have kitchens. I'll check in there."

"No. Now listen."

Here we go again. The colonel's giving orders.

"I'm serious," he argued. "Anybody can get into a hotel. I've got a place in Georgetown. There's plenty of space, big guest room, good security system. I can keep an eye on things, at least for the next few days. I don't think you should be alone. Not at night anyway. We can get a taxi for you if you really need to go in to work in the morning. That is, if you feel up to it. Let's wait and see about that."

Cammy leaned her head back and felt totally conflicted. "I don't know."

He softened his tone. "It's okay. Really. Look at it this way. You're working on something that could be important for the Pentagon and our guys in the field. My job is to keep track of these things. We've got a common interest here. I want to help you."

Does he really want to help me or just keep track of what I'm doing? And why would I go home with a man I met just two days ago?

She glanced over and saw the intensity in his eyes. Suddenly she felt a connection, as if there were an invisible thread linking their thoughts together. She was tired. Exhausted. Yet this man made her feel things she hadn't felt in a very long time. She had always been independent, in charge, on her own. Maybe it was time to accept an offer of help. Raj was helping her team at the lab. Maybe she should team up with Hunt. Just until they sorted out the threats. The trouble was, she wasn't sure she could trust Raj, and she didn't know about Hunt, either. Was she taking too much on faith? He did have a point about security, though. And surely she could take care of herself, even in another man's house

She sat still, staring out the window as Hunt turned left onto Dale Carlia Parkway toward Bethesda. "It's been a long night, Cam. Let's take this thing one step at a time. If we stick together, we'll be better off."

She pondered that. *I wonder.*

Hunt drove to her apartment building, and they both went upstairs to gather the suitcase full of clothes and toiletries she had taken to Mel's place. She went into the bathroom and washed her face, avoiding the bandage on her forehead. She stared at the mirror. Tired, sunken eyes stared back. *I'm a mess. Better get out of these clothes.* Bits of blood had dropped onto her beige sweater, and her black slacks had mud stains everywhere. *Let the cleaners worry about all of this. I've got too many other things to worry about right now.* She ran a brush through her tangled hair, and when she stepped back into the living room Hunt fished in his pocket and pulled out a blue cell phone. "Now that we're getting your things together, take this."

"I have a cell phone," she said, eyeing the small device.

"Not like this one. It has a security scrambler. I'll have one just like it when I head over to India. I want to keep in touch. Go ahead. Take it."

"How do I call you?" she asked, locking the door to Mel's condo and heading toward the elevator.

"You probably can't. I'll be in planes and meetings most of the time. But I'll call you whenever I can break free. I want to stay on top of this situation."

"You'll have enough to do over there without having to check on me," she said. "Aren't you trying to get the Indian government to slow down and not retaliate for that missile strike?"

"That's the plan. We've got to convince those guys that it wasn't the Pakistani government that ordered the strike, even if it was one of their missiles. What we do know is that three missiles were stolen, and we're still trying to figure out who took them."

"Three? They've only launched one of them. What about the other ones?"

"That's another problem. We've got to try and locate the terrorists and stop them before they decide to shoot off the rest of them."

"How long do you think you'll be gone?" she asked, pushing the button for the elevator.

"Not sure. If we can make some headway in Delhi, then we'll head over to Islamabad and get their people on board. Then the Special Envoy can come over and we can get some sort of a treaty in the works. The President would like to telescope the whole process . . . fast-track this thing. There's a big celebration coming up at the Taj Mahal." The elevator doors opened; they stepped inside and punched L.

"I read something about that. Aren't they inviting a bunch of world leaders and having a big party or something?"

"That's what we've heard. The President says that if we can get some sort of an agreement, maybe we can get the Paks and the Indians to sit down together and sign something while everybody's there."

"The Taj Mahal! That would be pretty spectacular," she said. "What are the chances of pulling it off?"

"That's why the team's heading over there . . . to put the pieces together. It's a pretty tall order. And speaking of orders, just keep that phone with you."

Another order. At least this one sounds reasonable.

As they walked out of the building, they heard a rumble of thunder off in the distance. "Come on," he said. "Maybe we can make it to Georgetown before that storm hits."

32

Rain pelted the brick sidewalk as Hunt hustled Cammy up the stairs and into the foyer. "You've got a nice place here," she said, trying to ignore the headache that had been plaguing her ever since the crash. She glanced into the living room at the brown leather chairs and prints of horses and snowcapped mountains on the wall.

"I went to camp out in Jackson Hole when I was a kid. Kind of reminds me of it," he said, pointing to a view of the Tetons. He set the security alarm to STAY and asked, "Want something? Beer? Wine? Anything?"

"We had plenty of coffee at the hospital, and I really need to get some sleep. If I can." She glanced at her watch. "It's one o'clock. When do you get up?"

"Around six, usually. But I may fudge it a bit in the morning. After all, it's a Saturday."

He turned on the light in the stairwell. "It's been quite a night. You're sure you feel okay?"

"More or less." She paused. "Actually, I feel like everything is coming at me all at once. Trying to get my program to work at the office. Trying to get an earmark from Metcher or funding from the Committee. Trying to get away from bad guys. And now, trying to find out about Melanie. God, it's like a perfect storm or something."

He reached for her hand, turned it over, and stroked her palm. A frisson of electricity shot through her as his fingers touched hers.

Still holding her hand, he pulled her into his arms. He kissed her forehead above the bandage and whispered, "We're gonna get through this."

She could feel the hard muscles of his arms encircling her in a velvet vice. She could feel his heart beating against her chest.

She gazed up into his eyes and felt that connection again, the invisible tether. She stared at him for a long moment.

He gently stroked her cheek.

It was tempting. So tempting to try to relax and shift some of her burdens to this man. He had gone out of his way to help her. He had come running every time she had called. But he was leaving in a few days. How could he help her when he was in India and she was in Rockville trying to elude a killer?

And now there was this tension building between them. Was it tension or attraction? She was so tired, she couldn't tell the difference.

A flash of lightning pierced the room. She pulled away and muttered, "We've got to get some sleep."

Another clap of thunder rattled the window.

He turned back toward the front door and showed her how to operate the security system. She memorized the code. He picked up her suitcase, led the way upstairs and down the hall. He switched on a light and dropped her bag at the foot of the queen-size bed covered with a moss green comforter and plaid shams.

"This is the guest room. Hope it's okay. Bathroom's in there. I'll be down the hall, and I'll order a taxi to be here in the morning. Do you really need to go to the office?"

She nodded. "I've got so much to do, and I want to go to the hospital first. So I guess I should leave around eight."

"Okay, but I'm going to try and make some other arrangements for you as soon as I get to my office."

"Other arrangements?"

"I want to see if we can't line up some protection for you."

"Protection? I'll be okay taking taxis for a while."

"I'm not so sure about that."

33

Rockville, Maryland—Saturday Late Morning

Cammy punched one more set of commands onto her keyboard and spun her chair around to answer the phone.

"Dr. Talbot."

"Just wanted to check on how you're doing and if there's any news on Mel."

Cammy wound the telephone cord around her finger. "Oh, Hunt. I've been upset all morning. The hospital wouldn't tell me anything. They just said she was still unconscious. I couldn't even get in to see her this time. So I'll go back in a little while and try again."

"God, I'm sorry. But look, she's getting the best care over there."

"But she hasn't come out of it!"

"I know it's hard to wait, Cam, but what other choice do we have?" When she didn't answer, he added, "Did you get any sleep last night? Storm was pretty loud."

"A little bit, I guess." In fact, she had tossed and turned, listening to the trees banging against the side of the house. Her thoughts had ping-ponged from worries about Melanie to questions about the man who had tried to kill her. She had finally fallen into a fitful sleep of perhaps a couple of hours. But she was grateful for the temporary sanctuary of Hunt's home, and she had to admit she liked hearing the concern in his voice. "Uh, thanks for the coffee and the taxi."

"Was he on time?"

"Yes."

"Good. Look, I need you to take a cab back to the house tonight, too. I've got some ideas about transportation for you, but I don't have it set up yet."

"What kind of transportation?"

"I want to see if I can't get you a protective detail. But it may take a while. There's a lot going on right now. I've got a bunch of meetings today, and I'm trying to get some information out of NCTC."

"NCTC?"

"That's the National Counterterrorism Center."

"Oh, the one they set up a while ago?"

"Yeah. They're trying to set up a whole new computer system. You know, to get the CIA and FBI databases merged and all of that."

"I suppose there are still a lot of turf wars going on," she speculated.

"Always. By the way, I know what kind of strain you're under just now with Mel, the guy who attacked you, the burglary, and all. . . ."

"Yes."

"But can I tell you a story on a lighter note?"

She sighed. "I've been wondering if there'll ever be a lighter note in my life. Sure, go ahead."

"Well, this morning we had a short staff meeting. We don't always meet on Saturdays, but in addition to our major problems, there were a lot of little things we needed to clear up. Guess I can tell you about it."

"What happened?"

"First, there's this new tank the Pentagon wants big bucks for. It's been in the papers about how they're building it, so I'm not exactly spilling anything."

"I think I saw something in the *Early Bird* a while ago."

"Actually, it was pretty ridiculous. You know how they get all set for a big field test, and everybody shows up, and it's all supposed to go according to plan?"

She thought back to the general's demands for her own field test. "Sure. That's what we're trying to do around here."

"Right. So the big boys at the Pentagon set up this field test of the tank and get all the contractors and Congressmen there with their staffs."

"When was that? I didn't hear about a field test."

"It was late yesterday. There hasn't been any press on it . . . yet . . . 'cause they're trying to cover it up."

"Why? What happened?"

"The tank would only go in reverse."

"Oh Lord! Now what?"

"Now it's back to the drawing boards. Anyway, after that debacle, we had a meeting, and Austin demanded to know who the MFWIC was on that project."

"MFWIC?"

"Mother-Fucker Who's in Charge. Sorry. That's a military term."

"Guess I never heard that one."

"So then our guy who works with the generals on acquisitions says that he sent a memo over to the Pentagon saying they should postpone the field test until they were sure it would work. But nobody read it until last night, so that was OBE."

"OBE?"

"Overtaken By Events. We say that a lot around here."

She'd heard military jargon over the years, but this guy used it a lot, and she was in no mood to learn a new language. She didn't respond.

"Listen, Cammy," he continued. "I just wanted to be sure you feel okay."

"I'm fine. Just tired and worried. Sorry, but I guess I'm just not very good company right now."

"Hey, no problem. Let me know if you learn anything about Mel, will you?"

The door to her lab opened and Stan Bollinger walked in. No knock. No call. He simply barged in, saw that she was on the phone, crossed his arms, and leaned against the doorjamb.

"I gotta go," she stammered into the phone, and quickly hung up. "Mr. Bollinger. What's up?"

34

Sterling, Virginia—Monday Morning

Wind-driven rain lashed the plate-glass windows of the conference room, sending rivulets of water cascading down the drainpipes. *Just like our profits*, he thought as he gazed out at the fury of the storm, *heading down the drain unless we do something fast*.

Nettar Kooner took his seat at the head of the massive table as half a dozen younger men filed into the room carrying notepads and pens. They took their assigned seats and poured glasses of water from the cut-crystal pitchers in the center of the table.

It was time for a strategy session. Not with members of his board. Not with officers of the corporation. No, this session was with his special hand-picked group of I-men. That's what he called them. If the FBI had their G-men, he had his I-men, eager, brilliant, ambitious, all graduates of top-notch universities in India, all specialists in their fields, all completely loyal to the boss. After all, he had found them, arranged their visas, brought them to the United States, and given each of them a special assignment within the vast reaches of Sterling Dynamics.

One was a mechanical engineer who already had several patents to his name. Another specialized in aeronautics, while yet another was a top linguist who could negotiate contracts in five languages. One wrote complicated computer programs, while the youngest proved to be the best psychologist of the group, always analyzing the behavior of government officials and Sterling's toughest competitors. It was a good, cohesive group and one Dr. Kooner was relying on more and more since he assumed the mantle of leadership of the company.

The CEO didn't pass out an agenda. Not for this group. He didn't need notes. He knew the questions and already had a few ideas about the answers. He got right to the point.

"You all saw *The Washington Post* on Friday." They nodded solemnly. "Don't believe everything you read, my boys. I'm not sure where that one came from, but I'm damn sure that Project Q-3 is much farther along than the papers indicate. I don't have to tell you what it means to us if this technology works in the field, to say nothing about what will happen if it gets an earmark.

"It's a little late in the game to duplicate their efforts, although we're going to try." He turned to the man on his left. "Arun, I know you've been tracking Bandaq, but now we're going to get serious. Pull out all the stops. I want a crash project on this idea of locking on to a missile's onboard computer. If we can even hint that we're on the same track, I'm pretty sure we can get a few members of the Committee to keep our appropriation at a decent level, let us have the time to develop the whole package along with our own missile program, and not be tempted to give Bandaq a dime."

The young computer programmer nodded his head and replied, "I'm already working on it. When I first heard about their new technology, I started to make calculations, and I've been coordinating them with our radar division. I didn't want to say too much until I made more progress."

"Good work. Keep on it. Shift into high gear and keep me posted." That's what Kooner liked about these men. They didn't wait. They anticipated. They were like Wayne Gretzky, who used to say that the object of the game isn't to skate to the puck but to skate to where the puck is going to be.

The CEO shifted his gaze to another man at the table. "They're talking about a field test. Get out to the Atlantic Facility and see what you can find out . . . timing, players, budget. I want everything you can get on what they're planning. We've got friends over there. God knows we've used them enough. They owe us. See if you can call in some favors. Maybe we call stall this thing."

To the man on his right he gave another order. "The Japanese are in town this week for a state visit. I've got a meeting scheduled with a member of their delegation to talk about a timetable for delivery of our new missile defense system. You'll go with me to translate. We can't let them cancel this deal. We have to emphasize our kill rate. Be sure to bring along the results of that last test of the sea-based model, along with the photographs. That should impress the hell out of them.

"And one more thing. We got word from Bangalore about that new rocket engine they've got now that uses supercooled liquid fuel."

"You mean the cryogenic engine?" one man asked.

"Yes, that's the one. It's a terrific breakthrough for our Indian Space Research Organization. This means they'll be able to launch high-altitude satellites or send a man to the moon. I have an idea for a partnership deal with them whereby we could produce intercontinental missiles using that engine."

A murmur of excitement went around the table as the young men exchanged knowing glances.

"I see that you like the idea. Got to stay a step ahead of the game. I want some plans drawn up along with mock-ups. I'll head over there next month for a conference with the Director. But first we have to win this fight on the Hill for our appropriation. Anyone have anything new to contribute at this point?"

The youngest man cleared his throat and checked his notes. "Sir, I figured this would come up today. I've taken the liberty of drafting a plan . . . an approach to the Members of the Committee, along with some background information on their commitments as well as a few things about their personal lives that might prove useful in your discussions. Especially useful with Congressman Metcher."

Dr. Kooner leaned back in his chair and smiled. He knew the young one would be good at this. He was another one who didn't wait to be given an order. He planned ahead. He was a goddamn crystal ball. And right now, he was also a godsend.

35

Capitol Hill—Monday Morning

Congresswoman Betty Barton was reviewing yet another energy bill when her intercom buzzed. "Sorry to interrupt you, but we just had a call from Davis Metcher. He wanted to know if he could stop by to talk to you about a couple of things."

A couple of things, my eye, she thought. *He probably wants to rehash his three d's—defense, drugs, and the deficit.* She could add a fourth d to that list—dames. But she was sure he wouldn't mention his latest conquest. At least not to her.

"Tell him I'm pretty busy, but if he wants to come by, I'll be here for the next hour or so."

"Thanks. He said he'd like to come in a few minutes. I'll tell him it's okay. Oh, and that group that wanted a meeting about money for ozone replacement. Shall I schedule that one?"

Betty rolled her eyes and scanned the ceiling. No divine revelation there. "They're constituents. Guess I'll have to find the time." She sighed. "Go ahead and put it on my calendar."

She went back to the Executive Summary of the bill they would be debating. *Here we are importing almost 60 percent of our oil and they just keep introducing bills to reduce that dependence by tinkering around the margins. It's been going on since the Nixon days.* She sighed in exasperation. As she reviewed the proposals she read a section calling for more of the same— increase the use of ethanol, demand higher fuel-efficiency standards, de- velop more windmills, except where anyone can see them. *Why don't we let the energy companies drill for oil and gas where it actually is? And why doesn't the President cut the red tape and let everyone get more inventive? What about new kinds of fuel cells, developing methane hydrates, or using thorium in new nuclear reactors?* She shook her head. *We've got too many entrenched interests buying votes so we'll just tweak the status quo . . . again,* she thought.

She made some notes in the margin and heard her buzzer. "Yes?"

"Davis Metcher is here."

"Send him in."

The door opened and the Congressman from Maryland came across the room sporting a wide smile. "Betty, how're you doin' today?" he asked jovially. "Thanks for letting me barge in on short notice."

"No problem, Davis. I figure you want to trade some votes," she said matter-of-factly.

"Got me there," he said as he settled into the red leather chair across from her desk.

"Let's see. Is it going to be for defense or drugs or the deficit?"

"Now, Betty, am I that predictable?"

"Usually," she said.

"All right then. Score one for the Gentlelady. I do need to talk to you about the defense bill. You heard the testimony in the Subcommittee. I have to figure out whether to earmark that new technology or give the nod to the missiles over at Sterling. I don't see how we can do both."

"Yes, the defense and the deficit. That's two out of three . . . so far."

Ignoring her gotcha tone, he said, "So here's the deal. I know you're com- ing down on the side of Sterling Dynamics, am I right?"

She nodded. "I think so. I just figure that it's a good idea to throw good money after good. I mean, their stuff actually works. Sometimes."

"Right you are. So if I throw Bandaq over the side and vote for Sterling on Defense, will you vote to extend the drug patents?"

"Extend the drug patents?" she exclaimed. "You can't be serious. Those companies are making a fortune. And you think they need even *more* pro- tection?" She shook her head. "It'll never fly, Davis. And you know it."

Betty Barton was a walking barometer. She could sense the reaction of the editorial boards of *The Washington Post* and *The New York Times* before anyone else could put together a focus group. She added, "It might fly on CNBC, but I doubt if Fox News would even buy that turkey."

Davis sat back and looked down at his hands for a long while, not saying a word. Betty stared at him. *What's the matter now?* she wondered. *He came in here like a long-lost pal, and now he's sitting there like a forlorn puppy.* She waited. Still no comment. She leaned forward and said in a soft voice, "Davis, is there something else going on here? Something I don't know?"

"Actually, it's an old buddy of mine," he said in a low voice.

"A buddy? What do you mean, a buddy?"

"We went to college together. His family contacted me. You see, he suffers from a rare type of lymphoma. There are some new drugs in the pipeline. But they're expensive to produce, and they'd only help a few people. So why should the big pharmaceuticals spend any time developing drugs that only a few people need when they can just churn out Viagra . . . or . . . whatever?"

She was momentarily taken aback. She had never heard Davis Metcher talk about his friends or discuss anything remotely personal. All she knew about the man was that he was single and probably the biggest rake on the Hill. She figured him for the total party boy after hours, although she had to admit he was pretty serious about the legislation and the committee work when they were in session.

"Davis. What does this man's family want?"

"They're grasping at straws. Thought maybe I could help somehow. Now I know that we can't let our personal concerns drive what we do up here. It's just that I've watched this whole thing unfold. I've met with the pharmaceutical guys. I've studied their numbers, their research costs, their production costs, how they make their profits. And sure, there are things that could be done better and drugs that are probably more expensive than they should be. But with the new drugs, there just isn't any incentive for them in this climate."

He shifted in his chair and continued. "Look at what happened to some of the vaccines. First, you've got that idiotic Vaccines for Children bill that passed. Well, that was before my time. But the government forced big discounts so they had to more or less give the stuff away. Then, with the threat of lawsuits if someone has a bad reaction, most of the drug boys said, 'Who needs it?' and just got out of the business. We've only got a few companies making some of the vaccines now. In the whole country. No wonder we get shortages once in a while. Whenever we need a new vaccine, the government has to call in the pharma boys and plead for their help. And now with the drugs for special cases . . ." He stopped and stared down at his hands.

Betty got up and came around her desk to sit in the chair next to his. "I understand your point. I really do. Let me take a look at the legislation. Maybe there's a way to reword some of the sections. Maybe we can do something on the importation provisions in exchange for patent protection. I don't know, but let me have a look."

Davis nodded. "Yes, that's good. You do that, and we'll talk some more about it later. And about Sterling, I'll go along with you on that one, if you feel strongly about it."

She paused and thought back to the Subcommittee hearing. She had to admit that the young Dr. Somebody certainly had spunk when she was describing her new technology. They couldn't prove it, though. At least not yet.

On the other hand, if they could pull it off, it would be unique. Something really different. Something we surely could use. Something that would give us a real advantage over a possible terrorist strike or problem in the field.

"Tell you what," she said. "I'm still studying my options on the defense bill. And if this situation over in India and Pakistan continues to heat up, we may have to spend even more money to tamp things down."

"I know," Davis said. "At least the President named Farrell to that Envoy slot. If anyone can get those two countries to the table, he can."

"Yes, I think you're right. Oh, and I heard something about a signing ceremony at the Taj Mahal. Know anything about that?" she asked.

"Only that the whole deal's a real long shot. Course if they could pull it off, I'd be willing to fly over there for the ceremony. It'll probably be a pretty good bash."

"Yes, probably. But back on the bill, I appreciate your offer to vote for Sterling. And yes, I have backed them in the past. I think the jury's still out on that other company. What's their name again?"

"Bandaq," he supplied.

"Right. I'll think about that one, too, and get back to you in a couple of days."

"Thanks, Betty. That's all I need to know." He turned and walked out of her office. She had planned to ask him to vote for a new provision in the energy bill, but that was pushing it. She had plenty of other Members she could talk to. Plenty of Members, plenty of issues. She couldn't spend much time on just one. Being a Member of Congress didn't afford her that luxury. As for casting her vote for Bandaq, at this point she didn't have a clue.

36

The White House—Monday Noon

"Good afternoon, Colonel Daniels . . . Mr. Jameson. Your table is ready."
The Maitre d' reached behind his walnut podium and picked up two
menus. He led the way past the large Plexiglas display case containing the
model of a tall ship, the USS *Constitution*, and into the White House Mess.

Hunt ate in this dining room just outside the Situation Room most days
along with other members of the senior staff. It had been run by Navy
Stewards since the days of Rutherford B. Hayes. The food was decent and
the service was quick.

They walked past the round staff table with open seating at the end of
the room and were led to a small table for two along the wall. They sat
down on the dark wooden chairs and picked up their navy blue menus
with the Presidential seal on the front cover and piece of gold braid down
the center.

The blue-jacketed waiter hovered discreetly off to one side, waiting for
their decision. Hunt closed the menu and set it down. "Make mine a BLT
and iced tea."

"I'll have the clam chowder and half a sandwich, thanks," Ted said. Then
he turned to Hunt. "Sorry I didn't make it in over the weekend. I've been

trying to talk my wife into moving back in. But no-go." He shook his head and said, "Anyway, tell me about that accident Friday night."

"It was pretty bad. Looks like somebody may have tried to kill Cammy."

"Kill her? Who? How?" Ted asked, incredulous.

"Somebody rammed her car. It crashed down a hill. Could have been fatal."

"Jesus! But she's okay, right?"

"A little banged up. Some cuts. She was lucky. She had a friend in the car who's still in the hospital, though."

"How is she?"

"She was unconscious for a helluva long time. She finally woke up yesterday. We went over there and turns out she had a pretty severe concussion. At least there was no spinal cord injury. But still. Poor woman looks kind of like a raccoon. Her eyes are all black-and-blue."

"But she'll be okay?"

"We sure as hell hope so. Doctor said she might be dizzy, have double vision. Who the hell knows?"

"But who did it? Any idea?"

"It's gotta be the same guy that broke into Cammy's apartment," Hunt said.

"So, what does she do now?"

"She's staying at my place"

"Your place?" Ted eyed his friend. "What are you going to do about her while we're gone?"

"Big problem. Woman needs protection."

"So what are you thinking?"

"I'm thinking FBI."

"You gotta be kidding! FBI's so busy now. They'll kick it to the local police."

"So it's a push. But the whole point is that she's working on a technology that . . . maybe . . . somebody wants to steal. Or stop."

"It's that *maybe* part that's going to stop you."

Hunt raised both of his hands in a defensive gesture. "We'll see. Anyway, back on our agenda. I've been getting more intel from your part of the world about how the Indians are trying to develop their own anti-missile system, and it sounds an awful lot like what Cammy and Bandaq are doing. If they got it, the Paks would be defenseless. It would be a one-sided deal. I mean, up to now it's been kind of a Mexican standoff with both sides having nukes. But nobody in his right mind thinks anybody over there would attack with nuclear weapons," Hunt ventured.

"Who says those militants are 'in their right mind'? What if those other two missiles have nuclear or chemical . . . or even biological warheads? That type of missile can carry just about anything."

"I know. And here's the big question. Do you think they'll launch another missile even if India doesn't retaliate?"

"If they've got two left. Why wouldn't they use them?" Ted asked.

"On the other hand, if they wait, and India gets a decent missile defense system in place, then retaliates against Pakistan or against the guys in Kashmir—"

Ted interrupted, "As you said, the Paks would be in deep trouble. About that defense system India's working on. It's for cruise-type missiles, right?"

"That's what I'm hearing," Hunt said. "And they could. I mean those Indian scientists are as smart as . . . or smarter maybe . . . than a lot of our people when it comes to clever inventions."

The waiter brought their drinks and quietly slipped away.

"As soon as we get over there, we've got to rev up the Indian military to find those missiles," Hunt said.

"They say they're working on it."

"Not working hard enough."

"The Paks say they're searching, too."

"Fat chance they'll find them. About the talks, are you getting any new vibes about whether the Indians will cooperate in coming to the table?"

"With the latest attacks in Kashmir, I don't know." Ted took a drink of water and added, "It's starting to look like Srinagar all over again."

"Srinagar?" Hunt asked.

"Remember, that's kind of the summer capital of India's part of Kashmir. Well, Jammu-Kashmir, as they call it. The rebels killed a ton of people in an ambush some time back. It was a real bloodbath, and everyone's afraid that more of those kinds of raids are on the drawing board."

"You know, the Muslims have been around for centuries and haven't caused this kind of trouble. But for the last several years they've been on a rampage. Against us, India, Russia, Spain, England . . . you name it, they're everywhere. Sometimes it's hard to figure out where they think they're going with all of this."

The waiter reappeared with their lunch orders. "May I get anything else for you gentlemen?"

"No thanks, I think we're fine," Ted said as he turned back to face Hunt. "Trying to put all of this in a historical context isn't easy when we have to spend all our time reacting to these attacks."

"Or preventing them."

"Which we've done in many cases. Trouble is, we have to be right *all* the time to protect our people. The terrorists only have to be right once and people die. Anyway, about Islam, we're not just talking about a religion. With Muslims, it's a whole way of life. There is no separation of church and state. The church *is* the state. At least that's what they're trying to pull off. And their laws are called 'Shariah.'" He paused to taste the chowder and then went on. "Right now there are a bunch of political parties in Pakistan who are trying to get that country to go back to Shariah."

"I know. Like the Taliban ran things in Afghanistan. Where women were really dumped on."

"Some of the hard-liners say it's the only way to maintain order and purity. Keep the women veiled, make them stay home and all of that because otherwise they wouldn't be able to control themselves, or some men would be tempted to take advantage of them. Then they'd end up as prostitutes or have kids outside of marriage and all of that. And since women are the keepers of the family honor, they'd better behave or it brings dishonor to the father . . . and the brothers, too. Actually, to the whole crowd." Ted stopped talking and ate his sandwich.

"So you get those honor killings you hear about."

"Yes."

"Seems pretty unfair to say it's always the woman's fault. What about the guys?"

Ted finished his soup and said, "In a way they have sort of a no-fault insurance policy. They hardly ever get prosecuted. But if a single woman has a child—"

Hunt interrupted, "She can get stoned to death."

"Sometimes. Now on the other hand, the Muslims do a great job protecting their own women. They revere their wives, their mothers, sisters, and so on. That's one reason they hate our society. They talk about our crime rate, how women get raped, how children are raised with only one parent, have abortions, do drugs; you name it, they hate it. And they're trying to protect their society from turning into . . . ."

"Us," Hunt answered. "I wonder if they've ever seen Madonna . . . or Paris . . . or Janet?"

"Get serious, Daniels!"

The waiter reappeared to ask if they would like coffee or dessert.

"Does the chef have any of those chocolate-chip cookies back there to-day?" Hunt asked.

"Yes. Would you like a plate?"

Hunt nodded. "That'd be great. And a cup of real."

"I'll have some decaf. Thanks," Ted said.

Hunt turned back to his colleague. "The Hindus. Now they're really different."

"About as different as you can get," Ted replied. "Islam has the one God, and the Hindus have sort of a supreme God, but then they have other gods and goddesses. The folks out in the country have their own fertility goddesses. Things like that."

"And what's the colored dot on the forehead mean?" Hunt asked.

"Oh, that. It's a sign of piety. It's like a third eye that's focused inward on God. And one more thing about Hindus and that Kashmir area. They believe the Himalayas are the stairway to heaven."

"No wonder they're fighting over it."

The waiter brought their coffee and a plate of cookies.

Hunt checked his watch. "I still have a few minutes, you okay on time?"

Ted nodded. "I've got a backgrounder at three. I'm fine for now."

"So, let me pick your brain on just one more point. I can see how the Muslims hate our society—"

Ted interrupted. "*Some* Muslims hate us. We have to be clear on this. Most Muslims have lived peacefully with other people for centuries. And there are a lot of changes going on. Elections in Afghanistan, Iraq, Palestine, Egypt. Women voting in Kuwait. Syria talking about political parties. It's just these fringe fanatics that have kind of hijacked the religion for their own bloody ends."

"As far as I can see, the problem is a lot bigger than fringe fanatics. And it's getting worse. Why now?"

Ted sat back in his chair and folded his arms. "I've been thinking about that for quite some time, and I think it's a combination of things. First you had the colonial countries trying to have their way. Then you had the creation of Israel right in the middle of their territory. And what do the Israelis do? They create a booming economy, out of practically nothing. Remember Golda Meir used to say that Moses led them 'to the one place in the Middle East that didn't have any oil'?"

"Yeah. She was right. And your point is . . ."

"That the Israelis are stuck in the desert, but they've built industries, universities, a democratic government with actual elections. The whole nine yards. And then to top it off, they have this Six-Day War back in '67 and completely humiliate all the Arab types."

"So they don't like being outdone. But way back, the Muslims were the smart guys. Baghdad was the center of science and mathematics." Hunt countered.

"Yes, but look at what's happened to them in the meantime. The rest of the world passed them by, and some of them are looking for somebody to blame. They'd never admit it, but think about it. When was the last time you heard about any Muslim country exporting a really good product you wanted to buy? A car? A computer? Anything manufactured? Where are their world-class universities? All of their bright kids try to get visas to study here. They've got all this oil, and what have they done with it?"

"Financed a bunch of terrorists?" Hunt answered.

"Yes. Groups that want to push us out of the Middle East and extend their brand of Muslim rule back to their boundaries in the fourteenth century."

They signed their tabs and got up to leave. "Back to our trip plans," Hunt said. "We're wheels up from Andrews at twenty/thirty tomorrow night. And as soon as we get to New Delhi, we've got to focus on finding those damn missiles."

"And preventing retaliation."

"But between now and then, I've got to prevent something else."

37

Sterling, Virginia—Monday Late Afternoon

Incredible. The report was incredible, incisive, and incriminating. And all from the youngest member of his team of I-men. How appropriate. Nettar Kooner read the brief paragraph again and reached for his phone.

"Come up here for a minute," he commanded.

A few moments later, a light knock on the door and the team member stepped inside the well-appointed office. "What can I do for you, sir?" he asked eagerly.

Kooner held up the report and motioned to the chair in front of the desk. "Have a seat and tell me how the devil you came up with this information."

The young man sat down, crossed his legs, and explained, "I have developed a contact at a bank in Washington. She's a clerk, she's smart, and she's from Delhi."

Kooner steadied his gaze. "Go on."

"I first met her at a party with other Indian friends. It became clear that she wanted to become more than friends. And in her position at the bank . . . it's on Capitol Hill . . . I thought she might prove useful."

"Good thinking."

"When I took her out for coffee, I mentioned that I was putting together a folio on Davis Metcher. I indicated it was important to us . . . and to India . . . that we find out as much about him as possible. She's not stupid. She's a patriot. She knows we have contracts in Delhi, and she also knows that Metcher has an important vote on the Armed Services Committee."

"And . . ."

"And she told me that she looked up his account and saw a curious series of regular transfers to another account. She told me the name on that account, and I did a bit of research. It turns out that it belongs to a young woman who was a Congressional Page four years ago and had to leave rather suddenly. And, as you can see," he pointed to the report Kooner was holding, "it all fits together."

"Amazing. And you believe this clerk is trustworthy?"

"Oh yes. Why wouldn't she be? Look at her motive. She's trying to please me, and so she dug up the information. There would be no incentive on her part to tell anyone else. After all, she could lose her job."

"Of course. Of course." He studied the page in his hand. "So ole Metcher got a teenage girl pregnant and has been paying her off ever since."

"To support the child, sir. As you can see, he also set up a custodial account for the little boy."

"Everyone knows the man has no morals when it comes to women. On the other hand, that description fits a few other Congressmen I could mention."

The young man looked up with a knowing smile. "This is true."

"So no one pays much attention to his usual antics. But this . . . this could ruin his campaign for reelection . . . if it got out."

"I couldn't agree with you more, sir," the young assistant said rather smugly.

The CEO got up from his desk. The young man rose as well, because their short meeting was over.

"Good work, my boy. Good work."

"Thank you, sir. If you need additional data . . ."

"No, this is enough."

As the assistant turned toward the door, Kooner added, "I don't need to tell you to keep this to yourself . . . and your young friend at the bank."

"No need at all, sir."

"Is Arun still in his lab? I wanted to get an update on his research on Bandaq's technology."

"No, sir. I believe he left a bit early for a dinner appointment."

"All right. It will have to wait." Kooner waved his hand toward the door, dismissing his young aide. "Thank you again for your investigative work."

"You're welcome, sir," he said as he quietly slipped out the door.

38

The White House—Monday Late Afternoon

Rain was still coming down in relentless torrents as Hunt dashed across West Exec to the West Wing and another appointment with Stockton Sloan. He wished they had an awning or something across that little drive-way, since the staffs were always running back and forth to meetings. No such luck.

Nobody ever had time to go down several flights to the tunnel. It was too out-of-the-way. So rain or shine, staffers were always dashing around outside the White House. Even the President had to walk outside down the colonnade next to the Rose Garden when he left the Residence to go to the Oval Office every single morning. At least that walkway was covered.

"Hello, Lucy. Busy day today," Hunt said, to the ever-present secretary. *That woman doesn't know the meaning of the words "vacation" and "sick leave,"* he thought. The only time she wasn't at her desk was when the boss forced her to take a few days off each year. And then she would only leave during the middle of August when the President was out of town and the Congress was in recess.

Then again, that's the only time the rest of the staff ever went anywhere on their own. There were no set vacations for White House staff. Everyone worked when they were needed, which was just about all the time. Even during the big snowstorms when *nonessential* personnel were told to leave early or stay home, nobody did because nobody wanted to be thought of as *nonessential*.

"Good morning, Colonel," Lucy said. "Busy day every day. They just changed the President's schedule again and added a drop-by in Room 450."

"Which group is it this time?"

"A meeting of the National Association of Professional Philosophers."

Hunt shook his head. "Maybe they think we need more sophists running our foreign policy."

"Perhaps," she sniffed. "And, of course, everyone is getting ready to welcome the Russian delegation. Before you ask, the answer is 'yes,' we got your backgrounder on the remaining weapons systems in Russia and the other Republics. It's been sent on to Mr. Gage."

"Thanks, Lucy. Uh, is Stock available now?"

"Let me check." She got up from her desk, walked to the Deputy's office, and glanced through the door. "Yes. He will see you now."

Stockton Sloan glanced up as Hunt walked in. "Afternoon, Daniels. Thanks for the paper on the Russians. I read a copy, and it looks pretty good. We still have a long way to go to cut back on some of those systems. At least we got the Ukrainians to give up their nukes." He pushed his files aside. "So what is it now? You said there was a problem involving that new technology we talked about."

Hunt pulled up a chair. "It's not exactly a problem with the technology. They're trying to get it ready for a field test."

"So what's the problem?"

"It's with the woman who created the whole thing."

"The one who testified about it on the Hill?"

"Yes."

"So what's her problem?"

"Someone broke into her apartment and stole her computer and—"

Stock interrupted, "Sounds like a job for the police."

"Right. But then the next night she was forced off the road and could have been killed. A friend of hers is in the hospital."

"Daniels, this is the White House. We don't get involved in things like this. It's a problem for local law enforcement. Why are you bringing this to me?"

Hunt shifted in his chair and leaned forward. "I have an idea that she might be the target of a foreign national."

"How would you know that?"

"Ambassador Bhattia told me about a member of a terrorist cell in Kashmir who may have slipped into the country. Look. I know it's a long shot, but first some group over there steals cruise missiles and shoots one off. Then there's the latest intel saying that some of the groups are trying to acquire more weapons, even defensive systems. So I figure it's just possible that one of them is here, trying to steal hers."

"Before it's even been tested?"

"Sure. Why not?"

"All right. For the sake of argument, let's say somebody is trying to steal it. They certainly wouldn't find it in a woman's apartment, unless she was a total idiot."

"She's not an idiot, I assure you," Hunt said.

"So, what could they possibly find in her apartment then?"

"Nothing. But if they're foreigners, they might not know that. Her computer was stolen, and that's all they took. No jewelry. No silver. Nothing else."

"Hmmm. And what did the police have to say?"

"We didn't tell them she was working on a classified project."

"We?"

"I was there. She called me when she saw the mess. So I went over to help out."

"I see. And you think some Kashmiri terrorist could be right here in Washington, D.C., staging two-bit burglaries?" Stock said wearily.

"I know it's far-fetched. It's just that I'm . . ."

Stock looked at Hunt over the top of his wire-rimmed glasses and frowned. "It's just that you're what? Personally involved? Is that it?"

Not yet, he thought. "No. I just don't want her to get hurt in some foreign plot here. If that's what it is, especially since I'm leaving tomorrow night," Hunt explained.

"So what are you suggesting?"

Hunt paused, "Well, first, I wanted to let you know what was going on. . . ."

"I always like to know what's going on. And . . . ?"

"And I'd like your permission to talk to Janis?"

"Janis?" Stock said, raising his eyebrows.

"Yes, sir."

"This is highly unusual."

"I know. All I can say is that sometimes I have to go with my gut. And my gut tells me that we have a big-time problem here. I don't want to see it get out of hand."

Stock sat back and folded his arms. "As if we didn't have enough on our plate searching for remnants of al Qaeda, now we've got to worry about Indians, Pakistanis, and Kashmiris coming over here, too? Did you brief anyone else about Bhattia's comments?"

"Yes, Field Rep at FBI and another contact at Homeland Security. NCTC is looking for militants that might be around here, too. They're all looking for the guy. But I want to set up protection for Dr. Talbot if I can."

The Deputy glanced at the files on his desk and then over at Hunt. "We've got major international developments to deal with here. The Japanese. The Russians. Indians. Pakistanis. And Janis has her hands full with domestic problems. Without more evidence that these attacks were staged by the same person or something that links a foreigner with something concrete, the FBI isn't going to touch this one. Go to the Montgomery County Police."

"And if they don't—"

"Daniels," Stock said in a firm tone, "I said go to the police!"

39

Washington, D.C.—Monday Early Evening

The dark-haired young man glanced furtively over his shoulder to be certain he had not been followed. He slipped inside the door to the Bombay Club, where his contact, dressed in a stylish charcoal gray suit, white shirt, and navy tie, stood in front of a podium asking about their table. He liked this restaurant just blocks from the White House. With its light blue shutters, beige walls, and ceiling fans, it resembled a private club in the heyday of British rule in India. Brass picture lights cast a warm glow over a series of old black-and-white photos of British royalty, big-game hunters, and pretty young women displayed along a wall of banquettes.

"This place always makes me think that Stewart Granger or Ava Gardner will walk out from behind those palm trees," the Indian Minister said.

"Yes, I have seen those old movies on the classic movie channel. They made it look so good, one wonders why the British ever gave up on us."

"They bloody well had to, my boy."

"This way, gentlemen," the Maitre d' said as he led them to their table near the baby grand piano where a pianist played a Schubert sonata. "May I check your attaché case for you, sir?"

"No thank you. I'll keep it with me," the man said, clutching it possessively.

"Very good, sir," the Maitre d' said, and then glided back to the front door.

"So you have it with you?" the Minister asked expectantly.

"But of course. I'll tell you all about it, but let's order first."

A waiter appeared and took their orders for tandoori salmon and chicken tikka masala along with a bottle of Neudorf Sauvignon Blanc from New Zealand.

"Now then," the Minister said, leaning across the table. "Tell me what you have for us."

The young man looked around the room, hoping he wouldn't recognize anyone. He was taking a big chance meeting his contact like this.

"I have Magellan with me," he said almost in a whisper.

"This is good. Very good. I can't tell you how long your uncle has been waiting for this very moment."

"But are you absolutely certain of its conveyance?"

"Absolutely!"

"The diplomatic pouch?"

"Of course the pouch."

"And there is no way it can be stopped or traced?"

"Absolutely not! It is the protocol. It is the rule of the operation of our embassies. Surely you must know that."

"One can never be too careful, my friend."

The Minister smiled conspiratorially. "I am sure you are correct. But as long as we have some time together tonight, tell me how you decided on the name for this part of the operation?"

"Magellan?"

"Yes."

The waiter brought their wine. After tasting and approving their selection, the young man began his story. "As you know, Ferdinand Magellan led the ships that were the very first to travel all the way around the world."

"Yes, I know of him. He was financed by the Spanish King, correct?" the Minister asked.

"Yes, but let's go back. Magellan was of noble birth. As you and I are as well," he said with a sly smile. "In fact, many say that he served as a page in the court of the Queen of Portugal and was educated there, as we were educated in the shadow of our government buildings."

"Indeed we were."

"As a young man he was in the East India service."

"I did not know of that connection."

"Many do not. But I digress. Magellan was a man of many talents and many curiosities. He believed that he could sail west and get to the Spice Islands."

"Like Columbus who went before him?"

"Yes. And he persuaded King Charles of Spain to give him the money for his voyage. He was able to buy five ships, and he sailed with a complement of 270 men. The year was 1519, and they set sail for the Canary Islands and then on to Brazil."

The waiter reappeared and poured more wine. This was turning out to be an interesting evening. The Minister had been quite concerned when he first learned that he was to be the contact for the transmission of important data from Washington back to New Delhi. He was new to the city and did not want to make waves. But when he learned the nature of his assignment, he realized how important his success would be to his government and, in turn, to his career.

He was worried about the situation at home. Ever since the cruise missile attack on their troops in Jammu and Kashmir, the Defense Ministry had been talking about retaliation, but their Prime Minister also had been talking to the President of Pakistan about renewing trade and opening more bus and rail lines. It didn't make any sense. There were mixed signals everywhere.

In addition to the missile launch, the Islamic militants kept crossing the Line of Control, attacking Indian villagers. And the Indian Minister was certain that the Pakistani government was funding their operation, even though they denied it. He couldn't trust them. After all, they were caught red-handed selling nuclear technology around the world and only gave their top scientist a slap on the wrist. How much more of this was his government supposed to take before fighting back? Perhaps they had a plan, a plan that had not filtered down to his level in the embassy. They needed a good plan right about now.

From what he did know, they might be preparing for war, even though they had agreed to sit down with an American advance team this very week. He didn't think much would come of those meetings, but his government had to receive these emissaries. While the Americans were pressing them for a cease-fire agreement, he knew his government was buying arms around the world. He knew they were working to receive approval to buy Israel's Arrow missile defense system. That was a good one, but it was for ballistic missiles.

Now they needed a system to defend against guided missiles like the one used just days ago. And his contact, this brilliant man, his very own dinner partner, had the key to their quest. He had to be careful how he handled his charge. He must encourage him to work carefully, quietly, and not bring attention to himself lest he be discovered and prosecuted. If that happened, they would lose it all. They would lose the system, their protection, their advantage. His embassy would incur the wrath of the U.S. government, something they could not afford in this delicate game of balancing off their allies against their adversaries. And most of all, he could not jeopardize his own career.

The waiter brought their entrées and quickly stepped back out of sight. The Minister took a bite of his salmon and listened intently to the young man's tale. It was a good one. It explained how he had selected Magellan, the name of the explorer, as the code word for this part of the defense puzzle.

"There were many problems along the way."

"Just as you have had problems. Yet you carry on."

"Yes. Magellan's ships sailed down the east coast of South America, losing one ship along the way. A second ship gave up, turned around, and sailed back to Spain, taking most of the food with them."

"What a traitor!" the Minister observed.

"Quite. One must be careful about deciding whom to trust."

The Minister nodded.

"So now Magellan was down to three ships, very little food, and the entire Pacific Ocean stretched before him."

"And yet he pressed on."

"But of course. He had a vision, just as I have a vision."

"Speaking of vision," the Minister said, "that article in *The Washington Post*, saying that the boomerang does not work, was a true eye-opener. It was perfect for our side."

"Yes, it was. It confused our enemies. I am sure of that. But back to Magellan. He sailed on, finally to Guam and then to the Philippines, where the explorer died in a tribal battle. But his last ship, the *Victoria*, was able to cross the Indian Ocean, go around the Cape of Good Hope, and make it back to Spain almost three years from the day they all had left. And so it was the very first ship to circumnavigate the Earth, just as the project Magellan circumnavigates the heavens."

"Amazing. I can see how he could be an inspiration to you in your work," the Minister said. "He faced dangers, as do we at home. We needed someone to act, and you have performed well. As it is said, all that is necessary for the triumph of evil is that good men do nothing."

"Ah yes. Edmund Burke."

"Please be assured that your efforts are appreciated at the highest levels."

A half smile crossed the man's face as he raised his glass in answer to the flattery. "I thank you, kind sir, for your comments and your encouragement. For, as you know, my work is not finished."

"Yes. And that is what we need to discuss now. I'm being pressed most urgently to send the last part of the project back to Delhi."

The young man shifted in his chair and hesitated. "This is the most delicate part."

"You must advance the calendar."

"I'm working as fast as I can, but I can't force others. . . ."

"Are there others who need to be, shall we say, supplanted? Moved aside? Perhaps permanently?"

He thought for a moment, carefully considering his answer. "I will analyze the situation and decide on a course of action."

"Just remember, the action is for the homeland." The Minister poured the last of the wine and raised his glass.

The young man joined the toast and nudged the attaché case toward his dinner companion.

"For the homeland."

40

Capitol Hill—Monday Early Evening

It was your basic drop-by. A reception for Members and their guests thrown by the Defense Contractors' Association in a last-ditch attempt to push their favorite projects before the vote on the authorization bill.

"Looks like a Ridgewells two-trucker," Davis Metcher quipped to the stunning redhead standing next to him at the buffet table.

"Pardon me?" she said, flashing him a bright smile.

"Ridgewells. That's the caterer you see all around town with their purple trucks," he explained. "And when you get a spread like this, I figure they had to fill up two trucks to get it here."

"Oh, you're so funny!" she exclaimed as she grabbed a plate and reached for the crab claws.

"Try the caviar, too. Looks like there's plenty of grub here. No need to even go out for dinner," he suggested, calculating exactly how long it would take to get her back to his apartment.

"Well, well, well. Looks like this is a party for the habitués and sons of habitués," the Majority Party Whip joked, slapping Davis on the back. "Defense boys sure know how to throw a doozy. I just stopped by the Frozen Food Filibuster Free-for-all. Lousy food at that one. It was all too cold. But after this thing, I'm heading to the Taiwanese event. I hear they're serving Tibetan barbeque. Just to piss off the Chinese, I would imagine."

Metcher chuckled and cocked his head toward his date. "I'd like to introduce a new member of my staff, Miss Roxanne O'Malley."

"Call me Roxy," the redhead tittered as she shook the other man's hand.

"Like the girl in that movie, *Chicago*?" he asked.

"Oh sure. Wasn't she somethin'? Wish I could dance like that."

You can probably do more than dance, Davis thought, as he watched her flirt with his colleague. "Uh, Roxy, why don't you run over to the bar and get me a scotch and water, would you?"

"Sure thing. Be right back."

"Where'd you find that one?" the Whip asked Davis.

"Daughter of one of my big contributors. Not the usual poli-sci major. At least she can answer the phones."

"I'll bet. How's your Committee coming with your markup? We've got to get this bill nailed down pretty soon."

"I know," Metcher said. "There're a lot of hands out for line items."

"And every one of them is at this shindig tonight," the Whip said, surveying the room. "I would imagine there's a good bit of arm-twisting going on. And all of our boys are hoping for contributions from our hosts. How're your coffers these days?"

"Not quite as full as I'd like. But I'm hoping that Sterling Dynamics will come through. Only problem is that the President's budget calls for a lot of things besides missiles. You know, the V-22 Ospreys, the F-22 stealth fighters, more money for pay raises. Not a big number in there for Sterling's pipeline, I'm afraid."

"Yes, I know, but we can probably juggle a few accounts here and there, depending on what you need. Do you have your votes lined up for our friends here?"

"I've been talking to Betty. She likes Sterling's stuff because it works."

"Oh, right, Betty. Can you actually deal with her? I've always thought she had pretty high bitch potential."

"Yeah. She's not exactly the BC type."

"BC type? What the hell is that?"

"The ones who are at my Beck and Call," Metcher said with a half smile. "Thing is, she and I talked about a trade. My vote for Sterling. Her vote for the patent bill."

"The patent bill? That turkey couldn't get a Presidential pardon on Thanksgiving morning," the Whip scoffed.

"I hear you," Metcher said. "But I really want that bill. And there might be more support than you know about."

"More support? From where?"

"I've been working on that issue, and I'm hoping we can put something together for the industry. They've really kicked in the bucks, you know. But besides that, there are some pretty good arguments about their research costs. And you can't say we don't need new drugs. There are a lot of variables . . . a lot of needs . . . I can fill you in later . . . I've got all the numbers," Davis said hopefully.

The Whip eyed him curiously. "Tell you what. You get your ducks in line for the President's defense program, and I'll see what I can do to get a commission appointed to look into the whole drug patent thing, and all the other problems in that industry."

Davis brightened at the thought. "That just might do the trick. But how soon could we get a commission together?"

"We can get it appointed right away. The trick is to be sure they don't submit their report until December, *after* the mid-terms. You know the game."

"I know. I know. Every commission I can remember, Social Security, Medicare, Global Warming, Space Shuttles, Tax Reform. They all were all told to report back in December . . . if it's an election year."

"Of course. No need to bother the folks with details before they cast their vote, now is there? But back on the defense bill, what do you know about that new technology over at Bandaq I've been hearing about? Sounds pretty terrific. If it works."

"That's a big if," Davis said. "I hear they're still tinkering with it and trying to set up a field test."

"They're running out of time."

"I know. I'm almost ready to take a pass on Bandaq and throw all the money to Sterling."

"Then again, if they can pull off a successful trial, we may have to go back to the drawing board and see what else we can knock out of the budget."

Davis sighed. "Let's wait and see about that," he said, furrowing his eyebrows.

"You don't sound too enthused. Guess Bandaq hasn't shelled out any campaign contributions for you lately, huh? They're usually pretty tight with the bucks."

"You're right. Nothing yet. But I made a pitch to their Chairman about hosting an event for me out there in Rockville."

The Whip chuckled and shook his head. "If you think you can pry big bucks out of that general, I've got some coastal property in Chad I'd like you to see."

"Coastal property?" Roxy asked as she sidled up to her boss and handed him his drink. "I love coastal property."

"Uh, it's not around here, Roxy."

Her face fell. "Oh."

"We were just talking about campaign contributions," Davis said to the girl.

"You know, my dad and my granddad have given oodles of money to the Party," she volunteered.

"Yes, I'm well aware of that, my dear," Davis said with a smile, happy to show the Majority Whip that he was working for the Party and not just for his own campaign.

The Whip turned to the girl with renewed interest. "You say your grandfather contributed?"

She nodded. "My family's into aviation. That's how we made our money."

"How interesting. And what did your grandfather do, precisely?"

"He was the last licensed zeppelin pilot."

The Congressman stifled a laugh. "I see. And what about your father? Does he fly those blimp things, too?"

"Oh no. He just owns the company. But you know, zeppelins aren't the same as blimps," she said confidently.

"Where did they ever get that name blimp anyway?" the Whip asked.

"Maybe it stands for 'Big Light Infrastructure Meant to be a Plane,'" she said with a giggle, and added, "That was a joke."

The two men exchanged a smile as she went on. "Now that I have your attention, I wanted you to know that Daddy hopes you'll continue to fund the blimp program for the Navy."

"Blimp program?" Davis asked. "Don't think I've heard about that one. I thought they just used blimps for advertising at football games."

"Oh no. Daddy says there's this new system that a blimp can use to see things under the water like submarines and mines. Daddy told me to ask . . . I mean . . . Daddy says it's called . . . wait a minute, I'll get it . . . it's called hyperspectral technology. There, that's it," she said triumphantly. "And it's just a small item in the budget, so we're sure you'll vote for it." She rubbed the arm of her boss and added, "Won't you?"

"We'll have to take a look, Roxy," Davis said, patting her hand.

"Well, I've got to go work the room," the Whip said. "And Davis, on that bill, see what you can do to keep the numbers down. We're fighting an awfully big deficit this time around."

"I'll do my best." Metcher turned to Roxy. "Now then, my dear, there's been no deficit of crab claws or caviar. Have you had enough?"

"Oh sure."

"Then let's try to work our way toward the door. I'm sure we can think of better ways to spend our evening than hanging around here."

He placed his hand in the small of her back and propelled her toward the exit. *It would be nice to have some new talent to play with,* he thought. He hadn't been feeling too sharp lately. Not since he got such a brush-off from that snooty scientist over at Bandaq. In a way he hoped that her test blew up so he wouldn't have to think about funding her damn project. On the other hand, if it worked, it would be quite a breakthrough for the President's missile defense program.

When it came to Bandaq, Metcher had to admit he felt pretty conflicted. Then he watched the way Roxy maneuvered her way through the crowd and sent him a dazzling smile as she headed out the door. At that point he knew that he wasn't going to have to face any conflicts tonight. Nope. Not a one.

41

"Damn shame we missed Metcher at that reception," Dr. Kooner remarked as he slipped the valet a tip, got into his Lexus LS 430, and turned on the windshield wipers.

"A real shame," the chief lobbyist remarked, fastening his seat belt. "At least we were able to get some time with Betty Barton."

"What's your take on that woman? I couldn't quite read her."

"I'm not sure."

"It's your job to be sure," Kooner snapped. He paid a handsome wage to a whole bevy of lobbyists who were supposed to keep score on every Member of Congress. Their needs, their wants, their wallets. Knowledge was power. Everybody knew that.

He didn't like having to hire the ex-staffers and former Congressmen he had on his payroll. But they gave him access. His K Street operation was damned expensive and didn't mean squat to his shareholders. The trouble was, if the U.S. government didn't set the price of everything from sugar to submarines, CEOs like him wouldn't need so many guys cozying up to Capitol Hill to protect their interests. As for his business, he had no choice. There was no such thing as a free market in military machines. If he could figure out a way to manufacture one component in every Congressional District in the country, his contracts would be a slam-dunk. The whole process didn't seem to have much to do with merit or cost-controls.

He turned the car toward Massachusetts Avenue, splashing water on a pedestrian in the process. His Vice President of Government Relations was droning on, making his excuses.

"About Barton. The bitch is cagey. She'll hold out until the last minute, cutting deals with the other members. She and Metcher are famous for exchanging votes on every issue on the docket."

"I know that. I'm not sure what else we can do to reel her in. We've already contributed the max to her campaign, haven't we?"

"Sure have."

"Got any more bright ideas?"

"We did come up with something kind of unique the other day, but we'd have to move pretty fast."

"What is it?" the CEO asked. "At this point, I'm willing to look at anything that's legal . . . or even . . ." He gave his Vice President a sideway glance and thought he detected a knowing smile.

"It's definitely legal. But it's something that would probably piss 'em off."

"What do you mean?"

"We were in a strategy session and came up with an amendment to the tax bill."

"The tax bill?" Kooner asked. "Why would you boys be spending your time on that piece of legislation? Unless they're going to raise the corporate rate or something equally asinine."

"Well, a lot of Members are talking about more tax cuts and simplification, and if they pull it off, it will likely lead to increased revenues. Every time they've cut the tax rate, they take in more money. Kind of counter-intuitive, but it works."

"I know that," Kooner said. "Cut taxes, create more jobs. More people working means more people paying taxes. So what's that got to do with us?"

"Increased revenues mean more resources for spending programs. And what's the most important spending program right now?"

The CEO glanced over at his chief lobbyist and replied, "Defense!"

"You got it."

"Trouble is, you're talking long-term here. Even if we could get a new tax bill through this session, there wouldn't be any payback for months . . . years probably," the CEO observed.

"Sure, we know that. But Congress always operates on the come. If they get this bill passed, they'll make all sorts of revenue projections, and then they won't feel so stymied by the current deficit."

"It all depends on who's doing the projections, the supply-siders or the static boys. So what was your new amendment?" Kooner asked as he turned and headed down K Street.

"It would stipulate that every Member of Congress fill out his own tax return."

"Why the devil would you want to do that?"

"Don't you see? If every Member had to fill out his own return, they would find out pretty damn fast how complicated the forms were and what the average Joe has to deal with every April 15th. And once they went through the exercise, we'd get a tax simplification bill pretty damn fast."

"You're right on both scores."

"Both scores?" the lobbyist asked, raising his eyebrows.

"Sure. You'd get a bill for simplification, but you'd irritate the hell out of them in the process."

"Guess you're right. Probably a bad idea."

"Probably," Kooner agreed. "But at least your staff is trying to be creative. I've got a couple of people in my office who are being creative, too."

"In what way?"

"The I-men are working on technology similar to Bandaq's. And we've got a couple of ideas involving Metcher."

"Metcher? He's the key, you know."

"Tell me something I don't know." Kooner pulled up in front of their downtown office and stopped the car. "Metcher's got some vulnerabilities we may be able to exploit."

"Vulnerabilities?"

"Stay tuned."

42

The digital readout said 5:45. Cammy flipped her pillow over. The cool linen did little to relieve her hot skin and the dull ache developing just behind her eyes. She reached up to massage her forehead and realized it was damp. She often woke up with headaches. She didn't know if a headache caused her bad dreams or if the all too familiar image of a burning plane crashing to earth brought on the headache.

In her dream, a missile blows up her father's plane. In her lab, the missile never gets blown up. She stretched, pushed the nightmare from her mind, and then remembered yesterday's dire developments. Even with Raj's help, her simulations weren't working. The general had sent around a memo setting the date for a field test. Stan Bollinger had requested yet another review of various departmental budgets and reminded her about next week's board meeting. And there had evidently been no progress in the search for the guy who was after her.

Hunt had come home late and was preoccupied in his library with plans for his trip to India. All in all, it had been a pretty lousy twenty-four hours, and it didn't look like things would improve any time soon. Even the weather was dismal, with intermittent rain squalls blowing branches against the house again.

She looked toward the window where slivers of light from the street lamps seeped through the venetian blinds, projecting a series of luminous tightropes on the wall. As she stared at the lines, she imagined herself trying to balance first on one, then on another. *This is a useless exercise.*

She turned on the bedside light, grabbed her robe, and stumbled into the bathroom. She brushed her teeth, splashed cold water on her face, and peered into the mirror. Her hair was a mess. She fumbled in her makeup kit for her brush and tried to tame the unruly strands. She could make herself more presentable later. Right now she needed coffee.

She crept down the stairs and into the kitchen, trying not to wake up Hunt. She walked over to the counter, filled the pot, found the coffee and filters in the cupboard, and turned on the coffeemaker. There were a couple of English muffins in the refrigerator. She pulled them out, along with some margarine and jam. As the coffee was perking, she heard a shuffling sound on the stairs.

She turned and saw him standing there, barefoot, in an old navy terry-cloth robe, running a hand through his tousled hair.

"Couldn't sleep, huh?" he said in a slightly hoarse voice.

"Not really. So I figured I might as well get the coffee started."

He sauntered over and touched her cheek. "You okay?"

"I guess," she said absently. "Just a few bad dreams on top of everything else."

"Yeah. I know how it is. Sorry I was so busy last night. I just—"

"Hey, you're not my babysitter. Besides, I know you've got a lot to do." She paused for a moment. "You're leaving tonight."

"I know. And things are piling up." He took two mugs out of a cabinet and started to pour the coffee. "Glad you made this. By the way, one of the guys at work told me a funny story about making coffee."

"Tell me," she said, accepting the cup and taking it to the kitchen table. "I could use something funny right about now."

"Well, it was about how this couple was arguing over who should make the coffee. The wife says to the husband, 'Since you always get up first, you should brew it.' Then the guy says, 'No. Cooking is your job, so you make it. I'll just wait.' Then she says, 'No, you should do it. And besides, it says so in the Bible.' And he says, 'Don't be silly. It doesn't say that in the Bible.

Show me.' And so she goes and gets the Bible and opens it and shows him that at the top of a bunch of pages, it says . . . 'Hebrews.'"

In spite of her mood, Cammy had to laugh. "Not bad. You usually do make me feel better, you know that?" *And starting tonight, there'll be nobody around who can do that.*

"At your service, my lady. Say, do you want one of these muffins?"

"Sure, thanks."

They shared their breakfast, talked about their plans for the day, and cleared the dishes. "I'd better go take a shower," Cammy said, heading toward the stairs.

"Wait a minute," Hunt said. "Come in the library. Let me show you the computer setup. Since the bastard stole yours, you can use mine while I'm gone. I mean, I know you've got nothing but computers at your lab, but I was just thinking that when you're here alone, you might want to do your personal stuff. E-mail, bills, whatever."

"Uh, that would be great," she said, following him down the hall.

"Let me just check my e-mail here, and then I'll show you the rest."

She stood behind him and watched as he turned on the computer, clicked on "Outlook," and keyed in his password. It was a series of numbers that she automatically committed to memory. Computers, numbers, passwords. They were her business. She worked with them all day long. She always seemed to remember the checklists, the algorithms, the ones that worked and the ones that didn't. It was all second nature to her.

He glanced at the list of a dozen e-mails and then ended the program. He turned to her and said, "Nothing I have to deal with right now. There are a lot of things here. Everything's pretty obvious to you, right?"

She looked at the various icons on the blue screen. "No problem. I can access my e-mail through Explorer. My system lets me use a different computer and still use my own passwords. I may try to do that later."

"Okay. Now I guess we both need to get ready. I'm sorry I have to leave tonight. I mean, with that guy chasing you around town."

"I'll be fine," she said. "I always tell the cabdrivers to go home a different way. And look, I really appreciate being able to stay here for a while, but I've been thinking it might be safer to stay in different places from time to time. Like I said before, maybe I should check into a hotel."

"No way. We've had this conversation before, remember? You stay here until I get back," he said.

He was standing next to her, but suddenly she felt lonely. Abandoned. Frightened. She realized she was going to miss this man. A lot. "When will you be back? Do you have any idea?"

"Not sure yet. We leave late tonight. . . . I'll head out to Andrews from the office, so I won't see you. It's a pretty long trip to New Delhi."

"How long?"

"About twenty hours or so. We'll be stopping to refuel. Anyway, we've got back-to-back meetings lined up at the Defense Ministry. Then if we make any progress in setting up the talks, we may head over to Islamabad to nail down Pakistan's part in the whole deal."

"What about the missiles?"

"They're on my list of things to talk to Indian Intelligence about. We'd sure like to find those babies before somebody decides to shoot off another one."

She walked over to him and put her hand on his arm. "Please be careful."

He looked down at her hand and then into her eyes. Almost in slow motion, he gathered her in his arms and lowered his mouth to hers. It was gentle at first. Then as he deepened the kiss, she heard a slight moan. She didn't know if it came from him or from her.

He framed her face with his hands and stared down at her. "You're the one I worry about, not me," he whispered. "I'll get back as soon as I can. Maybe a week. Maybe two. I'll call you."

She pulled back and tried to smile. "Okay. On the blue cell phone?"

"Yes, that one. Keep it with you. And keep it on. There's a charger on the desk. It should last a day or two." He pulled her to him again and murmured, "Trouble is, I don't know if I can last a day or two not seeing you." And with his words hanging in the air, he kissed her one last time.

43

Georgetown—Tuesday Early Morning

The cab was delayed. Hunt had left. Cammy had showered, dressed, and called for a taxi, but with the rain, the dispatcher said they were backed up. Cammy checked her watch and let out a nervous sigh. *With all I have to do today, it's just my luck that I'm going to be late. Damn.*

She looked out the window. No taxi yet. *Might as well not waste time.* She walked down the hall to the library, slid into Hunt's desk chair, flicked on the light, and turned on the computer. *That man is a turn-on*, she thought as she touched the control switch. She stared at the screen. *He said he'd be home in a week or two. Sounds pretty vague. Maybe he's planning on getting back sooner but doesn't want me to worry in case he gets all tied up over there. I wonder if there's a plan for a return flight after all. I wonder . . .*

She focused on the word "Outlook." *E-mail . . . calendar . . . I could just take a quick look. See if . . .* She clicked on the icon, saw the little box asking for his password, and quickly keyed in the memorized numbers. She clicked on "Calendar" on the left side and saw a bunch of letters and abbreviations entered for today. His first entry was listed as, "Dis Russ w/SS." *Hmmm. "Dis"? Maybe it's "Discuss Russians with SS." Secret Service? Could be. No. Wait a minute. The Deputy National Security Advisor's name is Stockton Sloan. That's it,* she thought. *Piece of cake.*

She didn't mean to snoop into Hunt's official life, or did she? She really wanted to know when the man was coming home. She was certain there wouldn't be anything classified on this machine. But a calendar. What was the harm in looking at a calendar?

She checked entries a week ahead, looking for anything like a flight schedule. But all she saw was a bunch of letters, probably acronyms. She saw references to IAEA. She knew that was the International Atomic Energy Agency. NNPT. She knew that one, too—the Nuclear Non-Proliferation Treaty. Then there was a reference to SECDEF and MDA. Easy. That's the Secretary of Defense and the Missile Defense Agency.

She looked at more dates. Most of his listings looked like a game of Scrabble—NSDD, INR, PFIAB. She recognized the last one as the President's Foreign Intelligence Advisory Board. Suddenly another entry for a date two weeks away read, "Get NK BA FLD TS."

She heard a honk outside. The cab was waiting. She stared at the screen again, trying to fathom what the letters meant. Of all the entries, this one made no sense at all. She grabbed a piece of paper from the phone pad and jotted down "Get NK BA FLD TS" and shoved it in her purse. She quickly shut down the machine, ran down the hall, punched in the security code, and slammed the door.

44

Washington, D.C.—Tuesday Morning

"A cruise missile costs between five hundred thousand and one million dollars. Therefore, it is a fairly expensive way to deliver a one-thousand-pound package." Jambaz read through the report he had found on the Internet. He wanted to learn more about the weapons his cell members had stolen from Pakistan, and he was fascinated to see how expensive they were.

Up to a million dollars for each one, and we got three of them for free, he mused. As for the thousand-pound package, it had turned out to be a rare gift indeed. He scrolled down and saw a picture of the GLCM (Ground-Launched Cruise Missile) launcher, which appeared to be a truck with a big trailer equipped with four long shafts to hold the missiles. It could be elevated to the proper angle for firing. Best of all was the accuracy of this type of missile. The article said, "It can fly 1,000 miles and hit a target the size of a single-car garage."

He was proud of Lashkar-i-Taiba for figuring out how to steal these things. It was the most important mission so far in their grand scheme. Yet these were only the first of many sophisticated weapons they would control when they won their Jihad. One day they would control the entire nuclear arsenal of the country of Pakistan.

Then they could target the Americans because they knew the spineless Western leaders would never use their own nuclear weapons. When the United States had dropped the atom bombs on Japan, the world was aghast. And since that day most every American had been afraid of nuclear power. Even though the hawks in their Pentagon kept writing papers about when it might be necessary to use those weapons, somebody always leaked the papers. Then after the press printed all the leaks, the plans were blamed on some lower-level bureaucrat making a mistake. No, the Americans would not use nuclear weapons again. And so, they would be a perfect target for blackmail. Every country in the world would force them to negotiate, not retaliate.

In the meantime, his group had a war to start and a war to win. There was much to do. Different cells had different orders. Jambaz had his own assignment, and he was frustrated by his failure so far. He did not want to report this to his leader or the other members of his cell. He hoped they would have patience, for the task was a complicated one.

He switched over to his new encrypted program to check for any new messages from Abbas Khan. Yes. There was one today. Jambaz quickly went through the motions and keystrokes and read the instructions. "Do not believe the reports in the newspapers about failures at Bandaq Technologies. These are lies. All lies to confuse the competition. We say again, you must acquire their system. And as I instructed before, if this is not possible, you must make certain that no one else acquires it. This means the scientist must be stopped before she is able to reproduce this Q-3 and make it available to her government or any other entity." He may have failed before. But tonight . . . *Inshallah* . . . the scientist would be stopped.

45

Washington, D.C.—Tuesday Afternoon

The White House driver swerved the car to the right and stopped. Hunt looked up from his notes and saw the flashing lights ahead. The Metro Police were clearing the way for yet another motorcade of shiny black cars. *Probably the Japanese heading for the Hill*, he thought. The number of cars in a Washington motorcade always seemed to be in inverse proportion to the size and importance of the country involved. The British Prime Minister had taken just two cars to travel to Capitol Hill, while some little dictator had commandeered eighteen limousines to transport his entourage around town.

The driver then executed a U-turn and took a side street to avoid the parade. He pulled up to the entrance of FBI Headquarters at Ninth and Pennsylvania, where Hunt asked him to wait, saying he was just going in for a short meeting. He leaped out of the car into the misty afternoon. The rain had tapered off, leaving a sky filled with gray clouds. He hoped it wasn't a harbinger of things to come.

He went up the stairs and into a reception area. The secretary asked him to wait a moment, so he sat down in a corner chair and opened his leather folder. As he reviewed his notes, he remembered the old story about J. Edgar Hoover running this organization and how he had demanded that all memos be no longer than a single page. The Director had received one particularly complicated memo and saw that the author had extended the margins almost to the edges of the paper to get all of his words on the one page. So across the top, Hoover scrawled, "Watch the borders!" And for the next week, additional agents were dispatched to monitor entry points from Canada and Mexico.

A few minutes later, Hunt was ushered into a large office with a dark wood desk, walls of bookshelves, and the familiar blue FBI seal on the back wall. He had tried to set up this meeting yesterday, but Janis had been out of town. He had no intention of going to the Montgomery County Police to beg for a protection detail. He knew it would be a dead end. So he decided to finesse the situation with Stock, if and when he found out that Hunt had used a family connection to go over his head. Besides, he'd always rather apologize than ask for permission.

Janis Prescott came around from behind her desk and extended her hand. "Hunt, it's good to see you again. How's your mother?"

"Fine, she's doing fine. Busy with her charity work. You know how it is."

"Yes, well, you give her my best. Please have a seat, and tell me what's on your mind. I was surprised to get your call."

Janis Prescott was an impressive woman. After attending Smith College, where she and Hunt's mother were classmates, Janis had gone on to get her law degree at Harvard and serve on the *Law Review*. She then worked in the United States Attorney's Office in Chicago and later served in the Department of Justice, where the President took note of her talents, naming her Deputy Director of the FBI. Even though she was considered an old family friend, Hunt respected her position and hadn't used that connection very often.

He sat down and checked his watch. He was going to be in and out in less than ten minutes. "I appreciate your seeing me on such short notice, especially with everything that's going on."

"Yes, I am a bit pressed today. But tell me, what brings you here?"

Hunt quickly described the new technology being developed by Cammy's team at Bandaq, its breakthrough design, its importance to the U.S. arsenal of defensive systems, and also its allure to foreign governments.

He summarized the tensions building between India and Pakistan, the growing threat posed by the Islamic militants fighting in Kashmir, and the likelihood that they had stolen and launched the cruise missile against Indian forces. Finally, he explained his suspicions of foreign involvement in the break-in at Cammy's apartment and the accident in Bethesda. He told her about the tip from the Pakistani Ambassador that an Islamic militant may be in town and said that Cammy needed protection. He was trying to make a cogent case for FBI involvement. Not just to find the bad guy. Hunt desperately wanted to protect Cammy. He knew this would be a tough sell, but at this point, he didn't know where else to turn.

He summarized his pitch. "While I know it may sound far-fetched, I think there's a thread here that ties in with the intel on these groups."

"Wait a minute. About the militant you said might be here in Washington. Who's working that angle?"

"I passed that along to two of my counterparts. One here at the Bureau and the other at Homeland Security."

"Good. I haven't been briefed on that yet. I'm sure I'll hear about it if they find him."

"Yes, but the problem is . . . until they find him, I'm very worried about Dr. Talbot. I feel her life is in danger." Hunt leaned forward and suddenly realized that he was holding his breath.

"And you think that's a job for the FBI?" the Deputy asked.

"I know you're swamped," he conceded.

"To say the least," she said. "Besides the terrorists we seem to be chasing around the country, we've got the drug lords, white-collar crime, and that whole new bill on child abductions that we're trying to enforce. I don't know, Hunt; my people are stretched awfully thin at this point."

"I know. I know. It's just that I'm concerned that this woman has become a target. And if it is an Islamic group, or even ISI or New Delhi . . ."

"From what you've told me, I do believe that the Pakistanis and the Indians could be interested in this new project. We know that they've been involved in the industrial-espionage game. They're not quite as good at it as the French. Not yet anyway," she said with a small shake of her head, "but they'd like to be. As for the militants, I doubt if they have the expertise. You were talking about Kashmir. You know we had a group here in Northern Virginia with ties to the Kashmir dispute. But they weren't exactly looking for sophisticated weapons systems. In fact, they were training with guns and paintballs, for God's sake."

"I know. And it's true, I don't know who's behind this. At least not yet. The police checked for prints, but we never heard any more about it."

"I do hate to disappoint you. But it really does sound like a job for local law enforcement."

Hunt was stymied. The FBI had been his last hope. "It's just that I don't think they—"

"Hunt, I'm sorry. I'm just so shorthanded right now. Until we have more . . ."

She needed more information. He needed more time. But time was running out. He glanced down at his watch. "I should get out of your hair. I'm leaving for India tonight. We've got an advance team going over."

"Oh yes, to pave the way for the Special Envoy. I heard about that. Good luck."

He tried one last tact. "But on this problem with Dr. Talbot, may I keep the lines of communication open on this one?"

"Yes, of course you may." She took out a card, jotted down her private cell phone number, and handed it to him as she got up from her desk. "Let's just hope that it was a random burglary and a bad case of road rage."

He knew that wasn't the case. He was frustrated, and right now he felt like the prosecutor in the old Perry Mason movies. The guy who always lost.

46

Kashmir—Tuesday Afternoon

"We have our next targets."

"Where?"

"How far?"

"Who are they?"

"When?"

The shouts mingled together as dozens of men crowded around Abbas Khan in the cramped bunker, their usual meeting place near the Line of Control separating Kashmir into Pakistani- and Indian-ruled areas. The room, built into the side of a mountain, was more like a cave than a cabin. There were small windows on only one side, and the air smelled of dust and sweat. But on this day, members of the cell were focused on revolution, not ventilation. The leader raised his arms to quiet the noise.

"The American team will be arriving soon in New Delhi." He turned to Rashid. "You sent their arrival plans to our brothers in Delhi?"

Rashid nodded.

"Very good. They know what to do. They will arrange a surprise for those American spies."

Two men in the back of the bunker raised their guns in tribute to their leader.

"Tomorrow we shall watch their progress on Aljazeera." Khan paused and added with a slight smile, "Or perhaps we will watch CNN. That may give us even greater satisfaction." The men nodded and murmured their approval.

Abbas Khan then unfolded a map on the floor. The men gathered around it. Some knelt on the dirt floor. Others squatted down behind them. All peered at the map and waited for Khan to continue.

"We have two missiles left, and you all know that we have recruited two more scientists. They will help us launch these weapons with pinpoint accuracy." He leaned down and pointed to the Indian capital. "Now then, if our information is correct, this so-called Special Envoy will be coming to New Delhi to arrange a peace treaty with Pakistan."

"But if we assassinate the advance team, won't they cancel the whole operation?" one cell member asked.

"Do not be a fool. Our attack on this group will only embolden their stupid President to show his muscles. He will not stop. He will call all the heads of state and promise them money and aid and anything else he can think of to get them to come together and talk about peace. He will need a good headline after we create a very bad headline. Don't you see?"

The young man sat very still, chastised by the harsh rebuke.

"Now back to the weapons. When this Envoy arrives for his meetings, that is when we will launch our next missile. It will easily destroy the Defense Ministry and everyone in it. We will make all the necessary preparations for the launch from our territory. It has sufficient range, and we do not believe the Indians have any way to shoot it down."

"Don't they have some defensive systems?" Rashid asked.

"Yes, some. But they are not very efficient. And even if they did have an anti-missile device, and they sent up another missile to intercept it, the explosion could cause some damage, as it would occur over their cities. Don't you see? We win no matter what they do."

"It has a conventional warhead, does it not?" Rashid asked.

"Yes. But don't worry. It will create much destruction, especially if it reaches all the way to the Ministry."

"And if India retaliates?"

"They have not yet answered our first missile strike. They do not know yet that we were responsible. If they did know, they would have fired back. No. They do not know."

"But if they did?"

"We are working on defensive measures ourselves." He glanced over at the table where the fax machine and his computer sat quietly. "I am still waiting for a report from Jambaz."

Rashid raised his eyebrows. "No word yet? Has something happened to him?"

"His last report indicated he was still working on his assignment. He was carrying out a plan tonight. He gave no specifics. But while we wait for him, we will work on our own plans."

"What about the last missile?" another man asked.

"Ah, that will be the best of all. It has a very special warhead, and I have waited to tell you its final destination until all our leaders had agreed. Now I can announce that we have decided to repeat the attack originally planned back in 2002."

"Which plan was that?" Rashid asked.

"The plan by our own Lashkar-i-Taiba to attack the Taj Mahal," Khan said forcefully.

"The Taj Mahal?" the others cried out simultaneously. The room erupted in noise and confusion as many of the men posed questions all at once. "Why the Taj?" "It's a Muslim mosque." "Our Muslim brothers pray there." "How can we do this?"

Abbas Khan sat back and waited for the furor to die down.

"I can understand your concerns, but we need the cooperation of every member. We do not need you to question our decisions. Therefore I will explain how we came to this conclusion. First, the Indians are planning a celebration of the 350th anniversary of the building. They have already invited many heads of state, including Western leaders. They are all our enemies."

The young men settled down on the floor again and gave Khan their rapt attention. He went on in a deliberate tone. "And if the American Envoy should somehow survive the cruise missile attack and persuade the Indians and Pakistanis to sign some sort of agreement, it will be signed at the celebration." He paused and said in an undertone, "But we don't need to worry about the Envoy. He will undoubtedly be destroyed." The men nodded.

"Then the American President will work even harder to get Delhi and Islamabad to agree to a treaty. It is obvious. It will happen."

"But the Taj Mahal. Can you explain why you want to destroy a Muslim monument?" a voice from the back of the room implored.

"Do you not remember just a few years ago when we had the first plan to destroy the place?"

A young man looked at his leader with a blank stare and replied, "We never carried it out."

"I know that, you fool. But we had a plan. The Indians found out about it. Careless e-mail. Bad communications back then. And when they found out, don't you remember how they put all their tailors to work sewing dark cloth to put over the whole place as camouflage? If you go there today, you can still see the steel hooks and eye-rings in the dome where they attached the tarps. Of course, they think this stupid cloth would protect their precious building from a bombing raid. What fools they are. We know the location of the Taj Mahal. And if we decide to blow it up or bomb it with a missile, then that is what we will do."

"But the Islamic heritage—"

"Silence!" he commanded. "I said I would answer your questions. You want to talk about Islamic heritage? I will give you Islamic heritage. Perhaps you all are too young to have studied your history properly. Perhaps you only listen to legends fed to the tourists who flock to Agra to look at a building. Let me tell you, there are many questions about that legend."

"How can there be, Khan Sahib? We all know the Taj Mahal was built by Shah Jahan as a tomb for his beloved wife, Mumtaz."

"Was it? Do you always accept everything you hear or read? Let me ask you a few questions, and then you can tell me if you are so sure. If it were originally built by a Muslim, then why does it not face Mecca as our other mosques do? If it were built by a Muslim, why does the style resemble a Hindu temple and contain so many Hindu symbols like the Lotus Canopy? Lotus is the sacred flower of the heathen Hindu gods and goddesses. It means nothing to us. And the border on the main gateway is decorated with the elephant trunk. You know we do not allow decorations of animals in Islam. So why are these things even present?"

The men stared at Khan and sat absolutely still.

"Another question. If it were built to be a tomb for his wife, why are there two floors below with many rooms for storing provisions? Hindus build basements. We do not need basements in our mausoleums."

Rashid exchanged a glance with the young man on his left, who had a curious expression on his face.

"And here are more questions," Khan continued. "Think about the arrangement of the buildings. The marble building in the center has two symmetrical buildings on each side. One is a mosque where our people pray. Why did they need the other one?"

Several men shook their heads in bewilderment.

"The long corridors leading up to the Taj Mahal are the type used in ancient Hindu capitals. And Hindus use octagons. They even have names for the eight directions. And what do you see at the front of the corridors? You see two octagon towers.

"Another building in the garden is the Naqqar Khana. What is that? It is the Music House. You know that a Muslim mausoleum must have silence. We never disturb the dead. But the filthy Hindus play music all the time, especially when they do their work."

"But the Qur'an . . . the lettering . . ."

"I did not say that Shah Jahan had nothing to do with the Taj Mahal. Yes, he had work done. Yes, he ordered marble and employed many workmen. Yes, his work took many years. But the lettering from the Qur'an was probably grafted onto the building."

"If he didn't build it, who did?" Rashid asked, wide-eyed.

"There are many stories. Many theories that it could have been built hundreds of years before as a palace, and he took it over. There was even a test of a wooden door."

"A door?"

"Yes. A radiocarbon date of a piece of wood from a door."

"What did it show?"

"The date came to the mid-1300s."

"But couldn't that door have been old to begin with?" another shouted.

"Perhaps. It is just one more clue."

"But the records . . . ," Rashid said.

"What records? There are very few records. They even argue over who the architects were. But yes, there are some records. They show that after his Queen died in 1631, she was first buried somewhere else, and then moved to the Taj Mahal in 1632. Then tourists were allowed to visit in

1633. And yet construction of the Taj Mahal, according to your precious legend, started in 1631 and went on for over twenty years. Now if Shah Jahan didn't even start construction until she died in 1631, and the work went on for over twenty years, why was she reburied in the middle of a construction site, and why were tourists visiting such a place twenty years before it was finished?"

The men began to mumble among themselves when their leader cleared his throat and continued.

"And I will tell you one more thing. This Muslim Shah was perhaps not worth our praise. There are also stories that even if his architects, whoever they were, only made improvements to an already existing palace, he didn't want them to create another Taj Mahal, so he had them killed. And so I ask you, why should we be concerned with such a place?"

The men sat in silence. Finally, Rashid raised his head and spoke. "There is another argument, Khan Sahib."

"And what is that?" he snapped at the young man.

"Even though there are many questions about the Taj Mahal, it is still a historic landmark. If we were to destroy it, even in the name of our Jihad, would this not bring down the wrath of the world upon us?"

The leader started to answer when another man interrupted. "Remember 1972? The Munich Olympics? Remember when our brothers killed the eleven Israeli athletes? They thought they could focus world attention to the plight of the Palestinian people. But instead, the world turned against them. And then the Spanish trains and the Russian school and the English—"

Abbas Khan waved his hand in frustration. "Those Olympics are long forgotten. We changed the Spanish government, and the Russians deserve even more than they got with that attack. They've been killing our Chechen brothers for years. And when they made their pre-emptive invasion of Afghanistan, it gave Osama bin Laden and our other leaders the strength they needed to develop and expand al Qaeda and the rest of our organization. Do you not see? When attacks are made by our side, more rally to our cause. And when we are attacked by our enemies, we get even more recruits. We win either way. That is why we must continue the fight right here in our homeland. We must never let the Americans talk about peace. There will be no peace until we control the governments . . . until we set up our own caliphates.

"It will be a long struggle. But we are getting stronger every year, every month, every day. And today we put these new plans into effect." He paused and surveyed the room. "Are there any more questions?"

Silence.

He raised his eyes. "We gather again tomorrow and watch the demise of the Americans."

47

"Okay, folks. We're going to do this again." Cammy had assembled her entire staff in her lab. Raj sat at a computer on one side of her, Ben on the other, and several other technical support people had crowded into the room with laptops and large display screens.

"Bollinger's given us until the board meeting to get a successful simulation, and you all know the general has planned a test at the Atlantic facility. This is no longer a marathon. It's a sprint. So I want new ideas, anything from anyone. I know Raj, Ben, and I have been taking the lead on this thing. But now I don't want you to genuflect. Stand up and be counted."

"I've got a mezzanine idea," a young woman announced from the side of the room.

"Lay it out," Cammy suggested.

"It may not get us to the Penthouse, so to speak. But it may get us off the ground floor."

"And right now, we're at Ground Zero," Ben mumbled.

The woman hit some keys on her computer, and a series of numbers showed on the screen at the end of the room. "It's another algorithm we could try."

Remembering the old adage that you never learn anything while you're talking, Cammy held her tongue and simply nodded her encouragement.

The test began when Cammy hit a button releasing a simulated missile attack. As the object traced a path across a series of screens, Cammy, Raj, and Ben tried the new formula. They combined it with others, reversed the protocol, and tried again. Then once more.

Nothing.

The white blip fell off the screen and a collective groan permeated the silence.

"Kind of makes you feel like Dilbert's in the next cubicle screwing things up, doesn't it?" Ben whispered.

Cammy shook her head. "That's okay. It was a good idea."

"Just not a good enough move to make the highlight reel," the young woman said.

"Come on, gang. Let's keep going here."

They worked for two more hours, then suddenly Ben leaned over and showed Cammy another formulation. She studied it, nudged Raj, and he said, "Why not? It just might help us break out of this chrysalis."

Cammy suddenly had a vision of a multicolored butterfly circling around her lab. *Color me nervous, but let's go for it.*

They geared up again as all eyes focused on her computer screen. Her wrist was aching again. This time the pain shot up her arm. She grimaced and tried to focus on her keyboard. She couldn't let her train of thought get sidetracked by a little discomfort. She sat up straighter in her chair, rubbed her arm, and began again.

Seconds stretched to minutes. Raj added an equation to Ben's idea. Then Cammy supplied a coda.

All of a sudden, a loud tone sounded, accompanied by the word SESAME flashing on her screen. There it was. A lock onto the missile. She quickly invaded the program and began to take control. The white blip had stopped moving. It simply hovered in the center of her screen.

"You did it."

"You locked on."

"You can redirect."

"That missile is ours!"

"Wait till the board hears about this one!"

"Yeah. To hell with Bollinger. We've got it made."

They all seemed to be chiming in at once. "What is this? The Hallelujah

Chorus?" Cammy laughed, glancing around the room. "Ben, you're a genius."

"Hey, it was a cameo."

"This show couldn't have made it without you," she said, leaning over to give her young assistant a hug.

"It gave me goose bumps," a fellow in the back volunteered.

"Me, too," the young woman agreed. "Mine are so big you could hang your hat on 'em."

A wave of laughter swept the room as Raj quickly made notes on the successful set of numbers.

Cammy ended the program, sat back, and beamed at her staff. "Okay, everybody. It worked. Q-3 really worked. That's it for today. You all deserve a little time off. And thanks. Really. Thanks to all of you." For the first time in weeks she felt excited. Elated. *We still don't know if it'll work against a live missile, but it's a damn good start.*

The support staff gathered their notes, computers, and props and began to file out of the room. Cammy turned to Ben. "Great work! How about a little celebration tonight? Dinner? I'm buying."

"Sure. Great. Just tell me where."

"There's a little restaurant in Georgetown right near the place I'm staying. You go down Wisconsin to N Street. Martin's. It's on the right."

She turned to Raj. "Want to join us?"

He raised his eyes and answered quickly. "No. No thank you. I still have work to do. And I'm going over to Sibley to see Melanie later."

"Oh, good. I'm going to stop there myself on my way home. I'll tell her to expect you." Checking the wall clock, she thought about how long it would take to wrap up here, get to the hospital, go home and change clothes, and make it to the restaurant.

"Ben, how about seven thirty? First one there picks the table. It's a weeknight, so it shouldn't be too crowded."

As she saved her notes and straightened her desk, she remembered Hunt's admonition about moving around town. Another one of his military terms: "Whatever you do, Cam, watch your six!"

48

Washington, D.C.—Tuesday Early Evening

"Hi, Mel, what's up?" Cammy said as she opened the door to the hospital room. Melanie was sitting up in bed, reading a copy of *Veranda* magazine.

"My spirits! The doctor says I can go home tomorrow."

"Tomorrow? That soon?" Cammy said, pulling up a chair.

"Yep. Well, you know how it is with insurance and all. As soon as you open your eyes, they find a way to kick you out."

"How true. But that's great. I'll come over tomorrow and drive you home. By the way, I really appreciate being able to use your car today. Waiting for taxis was getting to be a real hassle. The mechanics at your garage were pretty helpful. They brought your car over to the office."

"What are you going to do about your own wheels, though?"

Cammy sighed. "I'll have to buy another car. Mine was basically totaled. At least my insurance guy is taking care of the claim. But enough about that. How are you feeling . . . really?"

"I probably shouldn't operate any heavy machinery," she quipped, "but I'll be okay. I've been up and around. Even had a shower this morning. It's still hard looking in the mirror, though, with these eyes. I mean, the bruises and everything."

"How long before they clear up?"

"Few more days at least. The doctor said it was a basilor skull fracture. Guess I look like I've been in the ring with Mike Tyson, huh?"

Cammy chuckled. "You'll probably have women stopping you on the street saying, 'Honey, there's a hotline you can call.' But hey, you look a whole lot better than you did a few days ago. And are you eating anything? Is the food here any good?"

"It's typical. I'm trying to cut down anyway, you know."

"I know. But you don't—"

"Sure I do," Mel interrupted. "I've adopted a new motto."

"What's that?"

"Well, it's not really new, but I like it. How about this? Nothing tastes as good as thin feels," Mel said with a grin.

"Don't go overboard. I think Raj likes you just the way you are. And he said to tell you he'll be over a little later. He's still at the office, but I cut out early to come see you."

"Thanks, but it's not exactly early now. I mean it's, what, six thirty?"

"I know. Oh, wait till you hear what happened today," Cammy said, her eyes lighting up.

"Tell me."

"Well, I was working with Raj and Ben and the whole team. We were trying another simulation with new algorithms. Ben came up with a new idea. We tried it."

"And . . . ?" Mel asked expectantly.

"And . . . ta-da . . . we nailed the C^3 and redirected the missile," she said, holding up her hands triumphantly. "Of course, it was only a simulation."

"But that's fabulous!"

"I know. It was so exciting." She started flexing her fingers. "Only problem is, my hand still hurts every once in a while, and it kind of slows me down sometimes."

"You've been getting those pains for weeks now. You should see a doctor or something."

"Maybe later. Anyway, it's pretty neat about the test, though, don't you think?"

"Neat? It's absolutely terrific. But wait—"

"Wait? What?"

"I wasn't there to send out a press release."

Cammy shook her head. "Forget the press release. We can do that later. But can you believe it? I mean, after everything that's been going on with the general and Bollinger and the Committee breathing down my neck. Then with the burglary and now this," she gestured at the hospital bed, "to finally get a breakthrough. Oh, Mel, we really needed this."

Melanie reached over and touched Cammy's hand. "Know what? I'm really proud of you. I knew you could do it. Now all we need is a field test, and then Congress will come through with the funding and then—"

"Yes, well, let's take this one step at a time. I have to tell you that having Raj with us has been a great help. What a brain that guy has."

"I know . . . and a few other things, too," Melanie said with a glint in her eye. "I can't wait to see him. When do you think he'll get here?"

"I'm not sure. He just said he was going to make a bunch of notes to be sure we could re-create the scenario. So it may be a while, although Ben was helping out when I left."

"That Ben is really a sweet guy."

"He sure is. Best hire I've made all year."

"And he kind of follows you around like a puppy dog. Have you noticed?"

"Well, I wouldn't quite put it that way. I think of it more like mentor and student."

"You really are his mentor, aren't you?"

"Sure. I believe in bringing the smart ones along, if I can. I mean, the general did that for me when I got out of M.I.T."

Mel sat up and straightened the pillows behind her. "So what's your plan for tonight?"

"Since Raj said he was coming over here, and Hunt's not available . . . he's leaving for India, you know. . . ."

"Mmm-hmmm."

". . . I told Ben I would take him out to dinner to celebrate our little victory."

"It's kind of hard to celebrate anything without eating, isn't it?"

Cammy grinned. "Guess you're right. Anyway, we're meeting over at Martin's in Georgetown. Since it's cleared up, it's actually kind of balmy out there tonight, so maybe we can get a table outside. And I like their lamb chops. Their specialty."

Melanie picked up her magazine and opened to a particular page. "Oh, and speaking of food, I found another crazy recipe for my file. Look."

Cammy leaned over and read the page. "Chiles in a walnut sauce?"

Melanie chuckled. "And see how it's got twenty-eight ingredients, including twelve poblano chiles and the seeds of two pomegranates?" She set down the magazine and asked, "When you take me home, what about you? Want to come back to my apartment?"

"Not yet. Hunt told me to stay at his place until he comes back. He thinks I'm safer there, but I'm not so sure."

"Does he have a good security system?"

"Oh yeah. Place is like a fortress."

"And do you like it there?" Melanie asked coyly.

"It's a great house. Let's just say that I like it better when he's there."

"I know what you mean. When's he coming back anyway?"

Cammy paused, thinking about her foray into Hunt's private calendar. She felt guilty about using his password. But she kept telling herself she had only wanted to find out when he'd be back. It sounded like a lame excuse, though. Hardly something she wanted to confess. "I have no idea. He's leaving tonight and said it could be a week or so."

"Well, I'm sure he'll call you."

"I sure hope so." She checked her watch and got up to leave. "I'd better get going. I want to stop at the house to change, and then I'm meeting Ben. But you take care, and I'll be back tomorrow."

"Great. I can't wait to get out of this place."

Cammy was amazed when she found a parking place on N Street just around the corner from Martin's. Even though the restaurant was only a few blocks from Hunt's house, he had told her not to walk around Georgetown alone. She locked the car and hurried toward the restaurant. As long as there were a lot of people around, she felt pretty safe. As she turned the corner, she saw Ben already seated at a small dark green patio table under a green awning.

"Hey, Ben, great table. Looks like you snagged the last one."

"Yeah. On a night like this, I got lucky. This looks like a pretty good place. I've never been here before. What's good?" he asked, picking up the menu.

"Lamb chops," she responded, sitting down next to him.

He glanced up from the menu and asked, "Have you ever noticed how every restaurant always has white-meat chicken? You can never order chicken legs, you know?"

"I never thought about that."

"I figure there's gotta be a big silo somewhere filled with legs and thighs they can't sell."

Cammy started to laugh. "Stick with the lamb. It's better anyway. And would you like a beer? Wine? Order whatever you want."

Ben gave her a lopsided grin. "Thanks. Guess we deserve a little celebration. That simulation was awesome! The way you locked on to that sucker. Boy!"

"I couldn't have done it without you."

"And Raj," he added.

"Yes. But tell you what. We've been working on those calculations and programs for so many days now, what say we give it a rest and talk about something else."

"Okay. We'll park it, and I'll feed the meter," he said, peering over the rims of his glasses.

"Feed the meter?" she asked with a quizzical look.

"What I mean is, we'll park the subject of Q-3, and I'll think of something else to talk about."

Cammy sat back and began to recite, " 'If you can fill the unforgiving minute / With sixty seconds' worth of distance run, / Yours is the Earth and everything that's in it, / And—which is more—you'll be a Man, my son.' "

Ben stared at her for a moment, raised one finger, and said, "Wait. I've got it. Rudyard Kipling."

"Right you are," Cammy said with a smile.

"Here comes the waiter," Ben said. "Know what you want?"

"Sure do. Caesar salad, lamb chops, and a bottle of Pinot Noir, if you'll join me?"

"Sounds good to me."

"Speaking of sounds, is there a motorcycle convention in town or something?" she asked, looking out at the street.

Ben turned in his chair to follow her gaze and knocked a saltshaker off the table. As Cammy leaned down to pick it up, the sound of a shot pierced the evening air. Cammy jerked her head up just in time to see a man on a Vespa race the engine and careen around the corner out of sight.

The woman at the next table started screaming, the waiter rushed over, and Cammy looked at Ben, who was now slumped in his chair. Blood was streaming down his face. Her hand flew to her mouth to stifle a cry when she saw a bullet hole where his cheekbone used to be.

49

Georgetown—Tuesday Evening

A few blocks away on Prospect Street, the crowd at Café Milano was nois-
ier and more upscale. The regulars, like the former Chief of Protocol, had
already claimed their tables in front, while the tourists and other hangers-
on were shunted to the back of the place.

Dr. Nettar Kooner had requested a small table in the back. It was one
thing to be au courant, but in this case, he also wanted a small measure of
privacy for his discussion tonight. He ordered two bottles of Italian wine, a
white chardonnay, the Vintage Turina, and a Brunello red, along with some
Pellegrino. Then he sat back to wait for his guest.

He didn't have to wait long. Davis Metcher was making his way across
the crowded room, and Kooner smiled inwardly as he wondered if this
would indeed be some enchanted evening.

He stood up and extended his hand. "Great to see you tonight, my boy!
I see you know a lot of folks in this place."

"Yes, well, you know how it is." Davis smiled as he nodded to yet another
constituent.

"I took the liberty of ordering some wine for dinner. It's on the way, but
let's have a drink first."

"Good plan, Nettar. I could use one about now. There's so damn much going on these days, it's nice to take a little break."

"I'm just glad that you don't have to go jetting off to your district all the time like most of the boys."

"Pretty lucky to be representing part of Maryland. Of course, I don't get the frequent-flier miles this way, but what the hell. . . ."

A waiter materialized with their wine and Pellegrino. "Shall I pour the white for you, sir?"

"No, we'll order a cocktail first," Kooner said. "What'll it be, Davis? Scotch and water, I seem to recall."

"You're good. That's it."

"And I'll take a Bombay Gin martini with three olives."

"Certainly, sir," the waiter said as he hurried off toward the bar.

"Actually I just like gin-soaked olives," Kooner joked, picking up his menu. "They have quite a selection here. I suppose we should decide before we get down to the big decisions."

"Big decisions?" Metcher asked.

"Don't worry, ole boy. I'm not going to put you on the spot tonight. In fact, one reason I wanted to have dinner with you was to tell you that we had a staff meeting yesterday and decided to up the ante into your campaign coffers this time around."

Davis broke into a wide grin. "That's very good news. I know I can usually count on Sterling to come through. Got a tough race this fall, and I really want to beat that DA."

"We can't have some upstart coming in with no seniority replacing our friend Davis Metcher, now can we?" Kooner said soothingly.

"Glad to hear you say that, Doctor." He glanced at his menu. "I see what I want tonight, in addition to your support, that is."

"And what's that?"

"I think I'll go for the minestrone and that aged New York steak. Sounds mighty good."

The waiter appeared with their drinks and saw that Metcher had closed his menu. "Are you ready to order, sir?"

"Sure, why not?" He made his selections and the waiter turned to Dr. Kooner.

"I think I'll try the San Daniele prosciutto and the linguini with the Maine lobster."

"Excellent choices, gentlemen." He disappeared again, and the two men began a jovial conversation about the four sumo wrestlers who tried to give a demonstration on the seventh floor of the State Department, the continuing fight over windmills in the energy debate, and how a Congressman from Vermont had just dropped an amendment to the tax bill into the hopper.

"That idiot wants to put another tax just on millionaires. Says that the last time their taxes were raised, the economy improved," Davis said with a shake of his head.

"Post hoc ergo propter hoc," stated Kooner.

"Precisely. Fact of the matter is, the economy improved when we cut some spending, cut some other taxes, got a big jump in productivity, and lowered interest rates. It had nothing to do with taxes on millionaires, for God's sake."

"Couldn't agree with you more, my boy. Every time somebody on the Hill dreams up a new tax, I see it as political liposuction."

"I like that one. Think I'll use it in my next speech."

"Be my guest."

The CEO was enjoying this dinner. He and the Congressman were agreeing on most everything tonight. They had finished their cocktails, polished off the white wine during the appetizers, and were well on their way to emptying the Brunello. Maybe it was time to broach the real point of this dinner.

"Now, Davis, I imagine you saw that item in the *Post* the other day about Bandaq's new missile technology?"

"Couldn't miss it."

"Yes, well, they seem to be having their problems over there."

"Possibly. Still, they have a rather clever concept. Even you have to admit that," Davis countered.

"Yes, the concept is a good one. In fact, I wanted you to know that our boys have been working on a similar theory."

"Really? I had no idea. I thought you put all your eggs into the Patriot-type basket."

"Not all of them. Then again, our latest missile defense system has really worked. Our allies are lining up to buy it, you know."

"I'm well aware of that. Still, Bandaq does seem to be on the cutting edge."

"You're not saying you're considering giving them an earmark or cutting us back, are you?"

"I can't really say at this point. Now I'm mighty pleased with your support; don't get me wrong. It's just that I'm not sure yet how the other Members are going to vote."

Now it's time to play hardball, Kooner figured. He poured the last of the red wine and said in an offhand way, "By the way, I meant to mention that your little boy has your eyes . . . real chip off the old block, I'd say."

Davis choked on his wine. "What the . . . ?"

"He really is a good-looking boy."

The Congressman grabbed his water goblet, took a sip, and tried to clear his throat. "You must be mistaken. . . . I don't know what you're talking—"

Suddenly sirens blared outside the restaurant as three police cars flashed their blue lights and tried to maneuver through the crowded streets. The noise permeated the entire restaurant as patrons stared, and all talk turned to the commotion in front of them.

"What the hell's all that about?" Metcher asked, craning his neck.

Dr. Kooner figured his dinner guest was glad to change the subject. That was fine. He had made his point. The tipping point. He didn't have to repeat it. All he had to do now was wait for the expected result.

50

"Is he dead?" a woman shrieked as diners crowded around the table. Cammy hovered over Ben's body, feeling for a pulse in his neck. She couldn't find one. "Oh my God," she whispered as she stared at the eyes slightly rolled back into his head. She frantically leaned down to check his breathing. Nothing. The waiter pushed through the throng, grabbed a napkin, and held it to the wound, trying to staunch the flow of blood.

"It won't do any good," Cammy choked. "Somebody shot him. The man on the Vespa."

"Vespa? Vespa?" The word echoed through the crowd. "Anybody see a Vespa?" another man shouted. "Somebody call 9-1-1," the waiter called out. "Already did," a man standing nearby said as he shoved his cell phone back into his pocket.

The manager came running out the door and skidded to a stop. "Shot? Somebody shot? Here? Where? Oh no!" He pushed his way through to Ben's chair. "Get him inside. Inside. Now!" he bellowed to the waiter and others who were converging on the scene.

They lifted Ben's body as Cammy reached up to try to close his eyelids.

She was shaking. Her breath was coming in tight little sobs. "He's dead. Some-body killed him. But who?"

Three police cars with blue lights flashing screeched to a halt in front of Martin's. One policeman stayed outside to control the traffic and the crowds, while five others raced inside the restaurant. The first quickly walked to a se-ries of chairs where the waiters had placed Ben's body. Cammy was standing over him as if she were protecting him from prying eyes.

"What's going on here?" the policeman demanded.

"It's Ben. Ben Steiner. He's been shot. He's dead," she said haltingly.

"Where? Here? Inside?"

"No, we were at an outside table. I think he was aiming at me," Cammy sobbed.

"You were the target?" the officer asked, motioning his partner over. "Are you saying that somebody tried to shoot you and not that guy?"

"Yes," she said softly.

"Why you? Did you know the shooter?"

"I never saw him."

"So how do you know he was aiming for you?" the policeman pressed.

The waiter chimed in. "It kinda looked that way to me, too. I saw a guy taking aim. She leans down and next thing I knew *this* guy is blown away."

Cammy felt weak. She shuddered. The waiter grabbed a chair and eased her into it. The officer was taking notes.

"So you saw the shooter?"

"Well, sort of," the waiter said. "But not very well. It all happened so fast."

"What did he look like? Black? White? Tall? Short? What?"

"Um. Not black. But sort of darker skin. I don't know how tall he was. He was on a scooter. Skinny, I think. Not a fat guy. Dark clothes."

"Scooter?"

"One of those Vespa things."

"So he was aiming a gun while he was moving?"

"Yes."

"Must be some kind of sharpshooter," the cop said to his partner. "Okay, so this guy comes along on a Vespa, and he aims at the lady and he shoots the guy," he glanced down at his notes, "this . . . Ben Steiner, right?"

"Right," Cammy answered.

"Then what?"

"Then he takes off," the waiter said.

"Where?"

"Around the corner."

"What corner."

"From Wisconsin around to N Street."

The policeman turned back to Cammy. "So who is this Ben Steiner?"

"He works for me. He's a computer programmer," she said in a weak voice.

The officer took more notes, and the rest of the policemen fanned out to interview everyone else in the restaurant. Cammy stayed huddled next to Ben's body until an ambulance pulled up. Two medics raced in and loaded the body onto a stretcher.

"Where are you taking him?" Cammy demanded.

One medic replied, "Uh, to the morgue, lady. Sorry, but he's gone." He pulled a sheet over Ben's face and again said, "Sorry."

Cammy started to get up, but a policeman stood in her way. "Better stay here, ma'am. There's nothing you can do for him now."

"But I need to take care—"

"They'll handle things. Just stay here. We'll talk about notification in a few minutes. You can help us with that. And I need to talk to you some more about why you think you were the target. First we need to get some other statements. Just stay put for a minute, if you will."

Cammy slunk down into the chair once more. Then she reached into her shoulder bag and pulled out her cell phone. She punched in a familiar number and bit her lip, waiting for it to ring.

"Daniels."

"Hunt, it's me. I can't believe what just happened. Ben's been shot," she cried into the phone.

"Cammy? Ben? Ben who?"

"Ben Steiner. He works for me. We were having dinner here at Martin's. Outside. And this guy comes up on a Vespa, kills him, and gets away. But—"

"Kills him? What the hell? But . . . but what?"

"But he was aiming for me. I know it. I leaned over and, oh my God, there was this shot, and I know it was meant for me, but now Ben's dead."

"Jesus Christ! It's so noisy, I can hardly hear you."

"The police are all over the place. And an ambulance just took him . . . away. . . ." Her voice trailed off.

"Holy shit! Cam, listen. Just listen for a minute. First, are you okay? You weren't hit or anything?"

"No. i'm okay, but Ben—"

"Look. I'm in the car. They're taking me to Andrews. Our flight leaves in a little while. But wait. Stay right there with the police. I'm going to make a call. Cam, listen to me. Can you hear me?"

She got up and edged toward a corner of the room. "Yes, I can hear you."

"Now stay right there. Stay with the police. I'm making one call, and I will call you right back. Right back. Got that?"

She cupped the phone. "Yes, I'll stay here. They'll be here awhile. The place is completely crazy."

Hunt switched on the light at the back of the government sedan and fished out his wallet. He pulled out a card and dialed a number. As he heard the rings, he held his breath. *Be there. Please be there.* Finally, a steady voice answered.

"Janis Prescott."

"Janis. It's Hunt. We've got a development."

"Where are you?"

"I'm on my way to Andrews. But it's not me. It's Dr. Talbot, the scientist I told you about."

"Yes. What about her?"

"She's over at Martin's in Georgetown. She was having dinner with somebody from her office, and this guy comes up on a Vespa, aims for her, and ends up killing her friend."

"Oh my Lord! Is she all right?"

"Yes. Shaken up, of course."

"Of course. But what do you want me . . . ?"

"Look, I know it's late. And I'm sorry to hit you with this, but I wasn't sure who else to call right now. I'm leaving for Delhi in a few minutes and Cammy . . . Dr. Talbot . . . needs protection. Is there any way your people could help us out here?"

There was a short pause on the other end of the line. "The police didn't offer?"

"No," he lied.

"I guess it does sound like strike three, doesn't it?"

"Afraid so. The police can't handle this. I really think we've got some foreign crazy on our hands here."

"And they didn't catch the shooter?"

"No. He got away on the damn Vespa."

"I see. I wish I had more to go on, but under the circumstances . . ."

"Yes?" he said anxiously.

"All right. Can you get back in touch with her?"

"Sure. I've got her cell phone number. Let me give it to you, too." He read it off to the Deputy Director.

"Call her back, and tell her to stay there. I'll have a team on the way shortly. They will escort her home. Where is she staying?"

"Uh, actually she's been staying at my place because—"

"So this is personal?"

"Look, it's personal from the standpoint that I care about her. And I didn't think she was safe back at her apartment. The one they already broke into. But it's official because she's an important scientist working on a classified project and I honestly believe she's the target of a foreign national. And if not a foreigner, at least we know she's the target of somebody."

"True. I'd feel better about this if we had more about her work and who might be involved."

"I'll see that you get the latest from our shop on the Pakistan connection. Or maybe it's Kashmir. We're not sure yet. But there are a lot of people working on this, and I'll make sure you're in the loop on all of it."

"Yes, you do that. I realize you're leaving town. We'll keep an eye on the young lady. And get me that information."

"Will do. And Janis, thanks. I owe you. Big-time."

Hunt redialed Cammy's number. She seemed a bit calmer. She had given another statement and was just about to call General Landsdale to tell him about Ben. She said she was hoping her boss could notify Ben's family.

"Yes, that's a good idea," Hunt said. "Call the general. You shouldn't have to deal with anything else right now. Let's just make sure you're safe."

"How?" she asked plaintively.

"I just talked to Janis Prescott. She's the Deputy at the FBI."

"The FBI?"

"Yes. She's sending a team over there right now. They're going to stay with you 24/7. They'll take you back to the house and watch the place. They'll probably change shifts with another team in the morning. Stay with them, Cam. I'll call you when I can. You still got the secure phone with you?"

"Yes. I've got mine and that one, too. Oh, but I've got Mel's car now."

"One of the agents can take care of that. You stay in their vehicle."

"Okay. But when do you think you can call?"

"I don't know. It's a long flight. We have to stop and refuel at Shannon and then go on to Delhi. India is ten hours ahead of us. So by the time we get there, it'll be late Wednesday afternoon your time, but the middle of the night over there."

"Be careful, okay?"

"Don't worry about me. Just concentrate on taking care of yourself. They'll be some military types who'll be meeting us at the airport to give us the latest. Then I hope we can go to our hotel and get some shut-eye. So anyway, it'll be a while, but we'll connect somehow. Oh, and I was just thinking, if you don't feel like you want to stay in Georgetown, there are other secure locations—"

"No, I'm okay at your place. For tonight anyway." She hesitated. "But come to think of it, this guy must have followed me there . . . and then here."

"You're right. That's what I mean. At least from now on, you'll have protection."

"I'm going to take Mel home from the hospital tomorrow. Maybe I'll stay with her some of the time."

"Fine. That could be okay. Damn, I wish I didn't have this flight. I wish I could be there with you right now."

"So do I. I just can't believe Ben is dead. It's all so horrible." She stopped to wipe her eyes with the back of her hand. "And it's all my fault."

"Your fault?" he exclaimed. "That's what you said about Melanie. Now look, this is *not* your fault. This is the fault of some crazy lunatic who's running around town trying to kill people."

"I know. It's just that if only I hadn't invited him to dinner. If—"

"Stop! Now listen, you're one of the most rational people I know. We're going to get through this, you hear me?"

Her voice caught in her throat. "I know. I'll do the best I can."

"We're going to find this bastard. I've got some more calls to make before we take off. I've got to get more details sent over to Janis and try to get a few more folks working this thing."

"But I can't help feeling that it's not really your problem, it's my problem," she protested.

"Damn sure is my problem. I told you, it's our problem. You've got a piece of it with Q-3—"

"Which worked today," she ventured in a small voice.

"It worked in the lab?"

"Uh-huh." She sighed. "That's why we were having dinner. We were celebrating and . . ." Her voice trailed off again.

"So you locked onto a missile again?"

"Yes, and it was really Ben's input this time that got us . . . oh God! I can't even think about that now."

Hunt paused for a moment. "At least part of the puzzle, your puzzle, is falling into place. So as I said, you've got one piece of this thing, and I've got another piece. I'm just sure that somehow it all fits together. I don't know how . . . yet . . . but I'm sure as hell going to try and find out."

51

Washington, D.C.—Tuesday Night

Jambaz was furious. Not only had he failed in his attempts to steal Q-3 or stop the scientist from working on her project, but there it was: another demand from Abbas Khan to report his progress immediately.

He slumped down at his cluttered desk, turned on his small lamp, and examined the e-mail closely.

At least there was good news back home. Their Lashkar cells were working together on the next missile attacks. If India didn't retaliate to the first strike surely they would react to these. Then Pakistan's generals, who were even more trigger-happy, would respond in kind, and soon the entire region would be at war, with all kinds of missiles flying everywhere.

One problem, a huge problem, kept bothering him. It bothered Abbas Khan as well, which was why he had sent Jambaz to this city in the first place. If the new missile defense technology was completed and India was successful in purchasing it from the Americans, that would be like an ancient battle where both sides had swords, but only one side had shields. He could not let that happen. He had to make sure India never got the shield.

He doubted that the bureaucrats at the Pentagon would allow Pakistan to have it. Yes, they were selling F-16s, but not other sophisticated technology like this. And while Lashkar-i-Taiba wanted Pakistan's government to fall, they had to see that India did not end up the victor. No. They needed a stalemate and onetime elections where they knew they would win a majority in both Pakistan and Kashmir. They would then rule the entire area, control the nuclear arsenal, and be able to force America to do their bidding. He had heard it many times now. But Abbas Khan said it bore repeating so no cell member could doubt the outcome of the grand design.

As Jambaz stared at the message, a plan began to form in his mind.

He had not been able to eliminate this inventor. This Dr. Talbot. She would continue to work on Q-3. Then others would learn to operate it. He was certain of that, and he wasn't sure who they were.

Then he figured out what he had to do.

He simply needed to hobble the company itself. The place where all of the technology, the software, the systems, were housed. Yes, that was it. If he could destroy the Bandaq building they would not be able to focus on producing Q-3 for quite some time. A well-timed, well-placed explosion at an industrial complex, staged at the end of the day when most of the workers had left, could be just the ticket to Paradise.

He remembered that Dr. Talbot and a few others often worked late in that facility. He had been trailing her long enough to learn her habits. And if the blast happened to include just her, all the better for his cause.

He went to his bookshelf and pulled down two files. The first was filled with clippings and summaries of successful attacks by fellow militants in various parts of the world. It was gratifying to go back and read about successful operations. It often gave him new ideas, new insights.

The first articles were about a series of car bombs the insurgents had set off in Baghdad. All were done by remote control. And though the Americans had developed new jammers, the bombs still went off. They were being used everywhere. He underlined the words "remote control" and set one page aside.

He then studied reports about suicide attacks in London some time ago. Many had been killed and injured, but he was not ready to give up his life for Allah. Not just yet. He had more work to do.

His last reference was an old one. It was the story of the huge truck bomb blast that blew up much of the UN headquarters in Iraq back in August of 2003. The explosion had involved thousands of pounds of explosives. He couldn't handle thousands or even hundreds of pounds of explosives. He had to work alone.

He sat back in his chair and visualized his target, an industrial building, surrounded by parkland and woods. One could actually drive a car up to the front door of the building and park in a "Visitor" slot. Yes, that could be done. But it could be noticed. And if he was working alone, how could he park the car, get out, detonate the blast, and make his getaway? No, that wouldn't work.

He thought about the garage with the metal door. He had watched as Dr. Talbot and the other employees had used a card to access that garage. He had even made a note of how much time had elapsed between the entry of the car and the descent of the gate. There might be enough time to drive in directly behind another car, go and park in the center, and then find a way out of the building. Then again, if it was not a familiar car or a familiar co-worker, that could cause concern, too.

No. He would not use a car bomb.

He turned to his second file, the one on explosives. He had studied the effects of dynamite, which might be easy to get but would cause people to ask questions. He read about C-4, the explosive that the military used. That would be hard to get.

Then he thought about his favorite standby, Semtex. It was highly explosive, easy to get, and hard to detect. In fact, the stupid bomb-sniffing dogs had a hard time finding the stuff because it had such a faint odor. And it couldn't be seen on the X-ray machines at airports, either.

It was fairly stable and all he would need to set it off was a blasting cap or piece of detonating cord. The best part of all was that his cell had been storing small supplies of Semtex in several locations for the last several years.

They, along with many other militant groups, had purchased their supplies from Libya and countries in the Eastern bloc. Some of those militant groups had used it in their bombs, and you didn't need much to wreak a lot of havoc. He had heard that a small amount of the stuff had brought down that PanAm flight over Lockerbie, Scotland, so many years ago.

After 9/11, there was a demand to crack down on the big suppliers of Semtex. And that meant that the Czech government had to buy out the company that made it. A company with a great name, he thought. Explosia, based in eastern Bohemia. After that, it got a bit harder to buy from the Eastern bloc. So his cell had simply expanded its contacts in Libya. But then the traitor in Tripoli had caved in and turned from supporter to informer. Good thing they had concluded their purchase long before that debacle.

On Jambaz's last trip to America, he had been given a small block of it just in case it might be needed someday in the future. He had stashed it in a locker at a Greyhound bus station. No one ever checked those things. They were perfect places to keep anything truly important. It couldn't go off. There was no detonator with it. It simply looked like a lump of clay. A simple lump of clay that could be the perfect answer to his prayers.

All he needed now was the perfect delivery vehicle.

52

New Delhi—Early Morning

Hunt reset his watch to local time as the plane taxied to a remote hangar at the New Delhi airport. "I can't believe these ministry guys are going to meet us at two o'clock in the morning," he said, unfastening his seat belt.

"That's the plan," Ted said as he stood up and stretched. "We're here to try and prevent a nuclear war. They can jolly-well meet our plane."

Hunt reached for his briefcase as the other members of their advance team headed for the exit door. When Hunt approached the cockpit, he nodded to the pilots. "Good job, nice flight."

The captain shrugged. "We lucked out on the weather. Pretty smooth all the way. We'll all be at the same hotel, waiting for orders about the next leg."

"We don't know yet how long this is going to take," Hunt said. "If all goes well, we might be able to head over to Islamabad in a couple of days. We'll keep you posted."

As he walked down the steps to the tarmac, a blast of dry air hit his face. "If it's this warm in the middle of night, I'll bet tomorrow will be a scorcher," Hunt remarked to the major from the Defense Intelligence Agency.

"Yeah. Summer gets a head start in this part of the world."

The five team members huddled at the foot of the stairs and watched three men in dark suits approach with outstretched hands.

"Welcome to New Delhi," the first one said, shaking hands with Hunt. "I trust your flight was a good one?"

"Yes. Yes, it was. Thanks. I'm Hunt Daniels and this is Ted Jameson. We're with—"

"Yes, we know. The National Security Council." The Indian official turned to greet the others from the Pentagon, State Department, and CIA. "We will retrieve your luggage and, if you'll follow me, we have several cars here to take you to your hotel. We have some briefing papers prepared that you may wish to review before our meetings tomorrow."

"Good of you to arrange all of this at such a late hour," Hunt said.

"This mission is of the utmost importance to our country, Colonel Daniels. We are all anxious to get peace talks under way with the Pakistanis and lay the groundwork for the arrival of your Special Envoy. We are pleased with the President's choice of Senator Farrell. We know of his expertise in these matters."

Three black Mercedes sedans were parked off to the side. Their drivers began loading luggage into the trunks. "We brought three cars so we could split up and have more space for the drive to your hotel," the Indian explained.

"Thank you," Hunt said. "We appreciate that."

Ted had his overseas cell phone in his hand. He turned to Hunt. "Can I borrow your phone for a few minutes? Mine needs to be recharged, and I want to check in with my wife. I'm still trying—well, you know how it is."

Hunt had thought about trying to call Cammy, but he knew Ted was concerned about his domestic situation. He handed over the phone. "Sure. I'll make my calls later."

Ted dialed his number while the Indians were clearing the group through Customs. He talked for a few minutes, slapped the phone shut, and walked over to Hunt. "Great news. I can't believe this."

"What?" Hunt asked, shoving his passport back into his pocket.

"Remember how we've been trying to have a kid, but then we had all those problems?"

"Yeah."

"Well, my wife just got word that she's expecting a baby. She wants to come back."

"Hey, congratulations," Hunt said, slapping his colleague on the back.

"The doctor was on the other line, so she asked if I could call her back in a few minutes."

"Keep the phone. Call her from the car. No problem."

"Thanks," Ted said, a wide grin spreading across his face.

The Indian officials and members of the advance team got into their assigned vehicles and headed out of the airport. The little motorcade made its way through sparse traffic and out onto the highway.

Hunt was trying to listen to his counterpart outline the series of meetings that would take place in just a few hours. But he hadn't slept well on the plane and could hardly keep his eyes open. He had been too focused on Cammy. The idea that she was some terrorist's bull's-eye was gut-wrenching right now. He knew the FBI teams were good. They'd keep an eye on her. At least he had pulled that off. For now. But they couldn't shadow her forever.

He had made several quick calls to contacts at the Department of Homeland Security before he left, and he'd had a long talk with the CIA agent on the flight over. He knew that everyone was looking for this Jambaz Muhammad Sharif, if that was his real name. He also hoped the local police were looking for a slightly dented black Volvo and a Vespa in Georgetown. *Fat chance they'll ever find either one,* he thought as they sped down the highway toward the city.

His Indian host was saying something about new intelligence regarding an Islamic militant group based near the Line of Control in Kashmir. Hunt blinked his eyes and tried to concentrate.

They had pulled up behind the other two Mercedes at a stoplight when suddenly a gigantic explosion sent shock waves, shards of glass, and pieces of twisted metal up into the night sky. Smoke and flames engulfed the trio of cars as a truck swerved to avoid the conflagration. Gas tanks erupted into fireballs, and two cars coming from the opposite direction screeched to a stop. Their drivers jumped out and raced toward the ugly inferno.

53

The White House—Wednesday Late Afternoon

"How in God's name did those bastards know when our people were arriving?" the President barked into the microphone in the Situation Room.

The hastily arranged videoconference showed images of the Secretary of Defense and National Intelligence Director on the screen, while Austin Gage, the National Security Advisor, and Stockton Sloan, the Deputy, flanked the president at the long mahogany table.

"I believe the State Department put out an itinerary," the Defense Secretary said in response.

"What kind of morons are running their press operation anyway?" the President asked, skewering his NSC Advisor with a piercing gaze.

The unflappable Austin Gage responded, "The Secretary of State is in Africa, as you know, Mr. President. His press operation was undoubtedly trying to tout our overtures to the Indians and Pakistanis to come to the bargaining table."

"They can tout all they want, Austin. But they *cannot* put lives in danger. They publish schedules and look what happens. A car bomb blows up the best of the best." He turned to face the screen once more and addressed the Intelligence Director. "What do we know about the attack? Has any group claimed responsibility yet?"

"Not yet, sir. But the Indians are saying it could have been the Pakistanis. Then again, they're always trying to finger the Pakistanis."

"But you have a different take on this?" the President pressed.

"Yes, sir. The Paks have been running scared ever since that cruise missile strike. They swear on a stack of—no, wrong analogy . . . they swear that they had nothing to do with that missile, and they're already sending in word that they had no part in this car bomb, either. They keep issuing denials, but I'm not sure Delhi is buying."

" 'A man convinced against his will is of the same opinion still,' " Austin intoned.

The President gave Austin a sideways glance, "I'm not sure this is the time for pithy quotations, but I take your point. The Indians must be controlled."

"You're right, sir," Stockton Sloan said. "Does that mean you're still going to send Farrell over there?"

"Hell yes, I'm going to send him," the President replied, "that is, *if* we can get our collective press secretaries to shut up about his whereabouts."

"If I may," Austin intervened. "If we do send a Special Envoy over there, by definition it's a high-profile mission with meetings arranged between the Indians and the Paks. That's the whole point. And we can't control *their* press operations."

"I know that," the President snapped. "But we sure as hell can ask them to be careful about it." Everyone made notes as the President continued. "About our men. Have their families been notified? I need to make calls."

Austin consulted his notes. "We haven't been able to contact all of them, sir. I'll let you know as soon as we've tracked them down. Until then, we're not releasing any names. Not of the man killed or those injured. Nothing. We have to get to the families first."

"Well, let's hope we can at least keep that part buttoned up properly," the President said. "This is a real tragedy. Big goddamn tragedy. We send our brightest men over there to work on a peace process, and they get themselves blown to smithereens."

"I couldn't agree with you more, Mr. President. Our people are scouring Delhi for clues to this thing," the Intelligence Director said. "They feel pretty certain that it wasn't the Paks, but one of the Islamic groups. They have a few allies right there in India, you know. Muslims who are more loyal to their religion than they are to their homeland."

"Yes, I know. Keep looking and keep me informed. Losing this man is like losing a member of my own family. I'm not only mad about it. I'm damn mad."

"Of course, Mr. President. We're all in agreement on that score. We'll keep you updated throughout the weekend."

"All right. Now as for Farrell." The President turned to Austin. "Get ahold of him and tell him that his mission is still on. And tell him that if we can get something down on paper, we'll try our damndest to get all the parties to sign it at the Taj Mahal ceremony that's coming up." He turned to look up at the screen. "Are you both in concurrence with this?"

There was a slight pause. Then the Secretary of Defense spoke up. "I'm on board with the Farrell mission. We have to try to stave off some sort of retaliatory attack. The situation in Islamabad is quite unstable right now; with the President grabbing more power, the opposition is screaming. Then you've got the ISI refusing to carry his water and sympathizing with some of the militant groups. So all in all, a volatile mix. Our channels to their military are open, but there's dissension in the ranks. Bottom line . . . let's get Farrell over there to calm things down. If he can talk the Indians out of any sort of retaliation and get the talks back on track, maybe the Paks will simmer down and regroup."

"And the Taj Mahal ceremony?" the President prompted.

"I'm not so sure about that one, sir. You see, they've already invited a number of world leaders, and if the militants could get even close to that place, well, you can imagine."

Austin turned and spoke firmly. "Mr. President, if I may. I can certainly see that a celebration of that magnitude could become a target. However, before he left town, the Secretary of State emphasized that it would be a perfect venue for a signing ceremony. His point was that with most of the world watching, India and Pakistan would have to live up to their bargain."

The President sat still for a moment. "I'll take all of that under advisement. Right now I want updates from the CIA on the probable identity of these attackers." He then faced the Defense Secretary. "I want your boys to get me the latest numbers on the size of the arsenals in both India and Pakistan, force levels, and nuclear capabilities. And Farrell will need a complete briefing before he heads out." He then swiveled his chair to face Austin. "And about those families. Let's get to them ASAP. I need to make those calls."

"Yes, Mr. President," four voices echoed through the room. "But sir, one more thing," the Intelligence Director said, an anxious look on his face.

"What is it?" The President could see the man's image on the screen along with that of his deputy handing him a note.

The National Intelligence Director reread the note and looked up aghast. "I have just received word from our contacts at ISI that of the three cruise missiles that were stolen, we know the first one had a conventional warhead. That's the one that's already been launched in Jammu and Kashmir. . . ."

"Go on," the President said.

"Our people are now saying that of the two remaining, one is also conventional, but the last one may have a biological warhead."

54

Georgetown—Wednesday Late Afternoon

Flames engulfed the cabin. Engines screamed. The plane spiraled down and morphed into a car hurtling down even farther into a ravine. She tried to stop it, tried to see who had sent it crashing over the edge. But she couldn't make out the shadowy figure behind the wheel. Then he was taking aim. Right at her.

Cammy jerked awake and opened her eyes. Another horrible nightmare. *They're getting worse,* she thought. *What time is it anyway?* She groped for the digital alarm clock on the bedside table. 3:10. In the afternoon!

She lay there for a long while thinking about the dream. It was one she'd had before. The first part anyway. The part about her father's plane going down. The pictures of the fire and the engines had plagued her for years. She couldn't shake them. And lately the image of her car crashing down the hillside and the man with the gun had been added to the mix.

When would it stop? When would she ever be able to sleep peacefully again? When would it all be over?

She hadn't been able to sleep at all last night. After the agents had brought her back to Hunt's home, she had still been shaking, reliving the awful moment when the gun went off and Ben slumped in his chair. She shuddered again at the image and knew that she wouldn't sleep. She couldn't sleep. She had stayed up reading most of the night, only dozing off as the first rays of morning light had filtered through the venetian blinds at the bedroom windows.

Then she was aroused by the alarm she had set for nine o'clock. The general had told her to take the day off, which was just as well, since she had to go down to the police station and answer more questions.

She had called Melanie to tell her about Ben. Mel had been so shocked, she could hardly speak. She finally was able to say how sorry she was and how Cammy had to be careful and just concentrate on staying safe. Then Mel explained that there had been some delay in getting her paperwork squared away and she wouldn't be discharged from the hospital until later that afternoon.

Cammy had come back to the house, and the agents had thoughtfully suggested that she try to get some rest. They assured her they'd be right outside. So she had lain down just to take an hour's nap.

She never took naps. Not since she was thee. But today was different. She was different. Everything was different. She felt vulnerable and scared, and she was running out of options. She peeked through the blinds and felt somewhat reassured when she saw the FBI car right outside the front door.

She headed into the shower, washed her hair, and went through the ritual of blow-drying it, applying a modicum of makeup, and pulling on a pair of beige slacks and a matching sweater.

She hadn't eaten since last night, and even though she still wasn't very hungry, she figured she should try to fix something. She checked the refrigerator, found some eggs, tomatoes, and cheese, and put together a quick omelet. She poured a small glass of orange juice and sat down at the kitchen table, the same table where only yesterday she and Hunt had enjoyed a cup of coffee together.

Hunt. The mere thought of the man brought a wistful smile to her face. He had been gone less than twenty-four hours, and she missed him already. He hadn't called. And she had no idea when he'd be back. She thought again about the strange entry on his calendar. "Get NK BA FLD TS." It still didn't make any sense. But whenever he did call, she could hardly ask him about something she saw when she had stolen his password. It probably wasn't anything important anyway.

She finished her omelet, cleaned up the kitchen, set the security system, and headed out the front door to join the agents waiting at the curb. "Where to, ma'am?" one asked.

"I have to go over to Sibley Hospital to pick up a friend, if you don't mind. She's being released today. Oh, and since one of the other agents . . . who helped me last night . . . since he brought back my friend's car, do you think one of you could follow us and take her car back?"

"Sure thing. Hop in."

Cammy told the driver about the accident with Melanie as well as the break-in at her apartment and how the burglar had stolen her computer. He already knew about the shooting in Georgetown. He listened carefully but offered no observations except to say he and his partner would be with her 24/7. She thanked him but then sat there wondering how much longer she could receive such personal attention.

When they arrived at the hospital, one of the agents went upstairs with Cammy. She pushed through the door. "Hi, Mel. This is Mike," Cammy explained. "He's with the FBI. Are you ready to go?"

Melanie was dressed and perched on the edge of the bed. "Just about. One of the nurse's aides said she'd be by with one last form I have to sign. Why don't you both sit down for just a minute? We can check out the news or something."

Melanie aimed the remote at the TV set and churned through the channels until she found CNN. Cammy and the agent settled into a pair of folding chairs and began to listen to an interview with a professor explaining how we should expect another ice age because the cycle of warm ages and ice ages had gone on for millions of years and we were due for a change.

Suddenly the anchor cut off his guest, looked directly into the camera, and announced, "We have a breaking story about an attack on a group of Americans in India. We now switch to Fakhruddin Venkatanaman, our correspondent in New Delhi."

"Thank you, Rojas. A car bomb exploded near a motorcade carrying an American advance team from the New Delhi airport to their hotel just an hour ago and—"

Cammy shrieked and Melanie cried out, "Oh no!" The agent stared at the screen and muttered, "Sons of bitches! Would you look at that."

"Quiet . . . listen . . . ," Cammy implored as Melanie turned up the volume.

"It was a three-car motorcade carrying American representatives from the White House, the Pentagon, the State Department, and the CIA. Other motorists in the area are telling CNN that there were casualties. We are working to identify those killed or injured. No group has claimed responsibility for the incident—"

"Incident?" Cammy implored. "Incident? Was it Hunt? Was he a casualty?" she screamed at the set.

The agent turned to stare at her. "What? You know those guys?"

"Yes!" she wailed. "They just left last night."

"Who left last night?"

"Hunt Daniels from the White House."

"The White House?" the agent asked, incredulous.

"Yes. It's his house."

"Whose house?"

"The house where I'm staying."

"You live with this White House guy?"

"For now. . . . My God, Mel . . . do you think?" The CNN cameras were panning the entire area where cars were still smoldering, and a small crowd had gathered although it was still the middle of the night in India.

Mel got off the bed and went over to hug her friend. "Oh, Cam. I can't believe this. First you . . . us . . . then Ben . . . now Hunt?"

Cammy walked nervously to a side table, grabbed a Kleenex, and wiped her eyes. She stared back at the TV set and held up her hand as a command for silence. The reporter continued, "We have word that several bodies have been recovered from the motorcade and a series of ambulances transported other members of the party to nearby hospitals. For reaction in Washington, we now switch to our White House correspondent."

The image of an attractive dark-haired woman standing on the North Lawn of the White House came on the screen. "A senior administration official has just confirmed that the President held an emergency meeting with his National Security Advisor, the Secretary of Defense, and the National Intelligence Director on this attack in New Delhi. There are now three confirmed dead and numerous others injured. Names will not be released until notification of their next of kin. The President will be calling the families of the dead and injured shortly. The President has vowed to work with the government of India to find and prosecute those responsible for this latest attack.

"Meanwhile, plans are going forward for the mission of the Special Envoy named by the President just last week. A spokesman for the National Security

Council emphasized the President's determination to bring India and Pakistan to the bargaining table to negotiate an end to hostilities in the Kashmir region and restore trade and transportation. He went on to say that America will endeavor to defuse a volatile situation between two nuclear-armed countries that have fought three wars since receiving independence in 1947. Reporting live from the White House, this is Carmelita Morales for CNN."

Cammy sat transfixed by the pictures on the screen while she nervously twisted the strap of her shoulder bag. "I've got to call the White House," she announced, scrounging in her purse for her cell phone.

"Right," Mel said anxiously. "Call Hunt's office. They'll tell you what's going on. They have to know."

Cammy dialed the number and waited. And waited. Somebody must be there. Somebody had to be there. Three more rings and finally a voice said quickly, "Colonel Daniels' office."

"This is Dr. Cameron Talbot. I'm a friend of Hunt Daniels. Can you tell me if he's all right? I mean, in New Delhi? The car bomb? Have you heard if he's . . . ?"

"I'm sorry, ma'am. We don't have any information for you at this time."

Cammy heard other phones ringing in the background.

The aide sounded harried. "I just can't help you right now. Can you check back later please?" There was a click, and Cammy's face fell.

"They don't know anything."

"Or they aren't talking," Mel ventured. "No. I mean, you heard the report. They haven't notified the families. But Cam, wait; did Hunt tell you how many people were going over there?"

Cammy held the cell phone in her hand and stared at it in stunned silence for a long moment. "He said it was a team. Five. I think he said five. There was a friend of his from the NSC and then some others from the agencies. I think that's what he said."

"Okay. Okay. So there was a group," Mel said. "And there were three cars and drivers and probably some people meeting them. So that's a whole bunch of people, right? And sure they said there were three people killed. But three out of how many? He's probably okay. Think about it. The odds."

Cammy shook her head and glanced back at the TV screen, where they had switched back to the scene in New Delhi. Small knots of bystanders were being interviewed. They were describing the explosion, the fire, the quick response by Indian police. But nobody knew anything about the people inside the cars.

A nurse's aide opened the door and said with a cheery smile, "Here we are, Miss Duvall. All the paperwork is in order. Just sign here, and you can go home now."

Melanie, Cammy, and the agent were still focused on the TV screen. The aide said, "Excuse me, Miss Duvall, are you all right?"

Melanie turned around, a look of profound sorrow on her face. "I guess so. But would you do me a favor?"

"Certainly. What do you need?"

"Could you get a couple of Tylenol or something?"

"No problem. I'll be right back."

"Are you still getting headaches, Mel?" Cammy asked absently.

"No. It's not for me. It's for you."

55

Washington, D.C.—Wednesday Late Afternoon

Bubbling water spilled over the side of what looked like a gigantic cup atop the white marble fountain. The architect, Henry Bacon, might have been reading the Twenty-third Psalm when he drew the design. It cascaded down in three waterfalls intersecting a trio of sculptures, classical figures symbolizing the Sea, the Wind, and the Stars. A larger pool collected the water below and spread it in a circle surrounded by a stone ledge. A perfect place to relax and survey the scene that was Dupont Circle on a lazy afternoon.

A young man ambled out of the Kramerbooks store and into the Starbucks Coffee shop by the entrance to the Metro station. He bought two iced espresso caffe mochas and headed across to the Circle. He walked past groups of students in shorts and T-shirts lounging on the grass around the fountain and watched as they read textbooks and argued the finer points of philosophy and political science.

He found an empty chess table, one of many around the periphery where young and old could wile away a warm afternoon kibitzing or playing the ancient sport of kings.

He loved this game. After all, it was invented in India by a sixth-century philosopher. Back then it was called Chaturanga and symbolized a battle between four armies, each controlled by a different Rajah or King. Over the years, it had evolved from four players to two, and he was looking forward to challenging his contact today in this friendly setting. He had decided that meeting out in the open like this would be safe. After all, if he had something to hide, he certainly wouldn't be arranging a meeting in such a public place. At least that was the image he was striving to project.

He had been carrying a briefcase along with the two cups. He gingerly placed the espressos on the edge of the chessboard, sat down on a bench, put the briefcase next to his knees, and waited.

Two blocks away, a Minister emerged from the Chancery of the Indian Embassy on Massachusetts Avenue. Built in 1885, it was the oldest property owned abroad by the government of India. He was proud to be working there, proud to have an important office in the four-story granite and limestone building along Embassy Row. The Indian flag of red, white, and green horizontal stripes fluttered overhead in the breeze as he headed down the stairs and turned left.

He walked a few blocks, scanned the Circle, and spotted his collaborator. "A glorious day, is it not?" the Minister said as he settled on the opposite bench.

"Indeed it is. And since it is warm, I brought you an iced espresso."

"Ah, good. Very good. Thank you, my friend. It is good to get away from the office and reflect. Especially since the car bomb that killed two of our people."

"Yes, a real tragedy. Was it the Pakistanis?"

"They are denying it. This time, for once, we are inclined to believe them because there would not be a good motive for them to blow up an advance team trying to set up peace talks."

"Unless they don't want peace."

"You make an interesting point. It is still very tense in Delhi. All the more reason to get ready in case all this talk of peace goes nowhere."

"I agree. Absolutely."

"Of course, we already have a number of weapons on alert, and some excellent new technology. But the Defense Ministry was positively ecstatic to receive Magellan. Our people are already incorporating the software and advanced details you so carefully provided."

The young man took a sip of his caffe mocha and set up the chess pieces. He enjoyed receiving praise for his work. He had risked a lot to provide these materials to the Minister, and he wanted to prolong the encounter. "Are you up for a game today?"

"Yes. It is time to take a break from a difficult week," the Minister said, helping to arrange the board. "You begin."

The young man picked up his King's pawn and moved it two spaces to e-4 and said, "You were talking about technology just now. I was very pleased to see the announcement about *Chandrayaan I*."

"Yes indeed. Our very own spacecraft that will go to the moon in just a few years," the Minister said proudly, as he took his Bishop's pawn and moved it from f-7 to f-6.

"With all that is going on in our Motherland, I have been thinking that our scientists would undoubtedly have developed a version of Magellan on their own."

"Perhaps. But with your help, we have been able to save much time and money. You have no idea how much your efforts are appreciated in Delhi." He lowered his voice almost to a whisper. "And I assume you are ready to hand over the boomerang?"

"I have it right here under the table," he murmured as he studied the board.

"I am amazed that you were able to procure this for our country. Absolutely amazed."

"Let us just say that I was able to be in the right place at the right time."

"I must admit that I am excited. The fact that we are working together to transmit this most important project to enhance the safety of our country is . . . how shall I describe it?" He paused. "Very gratifying. Gratifying indeed. I almost feel like a boy with a new gift."

"Where did you grow up?" the young man asked.

"In the old Bombay. My father always took us away in the heat of the summer, though. And I remember one year when I was about ten years old, he took me to Kashmir."

"Ah, Kashmir. I, too, have visited the mountains there, the Pir Panchal."

"Yes, they are so beautiful. I remember we first went to Srinagar and stayed on a houseboat on Dal Lake. It was so cool, like a tonic."

"I've been to that area, and I'll always remember the colors in the highlands."

"The colors? You mean the way they changed?"

"Yes. In the morning the mountains looked like light violet. Then as the sun moved overhead, they became purple and bronze. But as evening came, I saw the setting sun turn the peaks into orange snow."

"Majestic indeed. And I remember the trees. The birch and the Himalayan spruce," the Minister said.

"Now that I think about it, with the trees and the mountains and the lakes, it looks a little bit like Lake Tahoe. Have you ever been out there?"

"No, I am yet too new to this country. I have heard of it, but I doubt if their Lake Tahoe has our red bear and our snow leopard."

"I'm sure you are right. The Americans have no idea of the beauty of Kashmir. In many ways, it is better than Switzerland."

"I couldn't agree with you more. Remember your history lessons and what the Mughal Emperor said about Kashmir, 'Gar bar-ru-e-zamin ast, hamin ast.' "

The young man chuckled and nodded his head. "Of course. 'If there is paradise on this earth, this is it.' It is all of this that we are fighting for, you know."

"Absolutely," the Minister said. "We must fight, and we must win."

The man picked up his Queen and moved it from d-1 to h-5. "Speaking of winning, that's Check!"

The Minister stared at the board and laughed. "A good game, my boy. Good game, good coffee, good conversation, and . . . ," he glanced under the table and reached for the briefcase, ". . . a good day."

He got up from the table and smiled broadly. "You have done admirable work here, my friend. And you do not think anyone will discover your . . . ah . . . cooperation with your home country?"

"I do not think so. I have been extremely careful."

"Good. Very good. We shall not meet again for a while. We wouldn't want the authorities to detect any special relationship." The Minister shook hands, turned, and carried his secret cargo out of the park.

56

Washington, D.C.—Wednesday Evening

IN HONOR OF THE HONORABLE STEPHEN P. KRAMER,
MRS. RICHARD S. McMILLAN
REQUESTS THE PLEASURE OF THE COMPANY OF
THE HONORABLE DAVIS METCHER
AT DINNER
SEVEN O'CLOCK

Davis glanced at the invitation again as he tossed a few papers in his brief-case and headed out his office door. He was going to be a bit late. Members of Congress were always late for dinner parties. They had the excuse of having to cast votes on the floor and attend prior receptions. Everybody knew that. Everybody expected it.

However, all the other guests would arrive at exactly seven fifteen for a seven o'clock event, unless it was an invitation to the White House. In that case the cars would line up before the appointed hour and everyone would alight and walk up to the North Portico at precisely the specified time, like racehorses at a starting gate.

This dinner was in Kalorama, a small but very prestigious area of the city. And while many of these affairs were boring as hell, this one might prove to be useful. After all, it was being given by the widow, the very rich widow, of a Detroit industrialist who had been a major donor to the Party. In exchange for his generosity, he had been named Ambassador to Belgium. Unfortunately, the old guy had died a few years back. But fortunately for the Party's sake, the widow, Adelaide McMillan, had remained in Washington and become the reigning doyenne of the social scene. And she had continued to donate to the cause.

Davis was glad she had stayed in Washington. But that was no surprise. Everybody who had any kind of important position in this town stayed here when the job was over. There was a cultural archaeology in the nation's capital. When Congressmen were defeated, they simply joined a law firm and kept the same house. They never even considered moving back to their districts in Nebraska or Alabama or Missouri. It wouldn't be nearly as exciting as Washington, D.C. Not even close. Unless they had to go home to campaign for higher office, they stayed. They all stayed.

As for the dinner, not only would Davis be able to pay homage to the widow McMillan, but he would have a chance to make some points with Steve Kramer. After all, what good was an event if you couldn't score some points? Steve was being honored because he was the new Chairman of the Senate Armed Services Committee, the previous Chairman having suffered a heart attack just a few weeks ago.

Yes, the evening could be useful, Davis thought, as he motioned to his aide to bring the car around. He could tell Steve that he had just about finished his markup of the defense bill and make sure that they were working off the same sheet of music.

And he could play nice with Adelaide. Hell, she might even kick in a few bucks to his campaign coffers. So tonight might also be a profitable one for his agenda. And whenever anybody went anywhere in Washington, even to a nice little dinner party, he always had an agenda.

Davis's driver headed through town and up Massachusetts Avenue to Twenty-fourth Street, where he turned right and then left to the McMillan address. Davis noticed that several other cars were parked near the house, their drivers quietly reading the paper or sipping coffee while they waited the requisite two and a half hours for the dinner to conclude. At least there was plenty of parking available. Good thing it wasn't time for those damn prayers at the mosque down the street, because then nobody could find a parking place anywhere in this neighborhood.

A butler in black tie opened the door before Davis had a chance to ring the bell. *Those guys must be watching out the window,* he thought, as he stepped into the luxurious foyer with its marble floor and entry table supporting a massive vase of orchids.

"Congressman Metcher, at last!" Adelaide McMillan exclaimed as she welcomed him into her spacious living room. "You were so kind to accept my invitation tonight . . . and to come alone. You are the most gracious extra man to have at my table. And tonight I have you seated next to my cousin from Brentwood. She's recently divorced, and I assured her that you would be a most charming dinner companion."

So that's it, he thought. *Oh well, no problem.* Brentwood was good. Lady must be rolling in it. Besides, as he looked around the room, he realized that he had made the A-list, or at least the A-minus list. An A-list dinner party would have included the Secretary of State and maybe even the President. But this President rarely went to local dinner parties. He preferred to have a few friends in to the White House. That way he was always in control and could go to bed early if he felt like it.

As Davis surveyed the room, he saw Janis Prescott. Interesting that the Deputy Director of the FBI would show up. She was usually so tied up with terrorists, white-collar criminals, and God knows who else, he rarely saw her out on the town. On the other hand, maybe she just needed a break.

He saw the former White House Counsel in the corner chatting up Russell Matthews, the Senate Majority Leader. The Counsel was no longer in his high-level job. But since he was now ubiquitous on the cable news shows as an analyst of every kind of legal question, he was still invited to all the good parties.

Over in another corner Davis spotted Richard Fairbanks and his wife, Ann. Fairbanks had been the U.S. Envoy to the Middle East and had actually been shot at, so he always had good stories to tell.

In Washington, no one invited individuals to dinner parties. They invited job descriptions. If you held a high-ranking job in the White House, you were invited to everything. If you were a Member of Congress with tons of seniority, you were asked to most things. If you were an Ambassador, well, it was catch-as-catch-can. After all, the name of the game was power. Power, proximity, and access. The center of power was the White House. An

Ambassador's power and access were back home. No proximity. Too far away to impress anyone here.

Of course, if Ambassadors represented really important countries like Great Britain or Russia, that was okay. In fact, that meant they were pretty interesting. Most of the other Ambassadors only met the in-crowd when they gave their own receptions on their National Days. That's when the White House and State Department were obligated to send a bunch of people to attend.

He remembered back during the Cold War days when the Soviets would have their National Day celebration, like our Fourth of July parties, and the White House had to send someone. But they would send only one very low-ranking NSC staffer to the event. Nobody wanted to draw that ticket, so they sort of rotated the dubious honor.

A few Members of Congress would show up and make an effort at détente, but they never stayed long, because all the Soviet boys ever served was six kinds of vodka and a bunch of jellied veal.

Davis figured that the dinner tonight would be a damn sight better than that. As if reading his mind, a waiter walked up and held out a tray of crab cakes with a remoulade dipping sauce. Davis grabbed one and popped the whole thing in his mouth.

Another waiter stood silently with a silver tray lined with glasses of champagne, chardonnay, and Perrier. Davis shook his head, looking for something stronger as he swallowed the hors d'oeuvre and turned to his hostess. "I'd be delighted to meet the lady from Brentwood. Always good to learn what's going on in Hollywood country."

"Yes, well, she's not one of *those*, you know," Adelaide said with a laugh.

"No. If she's related to you, I wouldn't think so."

"You'll be seated next to her at dinner, so of course you'll want to talk with others during cocktails. And I see you wish something besides champagne or wine?"

"A scotch and water if you have it," he said.

"Naturally." She motioned to the waiter and whispered Davis's request. "Now then, I'm sure you know everyone, so I'll leave you for now. I must get back to the front door."

He turned and walked toward Russell Matthews, the Majority Leader of the Senate, who was standing beside the large Steinway where a pianist was playing a Cole Porter song.

"Evening, Russ," Davis said, extending his hand. "Good to see you here tonight."

"Oh, Davis, hello. Yes, nice shindig here for Steve."

"Sure is. Lady throws a good party. So how do you think Steve will do as the next Chairman?"

"He'll do just fine. He's already up-to-speed on the defense bill. We were just talking about it. I hope you boys are able to reconcile a few things. The President wants his whole package, you know."

"Yes, that and then some," Davis said.

"So I've heard. Well, try to work it out with Steve. I assume you've got your Committee on board, and a majority in the House."

"I've sent out the usual 'Dear Colleague' letters about a few things. But yes, I've got it under control." He wanted to appear organized and powerful, especially in front of the Senate Majority Leader. After all, he had been thinking about running for the Senate in two years when one of the Maryland seats might open up. And it wouldn't hurt to have old Russ know that he was on top of things and a good team player.

A waiter appeared with his drink as another waiter offered a tray of smoked salmon canapés on black bread with chive cream. Davis took two.

He turned and chatted with the former White House Counsel and his wife and noted that they were about the same age. *Must be a first marriage,* he thought. That was fairly unusual for this crowd. Davis wondered how the man stayed interested. It was all he could do to stay interested in the pretty young ones he was dating these days.

He thought about Roxy and the job she was doing in his office. She wasn't very well organized, but he had his AA to keep track of everything. His Administrative Assistant was first-rate, had been with him since his first run for Congress. She really kept the place humming. He never messed with her. She was too important to screw around with. She knew it, too. They understood each other.

Roxy was a different story. He had only given her a job because her father made a personal request. And it was hard to turn down one of your major donors. So there she was, sitting at the desk right inside the door to his office, answering the phone and greeting the inevitable throng of constituents who poured through the place asking for help on God knows what. Everything from human cloning to a flag-burning amendment. At least the girl had a nice smile.

She had a few other nice attributes as well, he thought, as he remembered taking her back to his house on the Hill last night. She had been most obliging. Most obliging indeed.

He checked his watch and realized that it was seven forty-five. This meant that his hostess would be seating her guests pretty soon. Since the evening was scheduled to start at seven, and since no proper hostess ever extended the cocktail hour beyond the proper forty-five minutes, he could usually plan these things to arrive in time to get a drink, maybe two, check out the best people to talk to, but not get bored by having to stand around too long before the main event.

As predicted, Adelaide walked up to announce, "Dinner is served."

He followed her into the formal dining room where there was a long table for fourteen guests set with an ivory cloth reaching to the floor, ivory napkins, and a long, low centerpiece of spring flowers surrounded by votive candles, so everyone could talk across the table and not have a whole forest in front of them.

He found his place card and saw that the cousin from Brentwood was at least fairly attractive, even if she was a bit older than he might have preferred. On the other hand, she was probably rich as Croesus. And for that he could overlook a membership in AARP.

He stared down at his plate, where he saw a delicate soup bowl containing something that looked light green, with a slice of cucumber floating in it. He had no idea what it was.

He flashed a warm smile at his dinner partner. "So how are things in Brentwood?"

"Oh, we get by. We are in a bit of a pickle, though. Deficits and all of that," she said.

He noted what must be a five-carat diamond job on her right hand and figured she didn't have to worry about it personally. "Yes, we deal with those things all day long here in Washington. Major difference is that your state government is supposed to balance its budgets. We never seem to get around to doing that here."

"You talking about the deficit over there?" the guest of honor asked. "Here we are at this lovely dinner party, and we're already discussing our problems on the Hill."

"Oh, I love to hear about what's going on in Congress," the cousin urged. "Do tell me what you're working on."

That's all any of them needed to begin their usual friendly debates. It didn't take much encouragement. After all, they were doing the people's business. What could be more interesting then that?

Senator Kramer looked down the table and announced, "First of all, we're terribly shocked by that attack on our team in New Delhi." There was a murmur around the table. Even though the event had been announced just hours before this gathering, everyone knew about it because everyone who was anyone had the news on all day long, lest they be caught unawares in an important conversation.

"Shocking," Adelaide said. "Absolutely shocking. Do we know who did it?" she asked, employing the Washington "we" used by all insiders.

"Not yet," the Senator replied. "But I hear the President is mad as hell about this one and is promising to find them, come hell or high water." Whenever anyone could quote the President, he did so, especially at a dinner party.

"Here, here," the others responded.

"And speaking of troubles overseas," the Senator continued, looking directly at Davis, "how about the defense bill, ole boy?"

"Ready for markup," David assured him. "We just have a few small items to add."

"Add? My Committee is subtracting this go-around."

"Which items in the President's request are you going to subtract?" Davis inquired.

"We all want to support the President and especially our troops." Everyone nodded. "But there are a few things we can do without. At least this year. For example, the legislative affairs team from the White House has been paying me a visit. I expect they've hit you up, too, lately."

"Right you are," Davis responded. "I've had a call or two. I hear they're pretty keen on this new missile defense technology."

"New technology?" the cousin asked.

"Yes, pretty clever scheme. Takes over missiles, redirects them, and all that sort of thing," Davis said, waving his soupspoon. He whispered to his dinner partner, "By the way, what is this?"

She replied in a low tone, "It's grape and almond gazpacho. We thought it would be different."

"Yes, it is," Davis replied.

"That new technology from Bandaq sounds like something we should be funding. Don't you agree?" the Senator asked.

"I'm not sure we have the money for it," Davis said casually.

Janis Prescott cast a glance down the table. "I've heard about that technology, too. Seems that it's so effective that a number of other countries would like to get their hands on it." Then she added, "Of course we wouldn't sell it." Everyone nodded.

The Majority Leader intervened. "I'm sure we can find some other programs we can cut to make way for this new one. How about that, Steve?"

"Actually, the White House staff put together a pretty good list of recommendations. Tops on my list are the blimps."

"Blimps?" asked the former Counselor and current CNN analyst. "Trade blimps for missile defense? Sounds like a slam-dunk to me. Old versus new and all of that."

"Sounds reasonable," Russ said. "And if it's coming from the White House, and it means we can stay within our numbers. I'd call that a done deal, right, Davis?"

Oh boy. What now? He could hardly argue with the Senate Majority Leader, the Chairman of the Senate Armed Services Committee, and a TV commentator to boot. What the hell was he going to tell Roxy? It was her old man's company that built those blimp things and wanted that appropriation.

Then he reflected on his other problem. What could be a big-time problem with Sterling Dynamics. Those boys not only wanted to keep their R & D appropriation; they also wanted to knock Bandaq out of the box. And the bastard had the gall to threaten him with blackmail. Well, maybe it wasn't a direct threat, but it was a pretty goddamned big hint.

He'd been stewing over that one all day. He thought back to when it all had happened. Sure, the little page was cute. Sure she had come on to him. And sure, she had been hard to resist. But hell, he should have been more careful. He thought she was eighteen. She looked about twenty. He was shocked to find out she was only seventeen. Then he about had a heart attack when she calmly informed him she was pregnant.

He wasn't even sure it was his kid. But he had decided to do the honorable thing for once. He set up accounts for her and the boy. She had quit shortly after that and left town.

Now with Kooner making noises about the boy, Davis wondered how in hell he had found out. Washington was a sieve when it came to gossip and intrigue. Everybody knew that. But as he analyzed the situation, he finally decided he wasn't about to cave in to blackmail.

So he made a decision. He'd go along with the funding for Bandaq and leave Sterling's numbers alone. As long as they got a few contracts, they'd stay afloat. And what would be the point in Kooner going to the press about a piece of ancient history? What point indeed?

Davis paused for just a moment as a waiter removed his soup dish and placed a plate of rib lamb chops and steamed asparagus spears with a yellow pepper coulis and a grilled peach in front of him. He was grateful for the lamb. The rest of it might be colorful but wouldn't be very filling. It seemed that all of the hostesses around town were still trying to go with the low-carb thing at these dinners. And when he left one of these affairs, he always felt like stopping at McDonald's.

He turned to face the Majority Leader. "I think you make a very good point, Russ. Now that I think about it, the amounts for those two programs were about the same. So a switch would just about wrap it up."

"Well, I'm glad we settled that," Adelaide said with a smile. "Now I'd like to know what you all think about the renovations at the Kennedy Center and that new wing for the Corcoran that had to be canceled."

Davis knew about the Corcoran Museum. They had planned a modern addition to a classic building right across from the White House. He was glad it had been canceled for lack of funds. He always thought the plan, with its strange billowing walls, looked like a typhoon had blown through a sheet-metal factory. *Better not comment on that one*, he thought. *The cousin might have called it a modernist masterpiece.*

The rest of the dinner progressed with amiable conversation about new concert halls and the recent visits of the Japanese and Russian delegations.

Janis Prescott told a story about how some Russians had behaved on the first state visit of General Secretary Gorbachev back in the eighties. It was long before the Berlin Wall came down, before many of their people had been allowed to travel, and before their economy had improved.

It seemed that some of the FBI agents escorting them around town had taken them into Brooks Brothers, where they marveled at all the clothes that were available. They couldn't speak much English, but they all kept uttering one word, "Leemits? Leemits?"

The agents finally figured out that they were asking what the "limits" were to purchasing socks and shirts. When told there were "no limits" and they could buy as much as they wanted anywhere in America, they were positively stunned. Everyone loved that story.

Davis leaned back in his chair as the waiter cleared his dinner plate from the right and served a dish of chocolate mousse from the left. At least he'd have something sweet for dessert, although he would have preferred a nice slice of apple pie, preferably with ice cream on top.

He finished the mousse in three bites while he listened to the Brentwood cousin declare that she was enjoying Washington so much, she just might prolong her stay. Oh, great. Now he might have to go through this routine all over again. He glanced at his watch and saw that it was nine fifteen. He still had some cabernet left, so he raised his wineglass as he exchanged a glance with his hostess. She nodded imperceptibly, so he pushed his chair back and stood up.

"Ladies and gentlemen, I'd like to propose two toasts this evening." He turned to Adelaide. "First, to our most gracious hostess, who always brings together good fellows for good fellowship. We thank you for a wonderful evening."

"To Adelaide," they all said in unison as they sipped what was left of their wine.

Turning to Senator Kramer, Davis cleared his throat, enjoying his moment as the center of attention. "And to our guest of honor on the occasion of his becoming the new Chairman of the Senate Armed Services Committee. I know that the good Senator shares the wish articulated by President John F. Kennedy when he said, 'Let every nation know, whether it wishes us well or ill, that we shall pay any price, bear any burden, meet any hardship, support any friend, oppose any foe, to assure the survival and the success of liberty.'" He raised his glass. "To our liberty and your leadership." *There. That should make an impression,* Davis thought to himself as he sat down.

Everyone murmured, "Here, here."

The Senator rose to respond. "I wish to thank my colleague from the House and my hostess as well for this most delightful dinner. And on the subject of protecting our liberty, I, too, would like to give you a quote. It is from Thomas Jefferson, who said, 'Government big enough to supply everything you need is big enough to take everything you have . . . The course of history shows that as a government grows, liberty decreases.' And so I pledge to you tonight, that while I will work hard to maintain a strong defense, I will also keep an eye on your pocketbook," he said with a wink.

Everyone tittered and murmured their approval as they raised their glasses in a toast to the new Chairman.

The hostess rose from her chair and invited her guests into the living room for coffee. This always gave people one more chance to mingle and follow up on points they might want to make before the evening was over.

Davis held the cousin's chair and escorted her to the front room. Two waiters held sterling silver trays covered with demitasse cups of decaf coffee with tiny silver spoons, along with cream and sugar. The trouble was that the sugar bowl was filled with those little sugar cubes and tongs that looked like they belonged at a child's tea party. Davis could never make the damn things work quite right, so he took his coffee black.

He wished he could have had a nice steaming mug of real java. Oh well, Roxy would make him some first thing in the morning. Roxy. Jesus. What was he going to tell her? Of course, he didn't have to answer to his receptionist. On the other hand, he was kind of enjoying her talents these days.

He wondered if her daddy would pull her off his staff when he heard the bad news. No, he wouldn't be that dumb. He would figure that as long as she was in there, he had a shot at next year's appropriation. Yes, that's what he'd think. And that meant Roxy could stay for a good long while.

At nine thirty sharp, the guests began to bid their farewells. As they were moving toward the door, Davis found himself standing next to Janis Prescott.

"Janis, you made an interesting comment at dinner about other countries being interested in Bandaq's technology. I didn't know that word had gotten around already."

"Oh yes, it most certainly has," the Deputy said.

"Well, I hope to God they never get it."

57

Rockville, Maryland—Thursday Late Morning

"Excuse me, ma'am," the FBI agent said as Cammy was about to get out of the car.

"Yes?"

"Here. We'd like you to carry one of these," he said, handing her a small black device.

"Oh, a walkie-talkie."

"It's got a pretty good range. We thought it would be a better way for us to communicate, so you could let us know when you might be going out or heading home. If you'd just keep it with you, we could talk whenever we need to."

She dropped it into her purse and pushed the door open. "Thanks. I'll have it right on my desk."

"It has a clip there for your belt in case you leave your office," the agent advised.

"Oh, sure. I'll keep it close. And thanks again for the ride." She slipped out of the car and pushed through the front door.

Cammy gave a halfhearted wave to the receptionist, walked over to the security box, heard the door click, and went back to her office. She was feeling depressed, running scared, and constantly looking over her shoulder to see if a black Volvo or a Vespa was on her trail. She had also been watching the encrypted cell phone, willing it to ring, praying for a call from Hunt. A call that never came.

The only time she had turned it off was during Ben's funeral earlier that morning. It seemed as though everyone in the entire company had shown up. The ceremony was mercifully short. She had barely been able to keep her composure as she saw Ben's parents shaking with grief. Theirs had been a warm, loving family. A mother and father who had lost a son because of her. Sure, Hunt had said it wasn't her fault. It was the fault of a crazed terrorist who was probably after anyone working on Q-3. Still. She couldn't let go of the lingering guilt that taunted her memory of that awful night at Martin's.

As she sat down at her desk, she let her thoughts drift back to an earlier hour on Tuesday. The time when she had heard that piercing tone indicating her computer had a lock on a simulated incoming missile. It had been like ear candy. She had thought about the phrase from the Old Testament, "Make a joyful noise unto the Lord."

Then she remembered being told the phrase that was always uttered in the Jewish faith when you hear that someone has died, "Baruch dayan emet." "Blessed be the one true Judge." Would they ever find the man who had murdered her young protégé? Would he ever be caught and brought before a judge?

She sat down at her console and spent an hour going through some reconstruction exercises. She was using muscle memory, just rote routines. She stopped a few times and told herself she had to get a grip. If she could just concentrate on her calculations, maybe she could shut out the memories, the mourning, and the magnitude of all the other problems she faced.

The shrill ring of the telephone made her almost leap out of her chair to grab it, only to realize it was an office line and not the encrypted phone. "Dr. Talbot."

"Cammy, it's me," Melanie said. "Listen, can you stop by for a minute? I've got something to show you."

"I guess so. I can't seem to keep my mind on my work today." She clipped the walkie-talkie to her belt and trudged down the hall to Mel's office, wondering what was making her sound so chipper on a day like this.

"I'm still amazed you wanted to come to work today, Mel," Cammy said as she hovered in the doorway. "You should be resting."

"No. I'd rather be here. I'm fine, really. Besides, I have such a stack of stuff on my desk, I've got to get caught up." She motioned to a pile of newspapers and clippings. "Here. Read this. The best news of the day," she said, handing Cammy an article from *The Washington Times*.

She glanced at the page. "We got it?" Cammy asked, her voice rising. "It says here we got the funding for Q-3."

Melanie came around from behind her desk and pointed to a small paragraph. "Yep. See? 'A key member of the House Armed Services Committee said late last night that they will give Bandaq a line item in the defense budget.' Of course, the entire bill has to get reconciled with the Senate version and be signed. But right now, you're looking good. Metcher came through. Can you believe it?"

Cammy sat down in a chair next to the desk and read the short article again. "This is amazing. I knew the general was doing some lobbying. And Hunt said he was trying to get the White House to help. But to get it this quick . . ."

"Hunt?" Melanie inquired. "No word yet, huh?"

"No. And I just don't understand it. I've tried to call his office several times, but I keep getting the runaround. I mean if he's still alive, maybe he's hurt. Maybe he's in a hospital somewhere. But if he is alive, why hasn't he called? Why don't we know anything?"

"I don't know. It sounds like they couldn't find the family of the ones who were—"

"I guess. It's just that the waiting is so hard."

"Of course it is," Mel said. "Look, I'm working on a couple of press releases here. Why don't you take a break and go get some coffee or something. It's almost lunchtime anyway. I'll finish up here and be down in a few minutes." She glanced at Cammy's waistband. "What's that?"

"Oh, that's the walkie-talkie the agents gave me so we can always be in touch."

"With the cell phones and all that stuff, you look like a RadioShack outlet. At least you won't have any problems telling them when you're leaving, right?"

"Sure. And they can get to me if anything happens outside."

Melanie frowned. "You mean if some bad guys show up?"

"Who knows? But I was just thinking that I'm glad we work in a three-story building."

"And not in some high-rise?"

"Yes. I guess 9/11 sort of eliminated skyscrapers as good office space, wouldn't you say?"

Melanie sat down at her desk again, shuffled some papers, and said offhandedly, "Yeah. Kind of the way the French Revolution killed satin for men."

"And on that note, I'm out of here," Cammy said. "See you in a while."

Down in the cafeteria, Cammy put a small fruit salad, a carton of yogurt, and a glass of iced tea on her tray, paid the cashier, and walked over to a small table. "Mind if I join you?" she asked. "Mel's coming down in a minute."

Raj Singh looked up. "Not at all. I could stand some good company on a somber day like this. With the funeral and that attack in India . . . any word from your White House friend?"

"Nothing yet," she said, unloading her tray. "But at least there's one small piece of good news today."

"About the funding? Yes, I saw the item. That really is good news. Has the general said anything?"

"I haven't seen him yet today. But I'm sure Melanie told him all about it. He'll probably come down and celebrate or something."

"Yes, probably."

"You know, with everything that's happened, I haven't had much chance to thank you for all your help in my lab the other day."

"I was happy to be of service," he said quietly. "And now I have more to do on my side of the building. We're working on fine-tuning our detection and timing devices. We'll be busy on the upgrades for many months, I'm sure."

Suddenly the double doors to the cafeteria burst open and six agents wearing dark blue jackets with the letters FBI emblazoned across the back strode into the room.

"Oh my God!" Cammy exclaimed. "They didn't use the walkie-talkie. What could be going on?" She stared as the group made their way across the room. They were walking right toward her table.

All conversation in the cafeteria came to a stop as every employee sat still, watching the agents move through the room. Cammy recognized two of the agents as members of her morning team. She jumped up from the table and ran over to them.

"Joe? Mike? What's going on? Is there trouble outside?"

"Afraid not, ma'am. Not outside. It's inside. Would you identify Dr. R. P. Singh for us please?"

"Raj? He's right there. We were having lunch and—"

"Please step aside, ma'am."

Raj stood up from the table and looked around the room. The general was walking through the doors. Melanie was right behind him. General Landsdale rushed to the table and confronted the lead agent.

"What's happening here?" he demanded.

The agent ignored the question and spoke directly to Raj. "Dr. R. P. Singh?" Raj nodded.

"Come with us please."

"Wait a minute!" the general bellowed. "I'm the boss here. What the hell is going on?"

A second man took Raj by the arm as the first agent addressed the general. "Sir, I am Special Agent Joseph Frisby, and I have orders to arrest Dr. Singh on suspicion of transferring classified information to a foreign power. Information that impacts on the national security of the United States."

"What?" the general shouted. "Raj Singh? He's my employee."

"He may also be a traitor, sir."

Cammy stared at Raj, who stood stoically in front of her. "Raj, what? What are they talking about?"

Melanie raced to his side. "Raj? Raj? What's this about? What are they saying?"

One of the agents hooked a pair of handcuffs on Raj's wrists and started to lead him away.

"Wait just a damned minute," demanded the general. "I want an explanation. Do you have evidence that this man transferred information? I mean, what information? What evidence?"

"We can't discuss those details here, sir. We have to take him in. But we do have this." The agent pulled a piece of paper from his pocket and handed it to Raj, who took it in his manacled hands. Raj read the first paragraph and handed the paper to the general. Then he turned to Melanie. "I'm the one who told *The Washington Post* about the first failures in order to throw off others who might try to steal the technology." He turned his head to gaze around the room at the stunned employees gathered around the spectacle.

"*You* leaked that first story to the *Post?*" Cammy whispered. "I thought it was Metcher."

The general had been reading the first paragraph of the subpoena. He looked up at Raj, dumbfounded. "I can't believe this. You're charged with transferring the satellite system and Q-3 to India? You *took* them from us? You *spied* for another country while you were working here?" He waved his arm in a wide arc and shouted, "From here? Our project that was meant for the *protection of the United States of America?*"

His words echoed through the cavernous room. No one said a thing. Cammy stared. Raj stood mute. And a tear began to roll down Melanie's cheek as she closed her eyes in pain. The eerie silence was punctuated only by Raj's heavy breathing and Melanie's now muffled sobs.

58

Rockville, Maryland—Thursday Afternoon

"Hunt!" Cammy screamed into the blue cell phone.

"Yes, and I'm really sorry I couldn't get to you sooner, but—"

"I was so worried," she said breathlessly. "Are you all right? Tell me. Where are you? What happened? What about everybody else?"

"Hey, slow down. Take it easy. First, yeah, I'm okay, but it's been absolute hell over here."

"I can imagine. The news reports about the car bomb. They said three people were killed."

"The bastards set off the bomb, probably by a cell phone or something, and they had it all set to explode when we were stopped at a light."

"Oh no!"

"The bomb went off right under the middle car. And remember I told you about the guy I work with at the NSC, Ted?"

"Yes. What about him?"

"He was killed," Hunt said.

"Oh my God."

"He was such a good guy. Smart, team player."

"Have you talked to his wife? Where is she? Maybe I could—"

"That's one reason all of this took so long. She had gone to visit her mother, and they couldn't find her right away. They put a blackout on the whole thing. They finally got to her just a little while ago."

"Have you talked to her?"

"Just got off the phone. I had to make some other calls before I called you. You see—"

"That's okay. I understand. Don't even think—"

"And that's another thing. About the phone. When we got to the airport, the first thing Ted asked was whether he could borrow my cell phone. He wanted to call his wife, and his battery was low. We were in different cars, so when his was blown up, well, everything was blown up."

"But did he get to talk to her?"

"Yes. You see, they had separated, but Ted was trying like hell to put things back together. Turns out she had just found out she was expecting a baby. They had tried for years. Anyway, she had decided to come back. They were going to work it out. But that's the last time she heard his voice."

"Oh, the poor woman. Do you think I could talk to her? Go see her? Something?"

"That would be a nice gesture. But I think she's still at her mom's. Family's gathering around."

"Sure. Sure."

"But tell me about you," Hunt said.

"Me? I'm surviving. That's not the point. You still didn't tell me what happened to you with the car bomb and all."

"It was pretty horrific, I gotta say. When it went off, the pieces of Ted's car hit the rest of us. We got out just before the gas tanks lit up. Then we tried to get Ted and the other guys out, but everything was on fire. They never had a chance."

"The news said there were three."

"Yeah. Ted, an Indian Defense guy, and their driver."

"Didn't you say there were five people on your team? Where were the others?"

"The DIA guy was in my car, and the other two were in the lead. Ted was the only one alone with our host."

"But were you hurt?"

"Just some cuts and bruises. But as soon as the police showed up, they took all of us to a hospital and kept us there, doing tests and all sorts of bullshit. Finally our guys from the embassy got us out of there. But the phones, our luggage, my briefcase, everything was pretty screwed up. So this morning we regrouped and had a meeting and coordinated with the White House about the Special Envoy and all of that."

"What's going to happen now? Do they know who set off the bomb?"

"Not exactly. Nobody thinks it was the Pakistanis. So the Indians aren't about to lob anything in their direction."

"Thank God for small favors," she said.

"In fact, with the cruise missile attack and now this, the Paks are saying it has to be one of the separatist groups, and they're promising to work with the Indians to find them. So we've got that going on. And they're also saying they want to get the peace process going, so we're working out the details for the Special Envoy."

"You're dealing with all of that right after almost being killed?" she said in an astonished tone.

"That's why I'm here, remember?" he answered. "But now tell me, what's happening back there?"

"We all went to Ben's funeral this morning. And just now, you can't believe what happened."

"Raj Singh?"

"You knew? How could you know?"

"Remember I said I had to make a couple of calls?"

"Uh-huh."

"After I talked to Ted's wife, I got ahold of Janis, and she told me several things."

"About how they were going to arrest him?"

"Yes. She said that our guys have been keeping an eye on a certain Minister at the Indian Embassy. They also picked up some calls from a pay phone at Union Station. Calls to New Delhi."

"From a pay phone? I didn't know they could do that," Cammy said.

"They can do a lot of things you don't know about. Hell, they can do things I don't know about. I'm sure of that."

"But Hunt, it was so awful when they took him away. They put handcuffs on him. And now a bunch of agents are going through everything in his office. God, I just can't believe all of this. I mean, he was working with *me* on Q-3, and then he gave it away. He said he was doing it to protect his country."

"At this point, they probably need some protection. But not that way. Besides, do you think somebody over here could actually make it work? Don't they have to be trained or something?"

"Well, yes. They'd have to figure it all out. They do have a lot of scientific types over there, though."

"But, it would take a while, right?"

"Of course. I'm still working on a few things myself, but I think I've got a pretty good handle on it."

"That's what I thought. How's Mel taking all of this?" Hunt asked.

"She's devastated. She was really in love with him."

"Guy must have been pretty smooth."

"What do you think will happen to him?"

"I have no idea. We're pretty tough on espionage cases."

Cammy paused, leaned back in her chair, and stared at the ceiling. "At least you're all right. You have no idea how—"

"I know. Look, I'm sorry about not getting through. Oh, wait a minute, I almost forgot. Janis told me something else. She said that they may be closing in on this Jambaz guy and his membership in that Lashkar group."

"Really?" Cammy said, sitting up straight. "That would be so incredible. I mean, with the break-in and the crash and Ben . . . I've been feeling like I'm in some crazy human video game, but that lunatic has the controls all to himself."

"That's a pretty good description."

"Do they really think he's the one that killed Ben?"

"Not sure yet, but they've been working with the security people at every university in town along with the D.C. police. Evidently, the Pakistani Ambassador has been pretty helpful, too. She thinks they're going to find him pretty soon. I'll keep you posted."

Cammy let out a long sigh. "That's got to be the best news I've heard in ages. Oh, there was one other bit of good news today."

"Tell me. I could use some."

"Looks like we're going to get our funding from the Hill."

"That's great," he said. "I knew you'd pull it off. The technology is just too good to pass up. And on that score, I've got one more idea."

"What's that?"

"With all the talk about trying to get everybody together at that Taj Mahal shindig, the Indians are going ballistic about trying to protect it."

"I can imagine," Cammy said.

"They're starting to deploy their forces all around New Delhi and Agra—"

"Agra?"

"That's where the Taj is."

"Oh."

"And not only troops. They're trying to set up whatever missile defense batteries they've got in the country. It's kind of a mad scramble to get their act together."

"Can they really protect it?"

"Not if the terrorists are bent on blowing it up with those cruise missiles, which nobody has found yet."

"Oh Lord."

"But I've got an idea. I need to get to Austin."

"Austin Gage?"

"Yep. It's just a crazy thought at this point, but stay tuned."

59

Rockville, Maryland—Thursday Afternoon

He was grateful for the good weather. Allah was smiling upon him today, he thought as he parked his car just off a dirt road adjacent to the nature preserve. Jambaz opened the trunk and took out his new toy. The wings were in pieces he could easily put together later. They wouldn't fit in the trunk fully assembled. He gingerly placed them on the ground while he reached inside to retrieve his canvas bag containing all the other items he would need to complete his mission. He locked the door, pleased that everything operated in spite of the dent on the right side of the car.

He hadn't wanted to go to a body shop. Too much attention. Too many problems. He had decided to drive the car just as it was.

He slung the canvas bag over his shoulder, stooped to pick up the model and wings, and headed into the woods. He walked quite a distance until he reached a clearing, the one he had found on a previous surveillance.

He had already staked out this place. He had driven all around it and planned his approach with meticulous care. He figured he was just about the right distance away from his target, in a place where he could get a good line of sight to his prey and yet be protected on three sides by trees and bushes.

He had plenty of time. He could put everything together, make sure he had completely mastered the controls, and take some practice runs. The fact that the sun was shining and the wind was not blowing meant the conditions were perfect.

The FBI team was parked outside of the Bandaq building, sharing a thermos of coffee. "Hey, Joe, look over there," Mike said as he pointed toward the forest.

"I'll be damned. Looks like fun, doesn't it?"

"Yeah. I remember I had one of those when I was a kid. Used to fly it with my dad. Course mine was a damn sight smaller than that baby."

Joe peered through the windshield. "Sure is a big sucker. Wonder how far it flies?"

"Some of them can go a bunch of miles if they've got enough fuel. I heard there was this one model airplane called the TAM 5 that some guy actually flew from Newfoundland to Ireland."

"You're shitting me!"

"No, really. Like I said, I had a little model a long time ago, and so I've sort of kept up with those things. And that TAM 5 job was so cool, the way it stayed up."

"How the hell did the guy get it to fly so far?"

"I don't know exactly, but I read an article about it. Guess it was pretty fancy. He was able to keep radio control the whole way."

"Must have been a blast."

"Yeah. Don't have time for that stuff anymore, though. Not with this duty."

Joe turned on the ignition and pulled away from the parking lot. "Guess it's time to make the usual rounds."

"Yep. Let's drive around the complex. We never seem to find anything, but we've got our orders to keep an eye on the place. The whole place." As they turned toward the back side of the building, Joe watched the model plane fly around in circles and then disappear back toward the trees.

Cammy sat at her keyboard going through a compartmentalization routine. She had decided to go back and review her files, starting at the beginning of her research on the simplest systems, noting which computer programs and algorithms worked best. They were in the process of copying and automating many of the routines she had developed. She just wanted to be sure she hadn't left anything out along the way.

It was a long, slow process because there were so many different types of guidance systems. That meant there would be many different ways to invade and lock onto them. She had asked the new head of the radar and satellite division to stay tied into her system so she could incorporate their signals into her programs. She had to make sure that another operator, a commander in the field, for example, could call up the proper program to handle any expected attack.

There were programs for the very simplest of systems and other programs for the more sophisticated missiles that were being manufactured overseas. She had been working all day, and she was getting tired. But she wanted to stay and wrap up this first batch of programs even if it took her another couple of hours. She focused on the screen again and hit a few more keys.

Melanie was giving a tour and a mini-lecture at the same time. Seven young girls and two little boys gathered around her desk as she explained how she wrote press releases on her computer and sent them out to the wire services, newspapers, radio and TV networks. This was "take your children to work" day, and her job was one that seemed to fascinate these kids. They loved the media. Most said they wanted to be *on* television. But a few said they'd rather *control* what went on television or in the papers.

Spending her day shepherding these children around the building helped take her mind off the awful events of yesterday. The terrible reality that the man she loved might be a traitor to her country.

She focused on the eager young faces and talked to them about the importance of education. She told them to work hard in school and cultivate their dreams because, as she saw it, there were basically three kinds of people in the world. Those that make things happen. Those that watch things happen. And those that stand around and say, "What's happening?" The kids all laughed and said they wanted to be in the first group.

Melanie then passed out tablets and pens and showed them a DVD about Bandaq's latest satellite system. She asked each child to write a press release about what they had just seen. She explained that they should first figure out what headline they would like to read in the morning papers and then write the release so they'd have the best chance of getting that headline in print or the story on the air.

They sat on the floor in a circle and got to work. Melanie had told their parents she would handle this group for a while. She was happy to be surrounded by so many smiling faces for a change.

The two agents drove their staff car around the building once more and turned onto the road that paralleled the parkland. "Hey, look. Isn't that a car over there?" Joe said.

"Where?"

"Way over there kind of hidden in those bushes. See it?"

Mike squinted into the late-afternoon sun and replied, "You mean the black . . . oh shit!"

Joe gunned the motor and headed across the asphalt to the little dirt road that led into the woods. He pulled up behind the car, which was partially hidden by bushes and a tangle of vines. "It's a Volvo."

"And the right front bumper is all caved in. Holy shit. Call it in."

Joe grabbed the phone and dialed his headquarters. "I think we've got the black Volvo . . . yeah . . . yeah, that one." He read off the license plate while Mike went over to try to open the door. It was locked. They didn't need to break in to figure out they might have the missing car. The very car that every agent in town had been searching for.

"Get us some backup. Guy's gotta be around here somewhere. . . . yeah . . . right across from Bandaq. I'll tell the general right now." He listened to a series of orders and relayed them to his partner.

"Call the general on your cell. I'll get Dr. Talbot on the walkie-talkie."

"Dr. Talbot? We have a situation here. You may be in danger. We think we've located the Volvo . . . yes . . . black Volvo . . . here across from the building . . . he's gotta be around here someplace. Get away from your windows. Is there a secure area in the building?" He listened as Cammy caught her breath and listed some of the best places to go.

Joe heard a strange sound off in the distance and looked up.

"Oh no, oh no." He called into the walkie-talkie, "Dr. Talbot. Scratch that. Don't stay inside. Get the hell out of there. Now!"

60

Rockville, Maryland—Thursday Afternoon

"Why do we need to leave?" Cammy protested. "With our security system, nobody can get in here."

"Nobody has to get in there. Looks like something else is heading your way. And it's lookin' like trouble," the agent said as he scanned the sky and saw the model plane head slowly out of a bank of trees hundreds of yards away. "Now listen to me," Joe said firmly. "I'm giving an order to evacuate the building. I said evacuate!"

Mike was on his cell phone, giving the same message to the general, "Get your people out of there, General! . . . Why? . . . We're not sure, but there's something mighty strange going on here. I am ordering you to get your people out . . . now!" He hit the END button and turned to Joe, who was now shouting into the walkie-talkie.

"Look, Dr. Talbot, this is not the time to argue . . . it's . . . it's . . . I know this sounds crazy, but right now I am looking at a very large, very strange model airplane that is heading right for your building."

"Did you say a model plane?" Cammy asked.

"Yes, I said a model plane."

"What's it doing up there?"

"I don't know what it's doing up there, and I don't know what it's carrying . . . but it's not right and . . . wait a minute . . . I can't tell, but it looks like it's got a box strapped on top of it."

He turned to Mike. "I don't believe this! Look at that thing. It's moving slowly, but dead-on to the building."

Melanie was giving a tour of the kitchen in the cafeteria, showing another group of girls how their staff prepared lunches for several hundred employees When she heard the sound of the fire alarm, she stopped. *What could that be?* she wondered.

Then the general's voice came across the speaker.

"This is General Landsdale. We have an extreme emergency. All employees are to evacuate the building immediately. Repeat. Evacuate immediately!"

The girls looked scared. "What's going on?" one asked excitedly.

"I don't know, honey. Some kind of fire alarm, I guess. Don't you have those in your school?"

"Yes," they all said at once.

"Well, I guess we'd better follow orders. I'm sure your moms and dads are upstairs. C'mon, we'll find them."

Melanie started to herd the girls out of the room but saw that one was missing.

"Where's Stacey?" she asked the others.

"She had to go to the bathroom," one answered.

"Where? Which one?" Mel asked. The girl pointed to the back of the room. Melanie ran toward the ladies' room and called over her shoulder, "You girls head to the elevator. I have to find Stacey."

The speaker sounded again. "Evacuate *now!* I said get out now. No one is to remain in the building. Out . . . now!"

Joe saw dozens of people . . . men . . . women . . . and several children . . . streaming out of the building. "Good God, they've got kids in there." He shouted into the walkie-talkie once more, "Everyone else is getting out. Please, Dr. Talbot, get out while you can."

"You said it was a large model airplane . . . radio controlled . . . right?"

"That's how they do it. Radio. That's not the point. Just get out."

The agents jumped from the car and headed toward the woods. Maybe they could find him. Maybe they could find the radio and stop the contraption. But they didn't know where to look. It was a huge area, and he could be anywhere.

"I'll take the right!" Mike shouted as he drew his gun and ran.

Melanie pulled open the door of the rest room and shouted, "Stacey? You in there?"

"Mmm-hmmm," uttered a small voice. "I'll be out in a minute."

"We don't have a minute, honey. I need you right now."

"Oh, okay," the child said, flushing the toilet and opening the stall door.

Melanie rushed over, gathered the girl in her arms, and ran toward the elevator. She shouted, "Push the button. Push the button."

At that moment, the elevator doors opened and anxious parents poured out and grabbed their daughters. "Melanie, we have to get out," one father ordered.

"What's happening up there?" Melanie asked, hustling them all back into the elevator.

"I don't know," he said. "Let's just pray we get out in time."

The general dashed into Cammy's office and saw her pounding the keys on her computer while three screens jumped to life. "What the hell are you doing? Didn't you hear the order? Get out of here!" he demanded.

She didn't look up. She hit more keys as she concentrated on the second screen. "Can't."

"Can't?" he shouted. "We've got minutes, if that. What in God's name are you doing?"

Her hands were flying, sending a staccato of clicking sounds bouncing off the walls. "It's radio controlled. Early iteration. Simple," she mumbled, as a small image appeared on the screen.

"It could destroy the building and everyone in it," he said as he tried to grab her shoulder.

Her walkie-talkie beeped again. The general grabbed it. He heard Joe shouting his orders again. He was saying that the little plane had almost reached the periphery roadway and was beginning its descent. He was screaming now. The general held the receiver out so Cammy could head the agent's voice. She ignored it and hit one more key.

A piercing sound emanated from the computer speaker. "I've got a lock!" she cried triumphantly. "Where are they?"

"Where are who?" the general roared.

"The agents."

The general called into the walkie-talkie, "Where are you? . . . In the woods? . . . Trying to find the radio?"

Cammy shouted, "Get them out of there! I'm sending it back!"

The general stared at the second screen and watched in awe as the projectile hovered and then began to turn at an angle. "Joe, get out of there. The plane's coming back. . . . No. . . . Just listen to me. . . . It's Q-3. . . . Cammy's got a lock on the radio-control mechanism. She's turning it back. . . . Back to where it came from . . . get out of the woods."

Jambaz craned his neck and stared at the model plane. It had stopped moving. It was hovering. He looked down at the remote control. He hit the key and then hit it again. He aimed the device up in the air toward the model plane. It wouldn't respond. It still hovered.

He clutched the control, raised his hand, and waved it toward the plane as he pressed it again and again. No forward movement at all. *Batteries? No. Low fuel? Can't be. Frequency problem?* He stared at the black box again and jiggled a dial. Still no response. He couldn't believe it. He had built the model according to all the instructions. He had planned. He had practiced. Now, suddenly it was stalled.

He studied the plane and saw that it was beginning to turn around. *No. No. It can't do that.* He pounded the little box once more and then he began to panic.

Joe turned and started to run. He radioed Mike. "Where are you?"

"Looking for the radio. I think I see a clearing."

"Get your ass out of there. Talbot's pulled another one of her tricks. She's sending the plane back."

"She's what?" Mike exclaimed.

"You heard me. Get out of there. Look up. Can't you see it?"

"What the devil?"

"It's coming your way. Get back here, on the double. Did you ever see the guy?"

"I thought I saw something, and I was about to close in . . . ," he said breathlessly.

"Well, now the damn plane with whatever payload that bastard has strapped on top of it is about to return to Mama." He could hear Mike's heavy breathing as he ran through the woods. Joe hoped to God the man could run fast enough.

Cammy keyed in another code and the plane turned 180 degrees and headed back toward the woods. As soon as the general saw where the plane was headed, he got on the intercom and hit a button on the phone that broadcast inside the building as well as through speakers at all the exits. "To all Bandaq employees, this is General Landsdale. Do not, I repeat do not, move across the road toward the woods. We have a dangerous situation here. Stay back. Move to the other side of the building and take cover."

The employees who had gone out the front door were standing together on the sidewalk, staring at the sky. When they heard the announcement, they started to run to the side. The others who were in the back parking lot raced to a pair of delivery trucks and crouched down as they watched the plane change course.

Mike came running out of the woods and saw Joe next to the car holding a pair of binoculars. "What do you think?"

"I think we've got a maniac who's figured out how to strap a bomb on the top of a piece of balsa wood."

"Oh God. How big is it?"

"Not sure. Maybe big enough so it could have blown up the whole building."

"Holy shit."

"Backup should be here soon. I called Fire and Police, too. Hope they get here in time for the fireworks."

The plane flew in a straight line from the roadway across the trees and began a downward path. The agents watched in grim fascination as it headed toward the ground.

The explosion rocked the car. Flames erupted from the woods, and the blast propelled entire tree trunks into the air like so many matchsticks.

"Holy Christ!" Joe hollered as he raced around to the front of the car. "Okay, let's go." The two agents ran toward the blast, guns drawn.

"You don't think the bastard survived that one, do you?" Mike said as they sprinted through the trees.

"I doubt it. But we've got to find out."

They stumbled through underbrush and downed tree limbs. They got to the scene and had to stop as a bank of bushes burned in front of them. "No way he could have survived this."

"Unless he saw that it was coming back."

"I wonder. I suppose if the guy was smart enough to know about Q-3, he was smart enough to know how it worked." Joe scanned the area. "He could have figured out it worked like a boomerang, dropped the radio, and split."

"Where?"

Joe waved his arm. "Who the hell knows?"

They heard sirens in the distance. " 'Bout time," Joe said. "We could use a little help here."

"If he's in there, we'll find him," Mike said confidently.

"You're right, buddy. Dead or alive, he's all ours."

61

The White House—Friday Morning

"May I see a photo ID please?"

Cammy fished in her purse, produced her driver's license, and handed it to the uniformed guard in the small white building lined with windows. He checked his computer, smiled, and handed her a laminated pass on a long silver chain.

"Just hold that up to the machine over there. The one with the White House photo."

She followed his order, realizing that the machine must be registering the time she entered the White House grounds. She figured there would be a similar machine to keep track of when she left. *Clever,* she thought.

She then put the chain over her head and heard the guard say, "Please keep that pass visible at all times, ma'am."

"Sure will. Thanks."

"And would you put your purse down here, and step through the metal detector, please?"

At least this is quicker than airport security, she reflected, as she picked up her shoulder bag and walked through the door of the Northwest Gate. She proceeded up the driveway toward the entrance to the West Wing. She had never been to the White House, and she wondered if it would be like scenes in the old TV show *The West Wing*. In that one, everything looked so big and everyone looked so busy. The people were always making policy walking up and down the halls. She wondered if they did that in the real White House.

A smartly dressed military guard was standing at attention at the door. When she approached, he said "Good morning, ma'am," turned, and opened the door for her. She stepped inside and approached the reception desk. She was again asked for an ID, and while the woman was checking her log, Cammy glanced around the room. She noted a large painting of Washington crossing the Delaware. She scrutinized the picture and wondered why the artist had painted a woman riding in the boat. She made a mental note to ask Hunt about that sometime.

She was immediately led down the hall to the office of the President's secretary. As Cammy looked around, she realized that there weren't any glass walls or glass cubicles like the ones on the TV show. In fact, the place had an aura of a nicely furnished colonial-style home with camel-backed sofas, wingback chairs, and Chippendale coffee tables placed strategically throughout the reception areas.

"Good morning, Dr. Talbot," the secretary said brightly. "Congratulations. I read about what happened in Rockville. Remarkable story. Just remarkable."

Cammy blushed. The papers had all printed an account of how she had refused to evacuate the building and had stayed to take control of the radio frequency guiding the model plane with its deadly cargo. The reporters explained that Dr. Talbot had managed to turn the plane "like a boomerang" and aim it back at the attacker, whose body had been found later in the smoldering forest. She had been called a hero by her Congressman, Davis Metcher.

"Thanks. It was just something I've been working on," Cammy said modestly.

"Well, we were all mighty impressed." The secretary looked down at the mass of buttons on her phone and said, "Oh good, he's finished his call. You may go in now." She motioned to the President's military aide, who was standing by the door.

Cammy followed him into a bright oval room with a trio of tall windows at one end framed by four panels of gold drapery. While the rest of the building bore absolutely no resemblance to the TV show, the Oval Office did look familiar. The show set obviously had a good replica of the

President's desk, because there was the same Resolute Desk that Queen Victoria had given to President Rutherford B. Hayes. It stood in front of the windows, the polished surface gleaming in a shaft of sunlight. She had once seen the famous picture of that desk showing little John John poking his head out of the front panel when President Kennedy was working behind him.

She looked around and saw a painting of George Washington over the white fireplace mantel. There were three small statues on side tables along the curved walls. They were busts of Winston Churchill, Abraham Lincoln, and Dwight Eisenhower.

What a fabulous place to work, she thought, as she took a tentative step onto the plush gold oval rug with the Presidential seal in the center.

"Dr. Cameron Talbot," the aide announced. The President rose from his tall leather chair and extended his hand. Cammy stepped forward as the President said, "Welcome to the White House, Dr. Talbot. I understand we are all in your debt."

"Oh, that article—"

"Not just for saving one of our key defense suppliers and all the employees, but you are the lady who has invented a whole new concept for my missile defense program, and I like that."

"Yes, sir," Cammy said.

The President exchanged a glance with Austin Gage, who was standing off to the side. "First time in the White House?"

"Yes, sir," she said, not quite catching her breath. *Yes, sir. Is that all I can say?* she wondered. *Just "yes, sir"?* She was afraid she sounded like an echo chamber.

"Well, relax," the President continued warmly. "It's a pretty nice place, and we're glad to have you here. This is Austin Gage, my National Security Advisor." He motioned to one of the off-white couches in the center of the room. "Have a seat." She sat on the plush cushions and felt herself sink down several inches at least. The President sat opposite her, and the NSC Advisor pulled up one of the green-striped chairs that flanked the fireplace. "Now then, let's get down to business. Austin, would you like to brief our guest here on the situation in India?"

Austin opened a leather folder and began. "Dr. Talbot, we know that you are in touch with Colonel Daniels in New Delhi."

"Well, yes. He called and . . . oh, I was so sorry to hear about Ted. That car bomb!"

"Yes." Austin shook his head. "He was one of our best staff members. Damn shame. At least we've got a line on the group responsible for that tragedy."

"You do?" she inquired.

"I'll come back to that. First, we want to talk to you about a classified situation. We know you have a Top Secret clearance in connection with your work at Bandaq. But what you are about to hear today is strictly need-to-know."

"All right," she said in a steady voice.

"We've been working with India's Intelligence agents as well as with the top people at ISI in Pakistan. There is now a consensus that a group called Lashkar-i-Taiba may have set off the car bomb."

"That's the same group, I mean, the man who tried to crash that model plane into our building . . . when Hunt called, he said that guy might have been a member of that same group," Cammy said.

"Yes. It is all beginning to fit together. And we believe that may have been the group that fired the cruise missile at the Indian Army base in Jammu and Kashmir that killed so many people. Soldiers, but many innocents as well. We also believe that they have two other missiles, as three were stolen at the same time from a Pakistani depot." He studied her face carefully and went on. "Now, the need-to-know part of this equation is this. About the other two missiles. One is conventional, just like the first. But the other one may have a biological warhead."

Cammy gasped. "Oh my God!"

The President intervened. "As Austin said, we have a line on this group. But as you know, these terrorists have cells in many locations. They could be in Pakistan, Kashmir, India, and God knows where else. That man, that Jambaz who tried to kill you, he managed to slip in here right under our noses." He turned to Austin. "Make a note that I want an update on airport security and our new watchlist procedures. We've got to get tougher and figure out how to nail more than just Islamic rock stars."

Austin nodded and jotted down a reminder. He looked up again as the President continued. "So, as I was saying, we're trying to find this Lashkar group before they launch any more missiles. But we've picked up some chatter and decoded a few e-mails about the upcoming celebration at the Taj Mahal."

"You don't think they would target that beautiful building, do you, Mr. President?" Cammy asked. "I mean, it's a Muslim mosque."

The President waved his hand. "We don't know for sure. But this is the same group that had plans to attack it a few years ago."

"Really?" Cammy asked, wide-eyed.

"That celebration is going on as scheduled, but the Indians are doing everything they can to increase security, add guards, and install defensive systems around its perimeter. With such a large group of world leaders already planning to attend, India doesn't want to cancel because it might look like they're kowtowing to these terrorists and aren't strong enough to defend their country."

"Are you going over there, Mr. President?" Cammy asked cautiously.

"I'm not sure yet. First, I need to get Farrell in there to get the Indians and the Pakistanis to sign onto a formal peace treaty. They've already talked about trade and transportation, but we need much more than that. We need a no-first-use pledge in terms of nuclear weapons, among other things."

"Do you think they'll sign something like that, sir?" she asked.

"In the current climate, with so many eyes focused on that part of the world, they just might. They all have their hands out for economic aid, elimination of tariffs, and, in India especially, they want to be sure we don't clamp down on any outsourcing contracts. So, yes, I believe we have a window of opportunity here. But we want to do everything we can to ensure the safety of the next group of Americans going over there."

"The Special Envoy, you mean?" Cammy asked.

"Right," Austin said. "So here is the plan. In fact, I have to give credit where credit is due. I received an NSDD—National Security Decision Directive—from Colonel Daniels overnight. He has some interesting ideas. The President and I have discussed this, and we need your help."

"*My* help?" Cammy asked, turning from Austin to the President and raising her eyebrows. "What can I do?"

"You can take Q-3 to New Delhi and set up an additional defense perimeter."

"For the Taj Mahal?" she asked, her heart beating faster.

The President nodded. "We realize this is a very dangerous assignment, and we don't take it lightly We're talking about sending you and your Bandaq team over to a highly volatile area where there's a chance . . . and I have to say a very good chance . . . that some band of terrorists will try to launch a couple of missiles. And if they start playing around with biological warheads, no one can vouch for your safety."

Cammy hesitated. They wanted her to go to New Delhi. That meant she'd have to fly there. Get in a plane, probably a small government plane, strap herself in, and pray to God it didn't crash like all the planes in all her dreams. She had avoided planes for years.

"Dr. Talbot?" the Advisor prompted.

She took a deep breath and focused on the President. "If you ask me to go somewhere, of course I would go . . . anywhere, Mr. President," she said carefully. "It's just that if you want Q-3 to protect an area in India, I'm not sure if it will work." *It would be the triumph of hope over experience*, she thought ruefully. "I mean, we haven't even had a full field test against a live missile yet. Only simulations."

The President gave a half smile. "It seemed to work pretty well yesterday."

"But that was as basic as you can get. A model plane. Now we're talking about cruise missiles with guidance systems . . . sir," she said.

Austin consulted his notes. "Yes, well, Colonel Daniels seems to think it's worth a try. Then again, you could find yourself in the middle of a battle zone."

Cammy sat back against the down cushions and crossed her arms. This was it. A real test of her invention. An idea she had spent years perfecting. An idea that was born on the night she heard one President give a speech asking scientists to help develop a system for missile defense. And now she was sitting in front of *this* President who was asking a scientist for help to deploy it. Her help.

She had worked all her life for just such an opportunity. And now, at this moment, it was about to become a reality. But could she do it?

She looked up and announced, "I don't know if it will work, but I will try."

"That's all we wanted to hear," Austin said. "We know this is all very sudden, but we must move quickly. Do you think you could get whatever equipment you might need and get it on a plane first thing tomorrow?"

"Tomorrow?" she asked incredulously.

"Yes. We're sending Farrell over there. He arrives on Monday, and we don't know how long it will take to get both sides to agree on a treaty. We want you and your people in place so you can set up, tie in to our satellites, and test your system before the talks get under way. You see, as soon as they can hammer out an agreement, they'll all head to Agra."

The President spoke again. "About these militants. We still don't know where they are or just where they might strike next. They might not target the Taj Mahal. I think they'd be absolute fools to try such a thing. But we can't be sure. That's why we need you to go over there and work with the Indian Defense people. Obviously, they already have a copy of Q-3. Clever thieves that they are. But they haven't had time to study it and train enough people to operate all the systems. That's why we need you and your staff. Right now the Indians are pleading for our help and falling all over themselves to be cooperative."

Cammy thought for a moment. "Speaking of cooperation, there is one thing that could be really helpful."

"Name it," the President said firmly.

"This may be way out of line," she said tentatively.

"In this business, there is very little that's 'way out of line.'"

"Would you know what happened to Dr. Raj P. Singh?"

The President glanced over at Austin and narrowed his eyes. "You mean the traitor who stole that program out of your shop?"

"Yes, sir, that one," she answered.

"Why do you ask?"

"I know what he did. I know it was wrong. In fact, we were all shocked by the whole thing. It's just that out of all the scientists I've worked with, Raj was the very best . . . I mean, he knows how to operate much of the system, especially the satellite and radar components, and there isn't anybody else, yet, who can work with me on some of these calculations."

"So you're asking that he be allowed to work with you again?" Austin asked, furrowing his brow.

Cammy pressed on. "What I mean is, is he here? Is he in prison?"

The President replied, "No. The Indians were pretty upset having been caught with their hands in the cookie jar, so to speak, but they've been making the case that he wasn't trying to harm the United States but was only trying to protect his people from an attack. The man is not an American citizen. So instead of a public trial, we decided to deport him," the President explained.

"Never to return," Austin added with a shrug.

"When will he be leaving?" Cammy asked.

"He's already gone. We shipped him out last night," the President said.

"Then he's back in India," Cammy said excitedly. "That means he could help me. I mean, if he could be allowed to work with us when we tie into the satellite warning system and—"

Austin cleared his throat and exchanged a glance with the President. "Well, this is a first. She wants to work with a spy."

"It's only because he might be able to help us," she said quickly. "I mean we'll have to set things up so fast, he could—"

The President held up his hands. "Highly unusual, to say the least. But I take your point. Tell you what. You get back to Bandaq and get your team and your equipment organized for a morning departure. We'll have a plane on standby at Andrews and we'll give you vans to transport your people and whatever you need. Austin will contact General Landsdale and what's left of our team in New Delhi."

"You mean Hunt . . . uh, Colonel Daniels? He'll be there with us, too?" She suddenly felt a bit better just thinking about seeing him again.

"Yes," Austin assured her. "He'll be handling logistics, and he'll act as your go-between with the Defense Ministry."

The President added, "And I'll see what we can do about India's clever spy, although I'm sure they'll jump at the chance to have him lend a hand. Oh, and one last point. No publicity. No one, absolutely no one except the general and your own staff at Bandaq, is to know you're going over there. We don't want any more welcoming committees setting off car bombs."

She shuddered at the thought. "Yes, Mr. President. I completely understand."

62

Andrews Air Force Base—Saturday Morning

"Fasten your seat belts, folks. We're cleared for takeoff."

Cammy sat rigidly in her seat and pulled the belt even tighter across her lap. She gripped the armrests and took a couple of deep breaths.

General Landsdale glanced over at her from his seat across the aisle of the military jet. "You okay there, kiddo?" he asked in a fatherly tone.

"I just don't like . . . to fly," she said, gritting her teeth as the plane began to taxi toward the runway.

"I remember you said that, but this is a good plane, Cam. And the pilots are first-rate."

"Uh, right," she whispered. At least she was surrounded by familiar faces, her Q-3 team, the radar and satellite specialists, the General. If the plane crashed, she'd go down with friends. It wouldn't be like flying on a commercial jet where the only souls sharing a tragedy were total strangers. She shook her head to clear the macabre thoughts.

She tried to refocus and picture the scene in New Delhi where she would see Hunt once again. She conjured up his image, the deep blue eyes, the strong jaw, the whole rugged look. She thought about the way he had touched her face their last morning together. *A gentle touch can be as erotic as a strong embrace*, she reflected. But she could use either one right about now.

When she had left the White House the day before and returned to her office, it looked like total bedlam. Austin Gage had called General Landsdale, who in turn had called an emergency staff meeting to announce their departure for India. Everyone was scrambling to get the equipment ready to be transported on the vans that were already heading their way. Melanie had been briefed about a news blackout and given instructions on what to say if any hint of their trip leaked out.

It was probably good that Cammy had been so busy getting ready that she hadn't been able to dwell on the idea of flying across the Atlantic. She had tried to intellectualize the situation and tell herself that she was safer flying in the air than driving on the Beltway. But then, she got that nervous sensation again as she approached the building labeled: Terminal. Now, as the plane lifted off the runway and made a steep climb, she tried to relax and look out the window. The sun was a frosted bulb in the sky, its glow obscured by a foggy mist. At this steep rate, they would climb through the haze pretty quickly and fly above it all.

A pain shot up her arm. She tried to massage it away. She was wearing a small brace that she had picked up at the drugstore. She hoped that by keeping her wrist straight, it might increase the blood flow and cut down on the pain and occasional numbness in her fingers.

When they leveled off, the general asked the team leaders to gather at the back of the plane to go over their plans to set up and synchronize their equipment. Their conference then segued to a discussion of the defense bill and the Committee's sudden show of support. They talked about how Cammy had utilized Q-3 to redirect the model plane and nail the terrorist and how Metcher had then turned into a one-man cheerleading squad.

They also had a sober conversation about the tragedy of losing Ben and of Raj's betrayal. The general said he was so outraged at the man's actions, he couldn't imagine working with him again. Cammy had agreed with the general in principle but made the point that they were going to India to try to prevent a disastrous attack, so they'd all have to put their personal feelings on hold. The general had merely scowled. Then he suggested they all take a break and try to get some rest.

"Cam, what's that thing on your wrist?" Landsdale asked as they moved back to their seats.

"With all the computer simulations, my arm's been bothering me a bit. I'm sure it's nothing serious," she said, settling back in her window seat.

The general sat down next to her. "When we get back, why don't you see a doctor about that? You don't want it to get worse."

"I know. I'll try. It's just that we've been so swamped."

He patted her arm and said reassuringly, "I know. You more than most. But with your latest performances in the lab and then against that damn model plane, well, you're going to deserve some time off. And speaking of time off, now that our appropriation is coming through, along with the usual number for Sterling, maybe Nettar Kooner will take some time off and stop bugging everyone on the Committee to dump us and favor his production line."

"Kooner was pressuring the Hill?" Cammy asked.

"Of course. Guy's a real pro when it comes to lobbying. Even though both of our companies will get R & D money this year, I wouldn't put it past him to try and line us out next year, even after we go through our field test. But that's a long way off. We've got enough to worry about right now with this trip to India." He got up, went back to his seat across the aisle, pulled his briefcase onto his lap, and extracted a tiny Dictaphone. "I'm going to make some notes. I'll try not to talk too loud. Why don't you try to rest for a while? We'll be refueling at Shannon in a little while. Not much you can do between here and there."

She nodded and leaned her chair back. Maybe she could doze off before they landed in Ireland. At least there wasn't any turbulence. She closed her eyes and listened to the hum of the engines. She tried to breathe deeply, tried not to think about where she was. But instead of lulling her to sleep, the engine noise permeated her thoughts, and she imagined her father's plane once more. He was in his cockpit, checking his gauges, getting ready to fire his missile. *No.* She opened her eyes. *Not again. This isn't his plane. This one doesn't have a missile. Nothing's going to explode and we're not going to crash.* She kept repeating the words over and over, almost but not quite believing herself this time.

When they landed at Shannon, everyone got off to walk around a huge building filled with shops. She was surprised there were so many of them. Then again, the area catered to international passengers who were all taking a break from long flights and had nothing to do but wander around. She saw stores that were selling watches, perfume, leather goods. Finally, she spotted a small boutique next to a liquor store. She walked inside and saw a rack of silk negligees. *Hunt. I'll see Hunt. Maybe . . .*

She pushed a number of hangers aside until she found a lovely French silk gown. It was black with tiny straps and a deep V-neck bordered with fine lace. She checked the size and price tag and was amazed that it was such a bargain. *Duty-free*, she reflected. She also checked her watch and realized they were scheduled to take off again in about fifteen minutes. She slid the gown off the hanger, took it to the cashier, pulled out her credit card, and signed the receipt. She might be a scientist on a mission for the White House, but she was also a woman. And after all that had been going on, she wanted to feel like one.

She got back on board. Once again, they took off and headed east. She was feeling a bit better now that the first leg of the trip was out of the way. She was given a box lunch even though it was her dinnertime. She ate the fruit and took a few bites of the sandwich. She wasn't very hungry. It was hard to eat when she was still so anxious about the flight and what they'd find when they reached their destination.

She found a copy of *Aviation Week* in the seat pocket and flipped through it. There was an article about Sterling Dynamics' contract with the Japanese for a line of defense missiles. *Sterling. Why do I have to be reminded of those people all the time?* she wondered. Even the general had talked about them. He said Nettar Kooner was still on their trail. Of course, he would be. He was their major competitor. And now with the success of Q-3, at least in the lab and against the little plane, he'd be working harder than ever to knock them out of the box. She was sure of that.

Nettar Kooner. Nettar Kooner. N.K. N.K. Something about the initials jogged her memory. She pushed her food aside, leaned down, and reached for the shoulder bag she had stashed under her seat. She checked the side pocket, pulled out the little slip of paper, and read the letters. "Get NK BA FLD TS."

She'd been pondering that entry for days. The entry on Hunt's calendar for a day about two weeks away. Suddenly it began to make sense. "Get NK!" *Get Nettar Kooner. Get Kooner what?* "BA FLD TS." She stared at the abbreviations. *Could "BA" stand for "Bandaq"? And if it did, that meant the rest of it stood for "Field Test." "Get Nettar Kooner Bandaq Field Test." My God, that's it. Get that damn CEO the results of my test. Hunt had said he wanted to be there. He'd come and he'd watch everything I did and then feed it to their competitor. Could that possibly be true? Could he be planning to do such a thing? How could he? How could he be so two-faced? How could I be so stupid?* He had taken her into his home. He had organized FBI protection for her. *Of course he had. He wanted to keep me safe. He wanted to learn how I operated. He wanted Q-3.*

Her hands were shaking as she shoved the scrap of paper back into her purse and dropped it on the empty seat next to her. It was the Ken doll all over again. The charm. The pursuit. The endearing touches. The hopes. Her hopes for some sort of a relationship. She shook her head. *At least I didn't sleep with him.* She sat still for a long while and gazed out the window again. Through the darkness, she could imagine the clouds below. *Hopes are like clouds,* she thought. *The more you build them up, the more they turn into great big storms and dump all over you.*

After several minutes, she turned toward her boss across the aisle. "Jack. We have to talk!"

63

New Delhi—Sunday Night

The plane taxied to a stop. Everyone stayed seated while an Indian official came on board, checked their passports and declaration forms, and gave the pilots the high sign. Cammy and her team gathered their gear and moved toward the door. She had made it through the flight. But what now? They had a job to do, and just as the general would have to swallow his pride and work with Raj, she would have to figure out a way to work with Hunt. *Damn him*.

As she headed down the steps, she felt a strong arm encircle her waist and almost lift her off the ground. "Missed you, Cam," Hunt said with a grin. "Welcome to my world."

She pulled away and pushed a few strands of hair off her face.

"You okay?" he asked, eyeing her stern demeanor. "You probably didn't get much sleep. It's such a long trip."

She shifted her shoulder bag and kept hold of her carry-on.

"Here, let me help you with this stuff. The guys over there will handle the rest of the luggage, and we have vans for the equipment. But we've got a bunch of cars here to take us to the site. And don't worry. We're taking a roundabout route. There aren't very many people who know you're here.

And those that do, like the drivers, don't have a clue what you're here for. So I don't think there will be any trouble along the way."

"Thank God for that," she mumbled as she followed him to the lead vehicle. "Where are we going?"

"To an army base halfway between New Delhi and Agra. It's about an hour-and-a-half drive, but it's a good strategic site. They've got a staging area, and they're bringing in some extra computer types in case we need them."

"What about Raj? Have you seen him?"

"Not yet. I heard that you asked for his help. Our government says he's a traitor, but over here they talk about him like he's a goddamn hero."

"I can imagine," she said, looking away from him.

"How was your meeting with the President?" he asked.

"Fine. Just fine."

He looked at her and saw that she was avoiding his eyes. *They must have told her about the third missile,* he thought. *No wonder she looks upset.* "I want you to know that I really struggled over that memo I sent to Austin."

"Why?"

"Are you kidding? Here we are in the middle of what could turn out to be World War III and I get this crazy idea that Dr. Talbot . . . ," he tried to take her hand, but she pulled away, "*my* Dr. Talbot could come over here and save the world."

"Aren't you being a little dramatic?" she said, shaking her head.

"Well, you know what I mean. Anyway, I realize we're putting you and your whole team in the middle of a mess here."

"The President explained all of that," she said. "It was our choice. The general called an emergency meeting and told everyone what was going on. We know what's at stake, and we all agreed to come. So here we are," she said, waving her hand toward the line of cars.

"And I'm damn glad to see you. We've got a lot of work to do, though."

"I know," she said evenly. "It's going to take hours to set up. I just hope we can get our act together before Senator Farrell and his people get here."

"For the talks. Yeah, I know. They're due in tomorrow, so we'll be working overnight. Did you get any sleep on the plane?"

"Not much."

"Hey, what's with the wrist?" he asked.

She stared down at her arm. "Oh, that's just a little brace. It's there to keep my wrist straight. It's been bothering me and slowing me down a little.

On my computer. Nothing for you to worry about," she said without raising her eyes.

"I sure hope not. There's a lot riding on your skills, my lady," he said.

She didn't reply. She just kept walking toward the cars.

"About those missiles," he said, "we still don't know where they are. Every Indian soldier, agent, and policeman is on the lookout, and they still haven't found them."

She shrugged.

"You sure are calm and collected about all of this," he observed.

"That's just on the outside."

"And on the inside?"

"Never mind."

64

Northwest India—Monday Morning

"Remember the words 'buzz bomb'?" the instructor asked. A large group of bearded men was gathered around a trailer truck containing a number of silos. Most shook their heads. An older man came forward.

"Yes," Abbas Khan said. "The Germans made them. I was just a small boy, but we heard about them."

"Correct. It was the first cruise missile. The Nazis made it with a simple inertial guidance system propelled by a pulse-jet engine that made that buzzing sound. The real name was the V-1."

"Now we have better ones!" Rashid exclaimed as he peered at the launch vehicle.

"This is true. We have learned a great deal in the last half century. As you know, Pakistan has a number of large ballistic missiles for carrying nuclear weapons—weapons developed by our own Dr. A. Q. Khan's nuclear network, before they shut him down."

"Yes, brilliant man. A distant cousin. They may have stopped his sales of nuclear technology, but Pakistan still has the bombs . . . Weapons we will control very soon," Khan predicted.

The instructor continued his demonstration. "Yes, but these missiles are different. They don't just go up and come down. They are guided. When Pakistan tested these missiles back in 2004, the government talked about countering India's PJ-BrahMos cruise missiles that they developed with the Russians. A counterweight. Little did they know that we would procure their latest shipment, aim them, and be the first to launch them at our enemies. And when the Indians retaliate, we shall have the war we have been planning for years."

The men raised their fists and shouted, "*Inshallah*!"

"We have the commanders from the Pakistani Army here with us who have joined our cause." He inclined his head toward a group of uniformed officers nearest the truck. "They helped with the first launch, but this one will be more sophisticated." He pointed to one of the weapons. "Think of this as a pilotless airplane." The men craned their necks to look at their booty and nodded to one another. "Since they are unmanned, we do not have to conduct flight training for any of you. And since they are mobile, we do not have to worry about special hangars. Our mission today will be to target and launch the next missile at precisely the correct time to inflict maximum damage at the Ministry of Defense as soon as the peace talks get under way."

At the mention of the words "peace talks," one cell member chuckled and said in a derisive tone, "Peace talks. There shall be no talk of peace. We want war." There was a roar of approval.

The instructor pointed to the small building behind them. "This is a good location. Away from cities and nosey Indian soldiers. I commend you for infiltrating to this position."

"We have much cooperation from our Muslim Indian brothers, you know," Khan explained.

"Yes. They have performed well. And from this building we will monitor the talks on CNN. It makes our job very easy."

"You are right. We watched their stupid newscasts before. We knew precisely when to hit that motorcade. We can do it again," Rashid said.

"Yes, but that was to detonate a car bomb by remote control. This is a much more complicated operation," the instructor said. "We must carefully calculate the distance to the target and the flight time. We must also program the GPS with the latest terrain and physical features, as this will be a long flight."

"Can we be sure it will hit the right target, Khan Sahib?" Rashid asked his leader.

"That is why we have the experts with us. Do not raise doubts. Have faith. For even if this missile does not deter the negotiators from their talk of a treaty, remember we have one more missile. A very special one. For the Taj Mahal."

65

Northern India—Monday Morning

The place was crawling with titles. General Landsdale, the Director General of India's Missile Defense System, a Deputy Assistant Secretary of State, a major from the Pentagon, Lieutenant Colonel Daniels, and assorted Indian Ph.D.'s.

"Look at this crowd," Hunt whispered to Cammy as they stood in a corner taking a break. She sipped her third cup of strong coffee and nodded quietly.

"It's a pretty high-level group. Above whom, there are no whom-ers," he added with a slight laugh. "And they're all here because they want to work with your technology."

And so do you, she thought.

The entire Bandaq team had been up all night coordinating the satellite system, the radar detection system, the Command and Control system. A bank of computers sat in the center with three large screens above them.

Talk about pressure, Hunt thought. It was a little bit like a formal test of a new weapons system, except that this wasn't a test. He remembered the tension when the Navy had scheduled a trial of the sea-based Aegis Weapons

System. They launched one of their SM-3 interceptor missiles from the USS *Lake Erie* out in the Pacific near Hawaii. It was supposed to intercept an Aries target missile launched from the Pacific Missile Range Facility on Kauai. But one of the cells of solid fuel didn't ignite and, as the Navy's press release put it, "The SM-3 deployed its nonexplosive warhead, but an intercept was not achieved." *That was the understatement of the day! What was achieved was more like total humiliation*, he thought. So it had been back to the drawing board for the Navy to try to analyze the performance of all the components and see if they could find out which part had screwed up.

Today, there was no time to go back to the drawing board. If a missile were launched, it sure as hell wouldn't have a nonexplosive warhead. And if Q-3 didn't work, well, he couldn't afford to think about that right now.

There was a commotion by the door. A dozen Indian scientists jumped up from their chairs and surrounded a tall young man. They were clapping and cheering as he entered the room.

It was Raj Singh, the new King of Indian Espionage. At least that's what the newspapers had dubbed him. Raj looked uncertain as he glanced over and made eye contact with Hunt. "The prodigal son returns," Hunt murmured.

Hunt saw General Landsdale frown and turn back toward a computer console. But Cammy raced over to see her former partner. They exchanged a few words, and she pointed to a chair next to the satellite team. Raj walked over and took his place with the other scientists while Cammy came back to refill her coffee mug.

"So what did he have to say for himself?" Hunt asked.

"He apologized again for deceiving us." *And when are you going to apologize for deceiving me?*

"Did he ask about Melanie?" Hunt inquired.

"Yes. He wanted to know if she was okay. I told him she was devastated." *And so am I.*

"And?"

"And he just said he wished he could make it up to her. I hardly see how he can. He won't ever be allowed back into the United States. And I can't see her coming over here after what he did." *And I can't see myself coming over to your place after what you're about to do.*

"Yeah. I'm sure you're right. It is kind of strange seeing him again, isn't it?" Hunt asked.

"Yes. I've got mixed emotions about all of this," she said evenly. "But if things really get bad, I know I can use his help." *His help. Certainly not yours.*

Hunt squeezed her arm, "If you want my opinion, I think you can handle this all on your own. But I guess it's okay to have some backup."

Cammy took a sip of her coffee. "If those terrorists really do launch a missile at the Taj Mahal, think about it. The entire world would be up in arms."

"On the other hand, if they try to lob one and the Indian defenses fail, but you're able to stop it, think about that, Cam. It means you really do have the key to the balance of power here."

"You're sounding awfully dramatic again."

"I mean it. You intercept one of those babies, and this will not be a sui generis situation."

"Something unto itself?"

"Precisely. Not a lone event. It will have implications all over the world . . . for every country that needs to defend itself."

Cammy sighed as she surveyed the large room packed with equipment, consoles, screens, TV sets, scientists and officers rushing around, talking on cell phones. "At least we're almost set up here. But what I don't understand is why the Pakistanis can't give us more help in identifying the C^3 of these missiles. They were stolen from a Pakistani base. I mean, don't they know exactly what kind of guidance systems they had?"

"We've been all over them like a tent on this." Hunt said. "First of all, they say that they were just taking delivery on those missiles when they were stolen, so they didn't have any experience with their operation. But their biggest problem, one that they hate to admit, is that some of the people in charge of those missiles either have disappeared or are sympathetic to the militants."

"But don't they know where they bought them?" she countered. "I mean they could be British Sea Eagles, Chinese Seersuckers or Silkworms, although I doubt if they'd get those. They're pretty old. They could be French Apaches, German Kormorans, or Swedish RBS-15s. I mean, there are a dozen countries that export those things. Why won't they at least tell us who they're dealing with? It would give us a tremendous head start."

"I know. I know. I think there may be something else in play here. If Pakistan's archenemy is hit by a missile, it probably won't cause the Paks to lose any sleep at night, especially when they've told the world that they're not the ones who would be firing it. On the other hand, they have told us that they're scrambling and will try to get us some information before the Taj Mahal ceremony starts."

Cammy shook her head in frustration. "Well, let's keep trying."

"We are. I've got so many channels into Islamabad right now, I feel like a psychic."

She didn't respond. She glanced over at her team and finally said, "I think we should be set in the next hour or so. We've already run a few tests. Maybe we can wrap it up pretty soon and go get some sleep. What do you think?"

"I don't know why not. We're all wiped out. Besides, the Agra events don't even start for another two days. So, yeah, as soon as you're done, we'll get out of here. The Indian teams can hold the fort. Besides, it's getting pretty hot."

"Somebody said it was supposed to get up to one hundred degrees today. At least there's some air-conditioning in here. But a nice bath and clean sheets would certainly be in order."

He touched her cheek. She flinched. "Want your own room?" he asked.

"Yes," she said, and walked back to her console.

Hunt turned to watch the bank of TV sets arranged along the wall. They were all tuned to various news stations. He focused on CNN. "Hey look, isn't that Senator Farrell going up those steps?"

Cammy turned back and stared at the screen. "Must be. He looks like kind of a cross between James Baker and George Mitchell. And there sure are a lot of uniforms there to meet him. Is that the Defense Ministry?"

"Yeah. That's the place. I've been working in there for the last couple of days."

"So is he going to be meeting with the Prime Minister?"

"As far as I know. Of course, there's been a lot of horse-trading going on behind the scenes. You don't have a high-level meeting, even for a Special Envoy, without a lot of gophers playing with the agenda."

"I know. Do you really think they'll get some sort of treaty out of all of this?" she asked.

"After all that's happened, I sure as hell hope so."

Cammy went back to compare notes with General Landsdale and another technician. She was tired. She was disillusioned, and she had to admit she was scared. At the moment she felt like Sisyphus. And her arm still hurt.

Suddenly she heard the sound of an alarm and then Raj's voice shouting over the general noise in the room. "Incoming! Incoming!" he screamed, pointing to one of the large computer screens. "Northwest quadrant! Unidentified!"

66

Northwest India—Monday Morning

A cheer went up. Fists and guns were raised as the group of bearded men watched the missile blast out of the launch site. "For the glory of Allah!" they shouted joyously.

Abbas Khan watched from the periphery and glanced down at the fax he had just pulled off the machine in the small shack behind him. *What a fool. What a complete idiot,* he thought as he reread the article from the *International Herald Tribune* that another cell leader had just sent. The headline read, "American Scientist Foils Terrorist Plot." It explained how a certain Dr. Cameron Talbot had skillfully employed her new missile defense technology to capture and redirect a model plane with an explosive cargo away from an industrial complex, saving many lives. It went on to say that since she was able to take control of the radio frequency guiding the plane, she sent it back to the location of the terrorist who had launched it. His body was later found by FBI agents on the scene.

Khan shook his head and called out, "Rashid. Come here!"

The young man backed away from the uproarious group and joined his leader. "Yes, Khan Sahib. Isn't it wonderful? The missile is on its way to New Delhi. The cameras are there. They will all see the destruction of the top leaders of India. A most fitting tribute to their idea of negotiating a peace treaty with the American Envoy. Don't you agree?" he asked with excitement in his eyes.

Khan handed him the fax. "Read this."

Rashid quickly read the article and caught his breath. "She killed Jambaz? Our brother is dead?"

"Exactly. We sent him to perform a mission. He was to procure this new technology for us. For our cause. To defend against India's many missiles. And look what happened. He not only failed to get it; he got himself killed. And this scientist, this Dr. Talbot, is called a hero," Khan said in a furious tone.

"What are we to do?"

"We will persevere. That's what we shall do. We will find her, *and* her precious technology, and get it for our war effort. Once the hostilities are under way and we take over the government in Islamabad and control the nuclear stockpile, it will come in quite handy when other countries try to attack us."

"Of course you are right," Rashid said quickly. "What can I do?"

"You will replace Jambaz as our point man on this issue."

"Yes, Khan Sahib."

"Research this Bandaq corporation. Study this Dr. Talbot. Find out where she is and who else can operate the technology, and report back to me."

67

Northern India—Monday Morning

There was a stampede to the computer terminals, satellite and radar sensors. Cammy raced to her chair and stared at the screen in front of her. She saw a white object in the upper left corner moving very slowly across a superimposed map of the area. It looked like it was hugging the terrain as it inched its way across the screen. *Oh my God! They've done it. They've launched a missile. But it's not aimed at Agra. It's not for the Taj Mahal. It looks like it's headed . . . toward New Delhi,* she realized as her fingers began to fly over the keys. *Oh Lord! This is it!*

She sat transfixed for a moment, drew a deep breath, and began her calculations, working algorithms, analyzing possible passwords to the onboard guidance system. A sharp pain shot up her arm. She gave an involuntary shiver but forced herself to continue.

Raj shouted again, "Missile! Southeast trajectory!"

An Indian general frantically dialed a number on his cell phone. He was having trouble getting through. Every other official in the building had his cell phone out and was calling out evacuation orders, but there was precious little time.

———

Hunt rushed over to Cammy's console, keeping an eye on the TV set. He saw images of the Prime Minister of India shaking hands with the Special Envoy and his staff. It seemed as though all eyes in the room were shifting back and forth from the television to Cammy's computer screen, like a mesmerized audience at a bizarre tennis match, staring in horror as the incoming warhead inched closer.

The Indian general was now barking an order into his cell phone about launching countermeasures. Hunt knew they had Patriot-type systems arrayed around the Taj Mahal, but he doubted they would be effective in a missile attack on a building in the city.

Raj had pulled his chair over next to Cammy's and was scribbling some calculations on a tablet. Her hands were still flying over the keys. As each attempt to discover the missile's C^3 failed, she shook her head in frustration, glanced at Raj's numbers, and tried again. Her fingers were beginning to feel numb. She rotated her shoulder, ignoring the pain around her wrist. "Damn," she muttered. "Maybe this thing has been cannibalized. I can't seem . . ." Her voiced trailed off as the white image gained ground and a collective cry was heard in the room. General Landsdale held up his hands, demanding quiet, but he couldn't control the emotions of the Indian scientists and military men who were watching the missile weave its way to within miles of their beloved New Delhi.

Raj studied her screen and called out another set of entries. Cammy felt another pain shoot up her arm. The missile inched closer, closer to the city limits outlined on the computer map. Cammy started to enter another sequence of numbers when her hands froze. An excruciating pain in her wrist seemed to hold her fingers captive. One second. Two. Three. *Forget the pain . . . concentrate . . . think . . . pray.* She took her hands off the keyboard, massaged her arm, and forced the pain from her mind. She stared at Raj's numbers and then remembered one more possible combination. She forced herself to key it in.

Suddenly a high-pitched tone pierced the room and the word SESAME flashed on Cammy's screen. She cried out, "Yes! We've got a lock."

A huge commotion erupted as all eyes focused on her computer screen.

Now it's time to take control and try to redirect this thing. And like a worm invasion, she began to scramble its command signal and send a counterinstruction. The white image on the screen looked like it was slowing down and then beginning to turn. An astonished cheer went up. Hunt raced to her side as Raj was saying, "Send it back. Send it back."

Hunt shouted, "No, Cammy, you can't send it back!"

"Why not?" demanded Raj. "She knows how to do that. Q-3 can do that."

Cammy's hands were poised in mid-air as she looked from one man to the other. Then the National Security Advisor's words echoed in her mind. *"The need-to-know part of this equation is this. About the other two missiles. One is conventional, just like the first. But the other one may have a biological warhead."*

Which one is this? She thought for a split second. *It probably has the conventional warhead. They're saving the biological agent for an attack on the Taj Mahal. Yes, that's what they'd do. But if I send this one back, it will explode at their launch site, and that's where they probably have the other missile stored. That could create a cloud of deadly bacteria that could kill innocent people all over the place.*

She turned to Raj. "I can't send it back," she said defiantly.

"Why not?"

"Don't argue with her," Hunt said. "She knows what she's doing."

"How much fuel? How much range do I have? Where else can I send it? Give me a direction where there are less people," she demanded. "Can we get it over water?"

Raj bent over his calculations and scratched out a series of numbers. He pointed to the map on the screen. "No, that's too far. Aim over there. Northeast. Toward the mountains."

She tapped more keys and the missile responded to her commands. She turned to Raj once more, "Quick. Figure out the fuel expended. Then I can calculate the launch site, and maybe we can find them."

Hunt motioned to the Indian Army general hovering nearby. "General. We need you." The man rushed over. "Cammy . . . uh, Dr. Talbot is getting a lead on the possible launch site. Then your people . . ."

The general pulled out his cell phone and waited. Cammy huddled with Raj as they compared notes. Raj pointed to the map on the computer screen and then handed the general a slip of paper. "Try this area, sir. It looks like a place where the terrorists may have set up their launch vehicle. Can your people get there fast?"

"We can order an aerial bombardment immediately," the general responded as he began to dial a number on his phone.

"No!" Cammy cried out. "You can't do that."

"Why not?"

"You just can't," she said defiantly. "I am here as a representative of the President of the United States, and I'm saying that your people must not bomb the area. They could set off additional explosions that could be disastrous."

The general looked at her quizzically. "The President knows this area? This is inside India's borders."

Hunt intervened. "Dr. Talbot knows what she's talking about . . . sir . . . I'll brief you in a moment. But first, see if you can get your forces to round up that cell and take them alive if possible. That way you might be able to get intelligence on their other cells and also take possession of any other weapons they have there."

"Including the last stolen missile," Cammy muttered under her breath as she finalized her keystrokes.

The general hesitated a moment and saw the grim look on Hunt's face. "Yes, I hear what you are saying." He gave a series of orders on his phone, slapped it shut, and strode across the room to coordinate with his other officers.

On the screen, the image of the white object was now traveling slowly toward the mountain range northeast of the city.

She had done it.

Cammy slumped in her chair, exhausted, oblivious to the rest of the crowd. She closed her eyes, leaned her head back, and tried to breathe. She realized she hadn't been breathing right for the last several minutes. It had all happened so fast. She had heard the alarm and had gone into auto mode. Then there was the intense concentration during the chase, the calculations, the algorithms, the pain in her wrist and arm, the tension, the scrutiny of a room full of officials, the sound of the warnings. Then, finally, the exhilaration of success. Put it all together, and toss Hunt into the mix, and she had an image of a cue ball smashing into a rack, sending nine different emotions ricocheting off the walls.

Hunt crouched down beside her chair and took her hand. "You okay?" he whispered.

She opened her eyes. "I guess," she hedged. "Just catching my breath."

"Congratulations, Einstein! You really did it." He pulled her out of her chair as the ranking Indian officer walked over and stuck out his hand. "Good show, Dr. Talbot. On behalf of my country, I thank you. We are completely in your debt," he said, bowing slightly.

Cammy took his hand, winced at the pressure, and tried to smile. "Thank you. I'm just glad that the team . . . working together . . . I mean it was a group effort."

"Yes, yes. We know. But you were the key. Without your Q-3, those terrorists might have destroyed an entire section of our city with our Prime Minister and your Special Envoy right in the center. We are deeply grateful."

Cammy nodded. "I just hope that your people can find those terrorists. Do you have forces in that area?"

"Yes, not far. I have to say that I am amazed they were able to penetrate our border with their missiles. On the other hand, it is a fairly desolate region."

"Do you think they might have had help on the Indian side?" Hunt asked.

The officer paused. "I would hope not, but it is possible. We have had trouble with some of the Muslim groups. On the other hand, if we can wipe out these perpetrators and also get a peace treaty on the table, it would mean much progress. Much progress indeed."

"Let's hope it happens," she said. "Now, sir, if you don't mind, I think we would like to get some rest. It's been a long night."

"But of course," he said genially. "You deserve not only rest, but the very best that my country has to offer."

68

The Taj Mahal—Monday Night

The marble dome glistened gold and milky white in the glow of the moon. The four minarets, set symmetrically about the mosque, framed the intricately carved mausoleum and were reflected in a long shimmering pool of water.

Cammy stared at the sight from her hotel room balcony as she checked her watch. The general and their new Satellite System Manager should be here any minute now. The entire Bandaq group and what was left of the American advance team had slept much of the day and then had been honored at a lavish banquet.

Toasts were made to continued friendship between the United States and India, the world's largest democracy. A citation on behalf of the Prime Minister had been given to Bandaq with special recognition for Dr. Cameron Talbot and her missile defense system, which "promised to add a moral dimension—saving lives—to the complexities of modern warfare."

As for Hunt, he had been seated at a separate table, and she had carefully avoided him all evening. Now that the festivities were over, it was time to put her plan into effect. She heard a quiet knock on the door and walked over to open it.

"Jack, Bob, come on in. I thought those speeches would never end."

"Yes, they were pretty long-winded. Kind of like some of the testimonial dinners we have back in D.C.," the general observed. "But you have to admit it was nice having all those government types drinking toasts to your bravery."

"And to Q-3," Bob added.

"Speaking of Q-3, we've got a call to make," Cammy said, motioning to the telephone on the desk. "There are two more phones in here. One by the bed and one in the bathroom. Jack, why don't you listen in the bedroom. I'll take the other one."

"Are you sure this is the right way to go?" Bob asked.

"Damn right, I'm sure," Cammy answered forcefully. "If that bastard is planning to get his hands on Q-3 or even disclose our operating procedures, we've got to nail him now, before we get back to the states."

"Cammy's right," Jack said. "If we can get him to implicate himself, or even hint that he's willing to talk about a deal, we'll get our embassy to intervene."

"You know the script, right?" Cammy asked.

Bob sighed, sat down in the chair, and pulled the phone to the edge of the desk. "Okay, pick up your extensions. Let's get this over with."

"Colonel Daniels."

"Good evening, sir," Bob said in an even tone.

"Who is this?"

"Just a friend."

"What friend?"

"Someone who would like to do business with you."

"What kind of business? How did you know I was here?"

"With all the publicity about this mission and the success of Q-3 today, it wasn't hard to track you down."

"It's pretty late. What do you want?"

"Q-3."

"What do you mean, you want Q-3? It's not for sale."

"Are you sure about that? I have information that a number of others have been trying to acquire it. Strictly for defensive purposes, of course."

"What others?" Hunt demanded.

"Let's just say that with the demonstration this morning, the price that certain interested parties are willing to pay has gone up."

"What's that got to do with me?"

"I understand that you have a close relationship to this Dr. Talbot. So if you could facilitate the transfer of this software, my people would double any other offers you may have."

"What other offers?"

"Please, Colonel Daniels. Let's not be coy. We know there are many interested parties. Now then, shall we talk numbers?"

There was a long pause. Cammy held the phone to her ear, straining to detect Hunt's reaction to the proposition.

More silence.

"Colonel Daniels? I asked if you'd like to talk numbers. Do you wish to name your price?"

Another pause.

"I need time. Where can I reach you?" Hunt asked.

Cammy started shaking as she held on to the receiver.

"You can't reach me," Bob said, "but I can reach you. How much time do you need?"

"There's going to be a field test in another week or so," Hunt said.

"Yes. We have intelligence on that."

"You certainly are well-informed."

"We try to cover all the bases," Bob said. "But surely you'd like to reach an agreement . . . with my people . . . before the test. Am I correct?"

Hunt hesitated a moment. "I might. In fact, it's possible that I could get some preliminary information tonight."

Cammy shook her head in amazement.

"The sooner the better," Bob said. "Shall I call you first thing in the morning?"

"You're sure I can't contact you if I come up with something?"

"No. I'm moving around quite a bit. But it's good to know that we'll be working together. I can assure you, we'll make it worth your while."

69

The Taj Mahal—Monday Night

"I can't believe this," the general said, slamming down the phone and striding out of the bedroom. "A lieutenant colonel in the United States Air Force detailed to the White House willing to compromise a classified project? How the hell can this happen?"

Cammy stopped pacing across the room and put her hands on her hips. "Why not? First Sterling, then that Jambaz creature, then Raj, so why not a colonel? What do we really know about him anyway?"

"Obviously not enough," Bob ventured.

"Besides, he lives in a pretty nice house in Georgetown, and he drives a Jaguar," she said.

"On a colonel's salary?" the general asked, raising his eyebrows. "So maybe this isn't the first time."

Her phone rang and all three of them stopped and stared at it. Cammy glanced down at her watch again. "Who would be calling at this hour?" It rang again.

"Why don't you find out?" the general suggested.

Cammy grabbed the receiver. "This is Dr. Talbot."

"Cam, it's me."

Cammy covered the mouthpiece and whispered, "It's him." The general nodded for her to continue.

"Yes?" she answered matter-of-factly.

"I've got to talk to you. I'm right down the hall. Can I come to your room?"

She looked over at her boss and colleague. "Uh, no. Why don't I come to yours?"

"Yeah. That would be good. We need to talk."

She hung up the phone and sighed.

General Landsdale got up from his chair and walked to the door. "Wait here. I've got an idea."

"What?"

"Just give me a second. My room's next door. I want to get something."

Cammy turned to Bob. "I can just imagine what that guy's next move will be, so to speak."

"Sure sounds like he's got something up his sleeve."

"Or somewhere else," Cammy said with a wave of her hand. "Did you see how he was hovering over my computer all last night?"

"No. We were pretty busy with the satellite transmissions."

"Oh, right. Well, anyway, he was like a glue stick. Damn him."

When she heard the general's knock and opened the door, he was holding his tiny Dictaphone. "Here. We're going to turn this on and put it in your purse. Leave it open if you can, and let's see what the lieutenant colonel has to say for himself."

Cammy eyed the small device. "Brilliant. But can it pick up conversations at a distance?"

"Maybe. Keep your purse as close to you as you can. I've got the volume up all the way. It's the best we can do right now."

Cammy took a deep breath, straightened her headband, grabbed the purse, and headed out the door.

70

The Taj Mahal—Monday Night

"Thanks for coming over, Cam. I've got some incredible news. Let's go out on the balcony. The view's pretty incredible too."

"I know," she said, following his lead, sitting down on one of the two chairs, and placing her purse on the small patio table between them. "You said you wanted to talk. So talk."

"I just got a phone call."

"A phone call?"

"Yeah."

"At this time of night? Who?"

"It was pretty wild."

"Wild? Why?"

"Some guy called, trying to cut a deal with me to steal Q-3."

She didn't know what to say. Why was he telling her this? She paused and tried to sound surprised. "Somebody was trying to bribe you?"

"Yes."

"And what did you say?"

"I stalled for time."

"Why?" she asked cautiously.

"Why? For God's sake, Cam. Don't you see? If I can figure out a way to meet this guy, or his people, whoever they are, we've got ourselves another espionage agent. But I need to find out who he's working for."

"Who he's working for?" she echoed, her mind racing.

"Well, sure. We don't just want the messenger, like that Jambaz character. We got him. Well, you're the one that got him. What we really wanted was his whole cell. And with Raj, it wasn't just him; it was the Indian Minister and a whole bunch of other guys in the Defense Ministry. And now this. With that show you put on this morning, there could be any number of governments . . . competitors . . . bad guys . . . who the hell knows how many . . . who will want Q-3."

"But—"

"No buts. You're big news now. You and your technology."

"So what did you tell him?"

"I said I might be able to get some information for him tonight, and I said that there was going to be a field test in a week or two. I thought I could buy a little time with that. He already knew about the test, though."

"Hmmm."

"Hmmm? That's all you can say? Cam, this could be big. As big as the whole Lashkar thing. Or the Raj thing. How can you be so cool all the time? Come to think of it, you've been cool, cold really, ever since you got over here. What's the matter?"

She shifted uncomfortably in her chair and wouldn't meet his gaze.

"Hey, I know this has been pretty rough," he continued. "I mean, the missiles, the warheads, everything. I saw the pressure. Hell, I felt it, too. But you've hardly talked to me. After all the time we spent together in D.C. I thought we were a team. And now with this new group, whoever they are, we need to work together."

He reached over and took her hand. She didn't move. She just stared out at the night sky. *So maybe he wasn't going to cooperate with the caller. But what about the calendar? What about the reference to Sterling Dynamics?* She pulled her hand away and folded her arms across her chest. *Why not confront him? Let's see how he gets out of this one.* "Okay, yes. I have had something on my mind."

"Like what?"

"Remember when you left, you said I should use your computer?"

"Yeah. Sure."

"So I had it up and running, and I wanted to know when you'd be back."

"I told you I wasn't sure. Could be a week. Maybe two. You knew that."

"That's what you said. But I thought maybe you had made some contingency flight plans and, at the time, I was worried about you and how long you'd be away."

"So?"

She hesitated for a moment. "So, I thought I could just check your calendar to see your schedule."

"I have a password for that."

"I know. I used it."

"What? You hacked into my computer?" he asked, raising his eyebrows and studying her face.

She looked up and replied in a firm voice, "Yes. I saw you key it in, and I just memorized it. It's automatic with me."

"It's automatic?" he mimicked.

"More or less."

"So you got into my calendar. So what? There's nothing special or classified in there."

"That's what I figured. I was just looking for a flight schedule."

"Well, you didn't find one, because there isn't one," he said in an annoyed tone.

"I know that."

"So? So what's the big deal?"

"I found something else."

"What?"

"I found an entry for less than two weeks from now."

"What kind of entry?"

"It was strange."

"Lots of my entries would look strange to anybody else. That's why they're just *my* entries," he said. "What looked so strange? To you?"

" 'Get NK BA FLD TS,' " she ticked off the letters ingrained in her mind.

"What's the matter with that?"

"It was entered on a day right around the time of our big field test."

"Cam, I don't get it. What does getting baseball tickets have to do with your field test?"

She exclaimed, "Baseball tickets?"

"Yeah. I told you we sometimes catch a game when I can get tickets. That was a reminder to get some infield tickets for Nancy Kennedy."

"Who's Nancy Kennedy?"

"The head of our legislative affairs office. She's the one who spearheaded the efforts on the Hill. Efforts for *your* project, by the way. I went around Austin and got her to point out to some of the members how important Q-3 would be for the President's missile defense program. I thought it would be a nice gesture if I could get her some special tickets as a thank-you. See? 'Get NK,' Nancy Kennedy, Baseball Field Tickets, 'BA FLD TS.' "

"Oh God!"

"What did you think it meant?"

She looked up, took a deep breath, and explained in a halting voice, "You had said you wanted to come to our field test. And you also told me you knew the head of Sterling."

He nodded. "But what has that got to do with—"

"And when I saw those letters, I figured it meant 'Get Nettar Kooner Bandaq Field Test.' "

Hunt stared at her and shook his head. "Jesus Christ! I'd never do that. How could you even think—"

"I don't know. I just—it all made sense. The timing. The words. The past."

"What past?"

"My past."

He softened his tone. "Tell me."

"It's a long story. Let's just say that there was a guy in our industry that I used to go out with. For a while anyway. Until I found out that he was just trying to get information on how Q-3 worked. And when I wouldn't tell him, he . . . left . . . and went to work for Sterling."

"Oh Christ Almighty!" Hunt jumped up from his chair, walked to the railing, and turned to face her. "And you thought I was doing the same thing?"

"I didn't want to think that. But all the pieces fit."

"Seemed to fit," he countered.

He raked his fingers through his hair as she'd seen him do many times when he was upset or worried. "Look, I can see," he continued. "Well, I really can't see. But oh, to hell with it. There was a lot going on, so let's just drop it."

"Yes, we should."

"Because, as I said, we've got to work together now."

"Work together?"

"To find this new group, whoever they are. I'm going to meet with my team tomorrow. We'll figure out a sting op. And I may need you."

"No, you won't."

"No, I won't what?"

"You won't need me."

"Well, I might."

"No. Because there isn't any group," she said, staring down at the intricate stone on the balcony floor.

"What do you mean there isn't any group?"

"Just what I said. There isn't any group. It was a setup."

"A setup?" he thundered. "What the hell are you talking about?"

Cammy leaned back in her chair, stalling for time. "I set you up."

Hunt pulled her out of the chair and shook her by the shoulders. "You set me up? What are you saying?" he demanded, his eyes flaring.

She met his gaze and felt herself wilting under his harsh scrutiny.

"Tell me!" he said, pushing her away.

"When I figured out that calendar entry," she began.

"When you *thought* you figured it out," he interrupted.

"I went to Jack because I was afraid of what you were planning to do."

"And?"

"And we decided that our first order of business was dealing with the missiles. But then we had to protect the company."

"And?"

"And so we had Bob—"

"Who's Bob?"

"He's here with us. He took Raj's place on the satellite system."

"You had Bob do what? Place a call to try and entrap me?" he probed, his voice rising.

"We had to know."

"You had to know?"

"Yes."

"Wasn't it enough for you to know that I work in the White House? That I have a security clearance? That I came to help you after the break-in, the car crash, the shooting? That I arranged FBI protection for you?

That I took you into my home? *My home?* Who the hell do you think I am?"

Silence.

"I wasn't sure," she whispered.

"Well, that's pretty clear now, isn't it?"

"You had this fancy house in Georgetown. You drive a Jaguar. You're a lieutenant colonel. My dad was in the Air Force. I know what officers make."

He rolled his eyes and took a deep breath. "Fancy house? My wife and I bought that, with a little help from our families. When she left, she didn't want it. Didn't need it. I kept it. The Jag? Yeah, I like Jags. Got that one from a buddy at State who got assigned to our embassy in Nigeria. Got it for a damn good price, too. Satisfied?"

There was a knock on the door. Hunt barked at her, "Be right back. I think we need a time-out anyway."

A waiter walked into the room carrying a tray with a silver bucket, two glasses, and a bottle of champagne. "Would you like this on the balcony, sir?"

"Yes, thank you," Hunt said, pulling out his wallet and handing the man a tip.

"What's this?" Cammy asked, eyeing the bucket.

"Would you like me to open this for you, sir?" the waiter asked.

"Yes. Please," Hunt replied. The waiter pulled the cork, poured the shimmering liquid into the champagne flutes, and quietly left the room.

Hunt looked like he was regaining his composure. "After I called you, I ordered some champagne. I thought we'd toast your success and talk about working as a team again."

She slowly raised her eyes and stared as he picked up his glass.

His gaze met hers. "So where do we go from here, Cam?"

She paused and said quietly, "I was wrong. So wrong." She reached for her glass and took a sip. "Truce?" She took another taste. As the bubbles rolled off her tongue, she added in a soft voice, "I'm so sorry."

They sat down and stared at the marble building bathed in moonlight. They sipped champagne for several minutes and avoided each other's eyes. Finally, Cammy whispered, "The Taj Mahal really is a masterpiece."

"Yes, it is," he replied evenly.

She wanted to keep talking about something. Anything. "There was a brochure in my room," she ventured. "It said the building has dozens of precious stones. Diamonds, sapphires, jade, mother-of-pearl."

"Sounds like a Tiffany outlet," he suggested.

"Tiffany's doesn't have outlets," she said, anxious to lighten their mood.

"Our driver said it took a thousand elephants and twenty thousand men to build that place."

"You know, I read somewhere that there's a lot of controversy about who really built it."

"Does it make any difference?"

"Not really. From my standpoint, it's the most beautiful building in the world."

"And from my standpoint," he said, setting his glass down, getting up from his chair, and pulling her into his arms, "you are the most beautiful but also the most maddening woman in the world."

He kissed her forehead, then her eyelids, and finally crushed her mouth with his. Her lips opened as he deepened the kiss and encircled her with his arms. Her head was spinning. She had felt so angry, so hurt. Then so guilty and chagrined. Now she was feeling heady and relieved. Was it the effect of the champagne? The enchantment of the Taj Mahal? The embrace of this man? She wanted him. And she knew he wanted her. Was it just the range of emotions? When he picked her up and carried her back into the bedroom, she realized she really didn't care.

As the moon rose higher in the sky, they lay entwined, their breath evening out, their heartbeats settling down. She couldn't move. She was floating, floating from a great height slowly down through an energy-charged atmosphere. It felt like tiny electrodes were dancing on her skin, all over her body. Every pore felt alive and sated at the same time. It was an eerie feeling. Eerie because she had never felt quite like this before. She felt erotic and ethereal, enchanted and ecstatic.

"E-words," she murmured as she fluttered her eyes open and saw him gazing at her.

"E-words," he repeated. "What are E-words?"

"The way you make me feel. Erotic. Ethereal."

"That's the way you're supposed to feel," he said, gently caressing her face.

She leaned over and kissed his cheek, then settled down into his arms.

She tried to stifle a yawn. He stroked her hair and whispered, "Better get some sleep now."

"Mmm-hmmm." She had a fleeting thought about the Dictaphone on the balcony and the black silk negligee hanging in her closet. She could delete the recording. As for the gown, there was always tomorrow.

71

The Taj Mahal—Tuesday Morning

"More coffee?" Cammy offered, raising the silver thermos. Clad in hotel bathrobes, they were enjoying a breakfast of spicy eggs, fruit, and yogurt at the small table on Hunt's hotel room balcony.

He nodded and folded the newspaper he'd been reading. "Here, let me show you something,"

"What now? Haven't we seen enough articles? I'm not used to so much publicity," she said, taking a spoonful of fresh fruit.

"Well, that's just too bad. You'll have to hear a bit more, 'cause this one's pretty good."

"Which one?"

"The one in *The Times of India*. Says here, 'The brilliant American scientist Dr. Cameron Talbot demonstrated the viability of a brand-new technology for missile defense when she located, analyzed, and locked on to the guidance system of a missile aimed at the Defense Ministry in New Delhi. By executing a program that intercepted the deadly cruise missile, she was able to turn it away from its target and send it to the mountains northeast of the city where it landed harmlessly in an uninhabited area.

" 'She had been sent by the President of the United States to set up a defense perimeter around the Taj Mahal and the surrounding area, and she was working in concert with teams of Indian scientists and their array of missile defense systems. However, it was her technology, named Q-3 for its three components of radar, satellite, and computer systems, which was responsible for saving the lives of the Indian Prime Minster, the American Special Envoy, and a host of additional officials from both countries.' "

"Enough," she said, laughing. "All the papers have printed that story."

"No, wait. There's more. Actually, there's a quote here from the Chairman of Sterling Dynamics back home."

"Nettar Kooner?" she asked, sitting up straight.

"Yeah. Listen to this. 'When asked for a comment on the extraordinary new missile defense system, the Chairman of Sterling Dynamics, manufacturer of other missile components, said, "While we commend Dr. Talbot on the execution of her program in India, we are concerned that one lucky hit does not remove the threat of cruise missiles worldwide. I'm afraid that would be reaching." ' "

All of a sudden, Cammy saw the man in a new light. He was just another CEO vying for yet another defense contract. He was no longer a threat to her, merely an amusing irritant. "That's the sound of sour grapes being squished," she said with a smile.

"You're right. What a jerk. Anyway, it goes on here: 'The Indian Prime Minister issued a statement praising the heroic actions of Dr. Talbot, emphasizing that she came to India knowing full well that she and her team might be in danger of a terrorist attack. In addition to stopping the missile, Dr. Talbot was able to pinpoint the source of the launch, and Indian forces quickly routed the terrorist group, Lashkar-i-Taiba, killing ten and taking the rest into custody for questioning. A large cache of arms was recovered along with one other cruise missile which the Defense Minister said was part of the trio stolen from a Pakistani Army base two weeks ago. The government of Pakistan issued a statement praising Dr. Talbot's work and the actions of the Indian defense forces for eradicating a group that Islamabad had banned several years ago. Pakistan's President also announced his readiness to negotiate a peace treaty with India and will soon travel to Agra for a signing ceremony.' There. How about that?" Hunt said, slapping the paper down on his knee.

"Sounds like mission accomplished." Cammy said. "It was a pretty good day."

"And so is this one," Hunt replied. He raised his coffee cup in a salute, "*Carpe diem*, my dear."

"Indeed," Cammy said. "By the way, I got an interesting e-mail from the office."

"Yeah?"

"It was from our CFO, Stan Bollinger."

"What'd he say?"

"It was kind of amazing. He never thought Q-3 would work. He never thought any missile defense system would really work."

"A lot of people have felt that way. Guess you showed 'em," Hunt said with a grin.

"Well, I have to give Stan credit, because he sent a very gracious note of congratulations and said he was upping my budget."

"Sounds like the House Armed Services Committee," Hunt said.

Cammy finished her fruit and gazed back at the bedroom. "You know I can't believe they gave us these rooms. I've never seen such a gorgeous hotel. Well, of course, it's the only one with a view of the Taj," she added.

"Yeah. What does that booklet there say about the name? It's kind of weird."

"Let's see," she said, picking up a glossy folder. "They say, 'Oberoi Amarvilas is Sanskrit for 'Eternal Heaven.'"

"I'll buy that."

"You know what else they've got here?"

"What?"

"It says here that their spa has 'therapies to restore and rejuvenate the mind, body, and soul.' Maybe I'll head down and get a sandalwood wrap with the essence of rose, milk, and honey," she said with a lilt in her voice.

"Thought you'd be a little tired," he chided. "We didn't get much sleep last night."

"I was. I am." She tossed the brochure aside. "Just kidding."

"Speaking of kidding, I have one more thing for you from one of the papers."

"No more papers," she protested.

"But this one's for Melanie."

"Mel?"

"Yep." Hunt picked up the Asian edition of *The Wall Street Journal* and shuffled the pages until he found a lifestyle feature. "Didn't you tell me she was collecting crazy recipes or something?"

"Well, yes. At least she used to. Things have been a little too busy lately to do anything that resembles fun, if you know what I mean."

"Gotcha. Anyway, clip this one, and take it back to her." He handed her the paper.

Cammy read the title: " 'Grilled Kangaroo on a Coriander Falafel, with Tahini Lemon Sauce and Green Pepper Relish'?" She burst out laughing.

"Tell you what. Before we head out for the whole sightseeing thing, I'm relishing the thought of spending a little more private time with you, my lady."

They walked hand in hand from the terrace back to the bedroom, where they shed their robes. Once again, he noticed the scent of vanilla as he guided her down onto the cool white sheets and wound his fingers through her hair. He could get lost in all that silk. It framed her face and made him think of Botticelli's *Birth of Venus*. This was the birth of something all right. He didn't know quite what, but he knew he had to have her. Again.

He was gentle at first. Forceful later. He touched her. Stroked her. Moved with her. Kept pace with her. Until she cried out his name.

Cammy still had her eyes closed. This time she felt like she had just jumped out of an airplane. But it was a nice plane. A beautiful, shining plane. She was with an instructor, sharing a parachute on the long dive. They were joined, entwined, protecting each other as they fell down, down, down. The parachute had fluttered open, and they continued their descent, buffeted by warm gentle winds all the way.

She felt a breeze and realized that Hunt had left the terrace door open. The early-morning air cooled her skin as she lay damp and spent in his arms.

72

The White House—Later

"Welcome back!" the President said, smiling broadly as Cammy and Hunt walked into the Oval Office. "Congratulations all around, to both of you," he added, motioning for them to sit down.

"Thank you, Mr. President. It's really good to be back," Cammy said.

"As you know, a lot has happened since our first meeting. And besides saying 'thank you' for your incredible performance in India last week, I wanted to let you know the final chapter in the negotiations."

"We read about the peace treaty," Hunt said, "and I saw a stack of briefing papers about how India and Pakistan finally signed a no-first-use agreement on nuclear weapons, along with protocols on trade, transportation, and energy."

"Yes, they're going ahead with that pipeline deal. And, of course, they're moving toward elections in Kashmir, which could result in a new level of autonomy for that entire region."

"May I ask a question, sir?" Cammy said.

"Certainly."

"One article said that the agreements contained some sort of secret protocol and I wondered . . . maybe I'm not cleared to know, but—"

"Actually, that's why I brought you here, Dr. Talbot. Yes, we did add something new. You see, now that India has procured this Q-3 of yours and is evidently figuring out how to use it, we have decided to *give* the same version to the government of Pakistan."

"You're *giving* it to Pakistan?" Cammy exclaimed.

"Yes. Our government will cover the cost, of course. At least the Paks wanted to buy it legitimately through State, Defense, and the Commerce Departments. And now with both sides having a shield against certain classes of guided missiles, it's a checkmate. And we all win. Neither side can make another move. No one will launch because neither side's missiles will get through."

Cammy sat back against the soft cushions of the sofa, her mind racing. *That's it*, she thought. *The President is absolutely right. Missiles would not be launched, and that means lives would be saved. And isn't that the whole point?* She glanced back at the President, saw him get up from his chair and pick up a box from his desk. It was wrapped in heavy white paper. He handed it to her.

"Go ahead. You can open it."

Cammy carefully removed the paper and lifted the lid. She saw a pair of cut-crystal champagne glasses embossed with the Presidential seal.

"These are beautiful, Mr. President," she said, holding up one of the glasses. A ray of sunlight glinted off the edge, creating a momentary rainbow.

"I just wanted you two to have a little memento of this occasion. I figured you could drink a toast to our collective victories."

"Thank you, Mr. President. Thank you so much," she said, getting up from the couch and shaking his hand.

"And we thank *you*." He walked with them toward the door and added, "I look forward to keeping in touch, Dr. Talbot."

"Keeping in touch?" she said quizzically.

"Yes. You see, I just might have another assignment for you."